Robot
Dreams

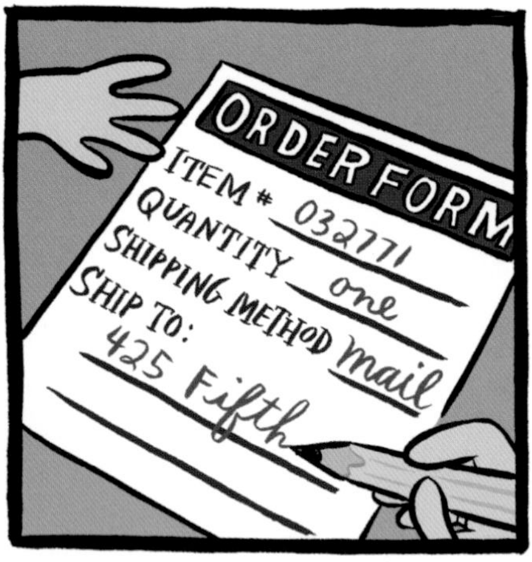
ORDER FORM
ITEM # 032771
QUANTITY one
SHIPPING METHOD mail
SHIP TO:
425 Fifth

ROBOT DREAMS

Sara Varon

SQUARE
FISH

First Second

New York

Special thanks to my mom, Maureen Panzera & Tanya McKinnon.

SQUARE
FISH

An imprint of Macmillan Publishing Group, LLC
120 Broadway,
New York, NY 10271
mackids.com

Our books may be purchased in bulk for promotional, educational, or business use.
Please contact your local bookseller or the Macmillan Corporate and Premium
Sales Department at (800) 221-7945 ext. 5442 or by email at
macmillanspecialmarkets@macmillan.com.

Cataloging-in-Publication Data is on file at the Library of Congress.

ISBN 978-1-250-07350-1 (paperback)

Originally Published in the United States by First Second
First Square Fish Edition: 2016

Square Fish logo designed by Filomena Tuosto

10 9 8 7 6 5 4

August

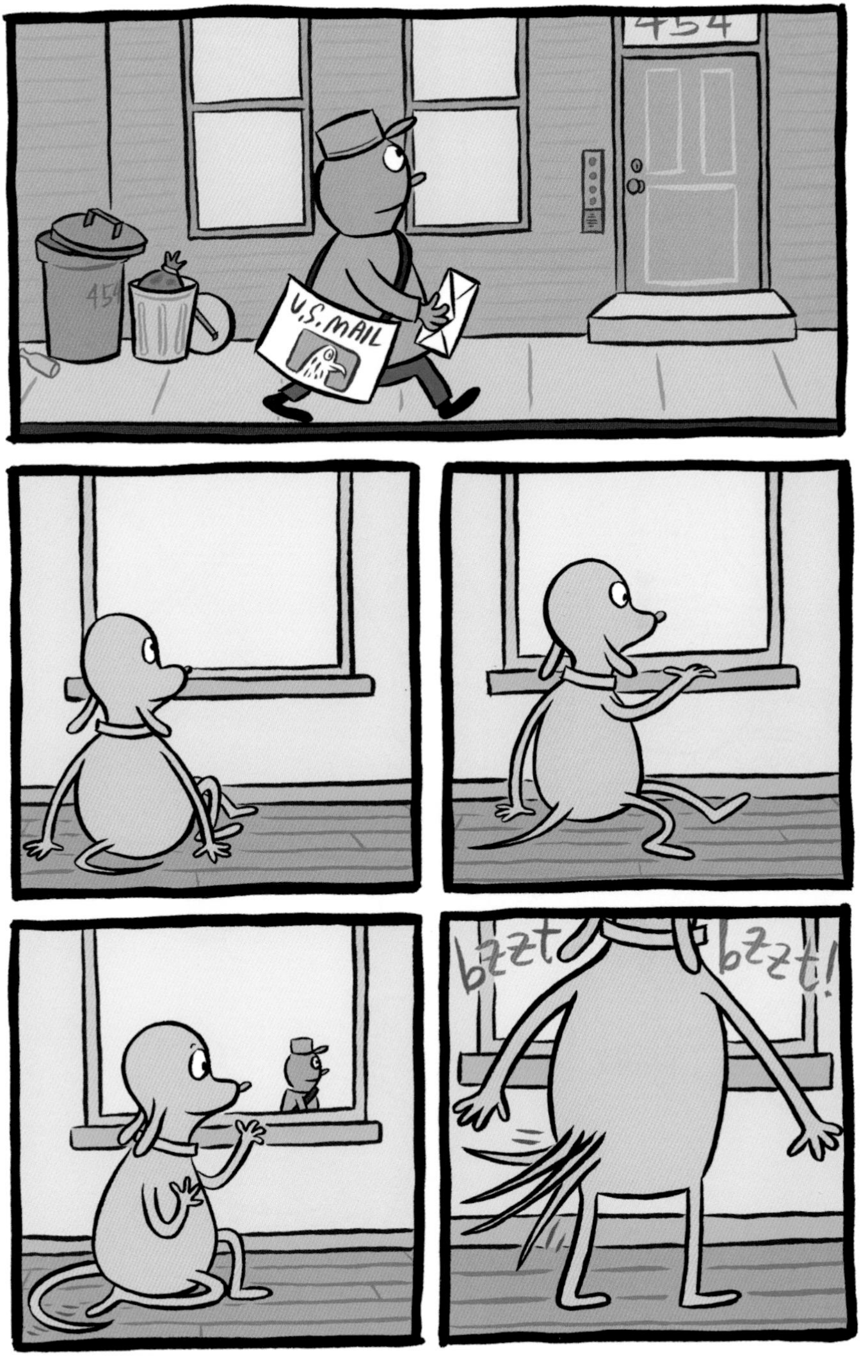
454
454
U.S. MAIL
bzzt
bzzt!

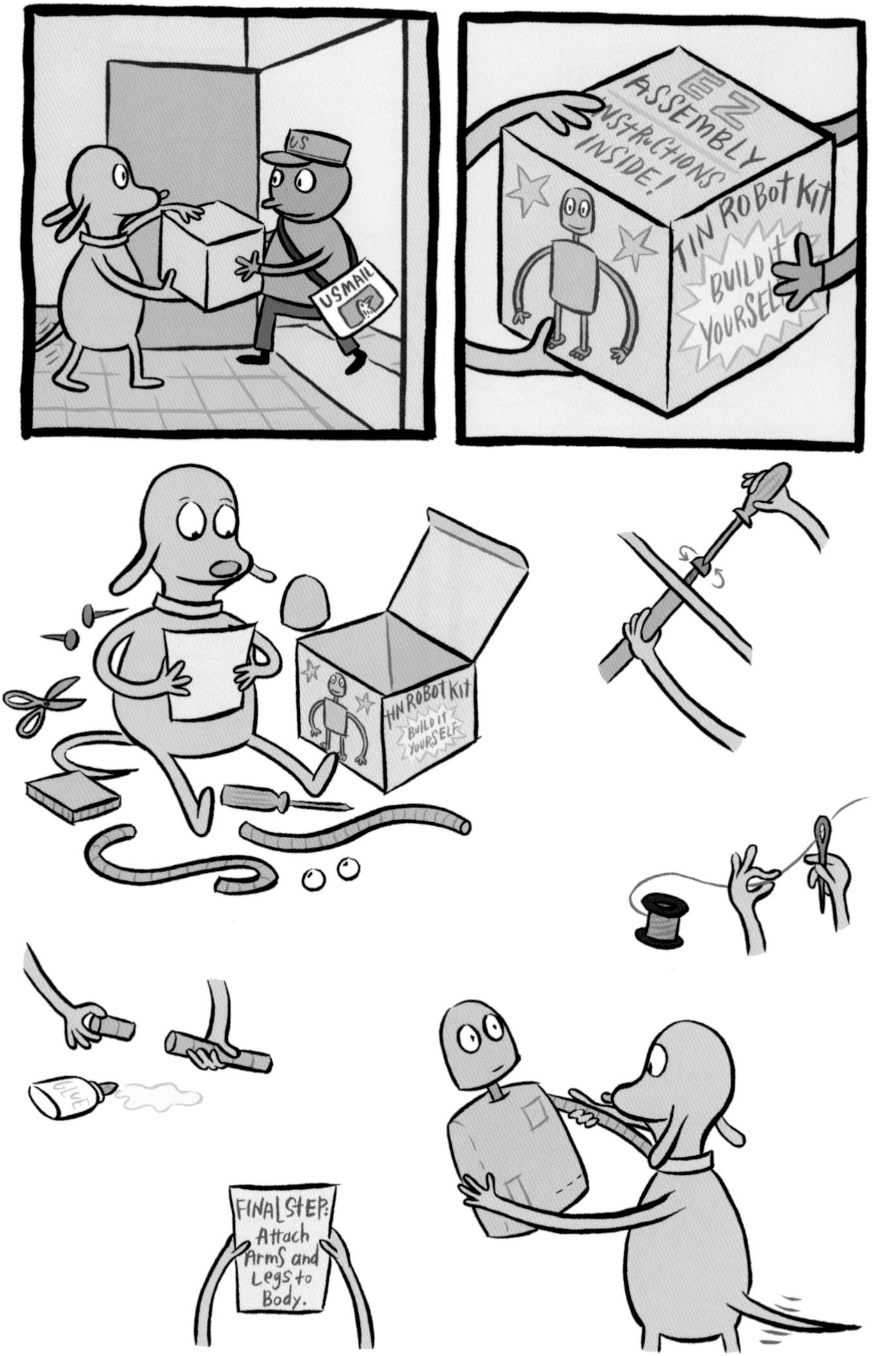
US
US MAIL
EZ ASSEMBLY
INSTRUCTIONS INSIDE!
TIN ROBOT KIT
BUILD IT
TIN ROBOT KIT
BUILD IT YOURSELF
FINAL STEP: Attach Arms and Legs to Body.

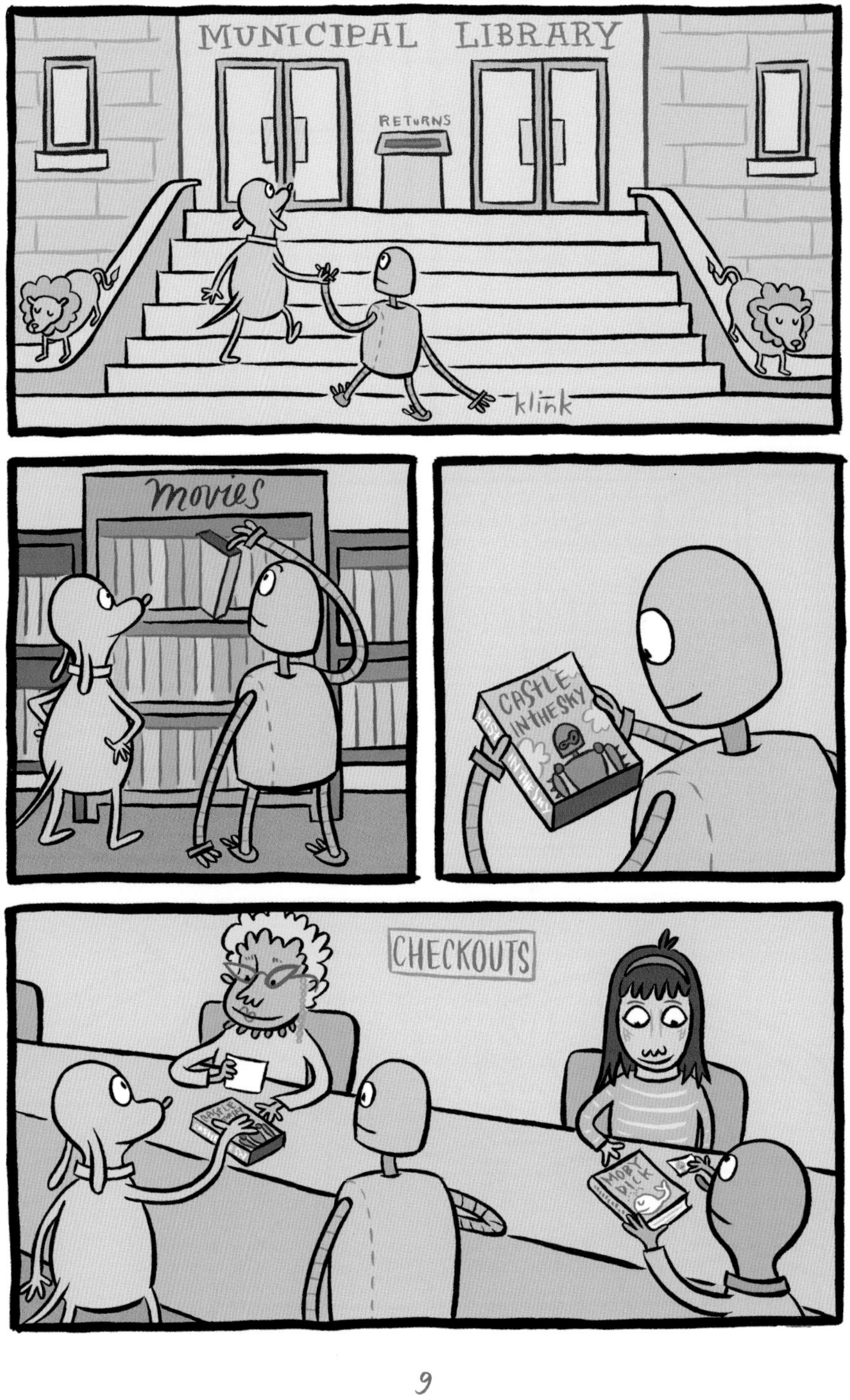
MUNICIPAL LIBRARY
RETURNS
klink
movies
CASTLE IN THE SKY
CHECKOUTS
MOBY DICK

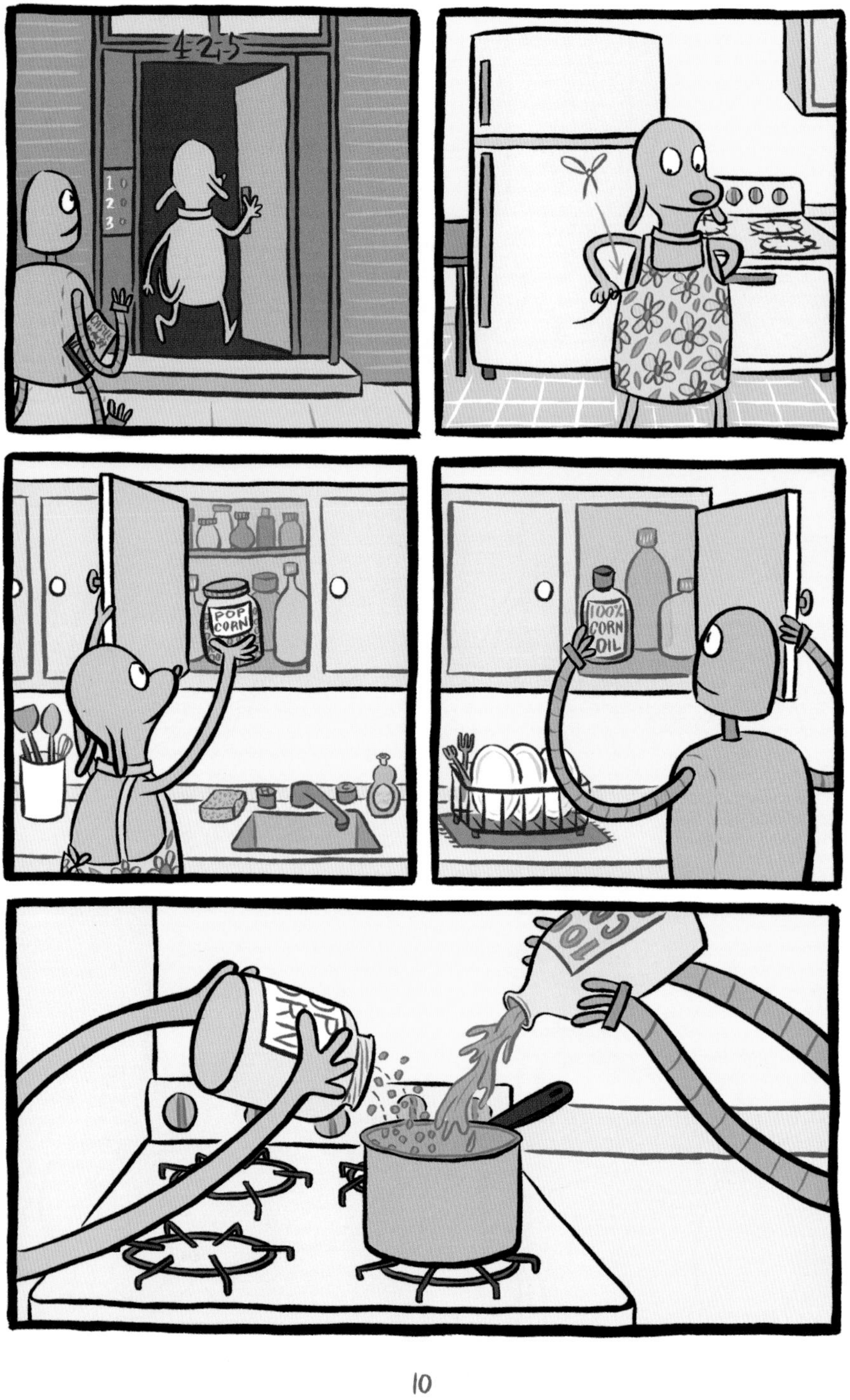
425
1
2
3
POP CORN
100% CORN OIL

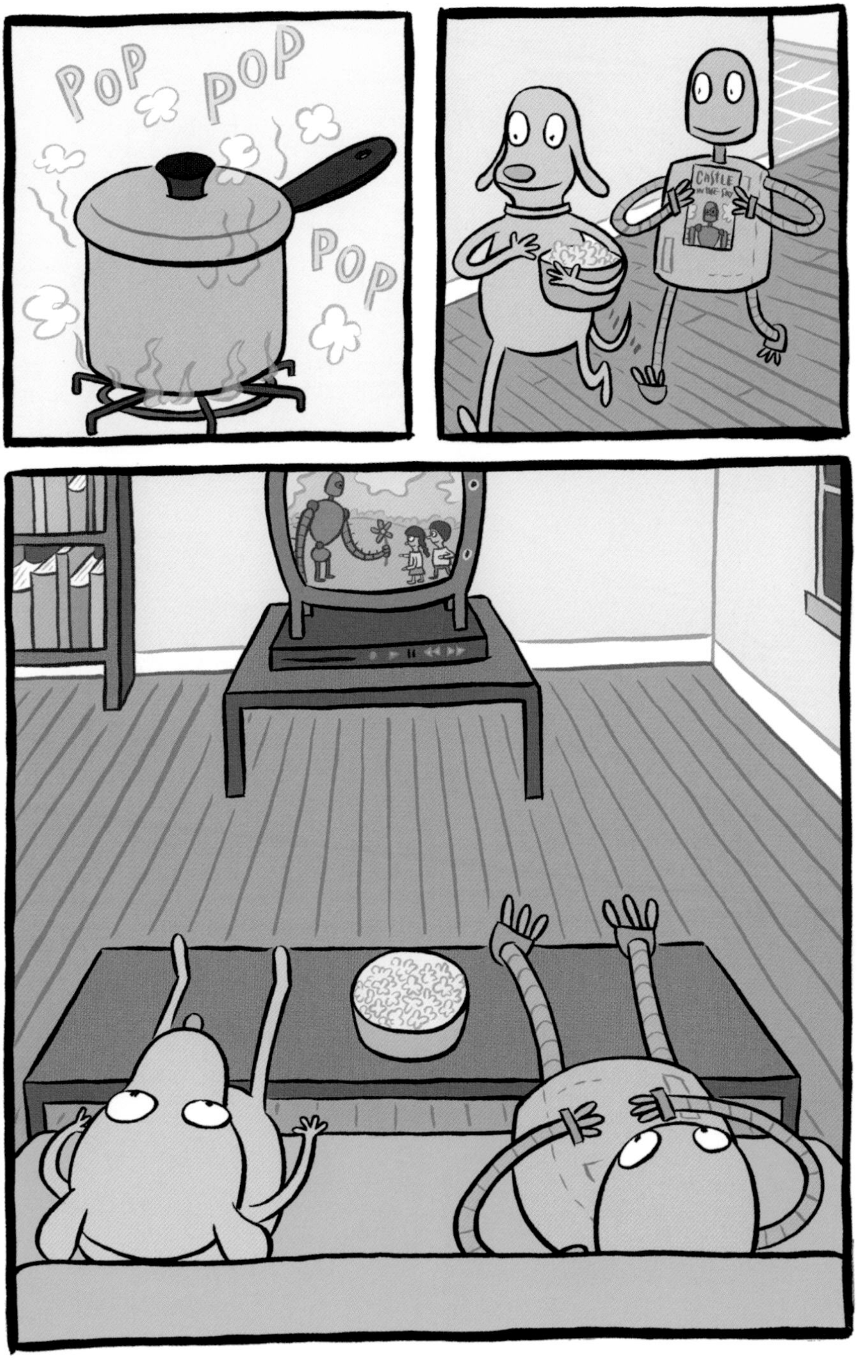
POP POP
POP
CASTLE IN THE SKY

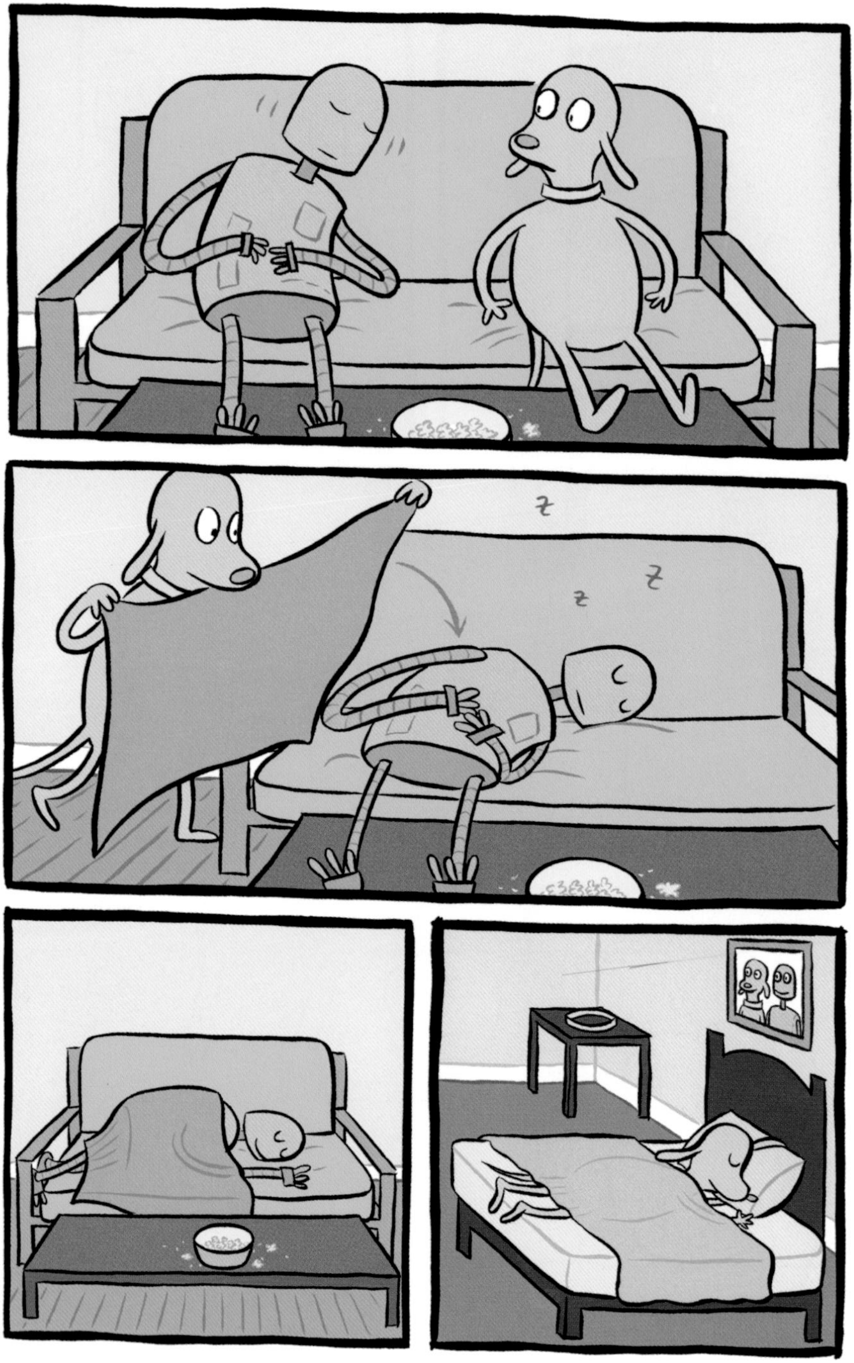
z
z
z

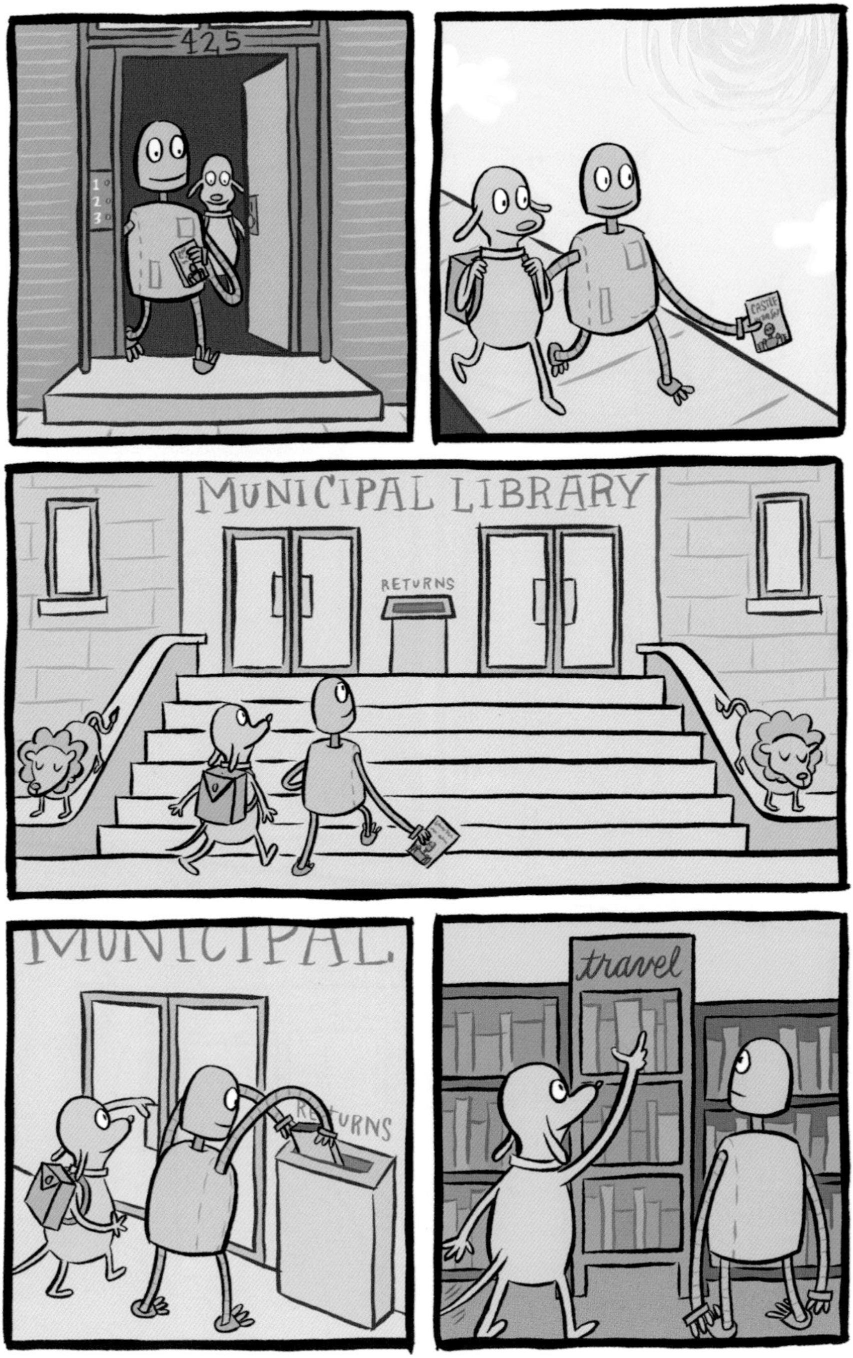
425
1
2
3
CASTLE
MUNICIPAL LIBRARY
RETURNS
MUNICIPAL
travel

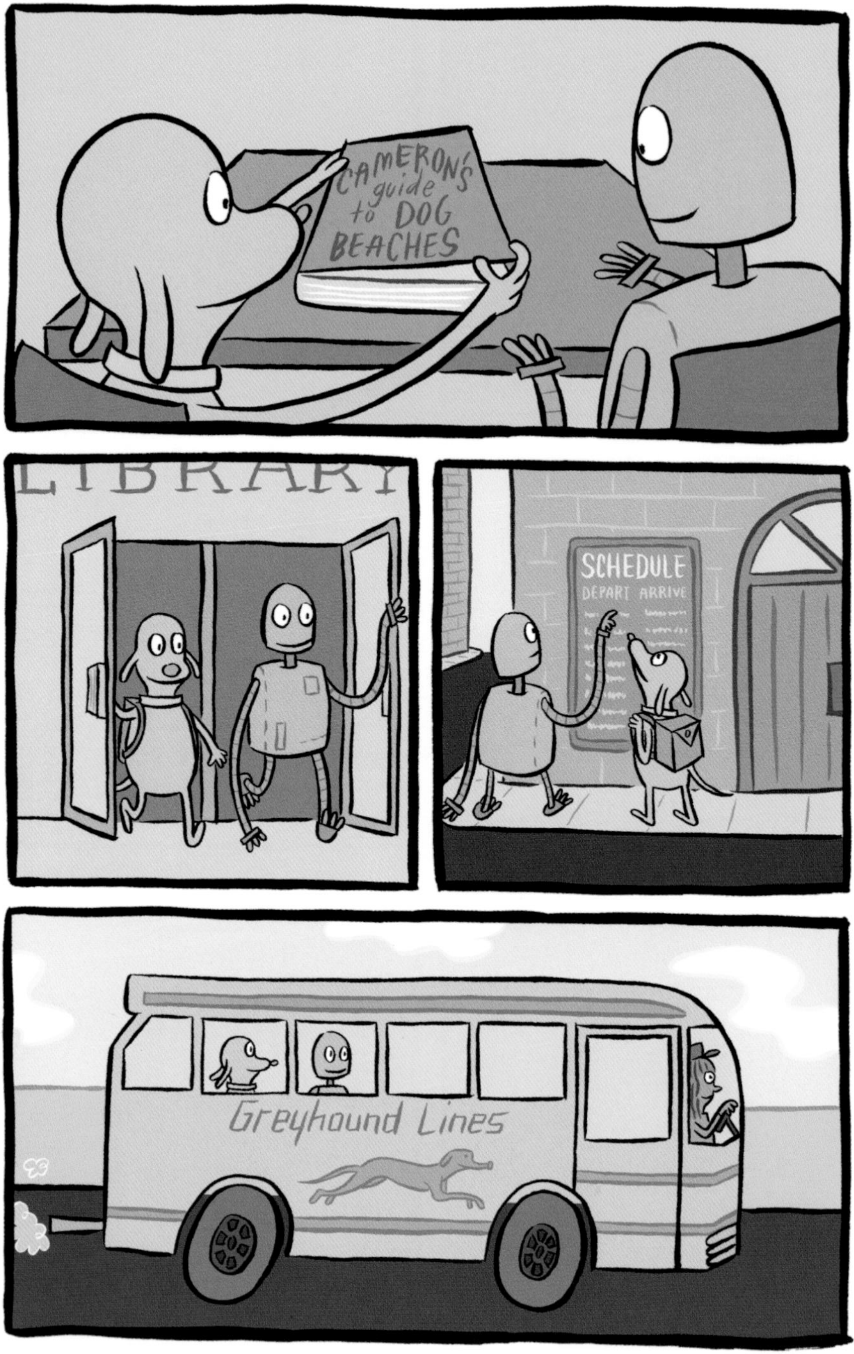
CAMERON'S guide to DOG BEACHES
LIBRARY
SCHEDULE
DEPART ARRIVE
Greyhound Lines

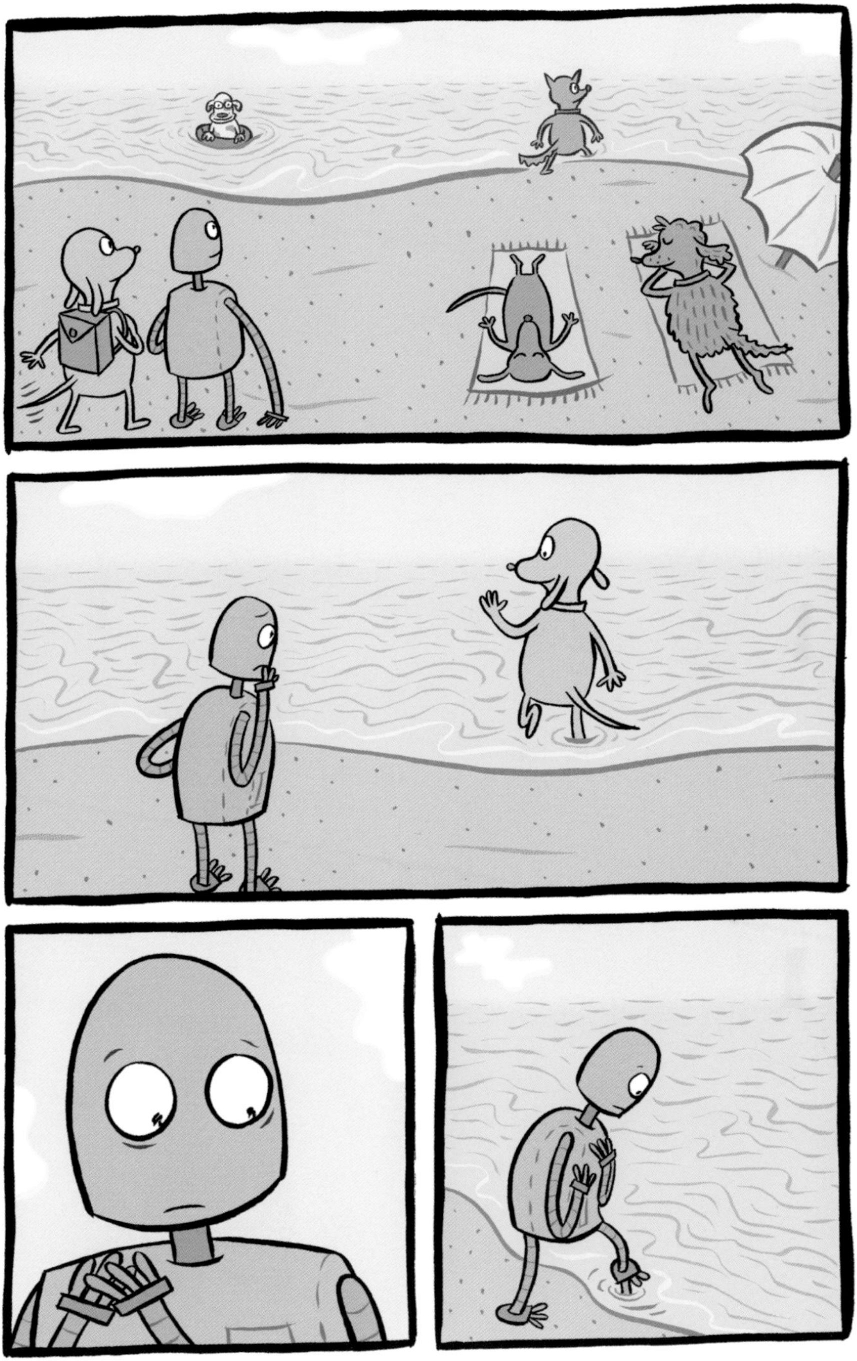

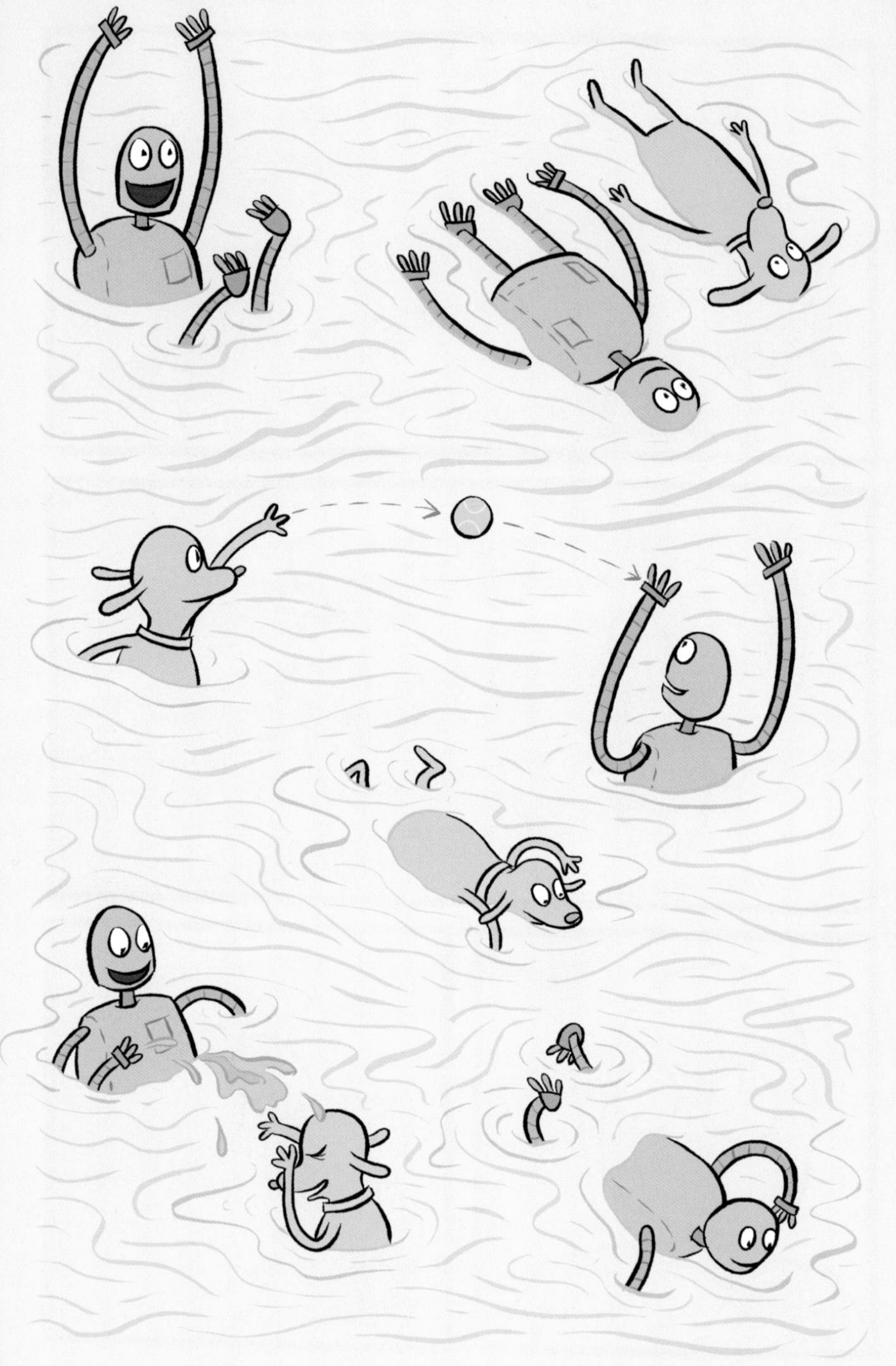

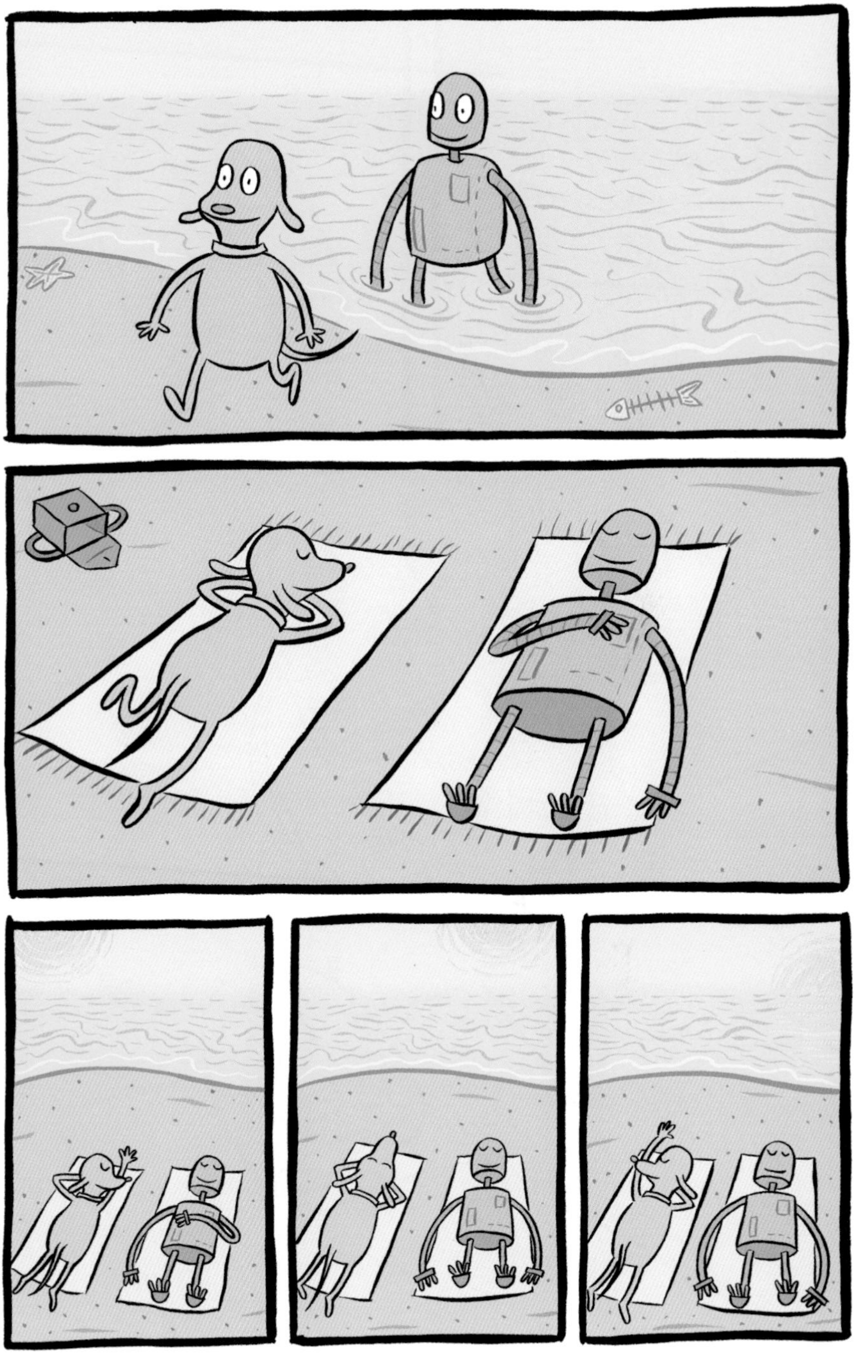

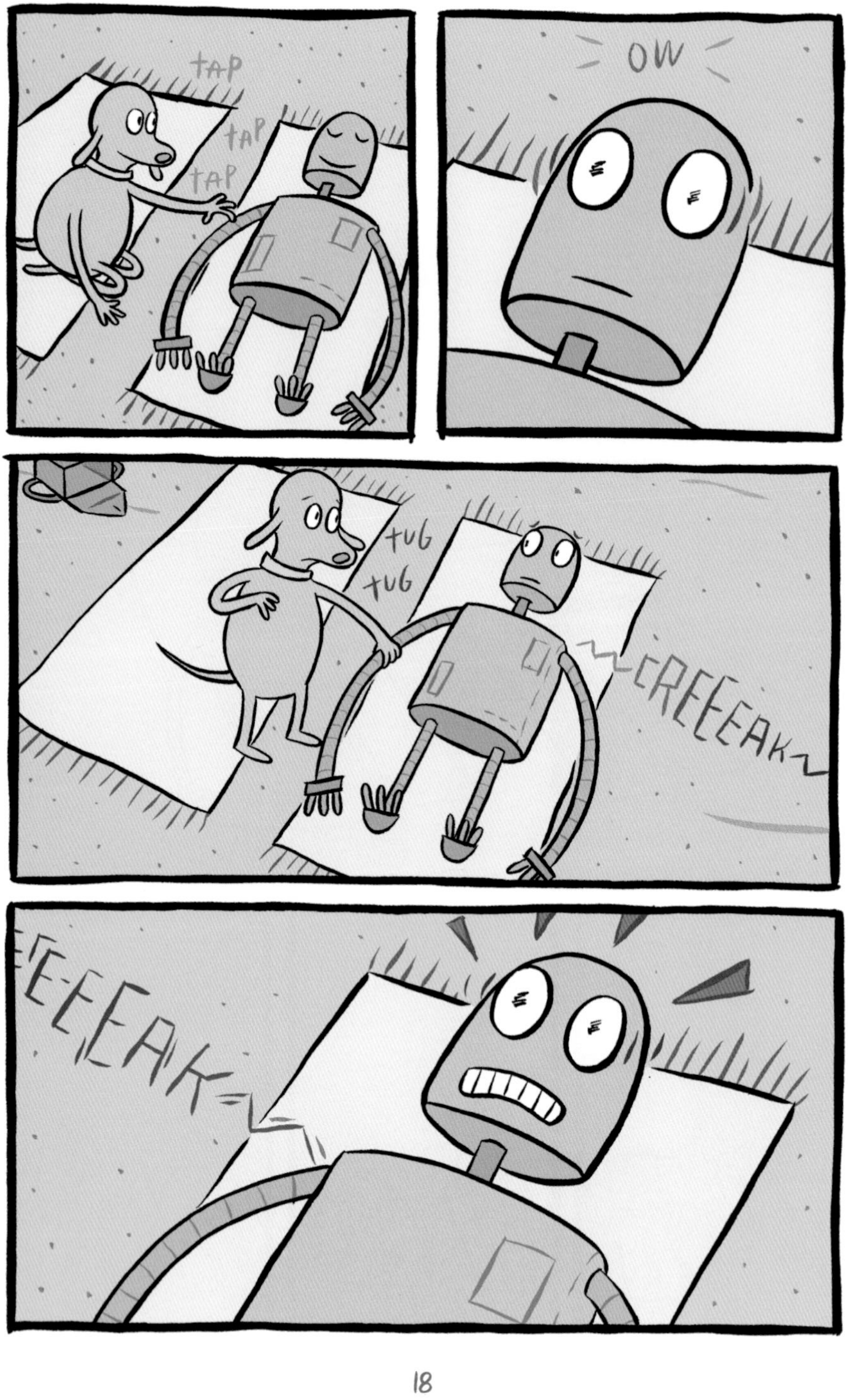
TAP
TAP
TAP
OW
TUG
TUG
CREEEAK
EEEAK

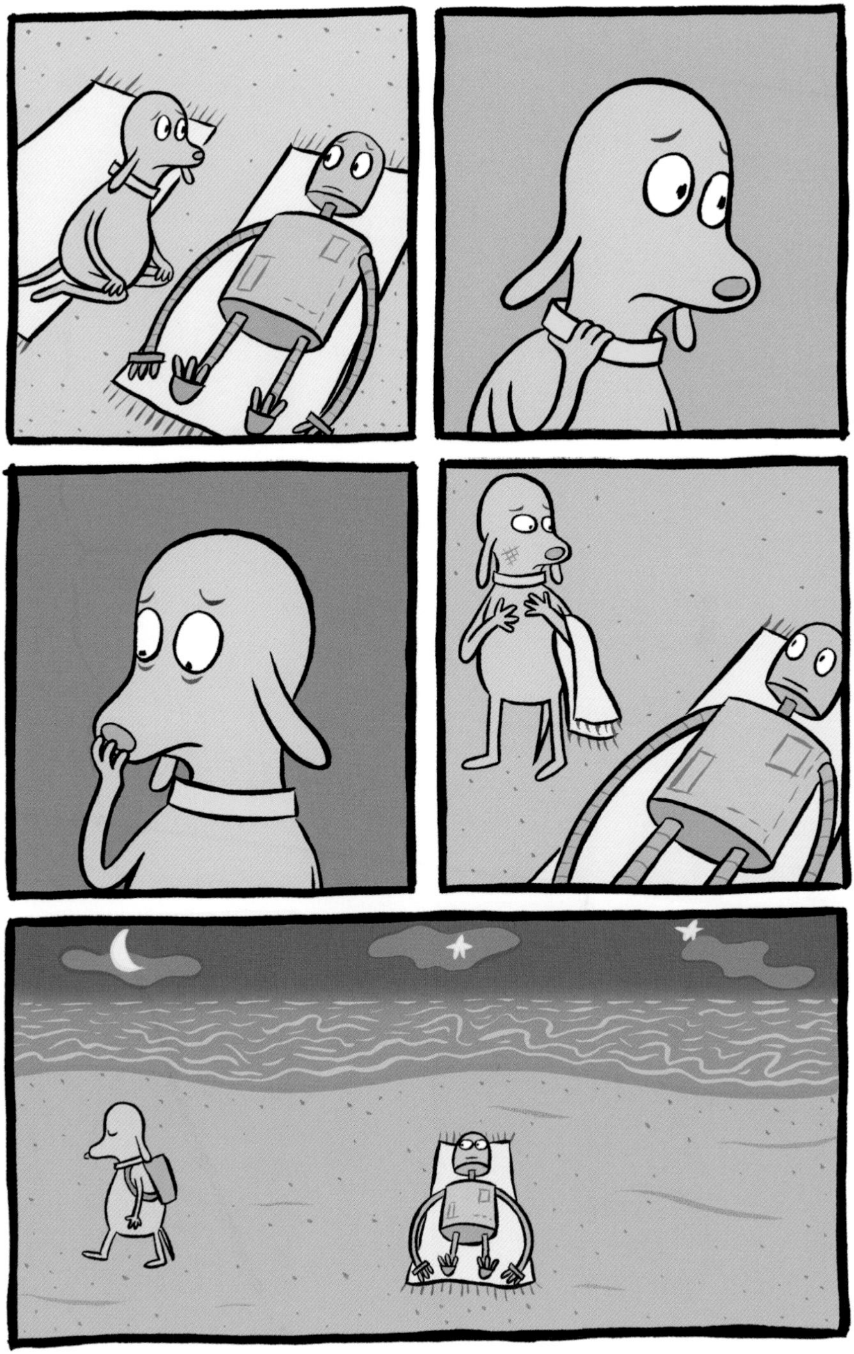

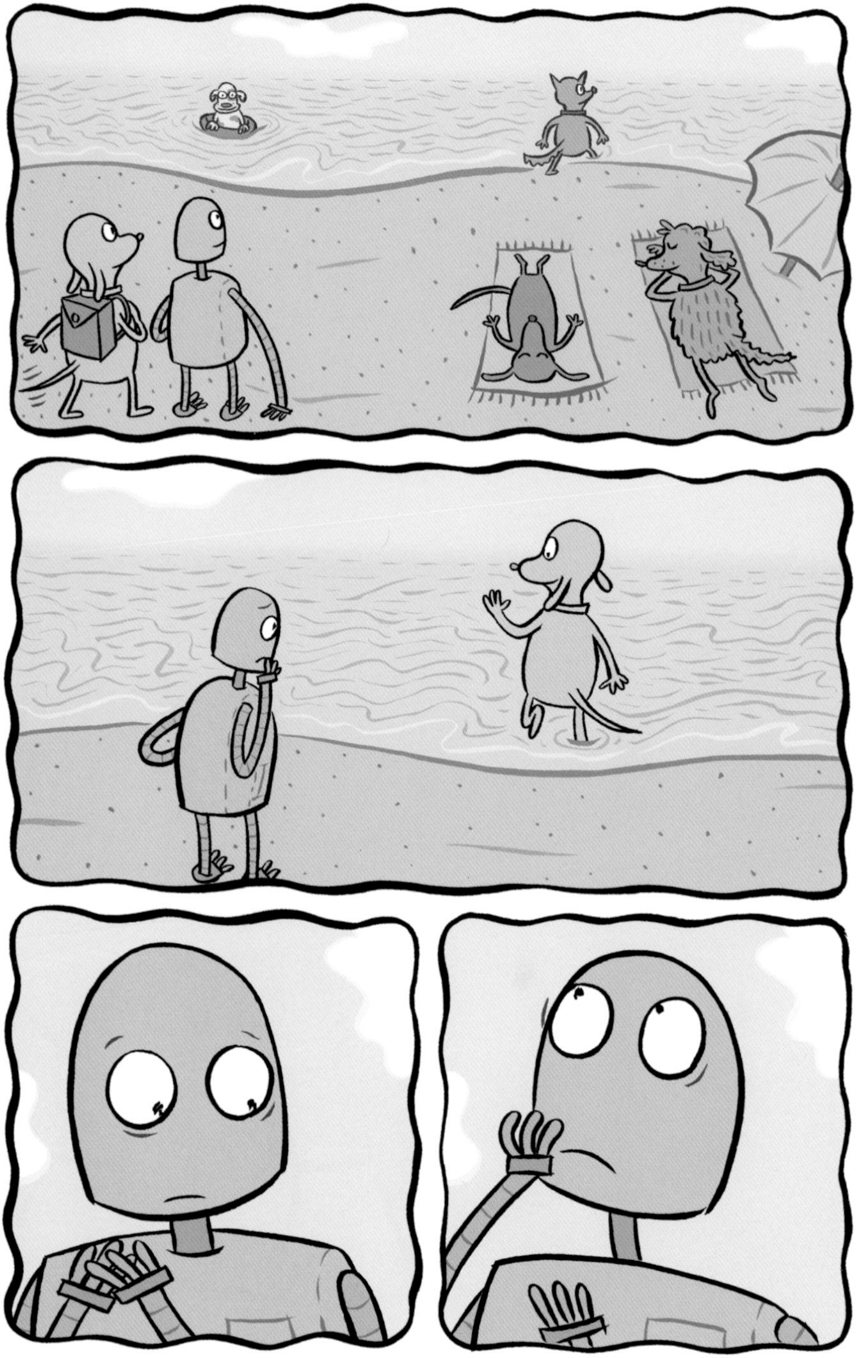

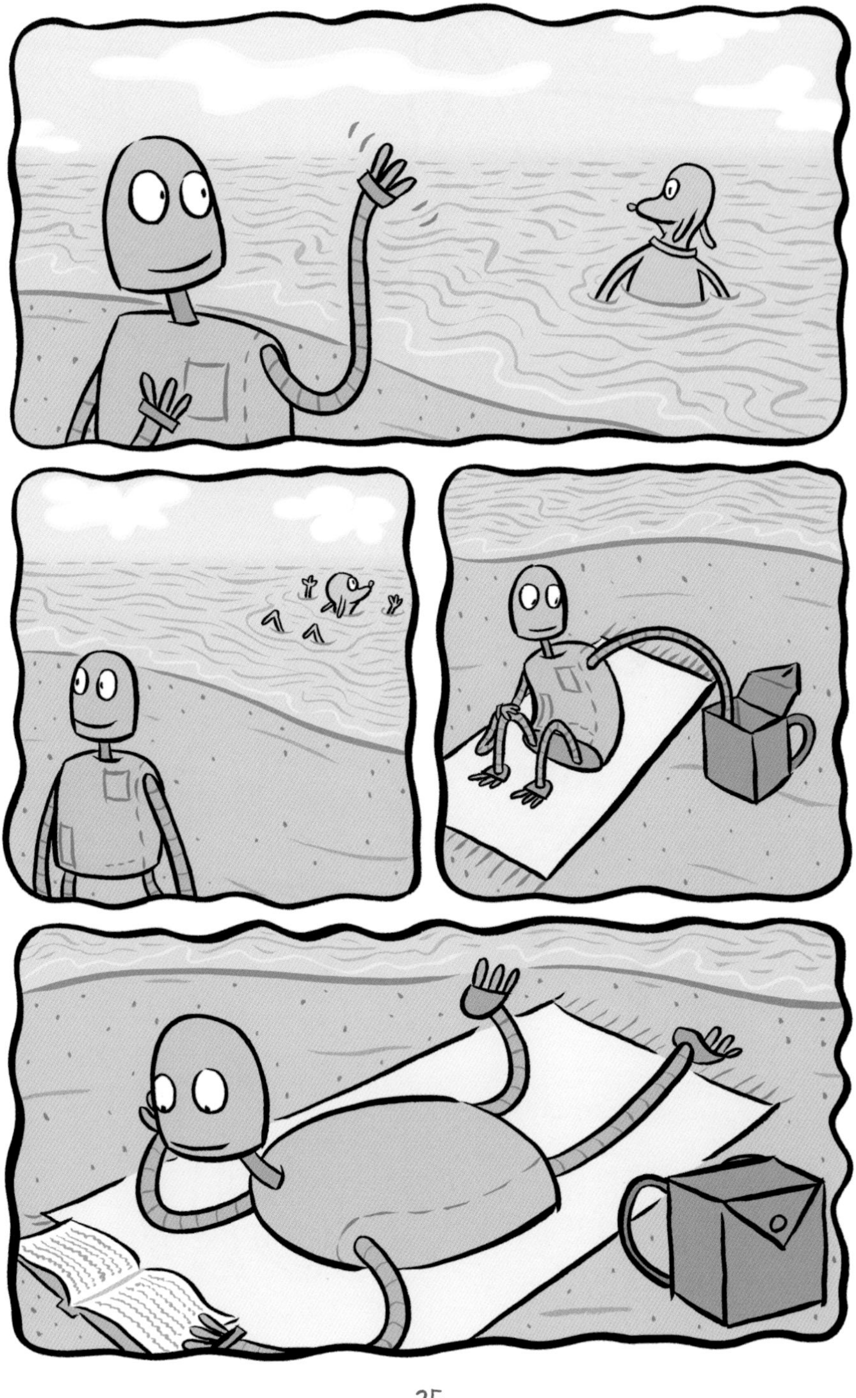

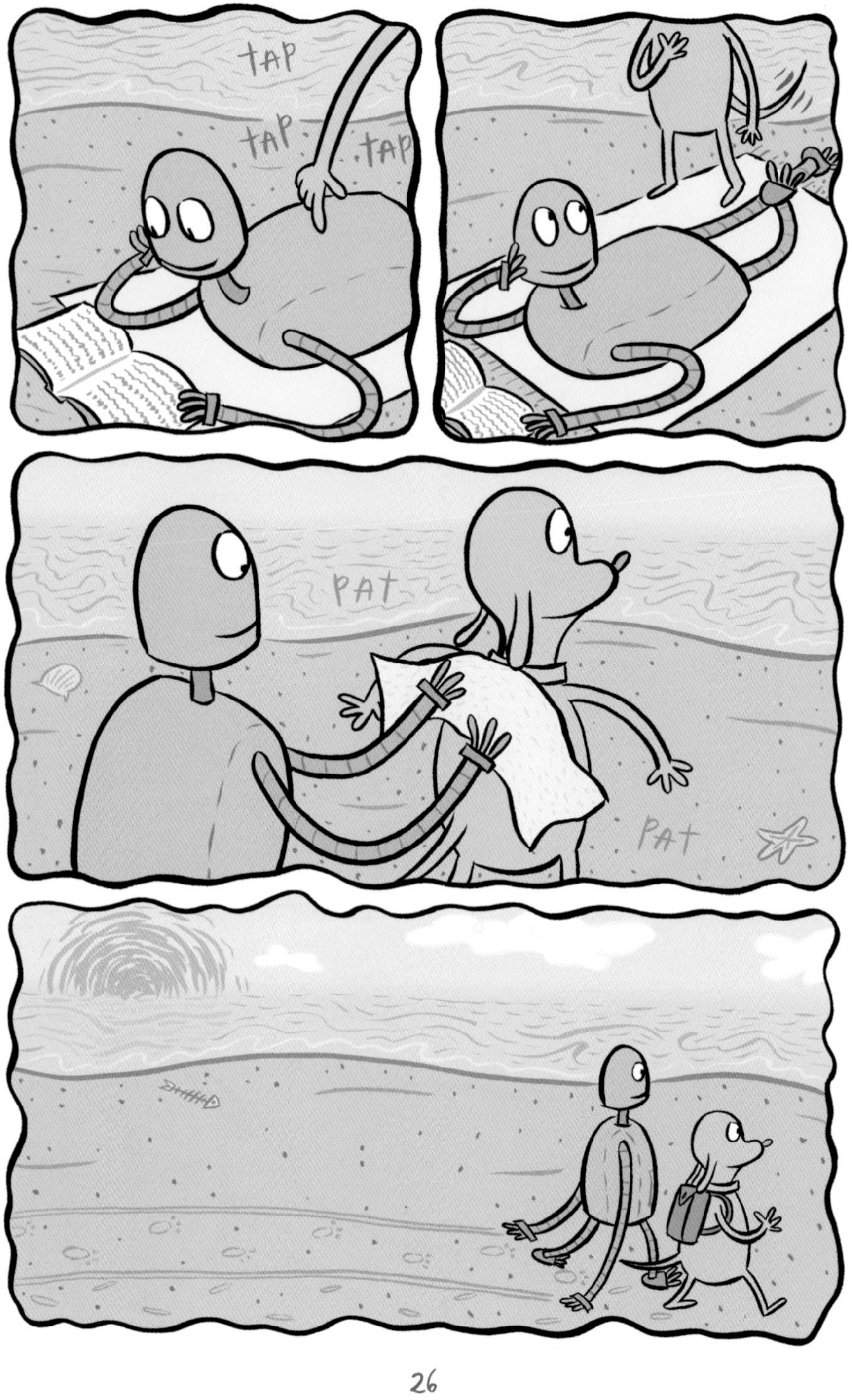
TAP
TAP
TAP
PAT
PAT

September

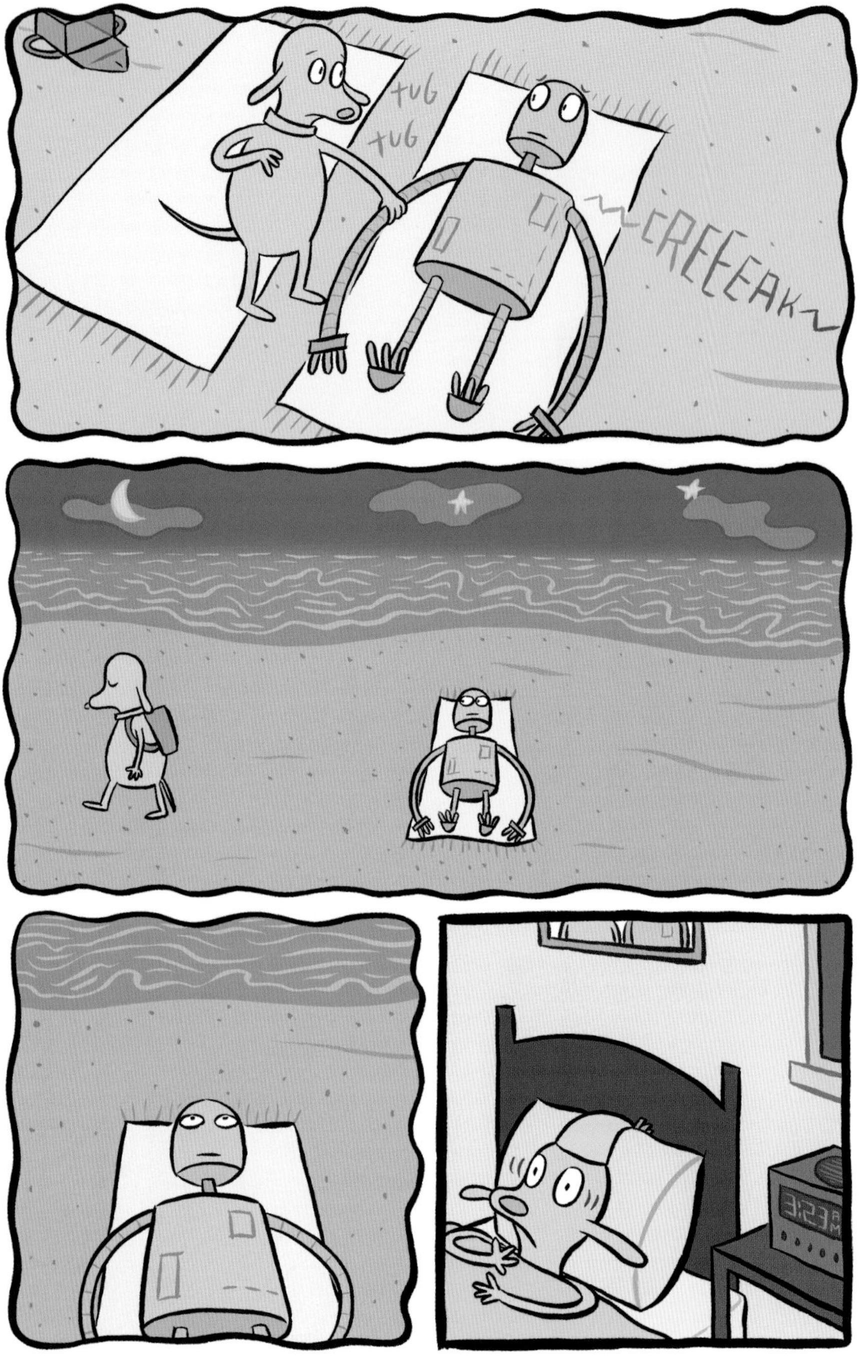
TUG
TUG
CREEEAK
3:23 AM

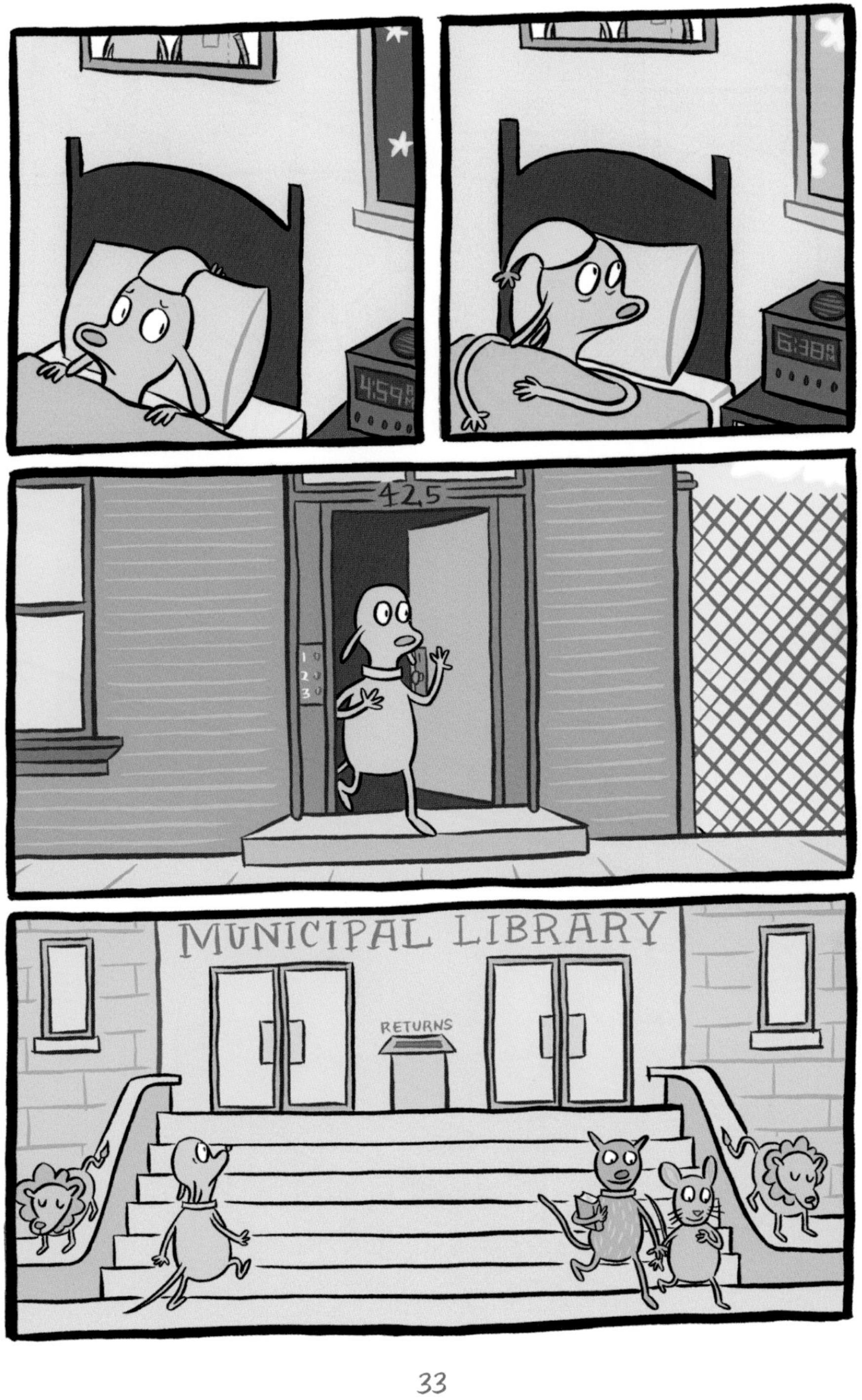
4:59
6:38
425
MUNICIPAL LIBRARY
RETURNS

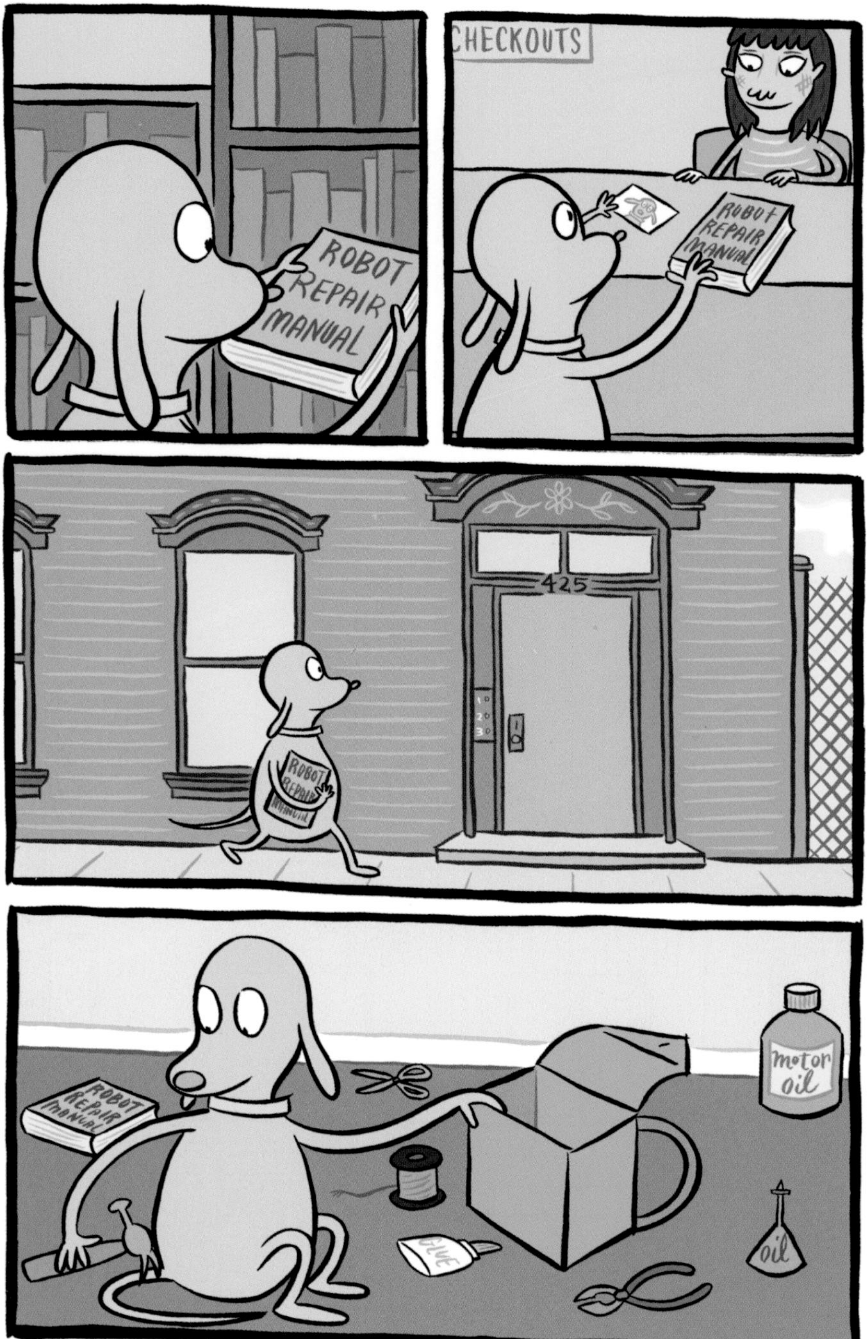
ROBOT REPAIR MANUAL
CHECKOUTS
ROBOT REPAIR MANUAL
425
ROBOT REPAIR MANUAL
ROBOT REPAIR MANUAL
motor oil
GLUE
oil

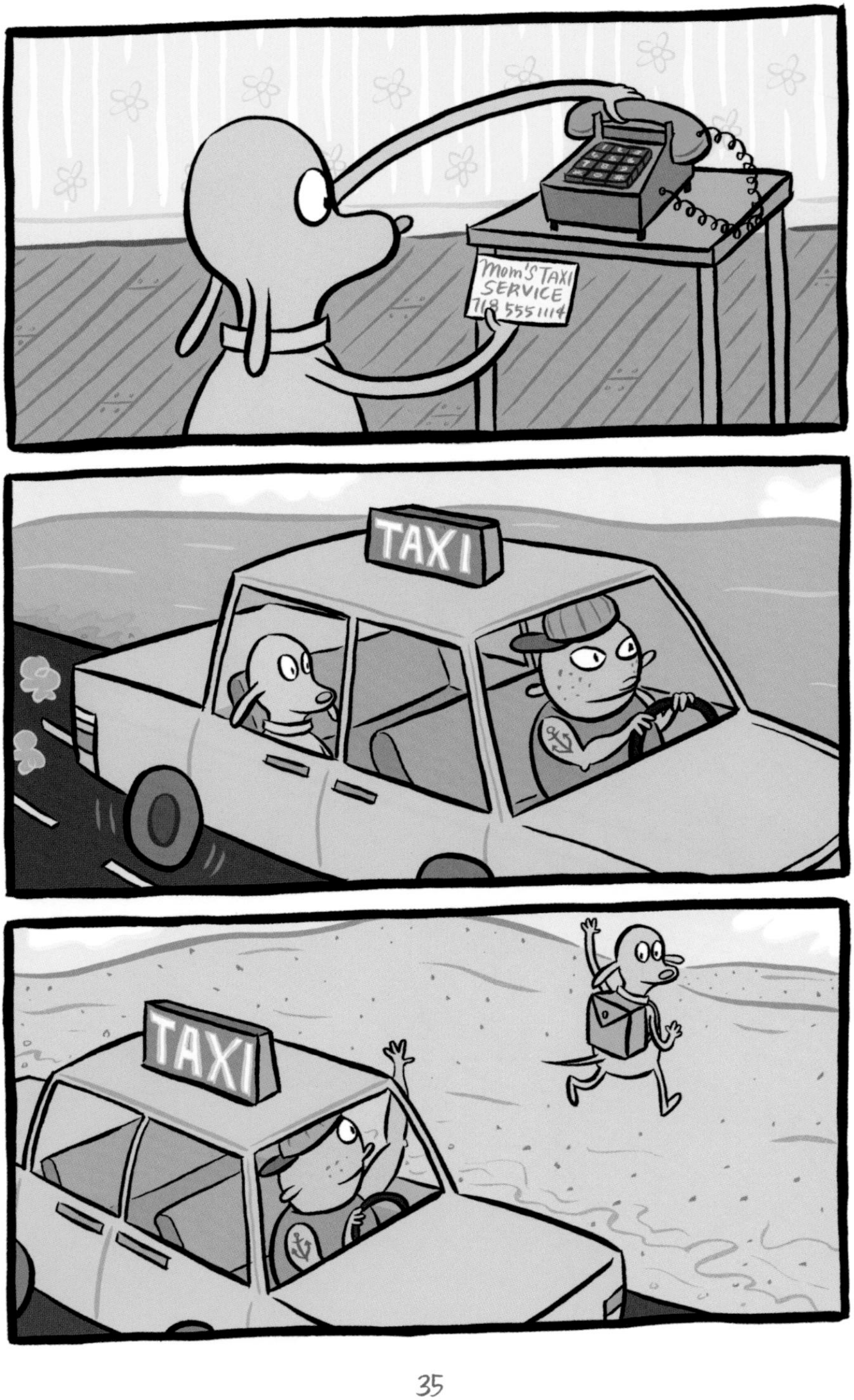
Mom's TAXI SERVICE 718 5551114
TAXI
TAXI

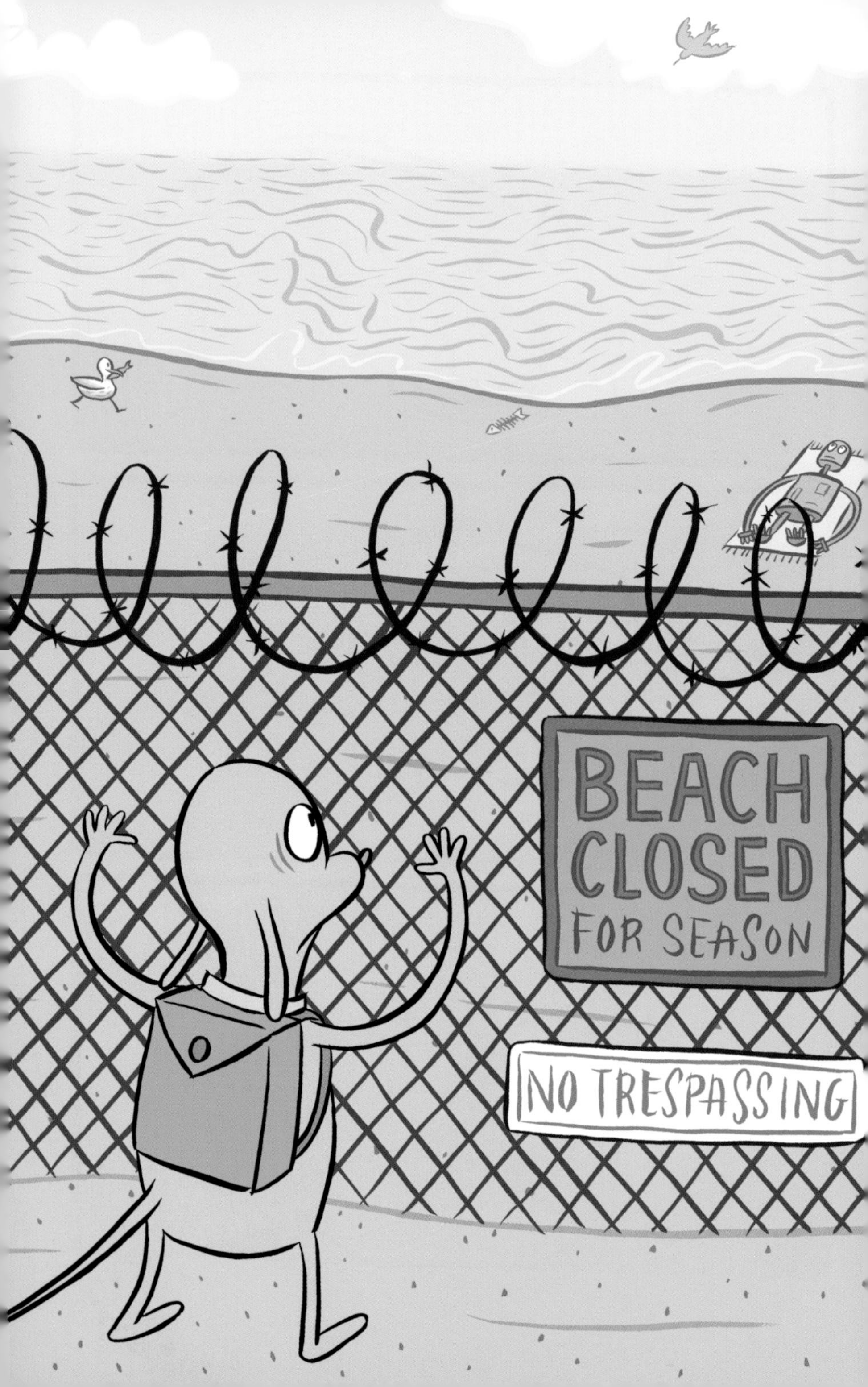
BEACH CLOSED FOR SEASON
NO TRESPASSING

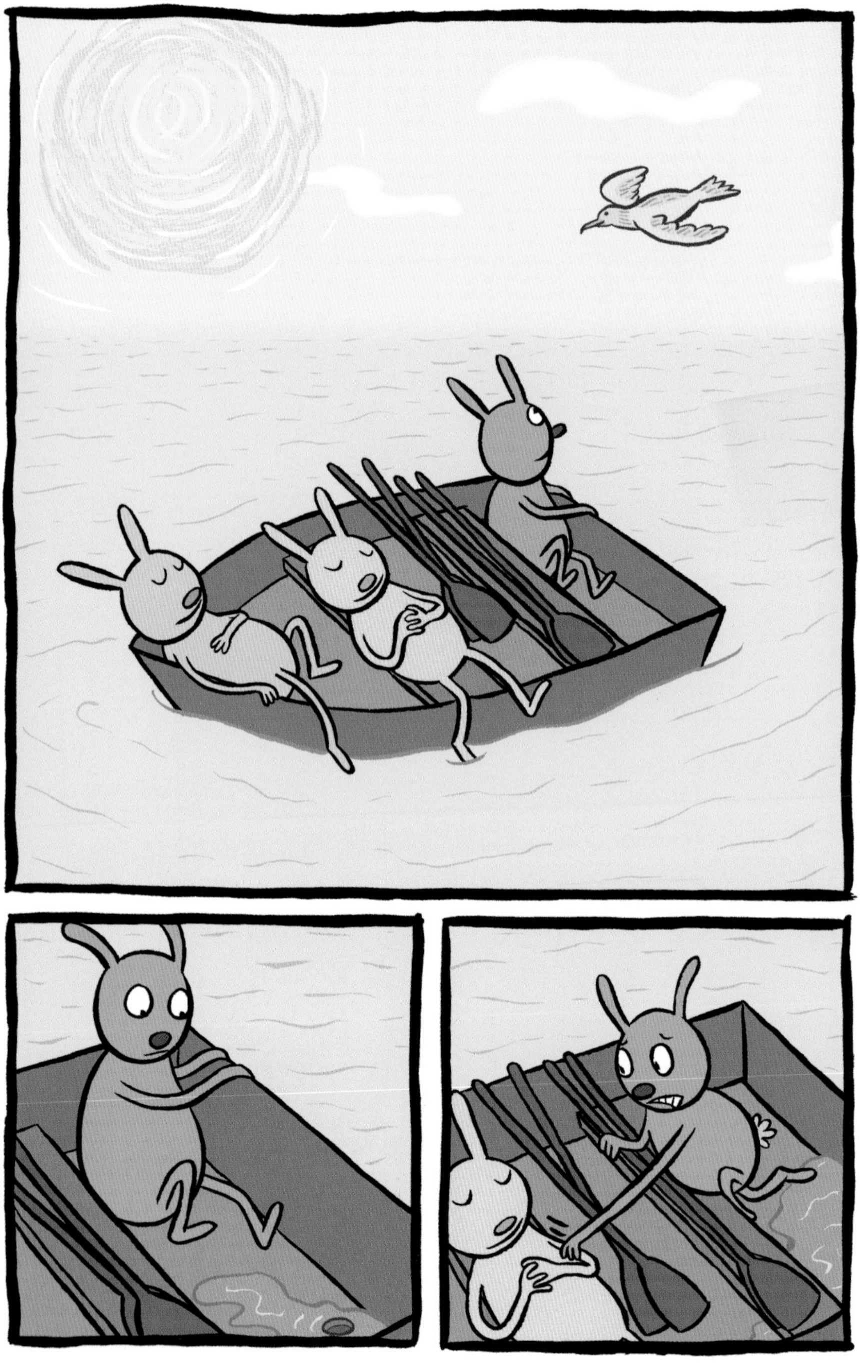

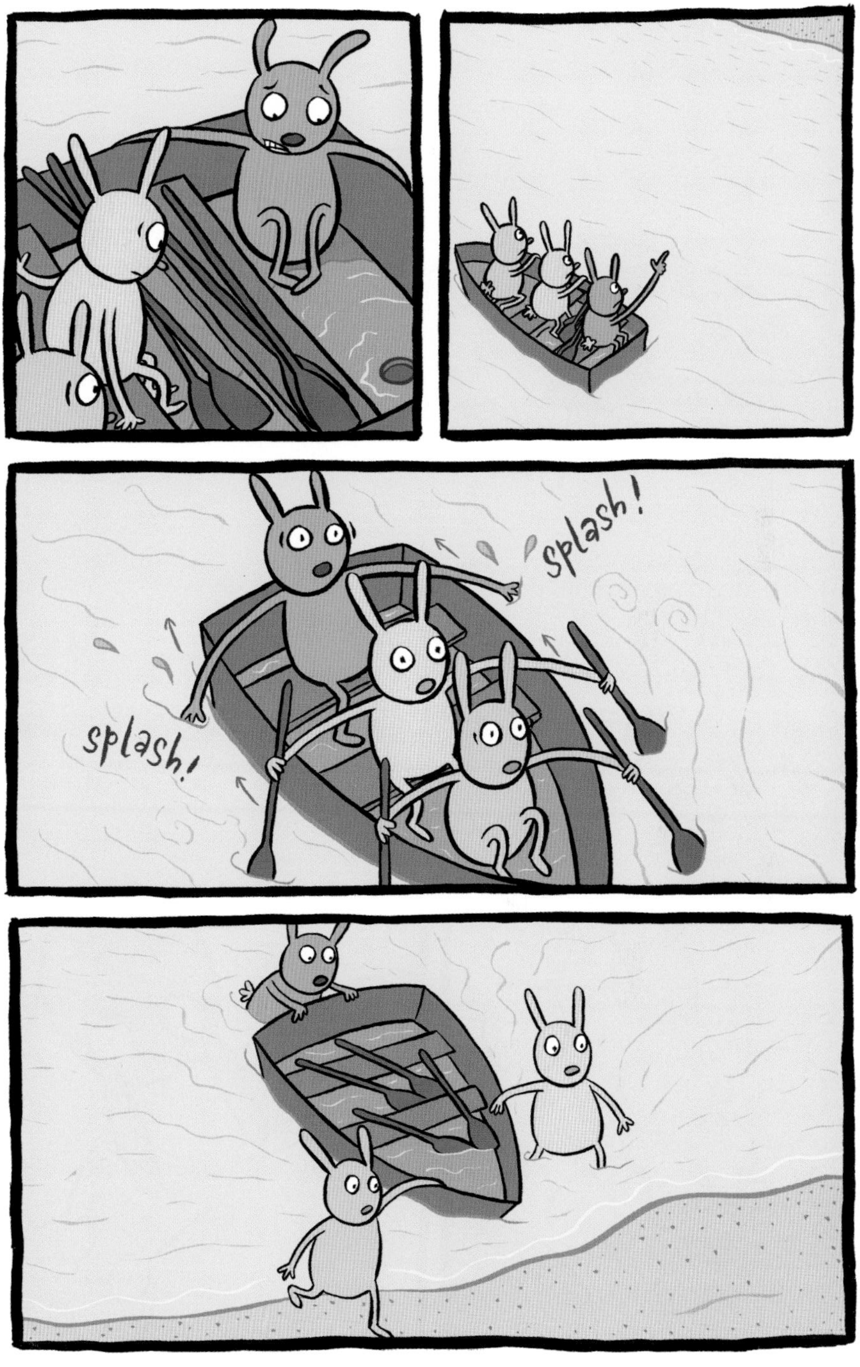
splash!
splash!

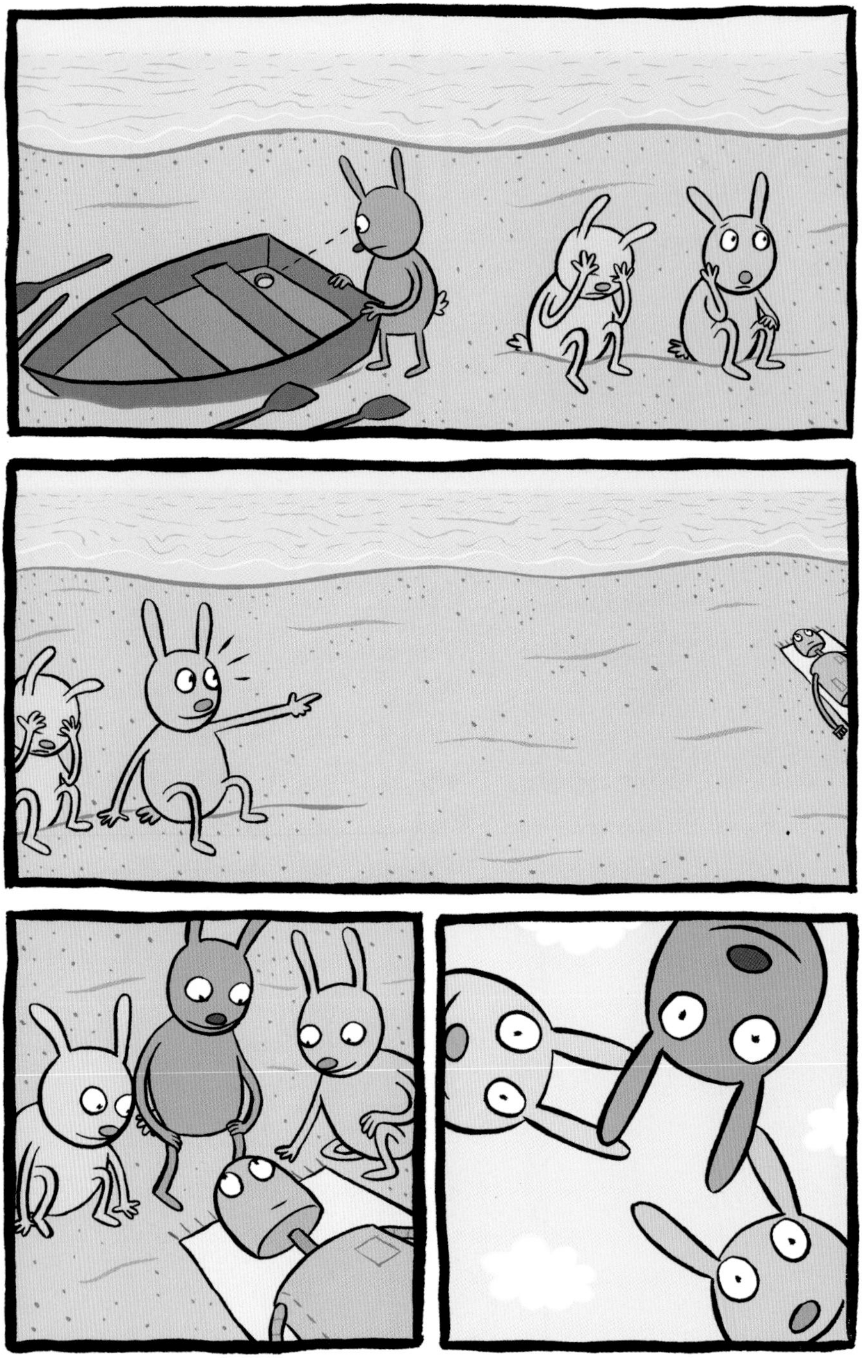

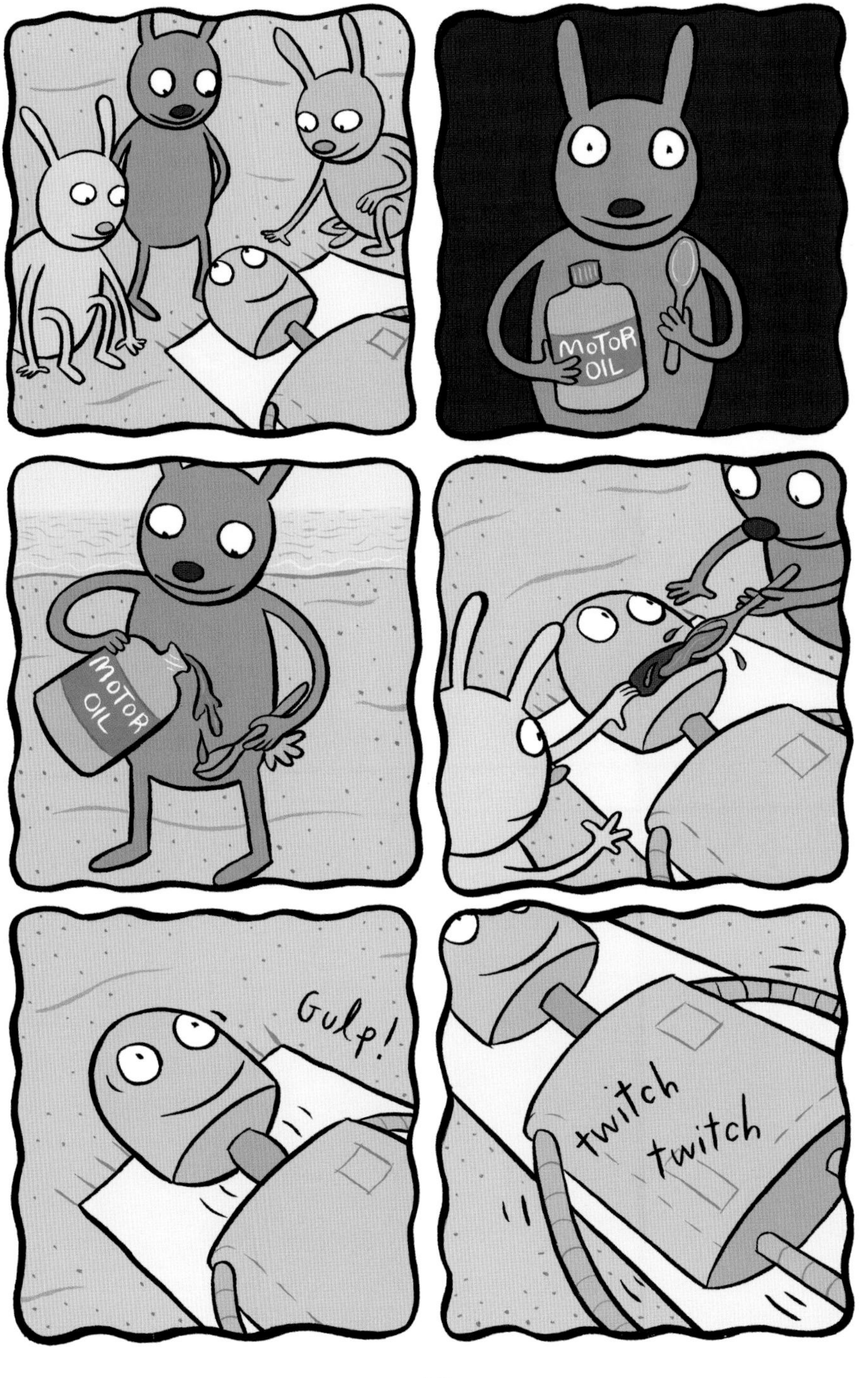
MOTOR OIL
MOTOR OIL
Gulp!
twitch twitch

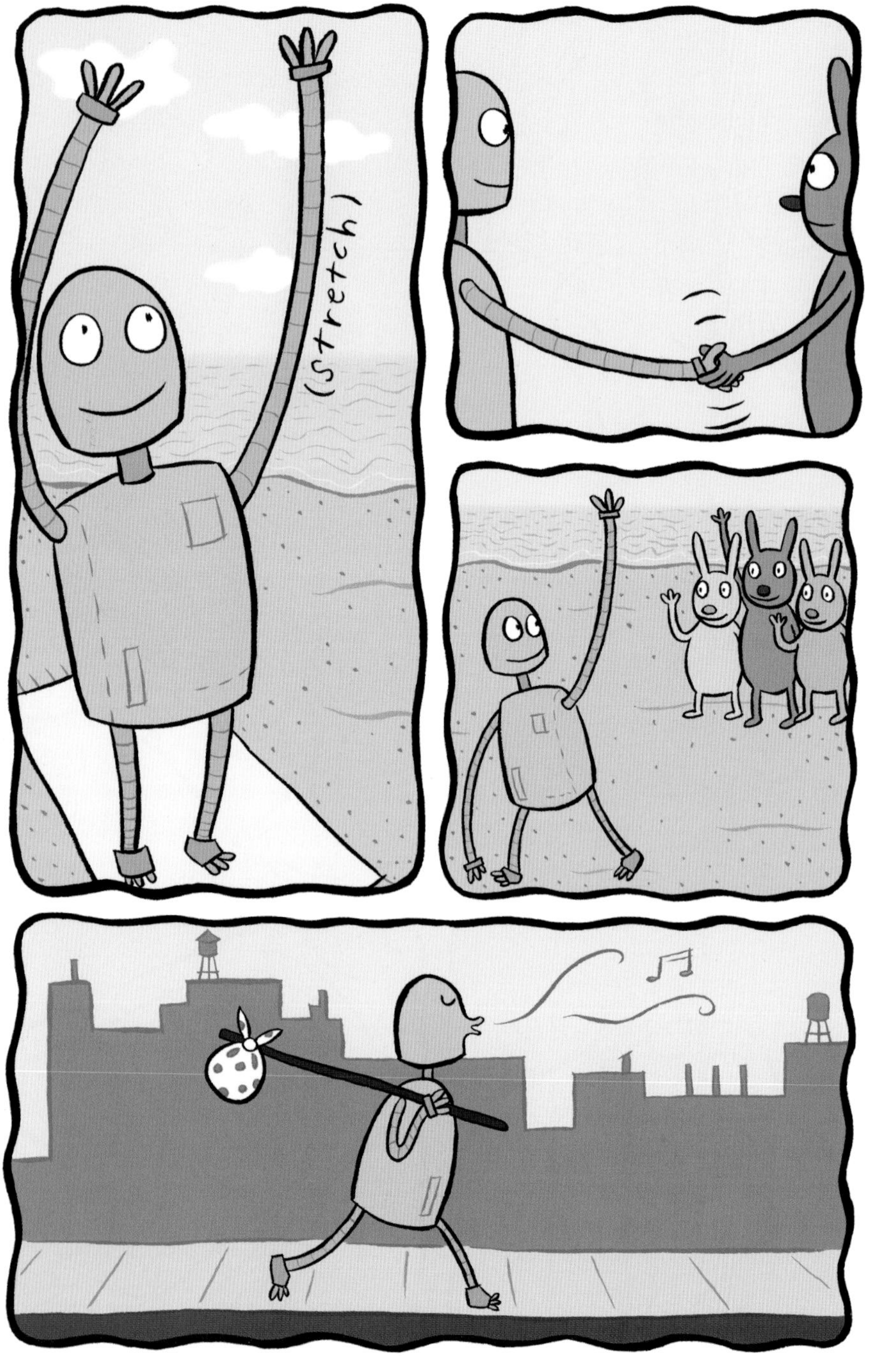
(stretch)

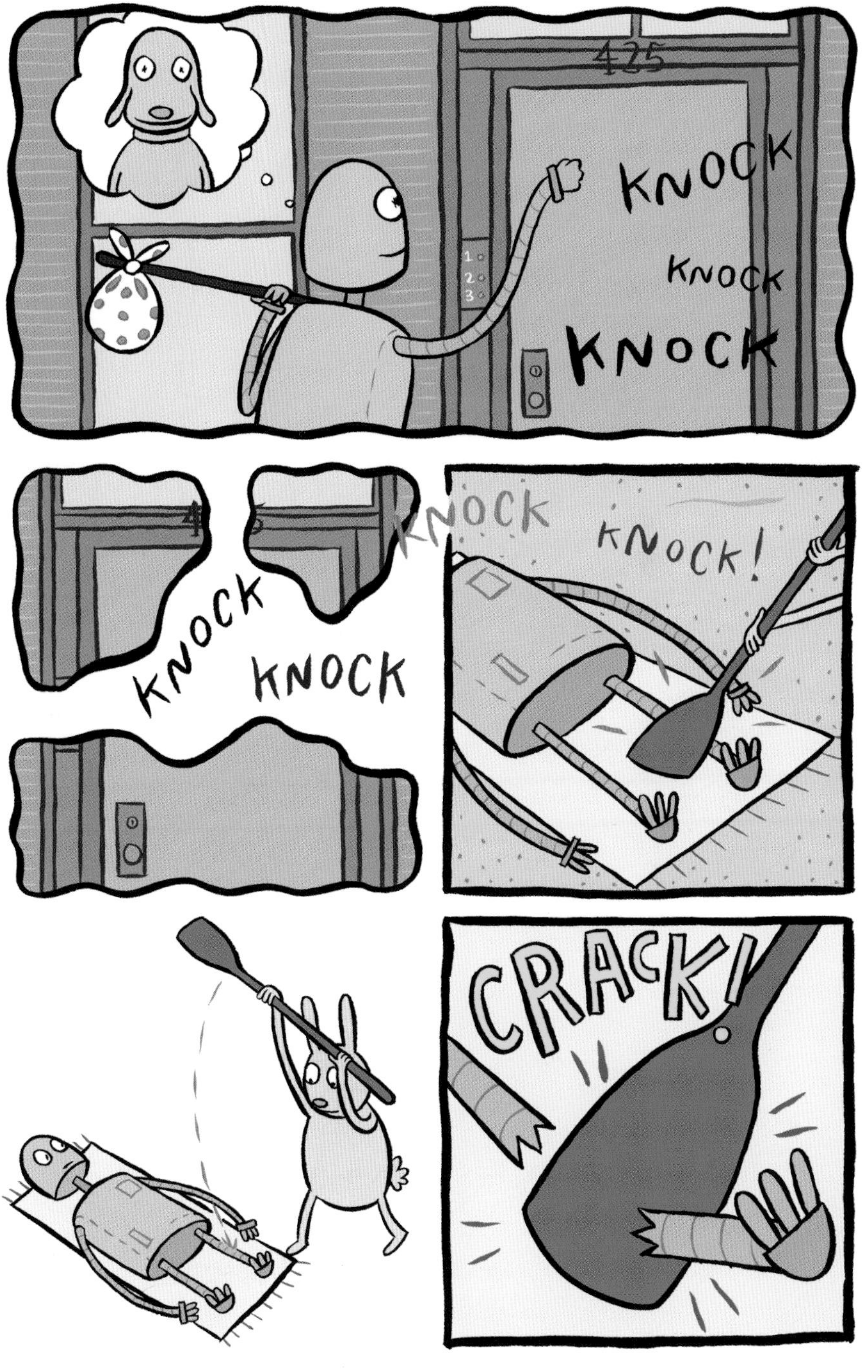
425
KNOCK
KNOCK
KNOCK
KNOCK
KNOCK
KNOCK
KNOCK!
CRACK!

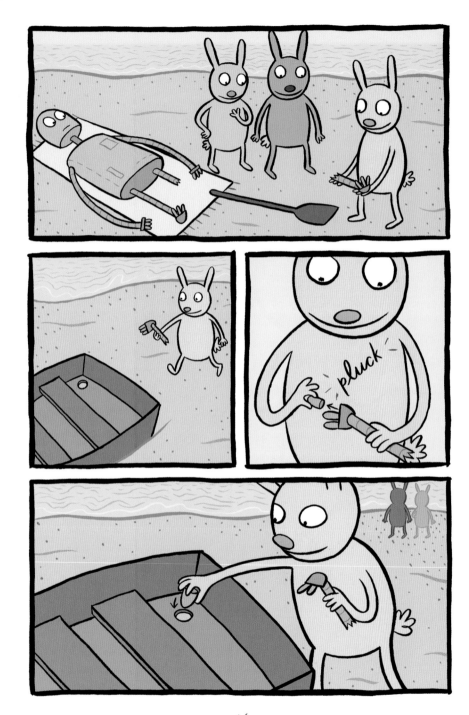

pluck

46

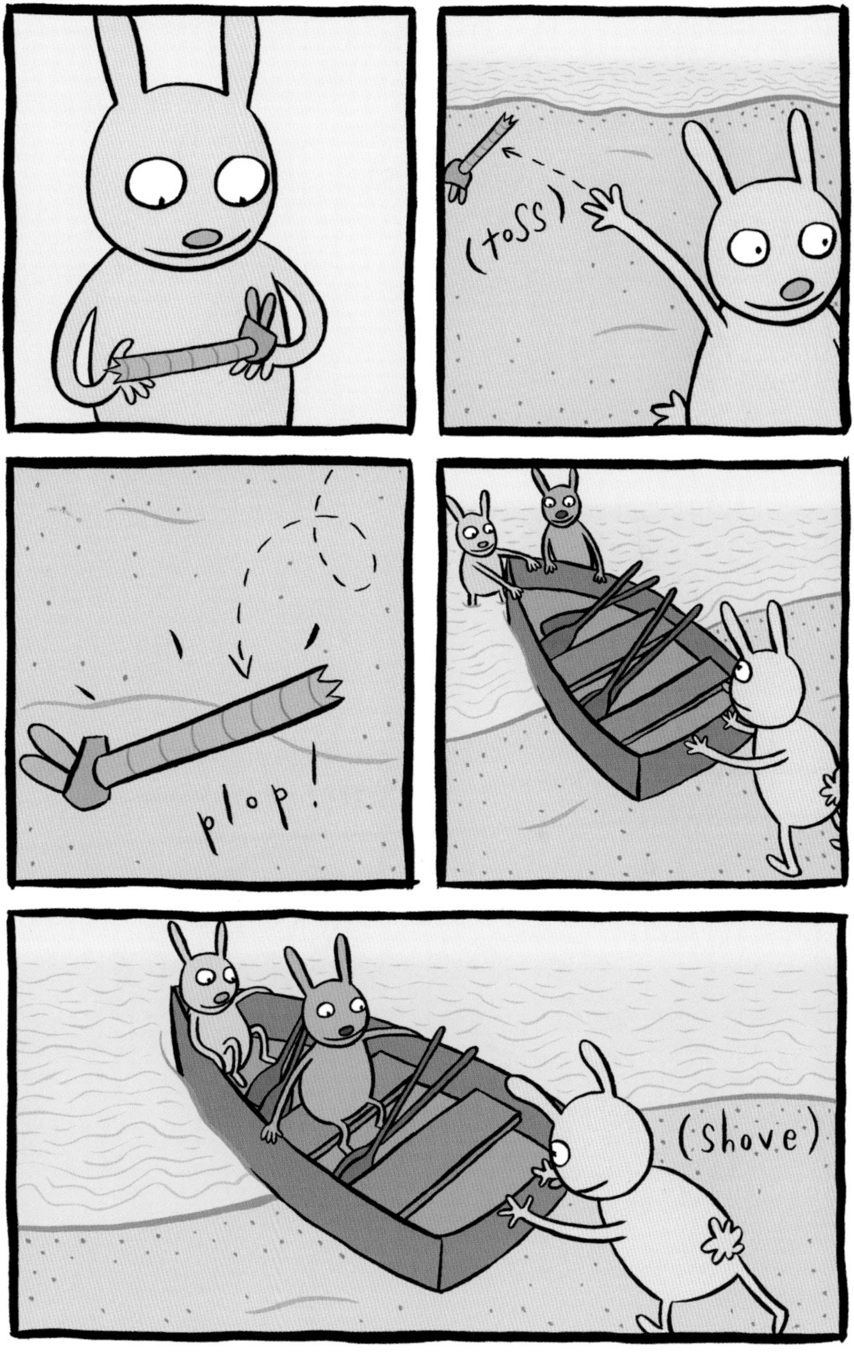
(toss)
plop!
(shove)

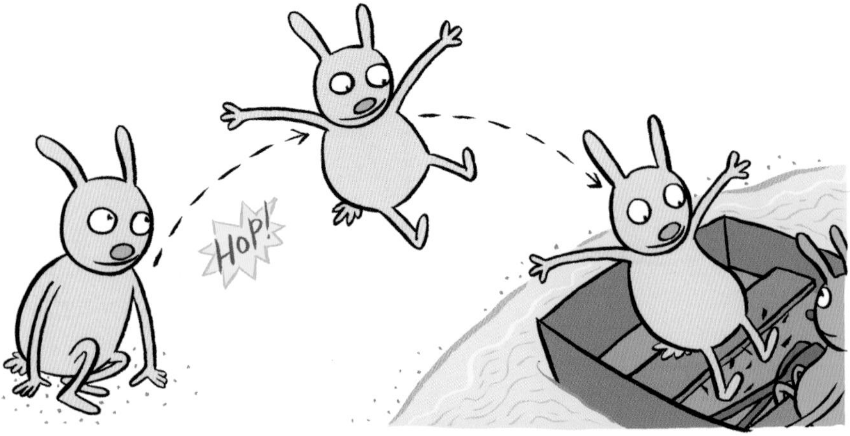
HOP!

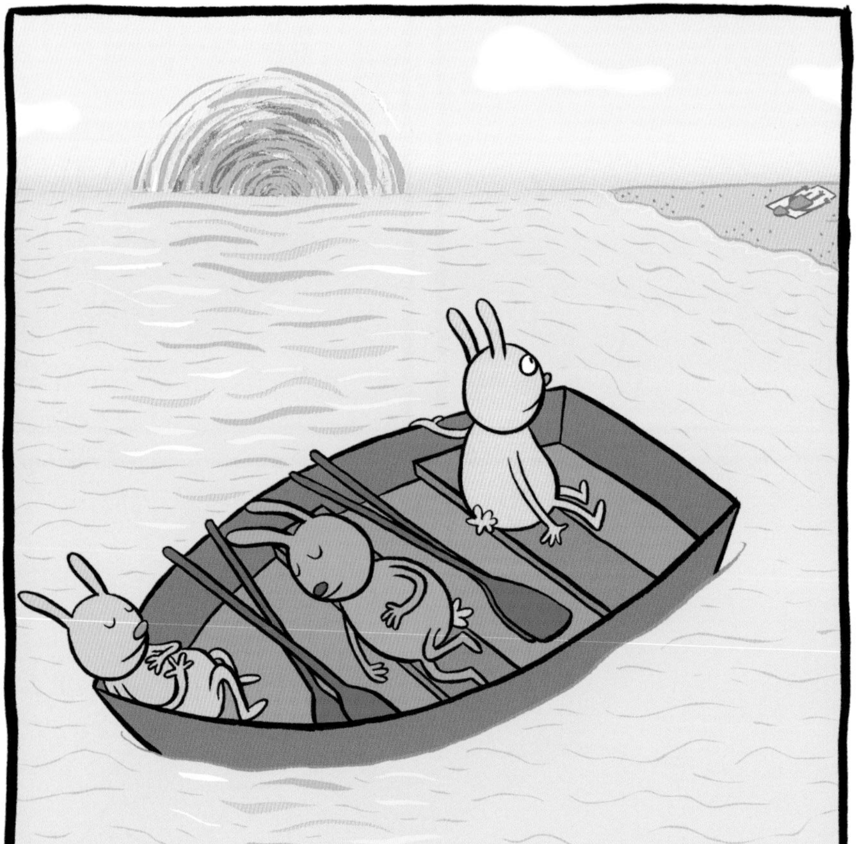

October

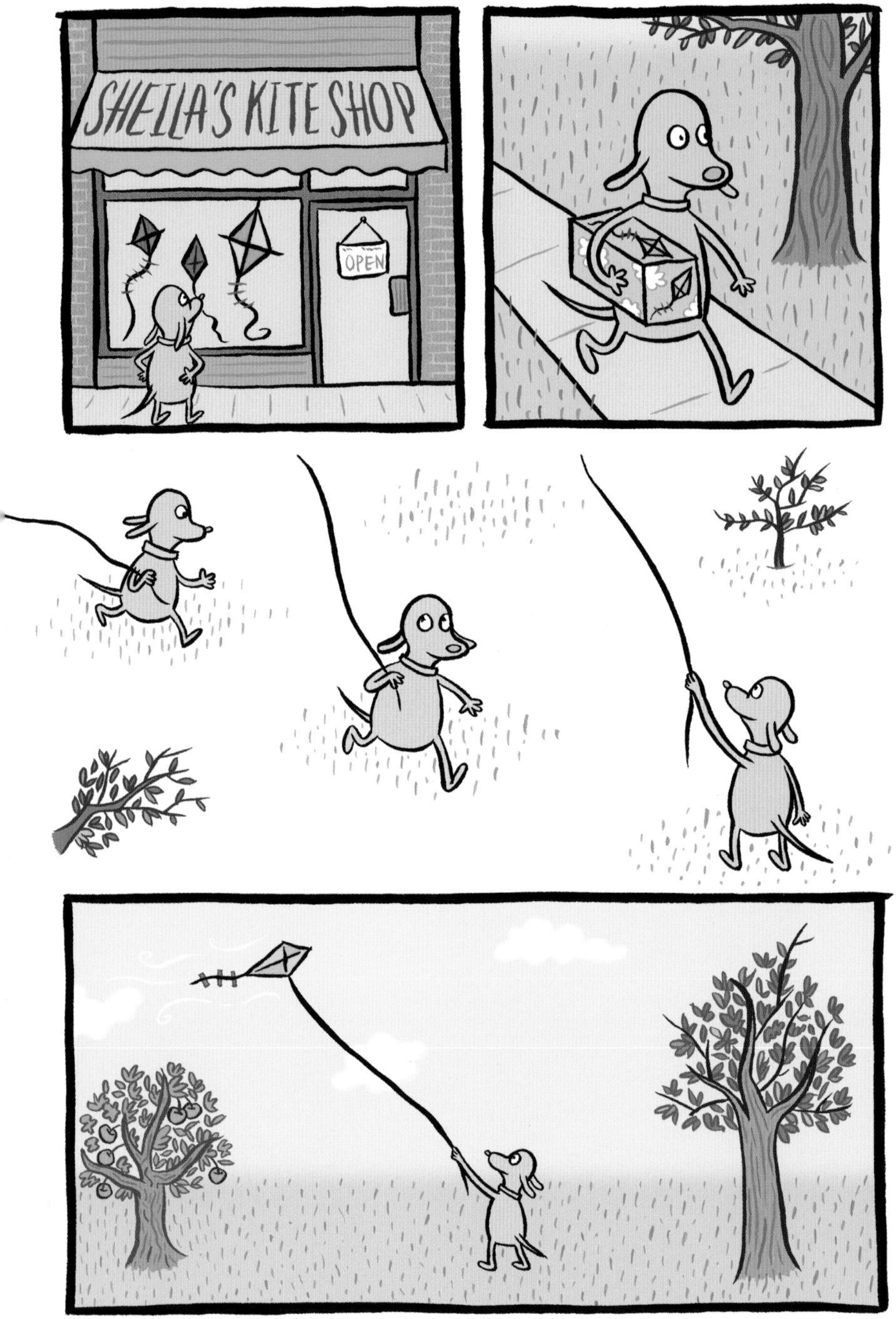
SHEILA'S KITE SHOP
OPEN

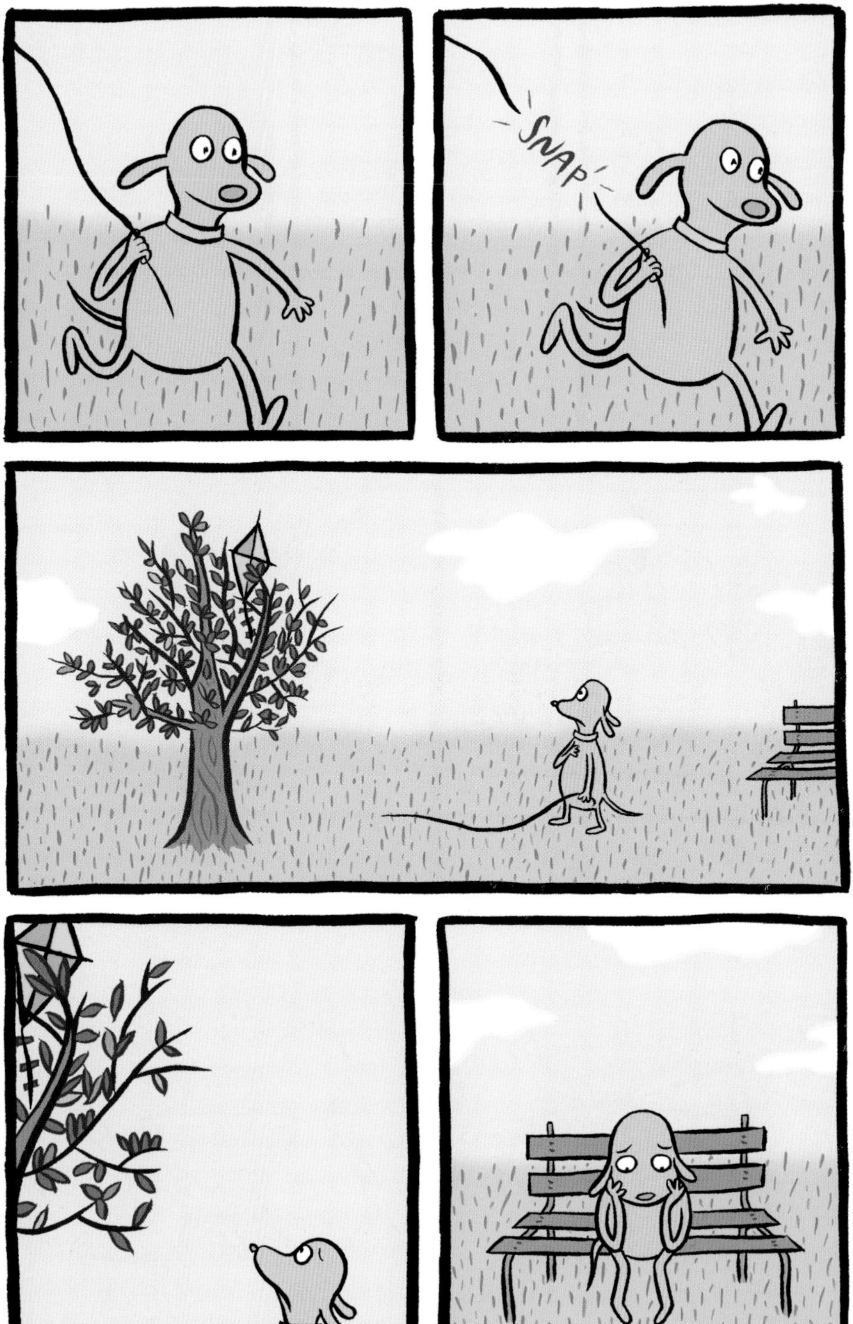
SNAP

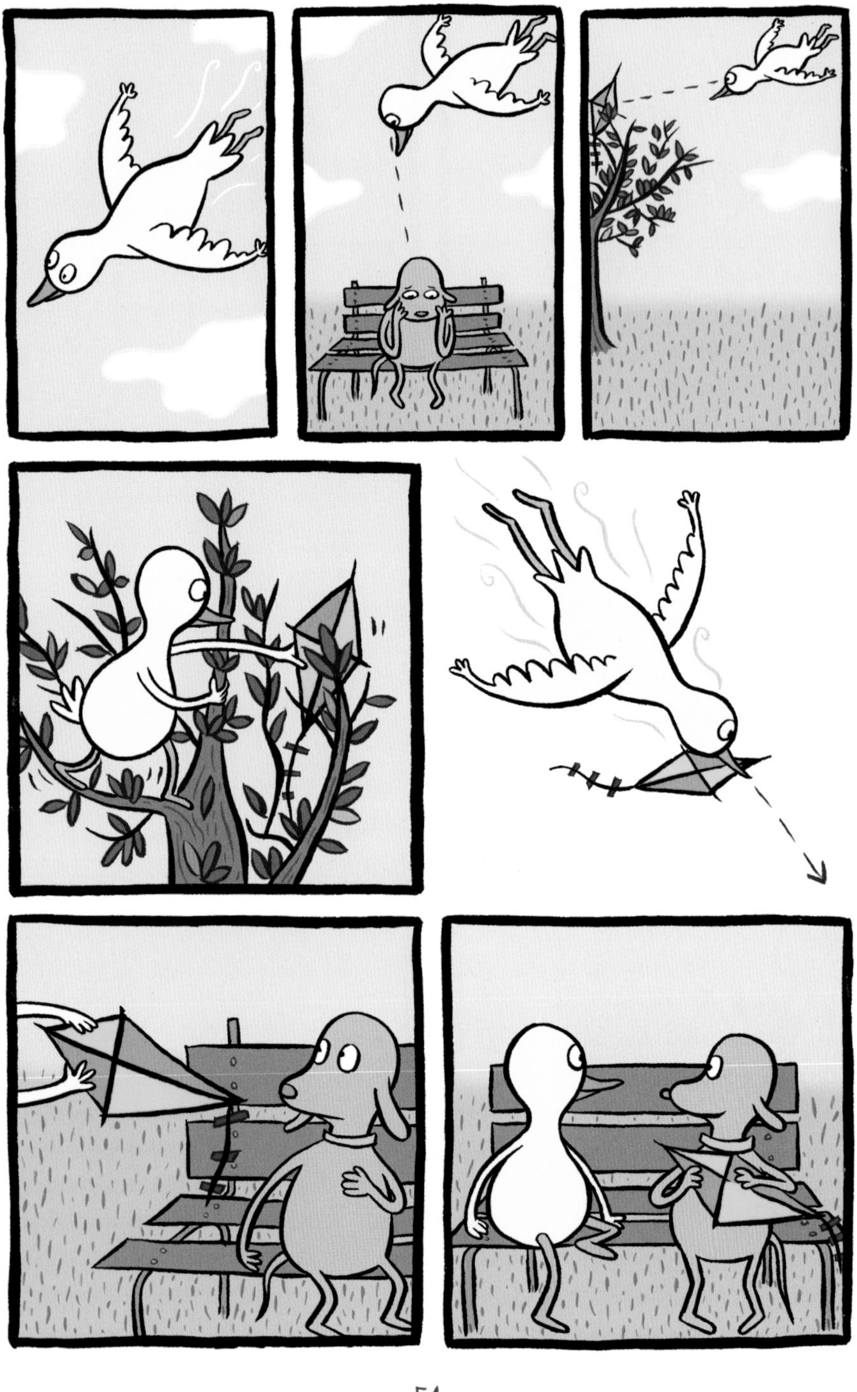

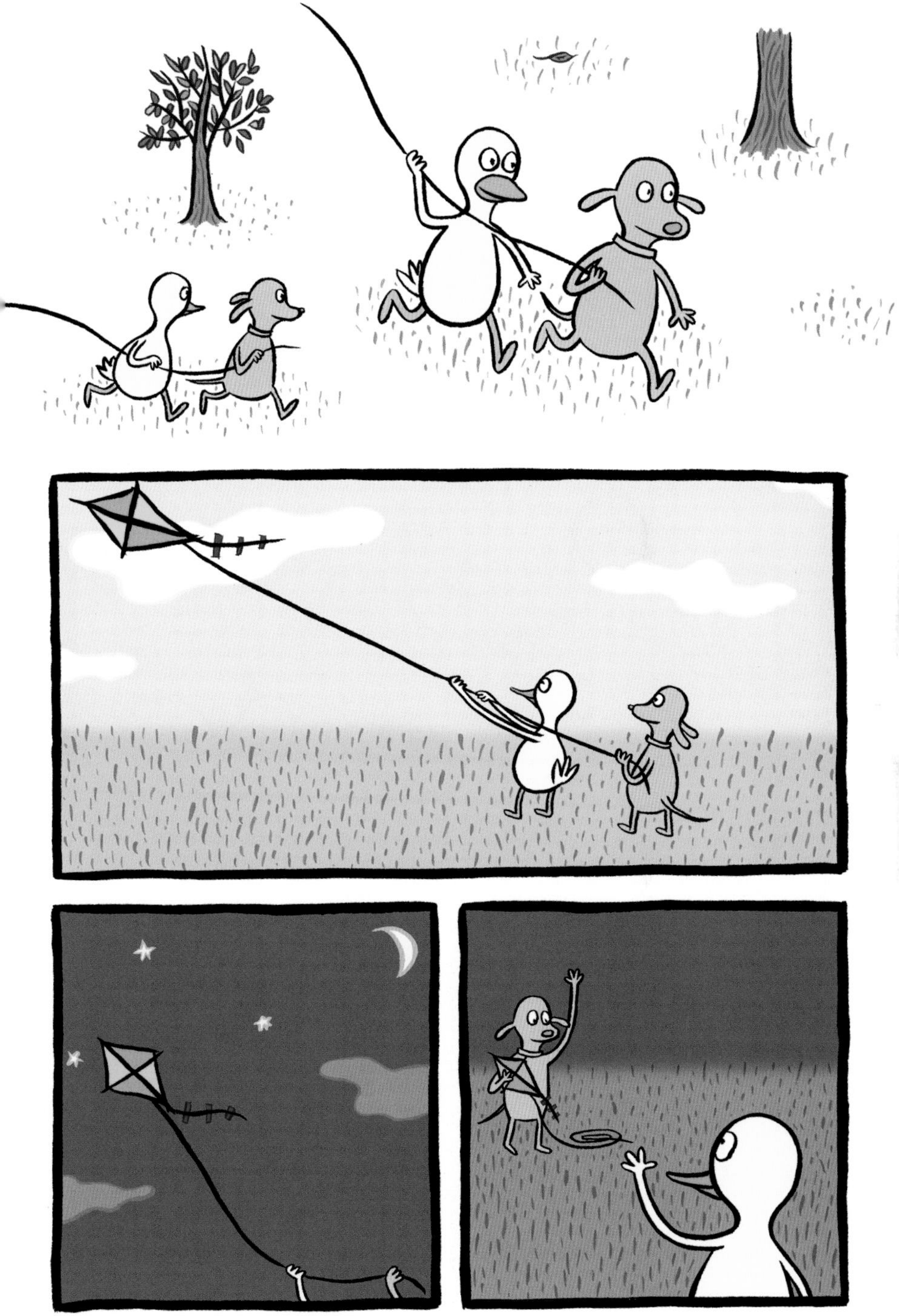

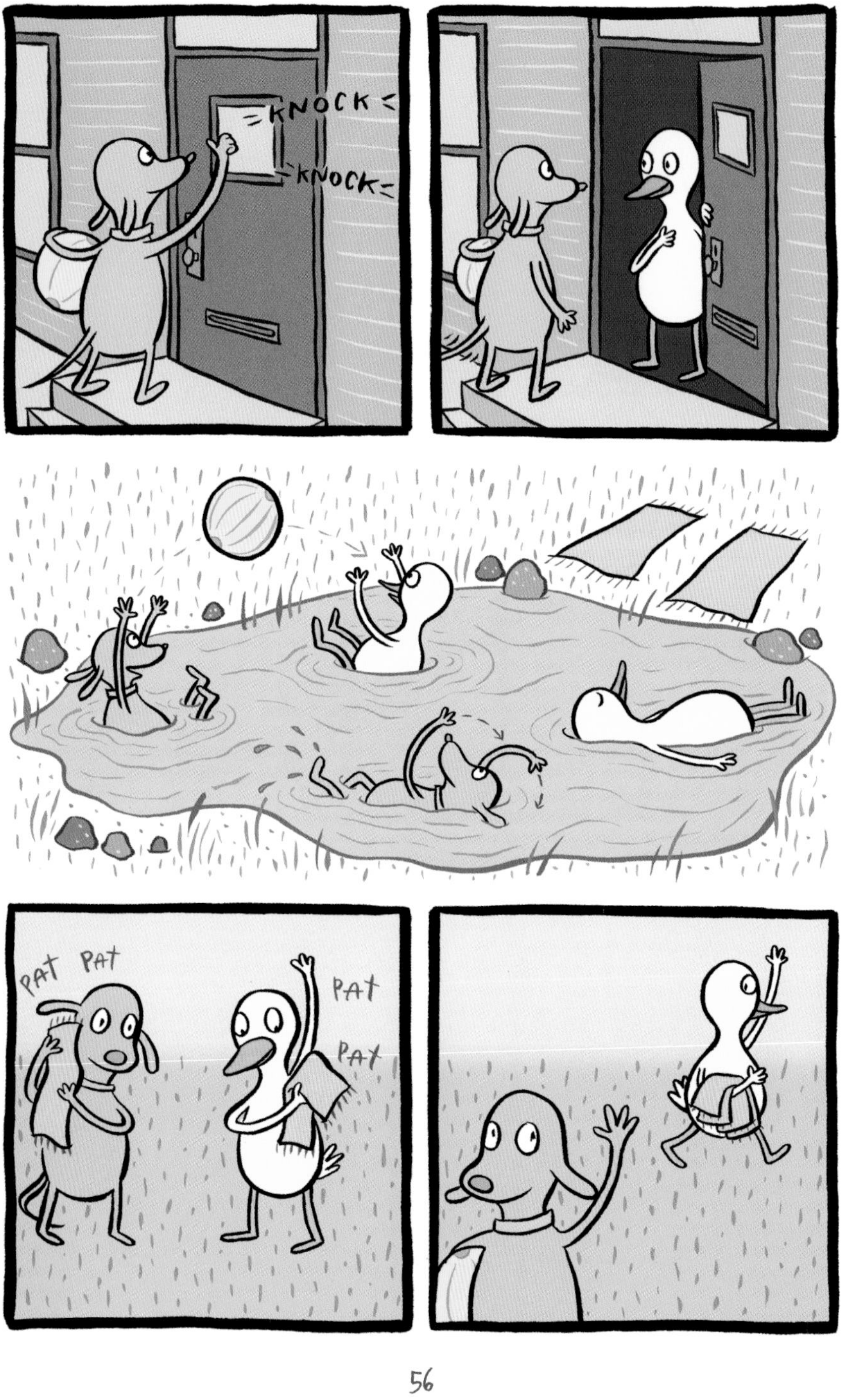
KNOCK
KNOCK
PAT PAT
PAT
PAT

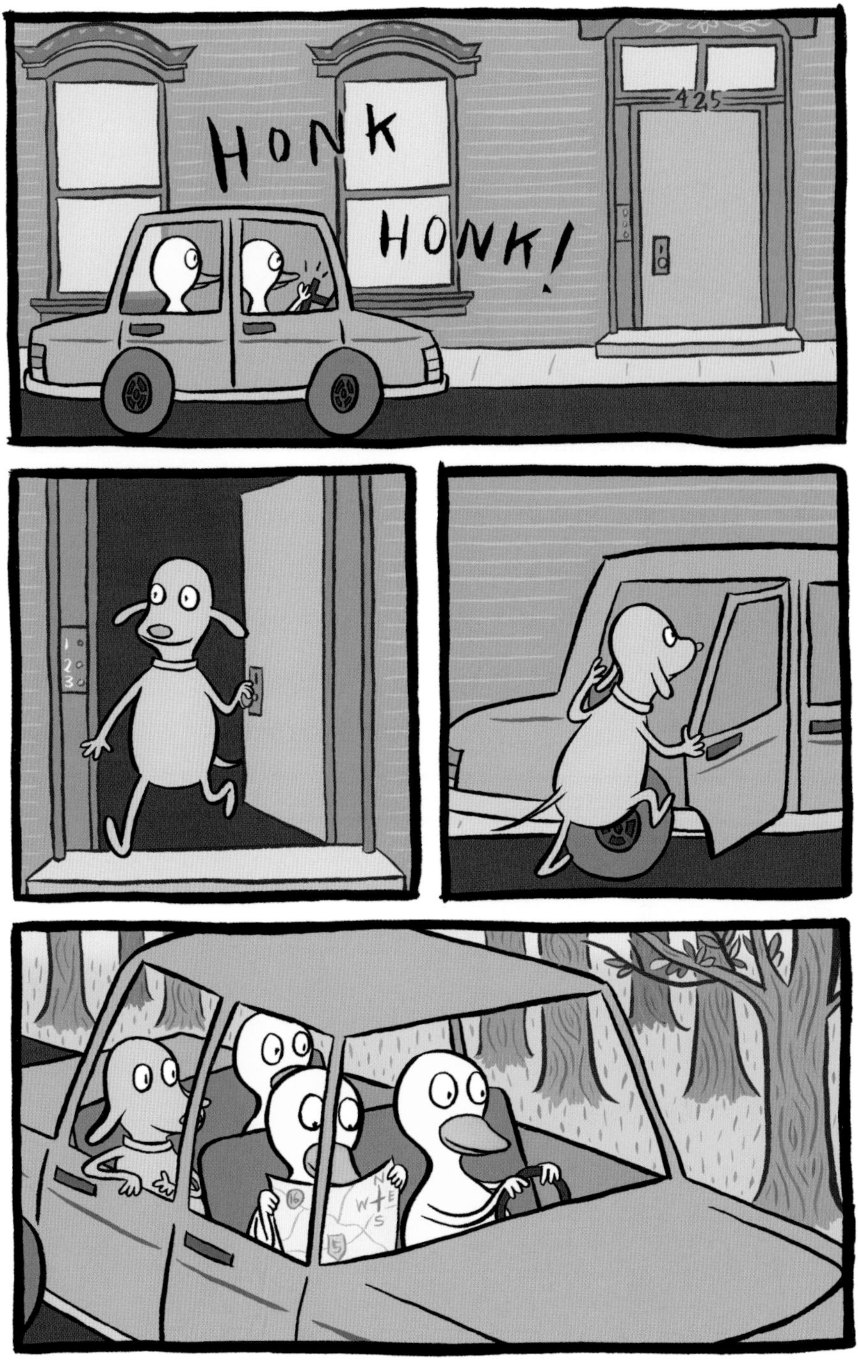
HONK
HONK!
425

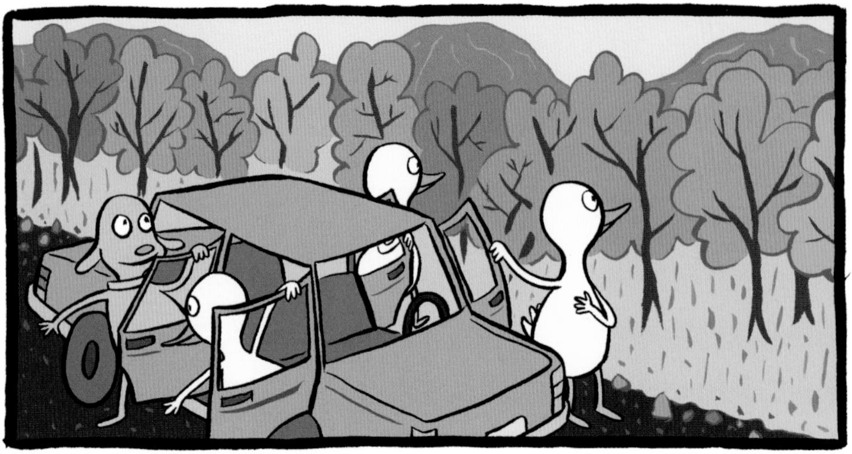

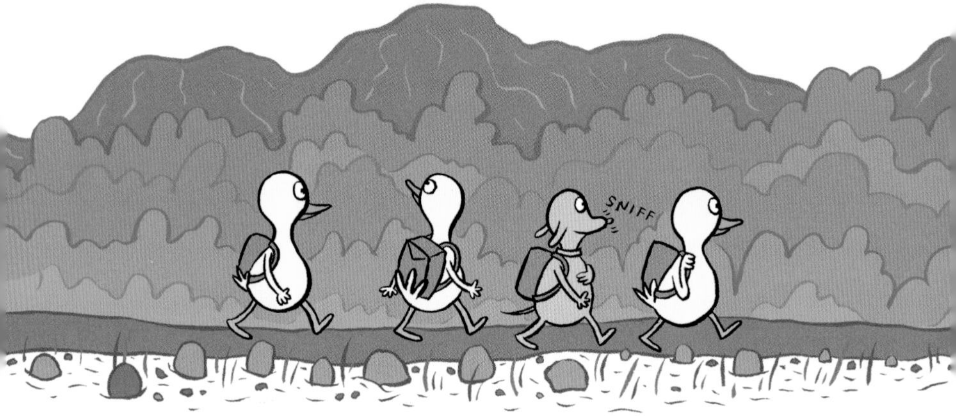
SNIFF

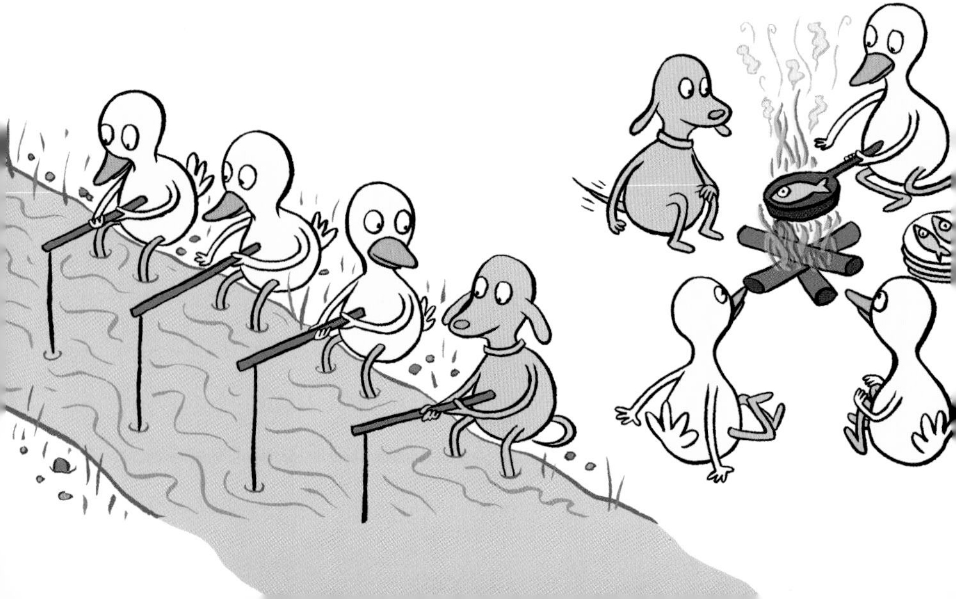

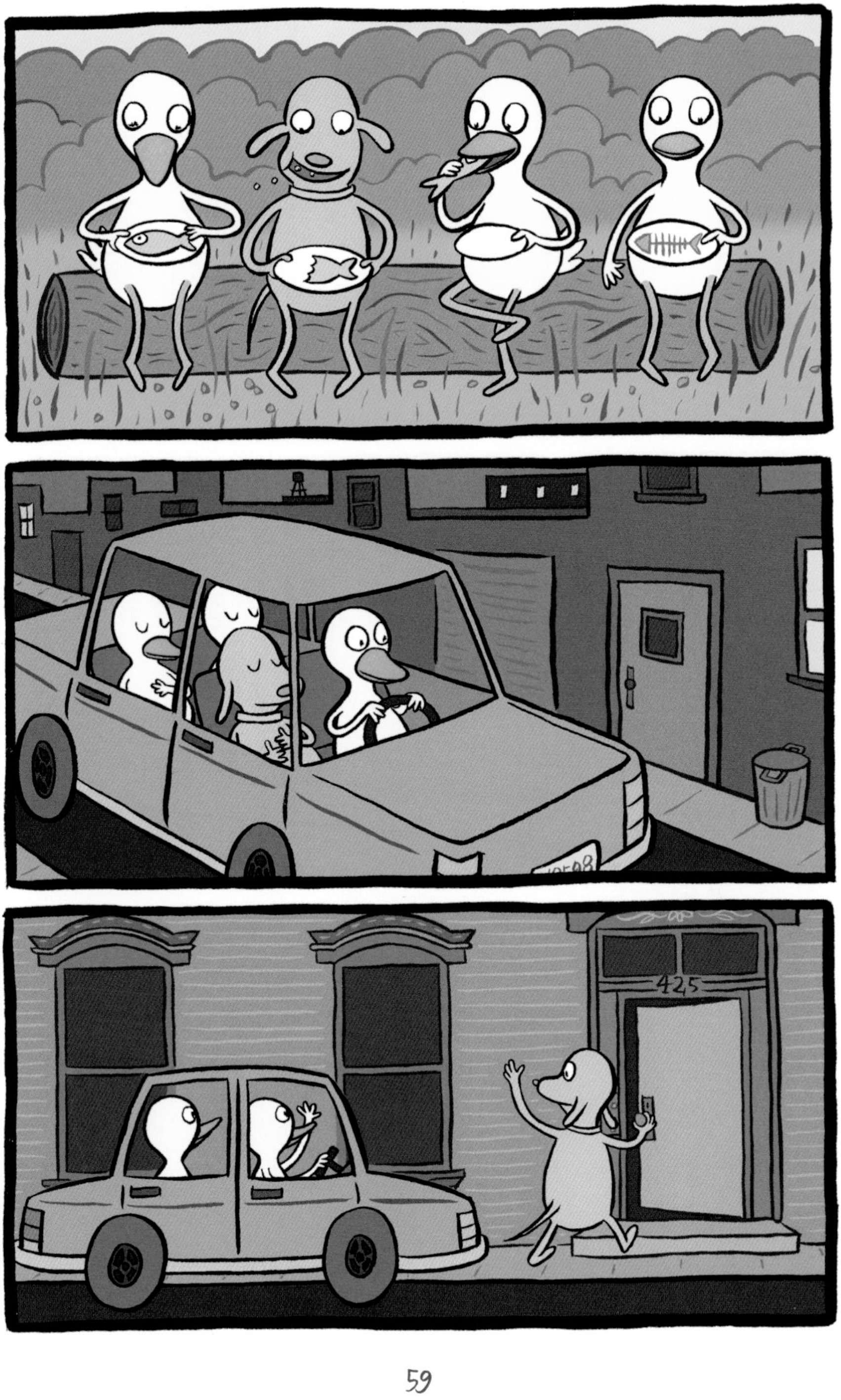
425

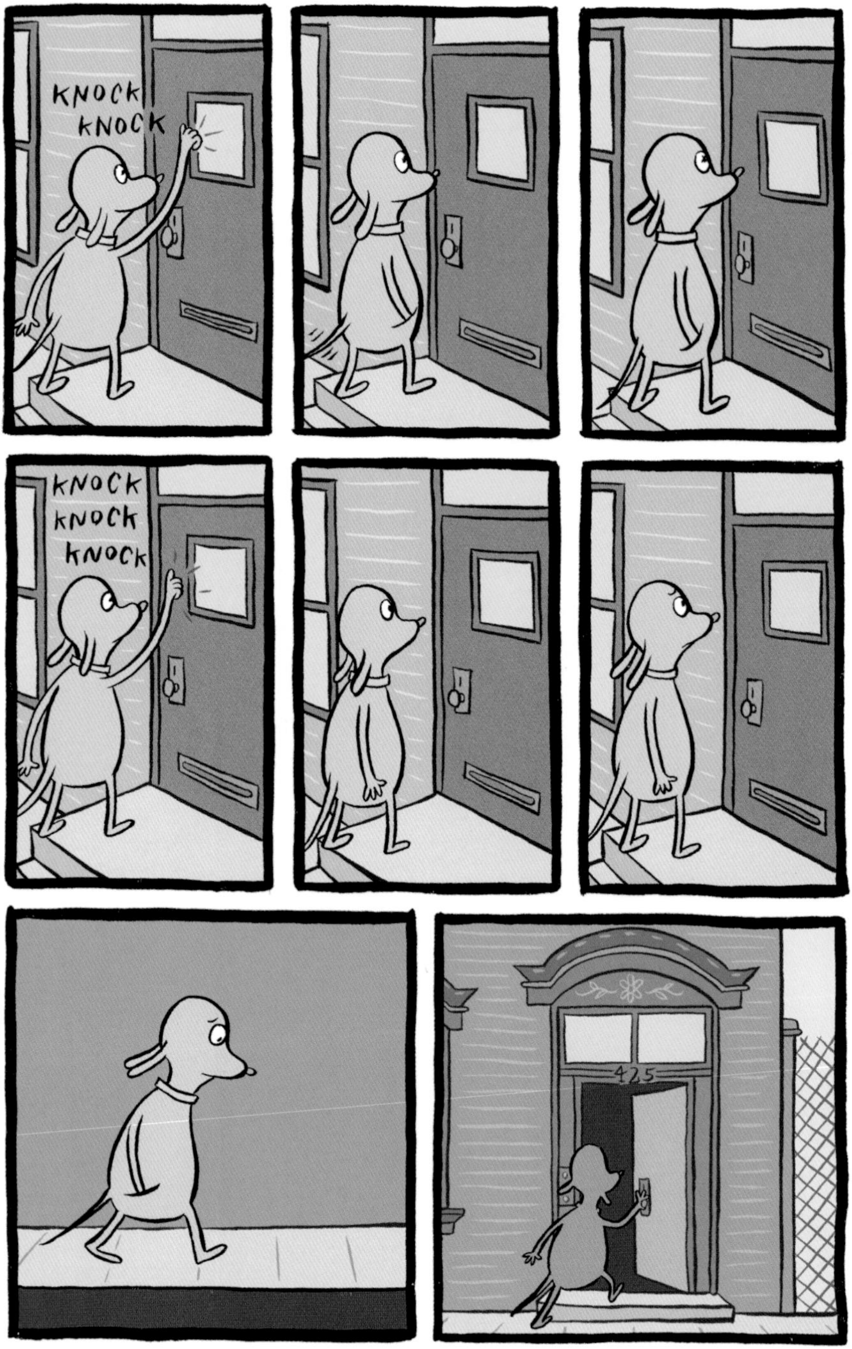
KNOCK KNOCK
KNOCK KNOCK KNOCK
425

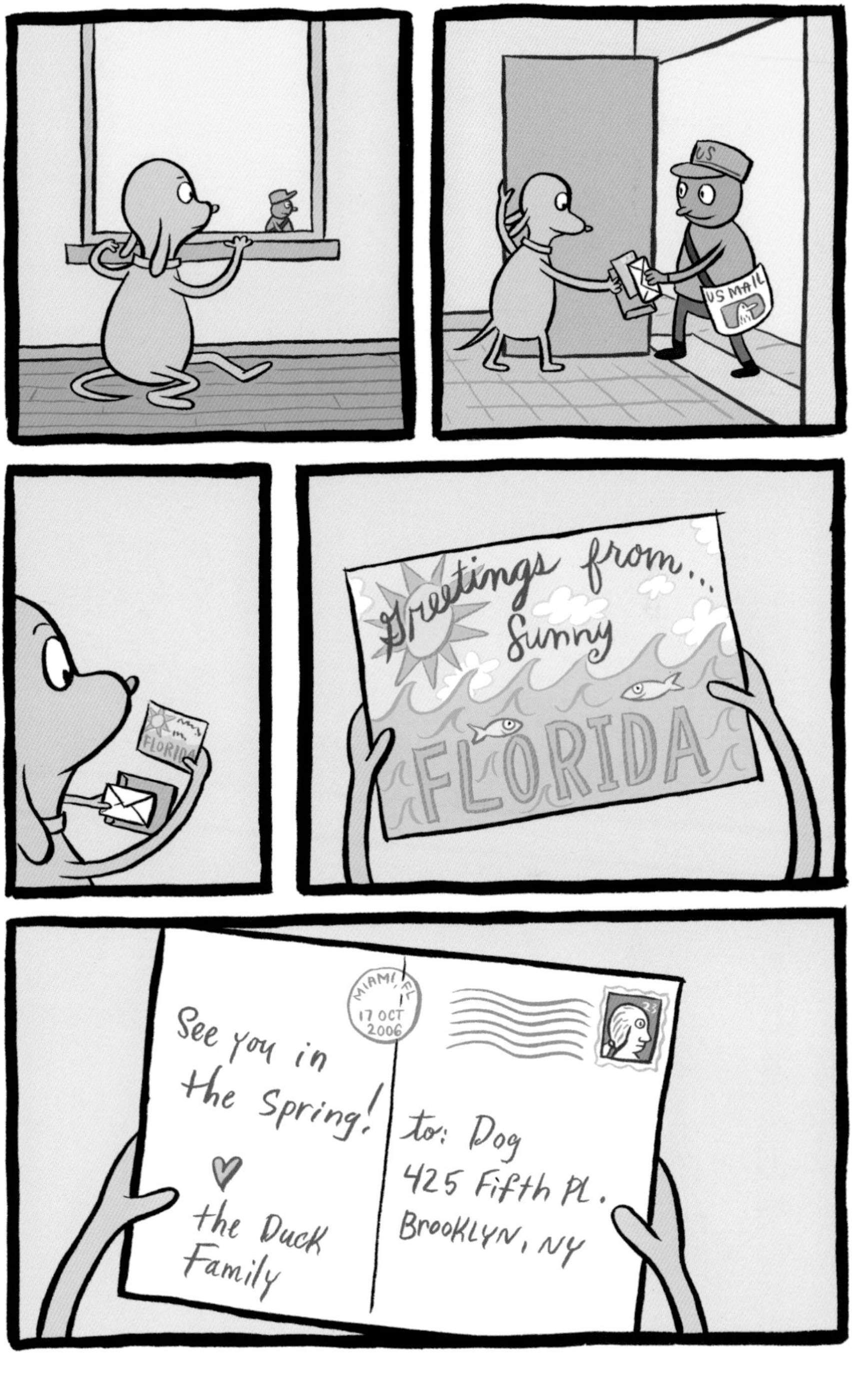
US
US MAIL
Greetings from...
Sunny
FLORIDA
MIAMI, FL
17 OCT
2006
See you in
the Spring!
the Duck
Family
to: Dog
425 Fifth Pl.
Brooklyn, NY

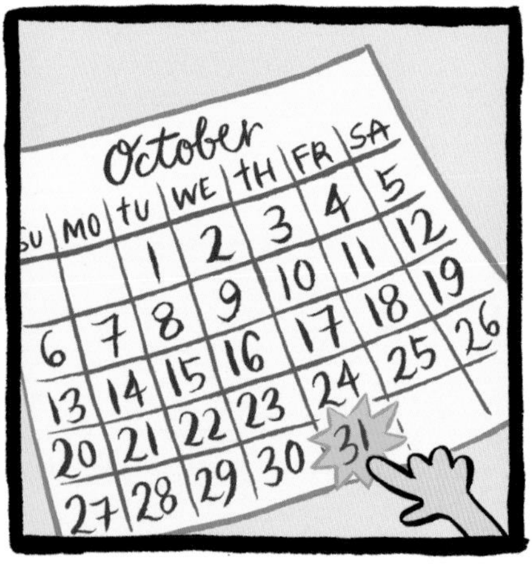
October
SU MO TU WE TH FR SA
1 2 3 4 5
6 7 8 9 10 11 12
13 14 15 16 17 18 19
20 21 22 23 24 25 26
27 28 29 30 31

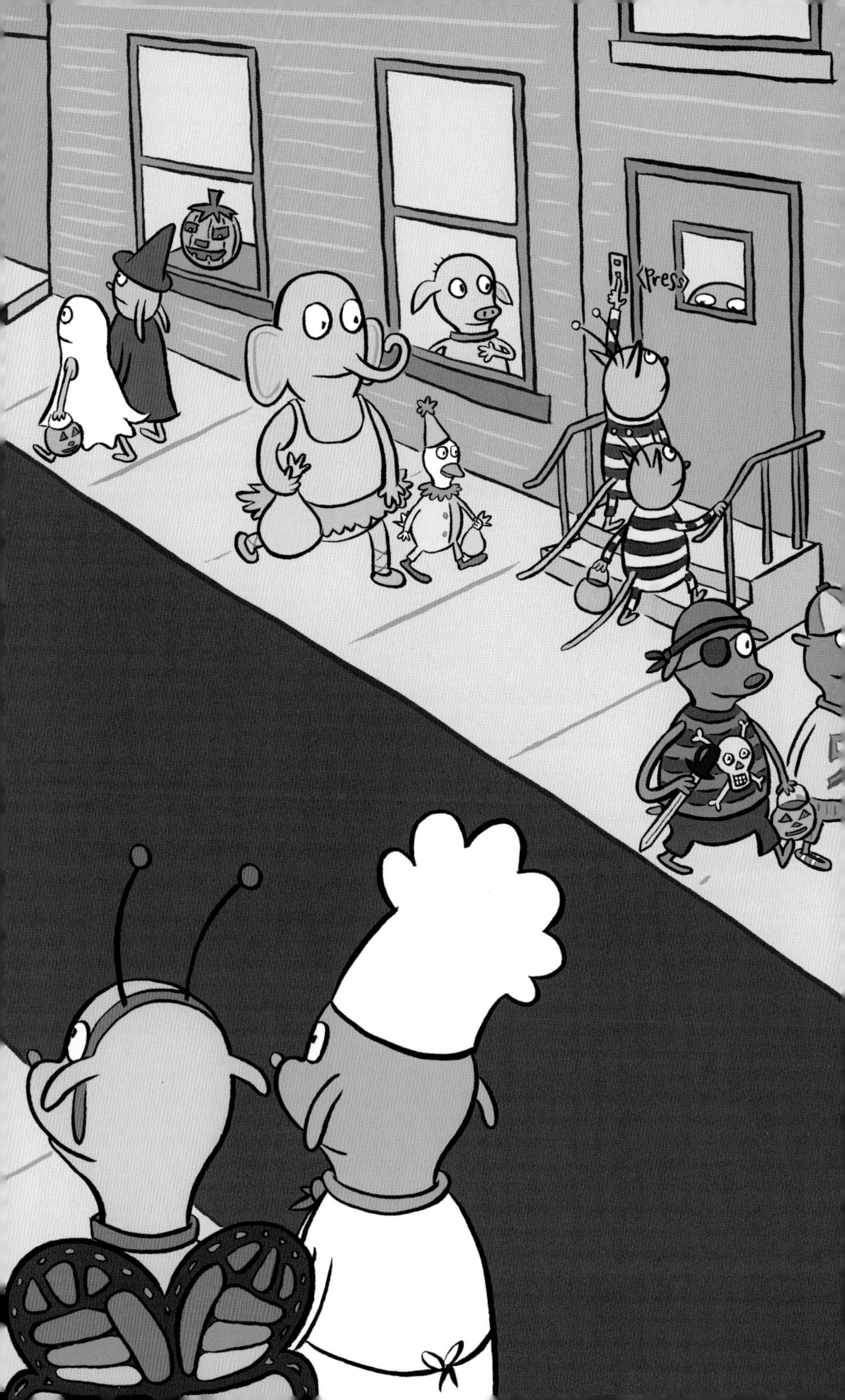
Press

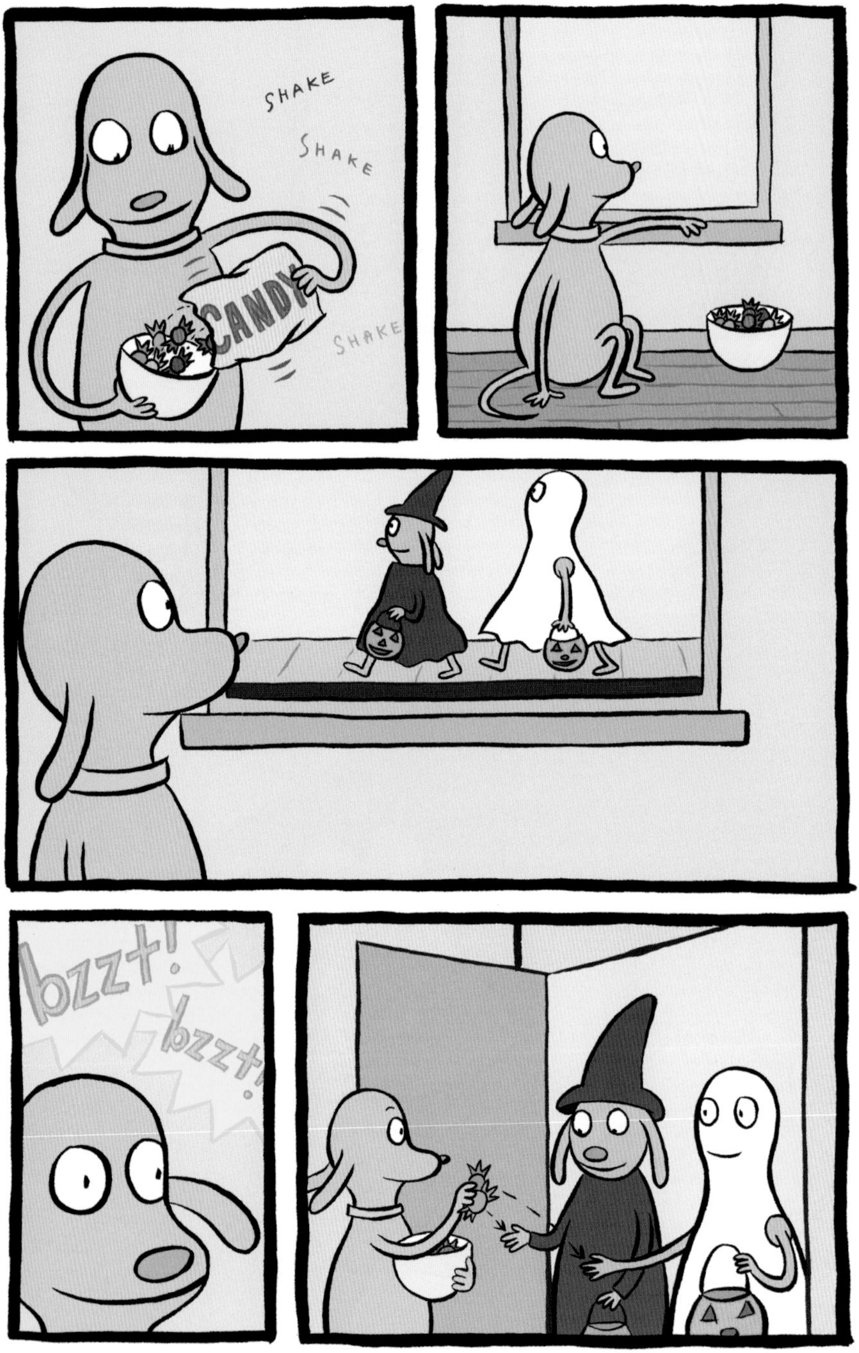
SHAKE
SHAKE
CANDY
SHAKE
bzzt!
bzzt!

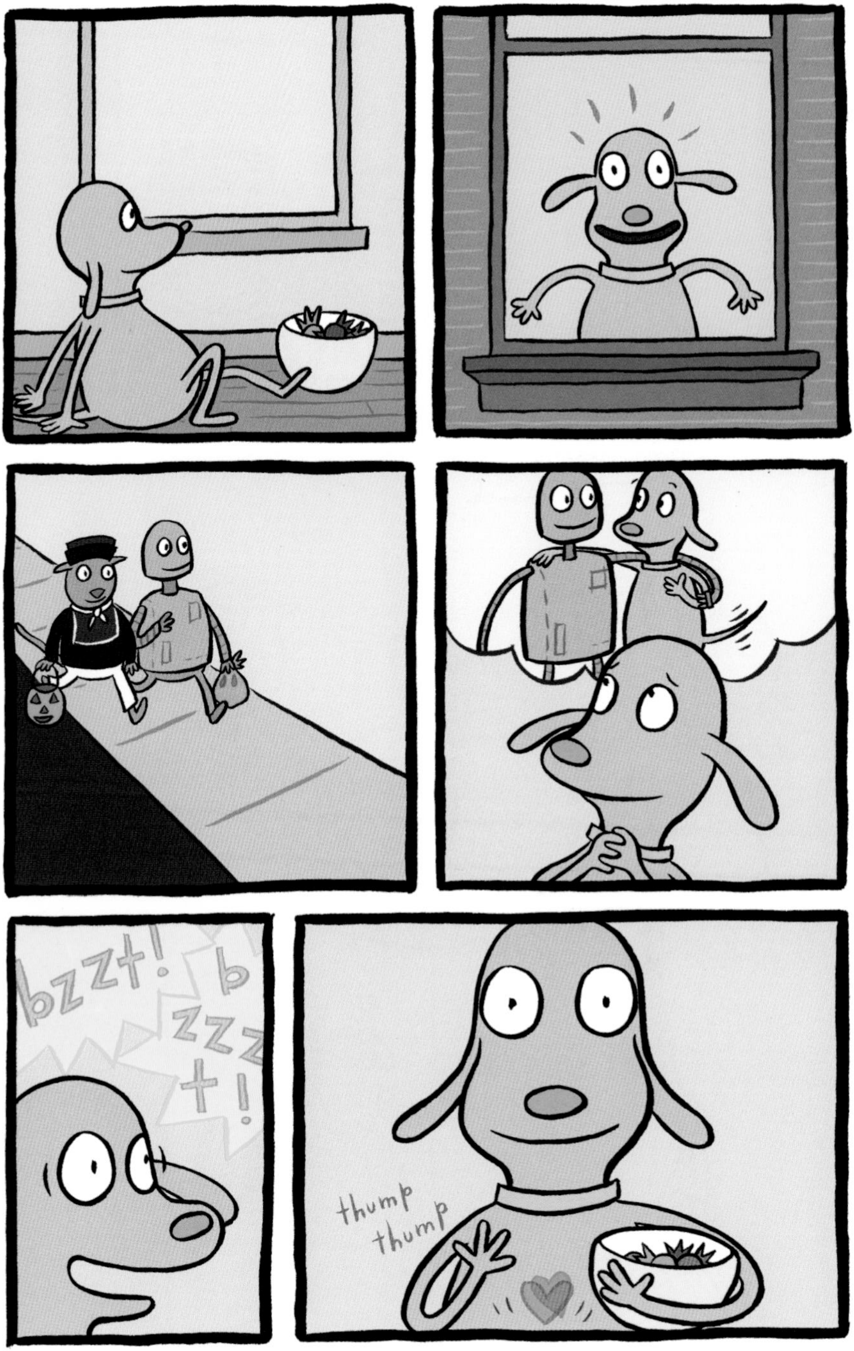
bzzt! bzzzt!
thump thump

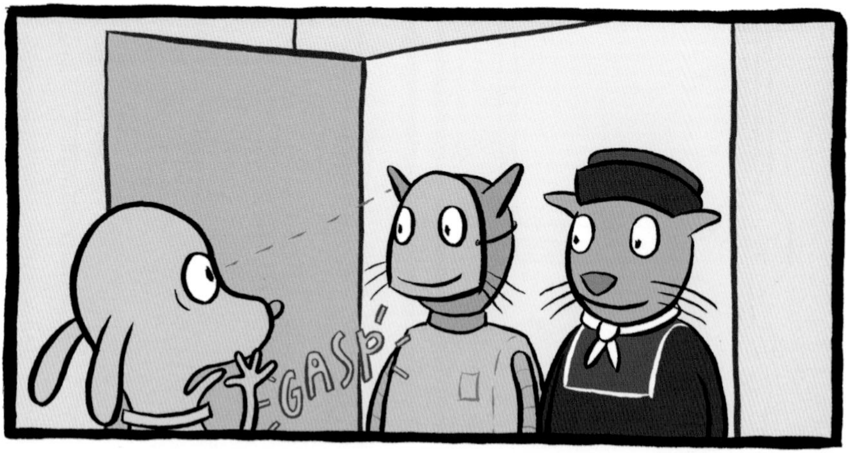
GASP

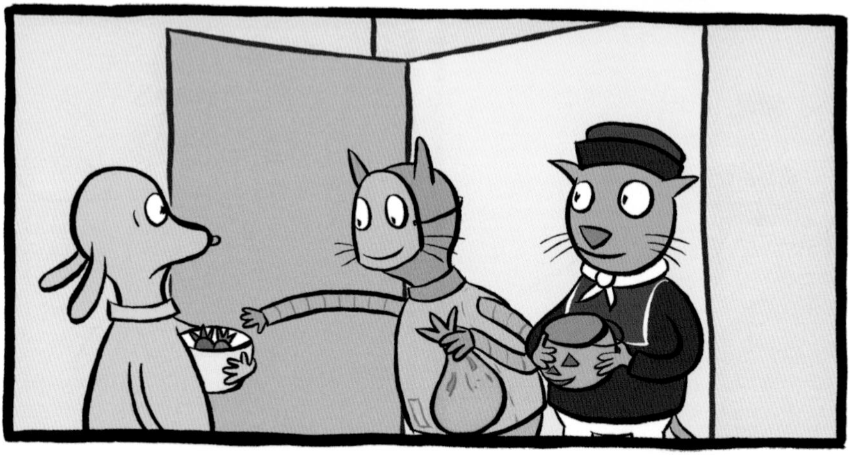

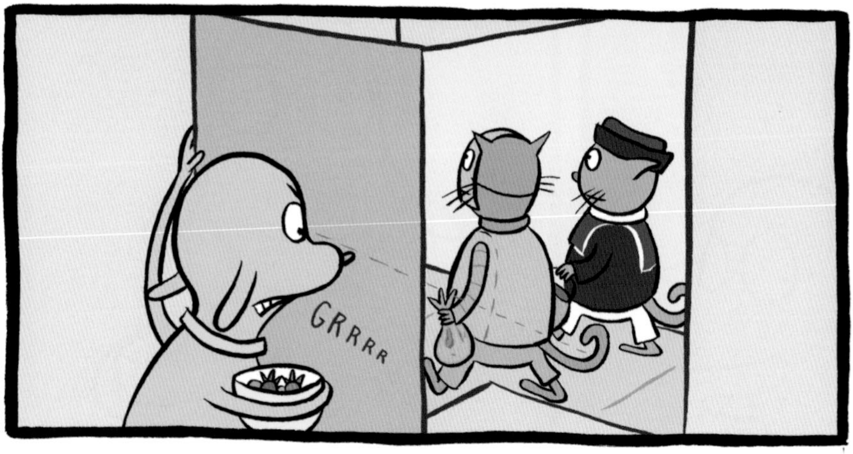
GRRRR

November

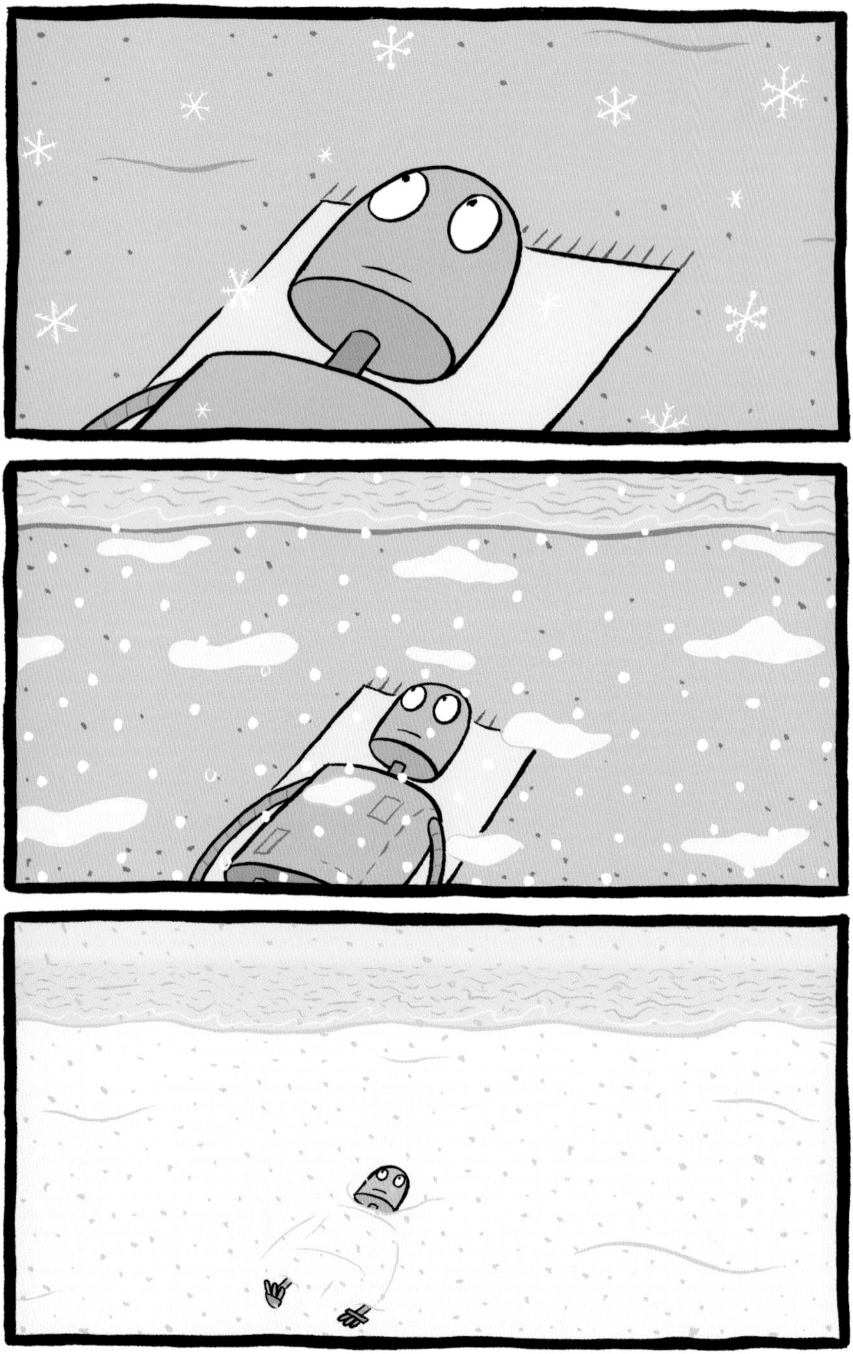

December

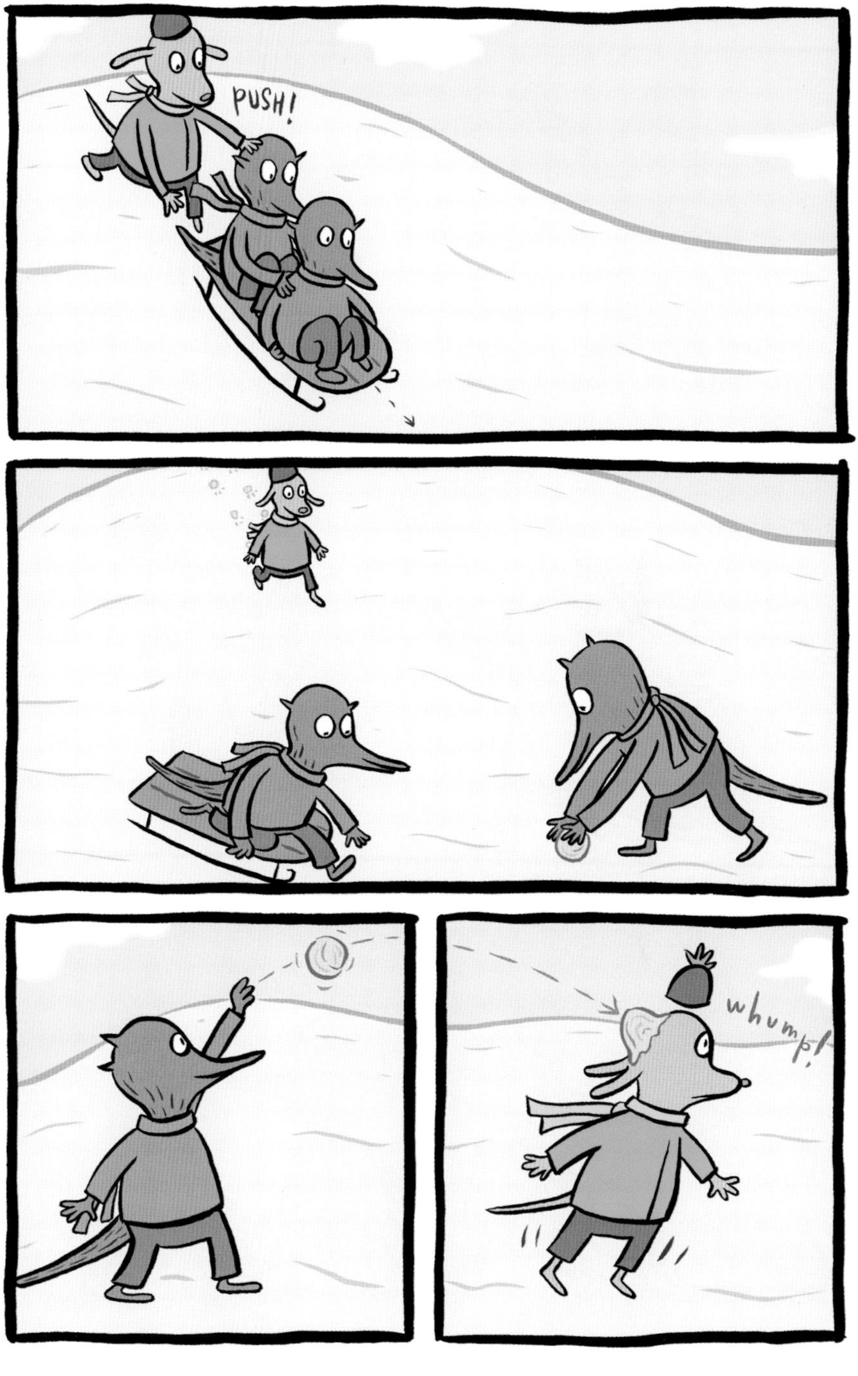
PUSH!
whump!

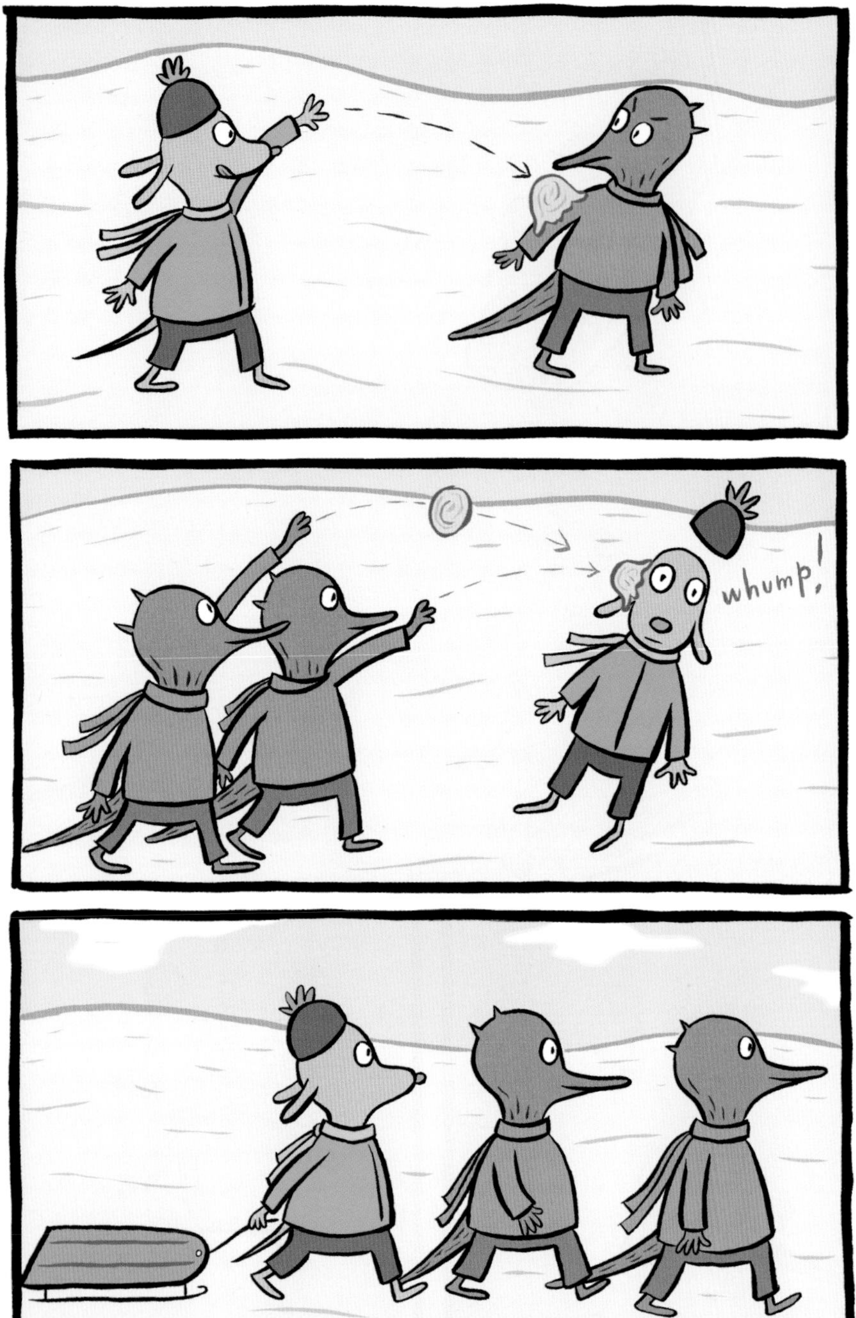
whump!

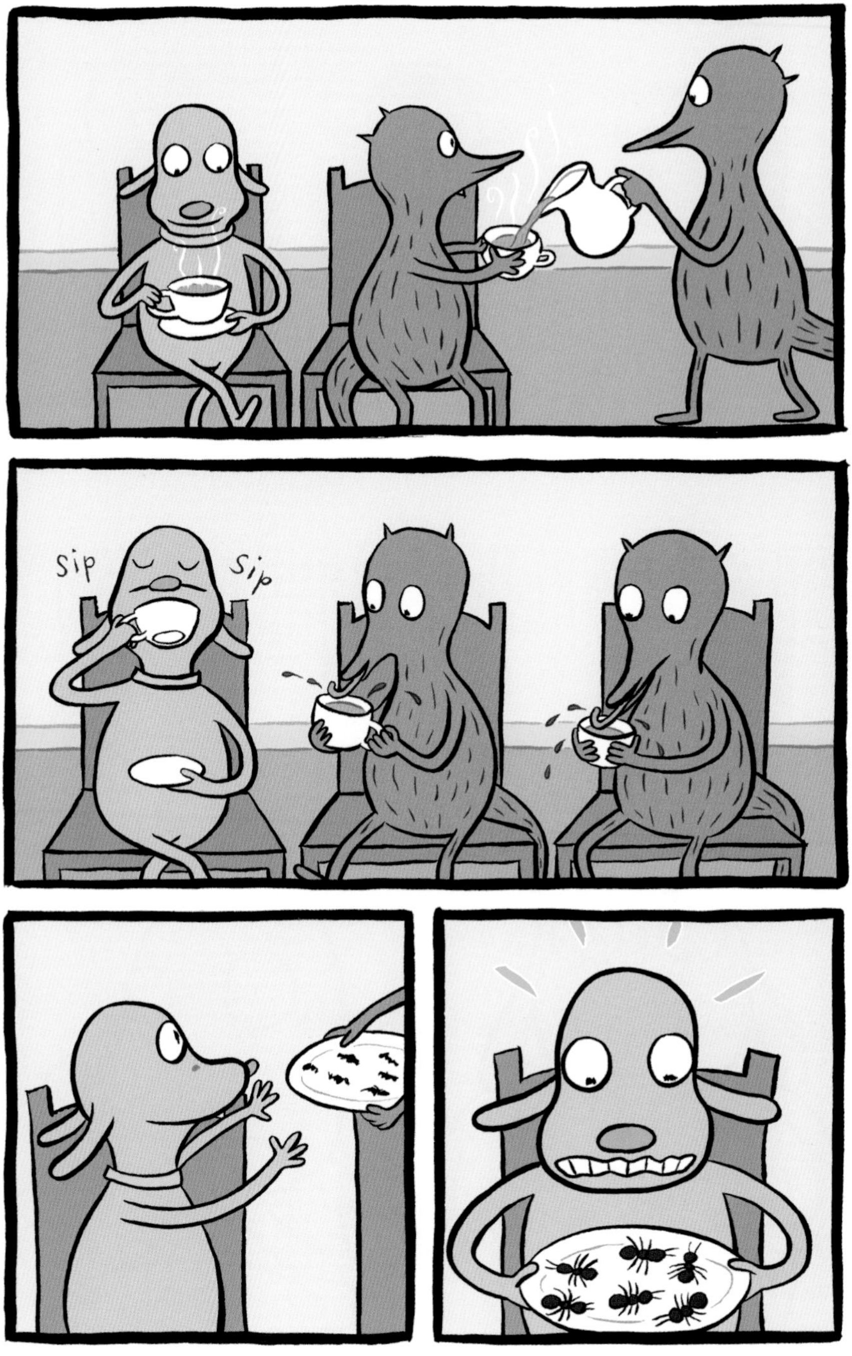
sip
sip

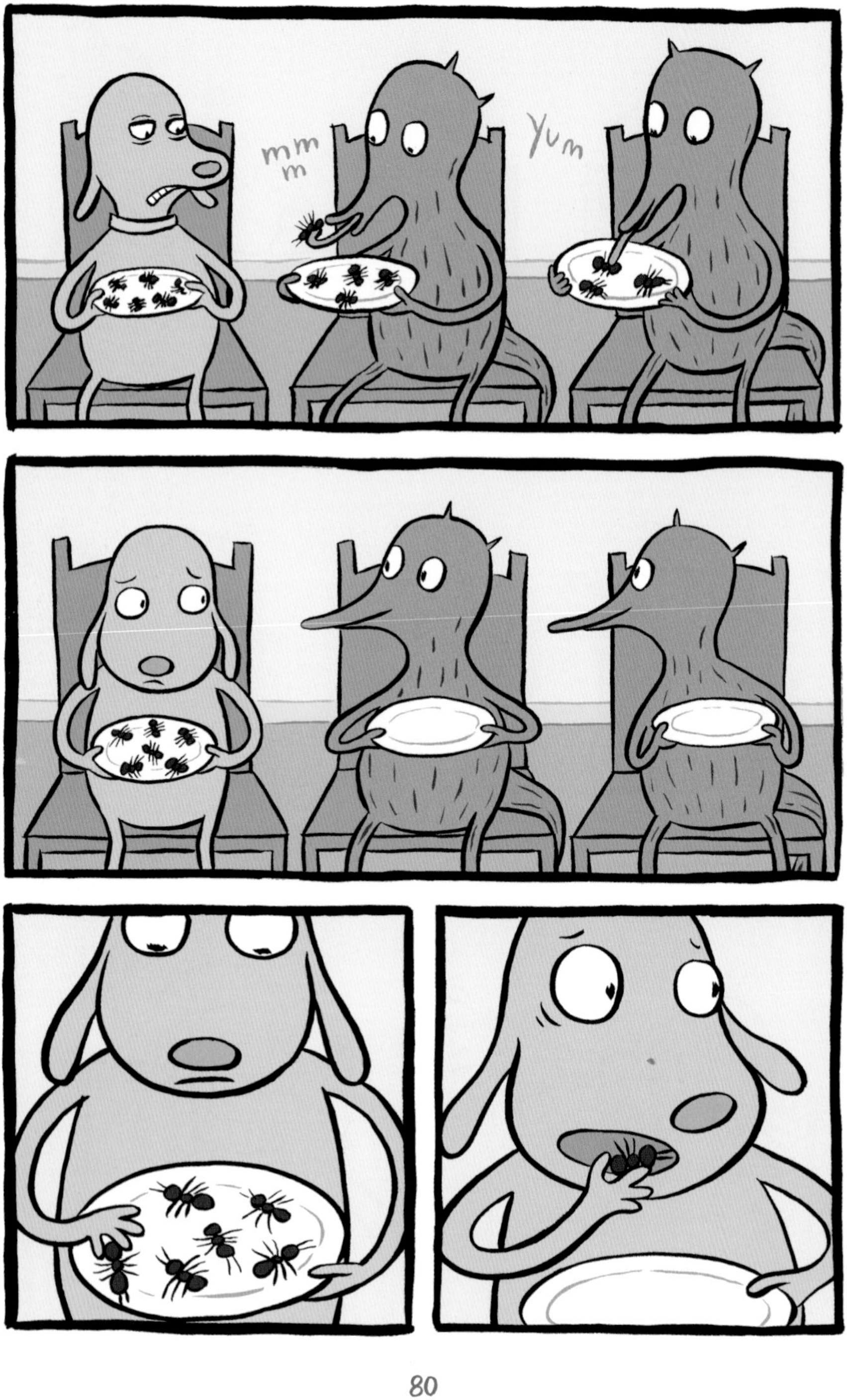
mmm
yum

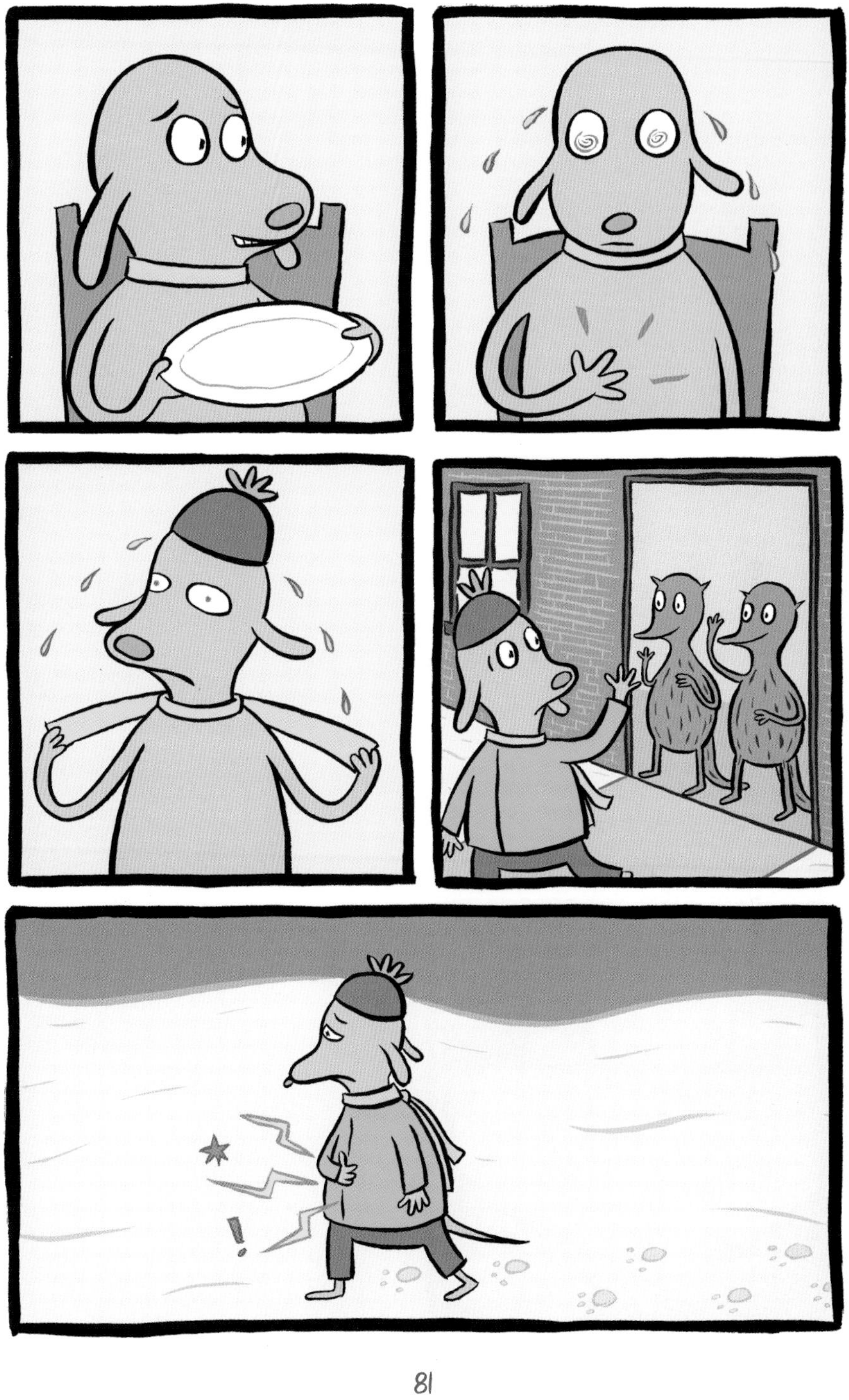

January

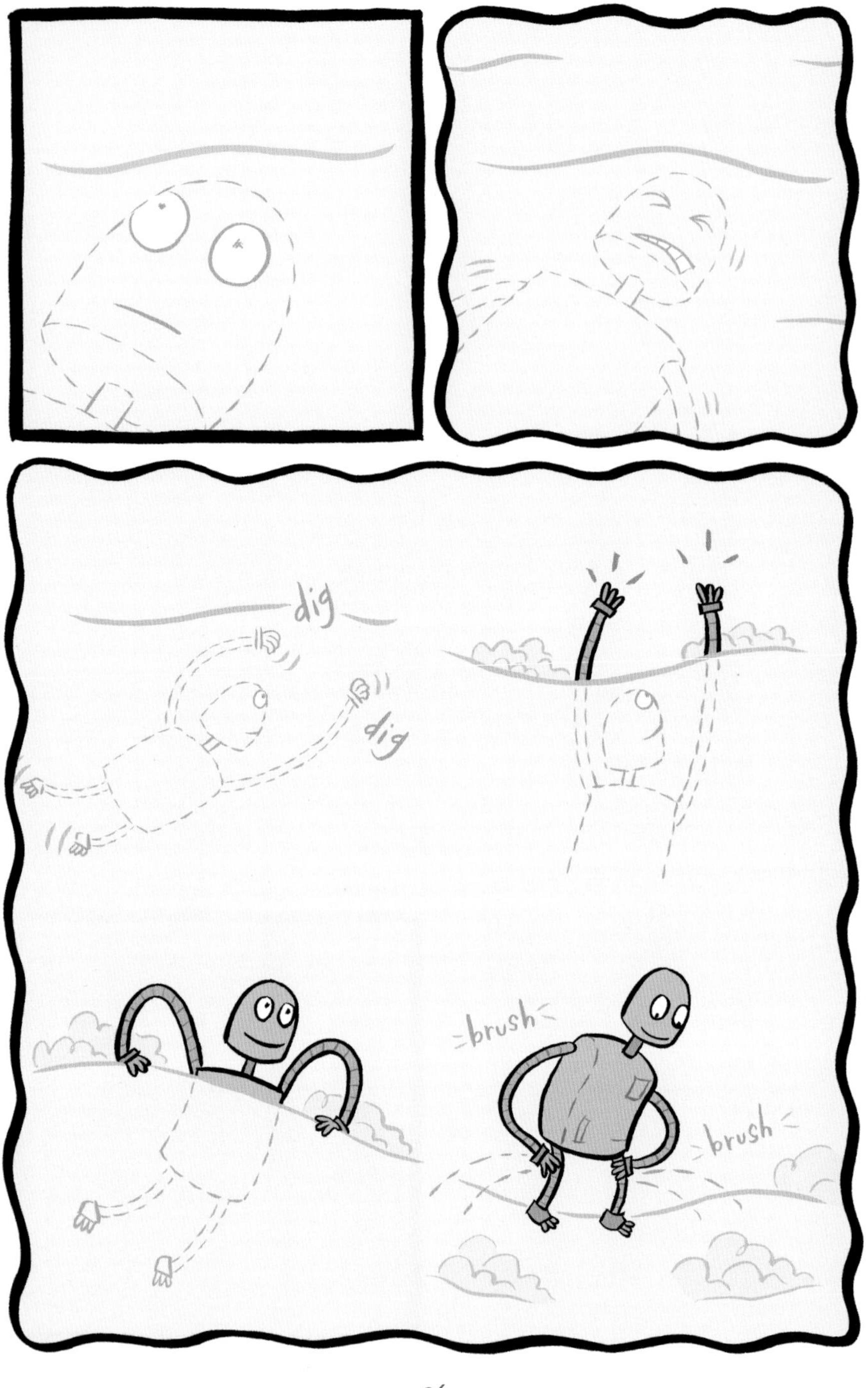
dig
dig
brush
brush

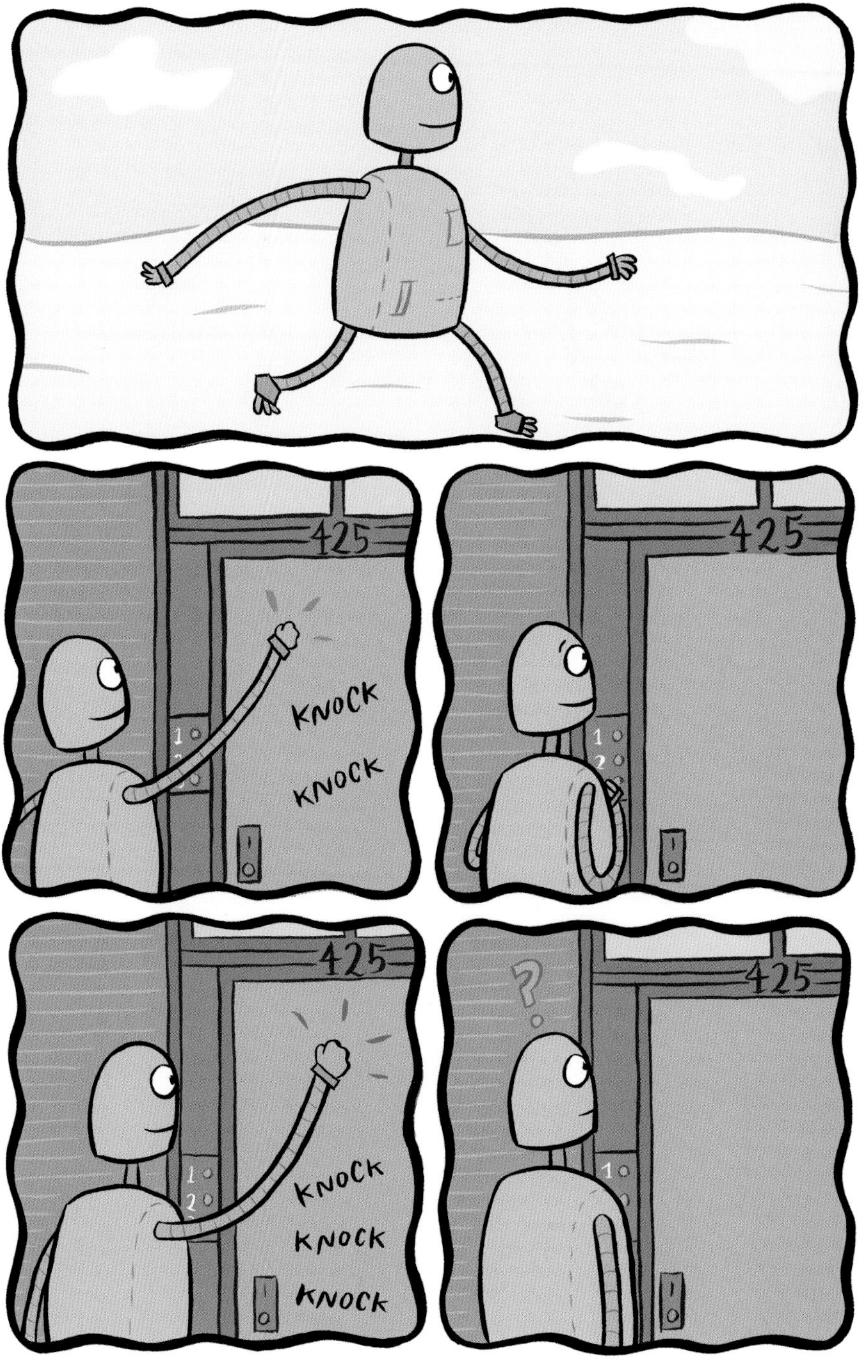

425
KNOCK
KNOCK
425
425
KNOCK
KNOCK
KNOCK
?
425

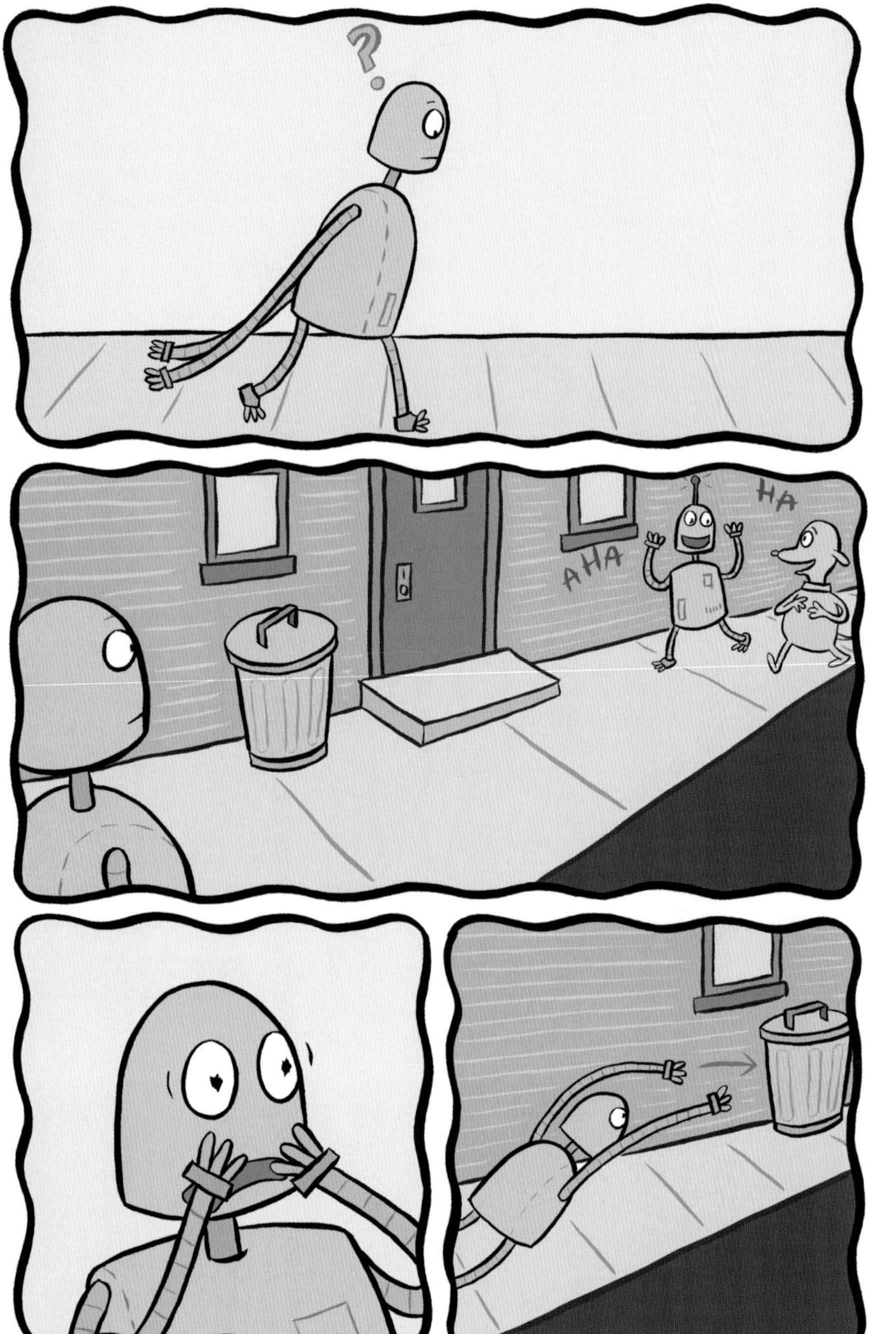
?
AHA
HA

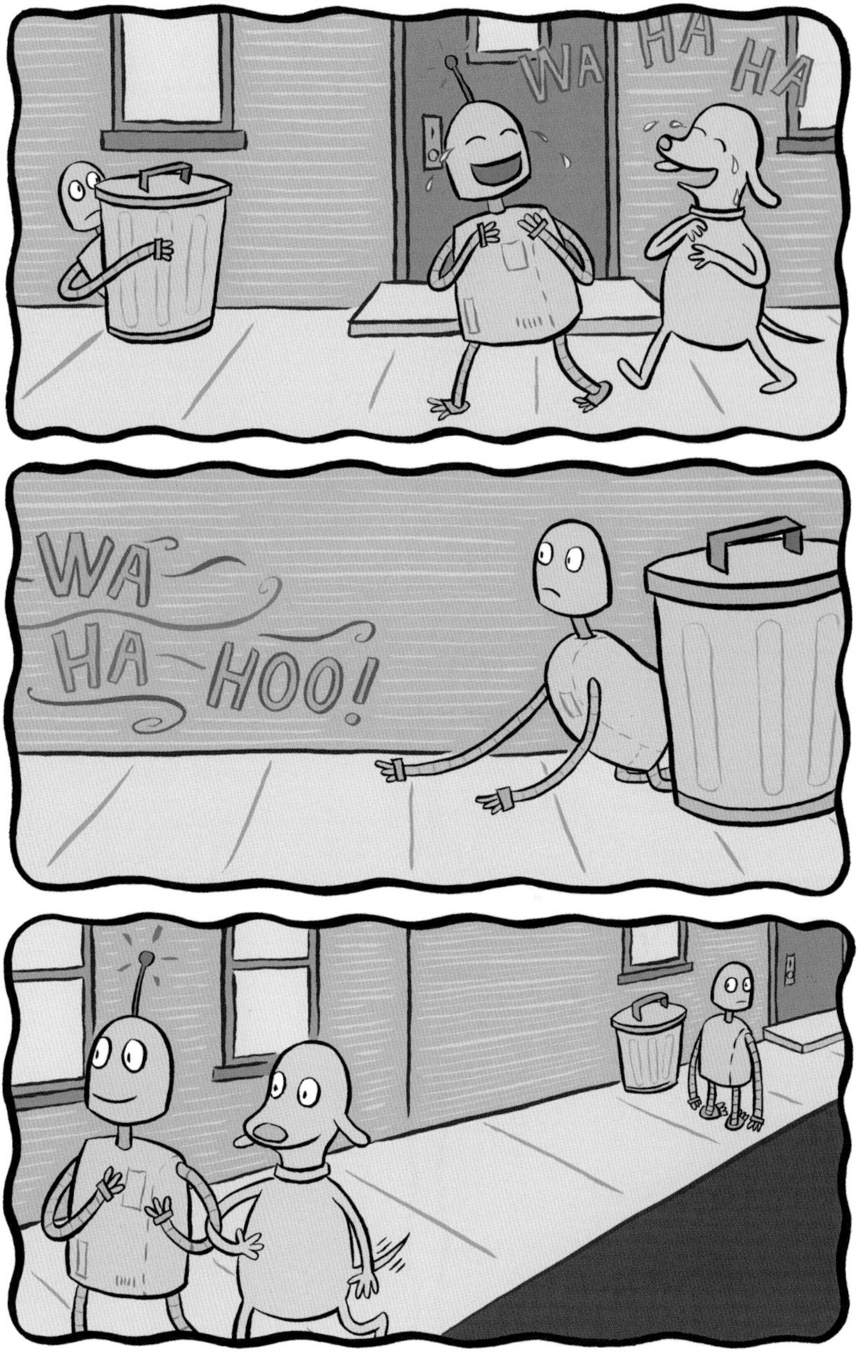
WA HA HA HA
WA HA HA HOO!

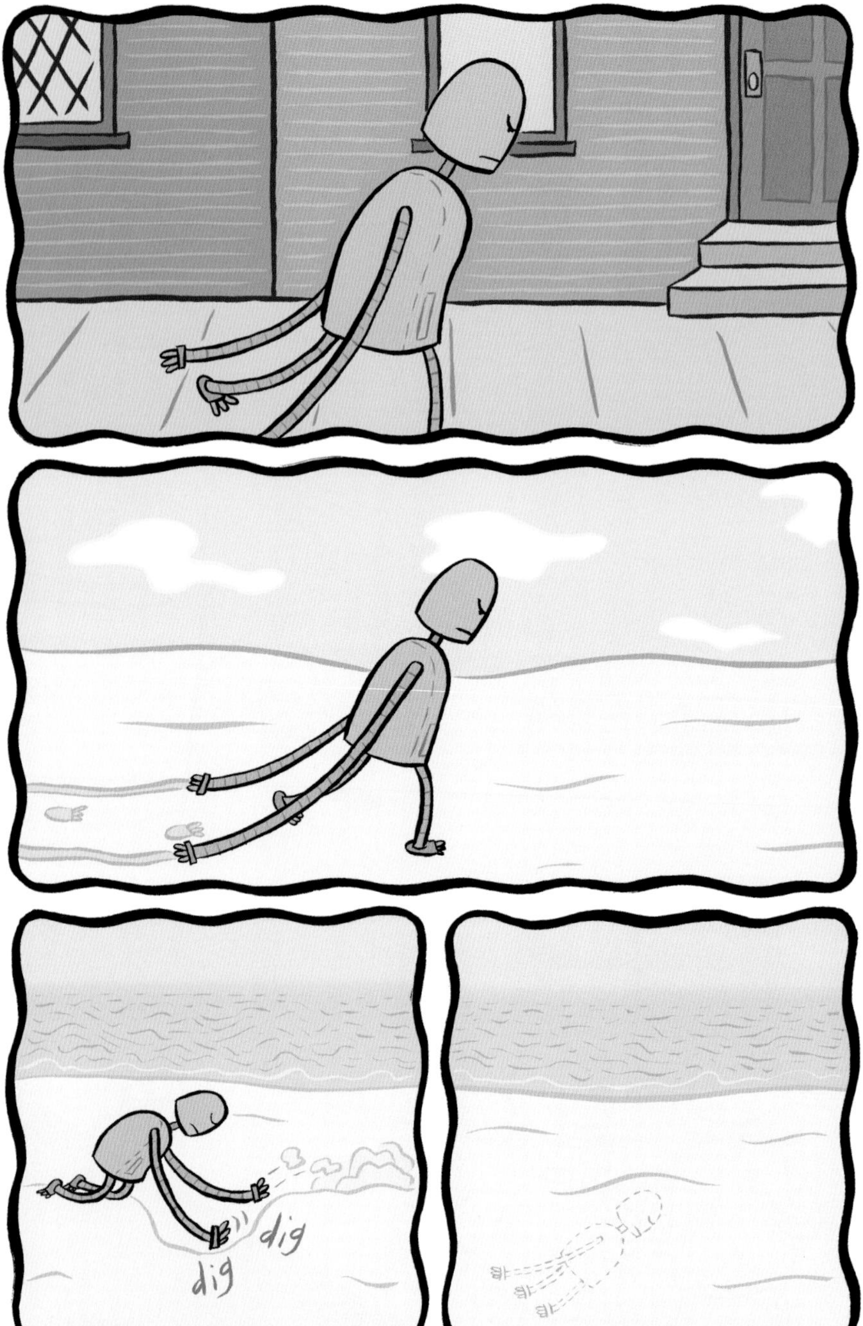
dig
dig

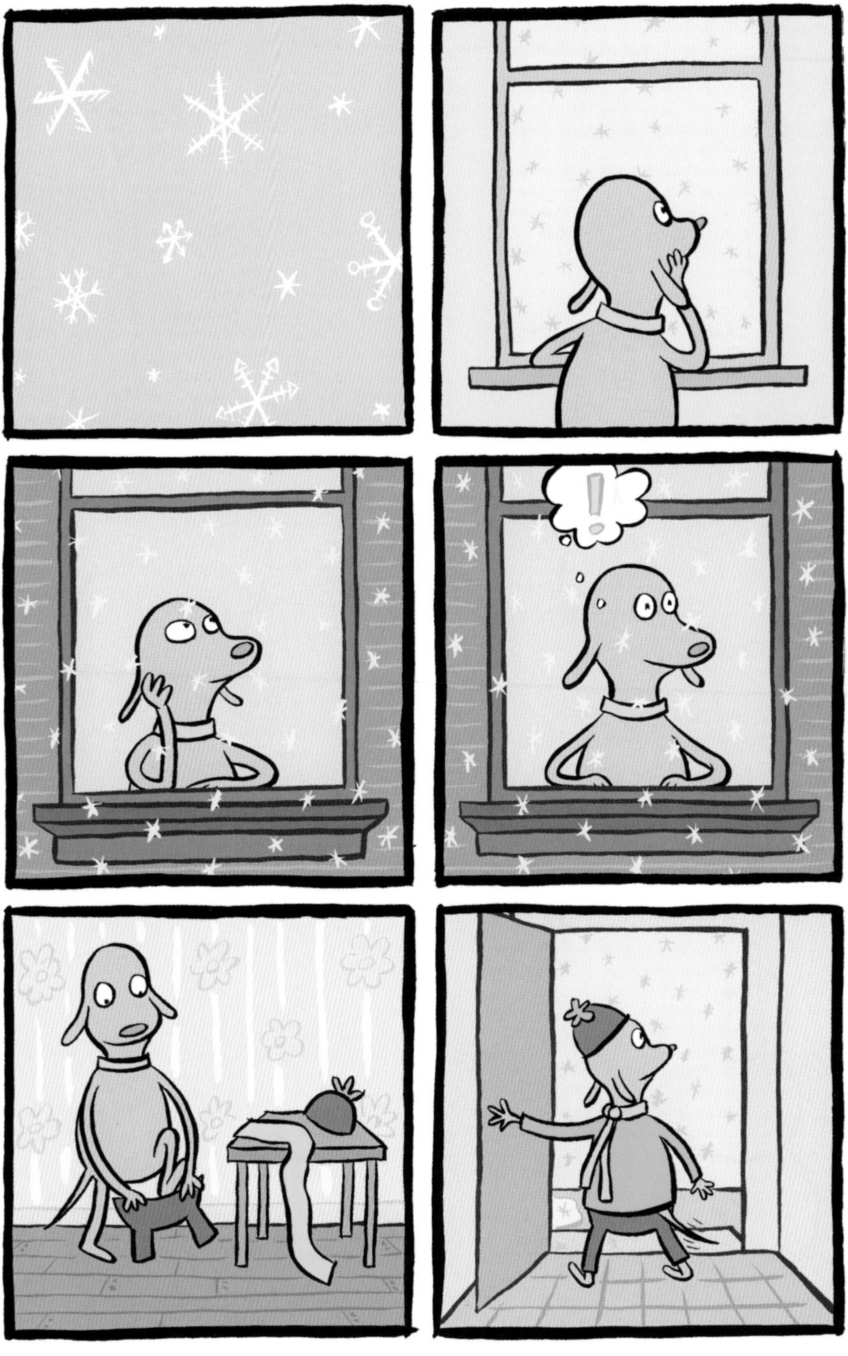
!

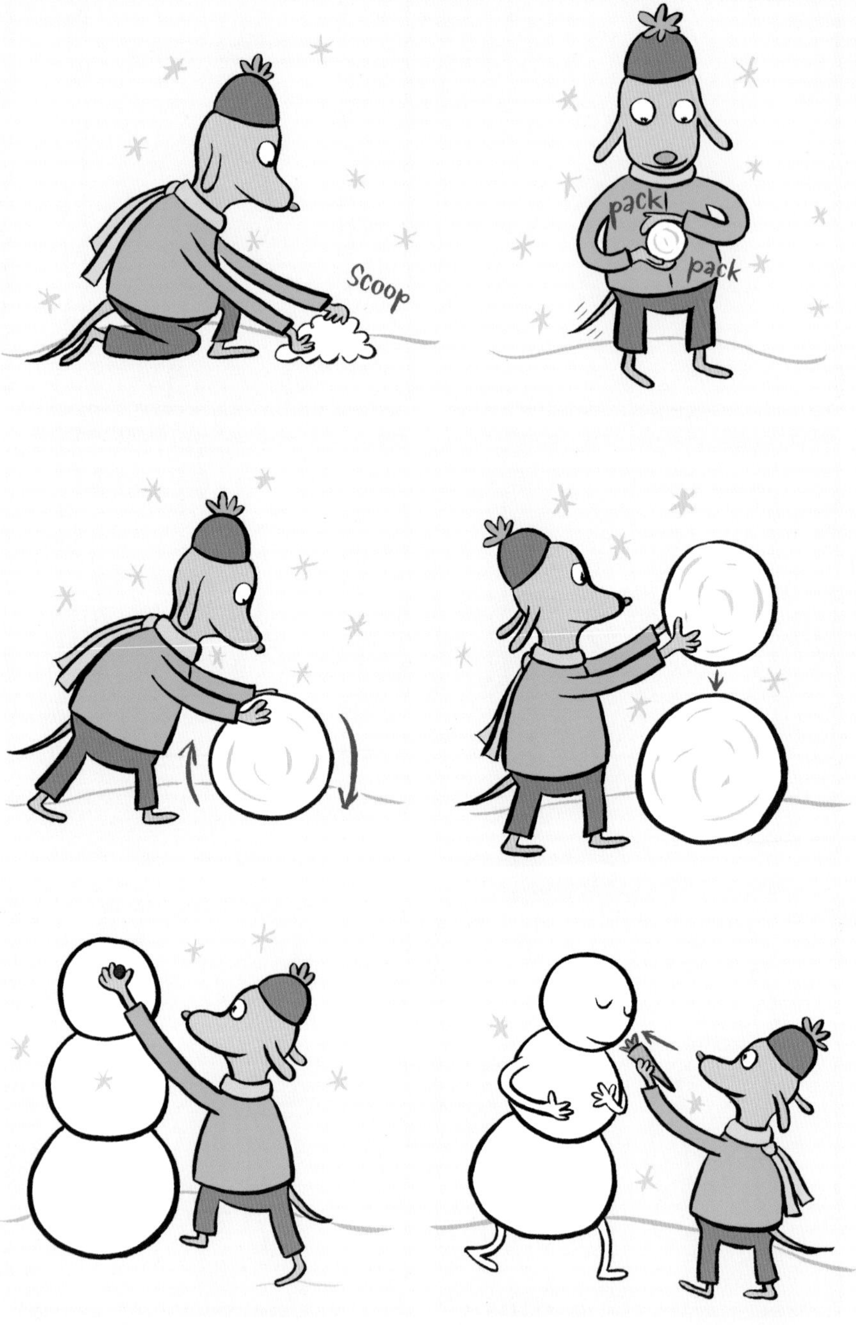
Scoop
pack!
pack

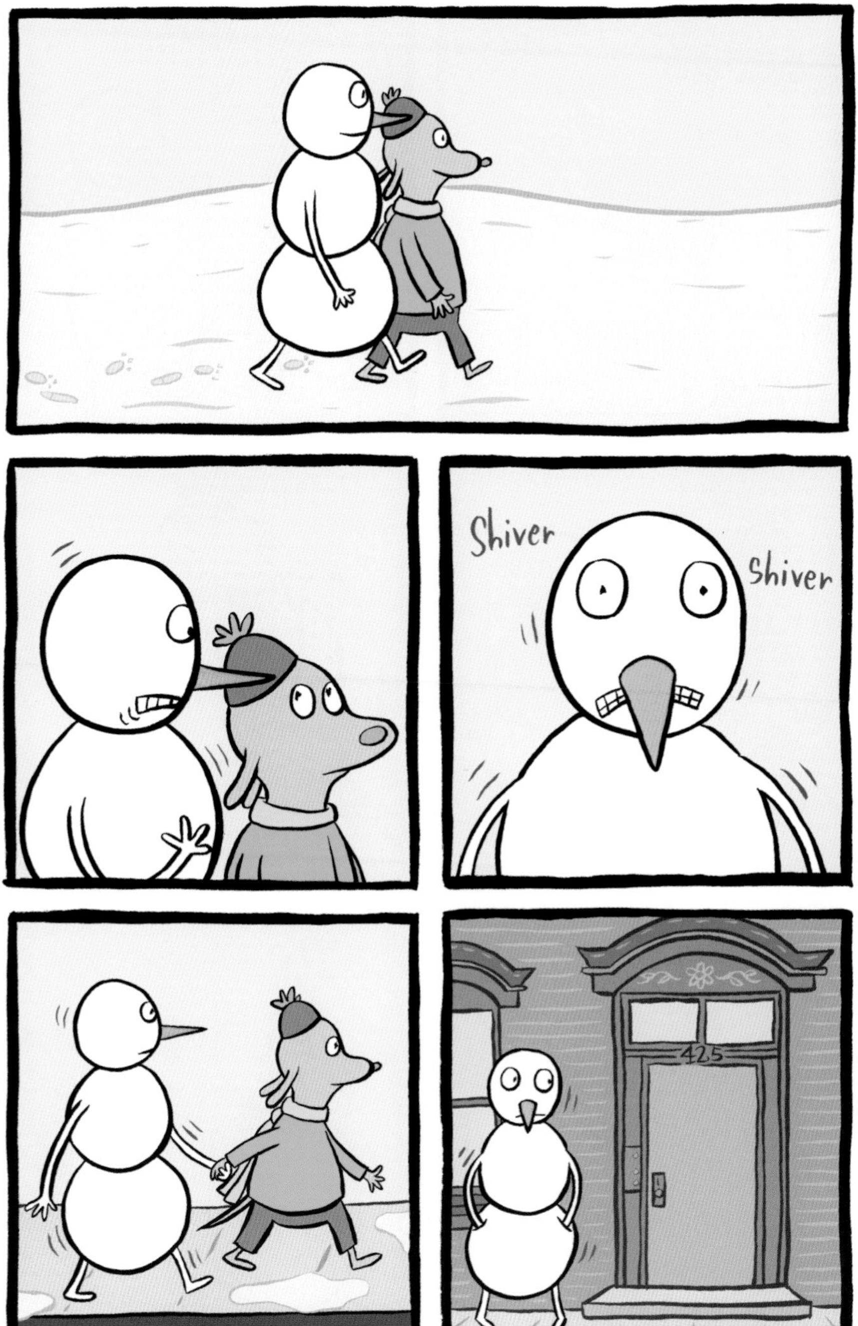
Shiver
Shiver
425

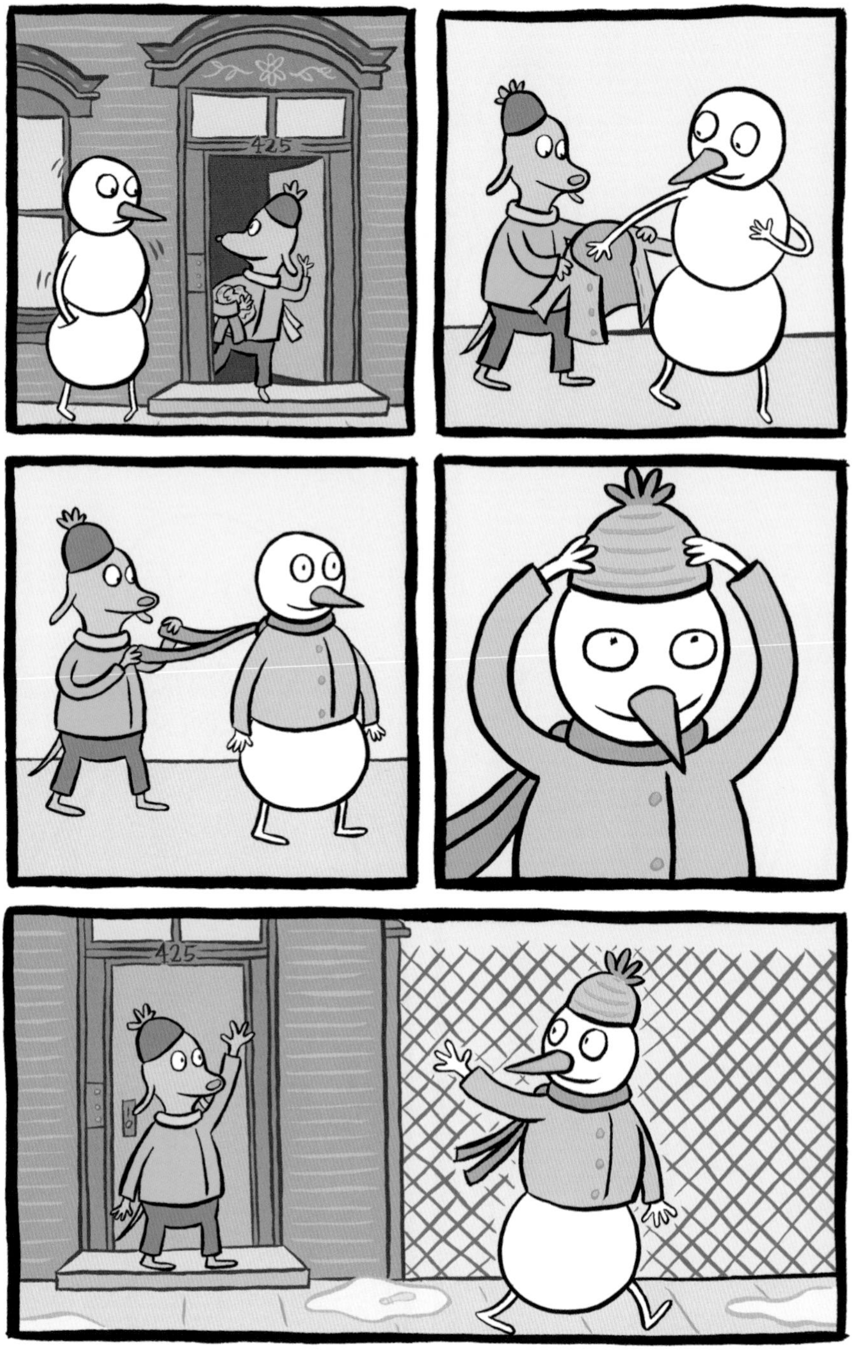
425
425

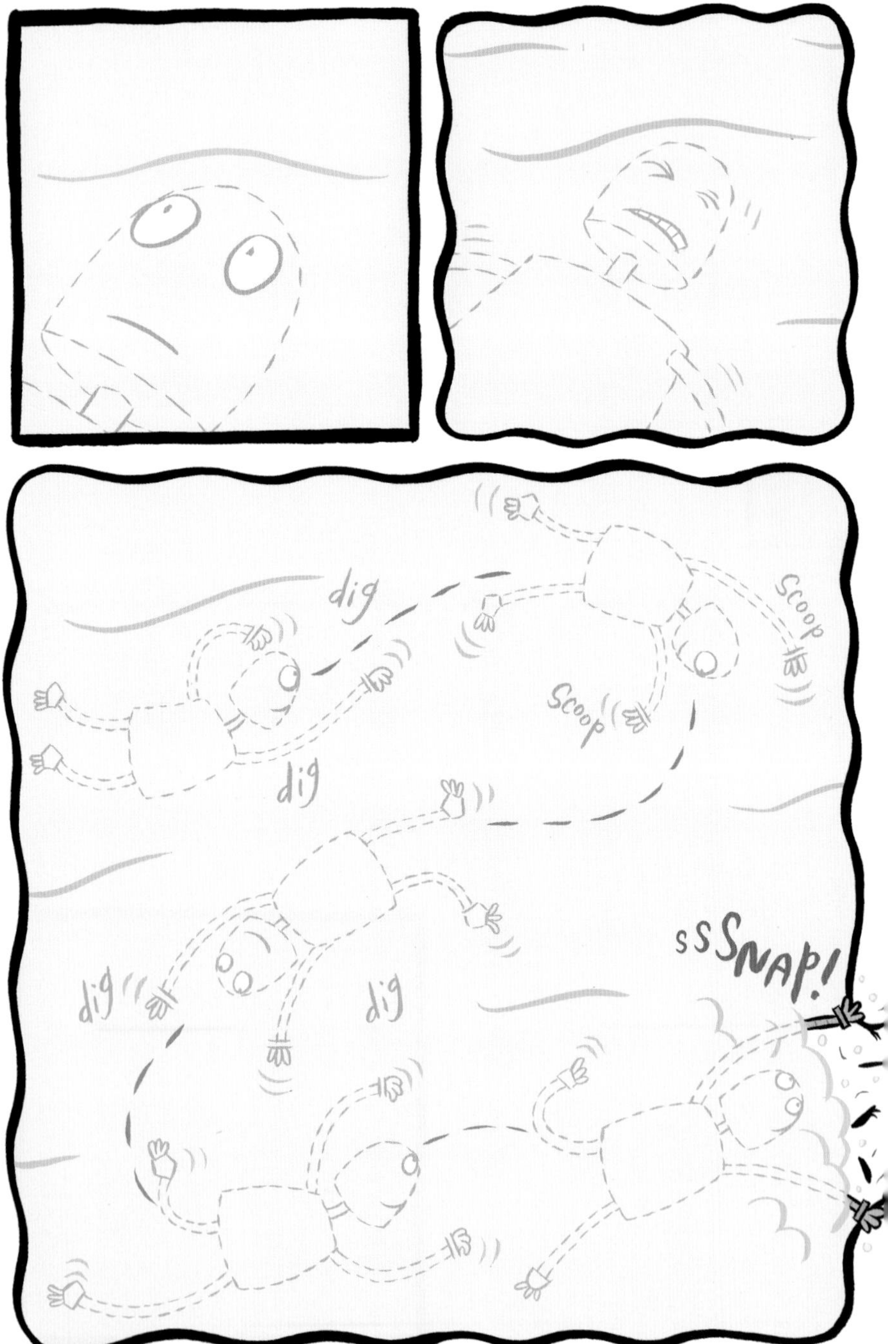

dig
Scoop
Scoop
dig
dig
dig
sSSNAP!

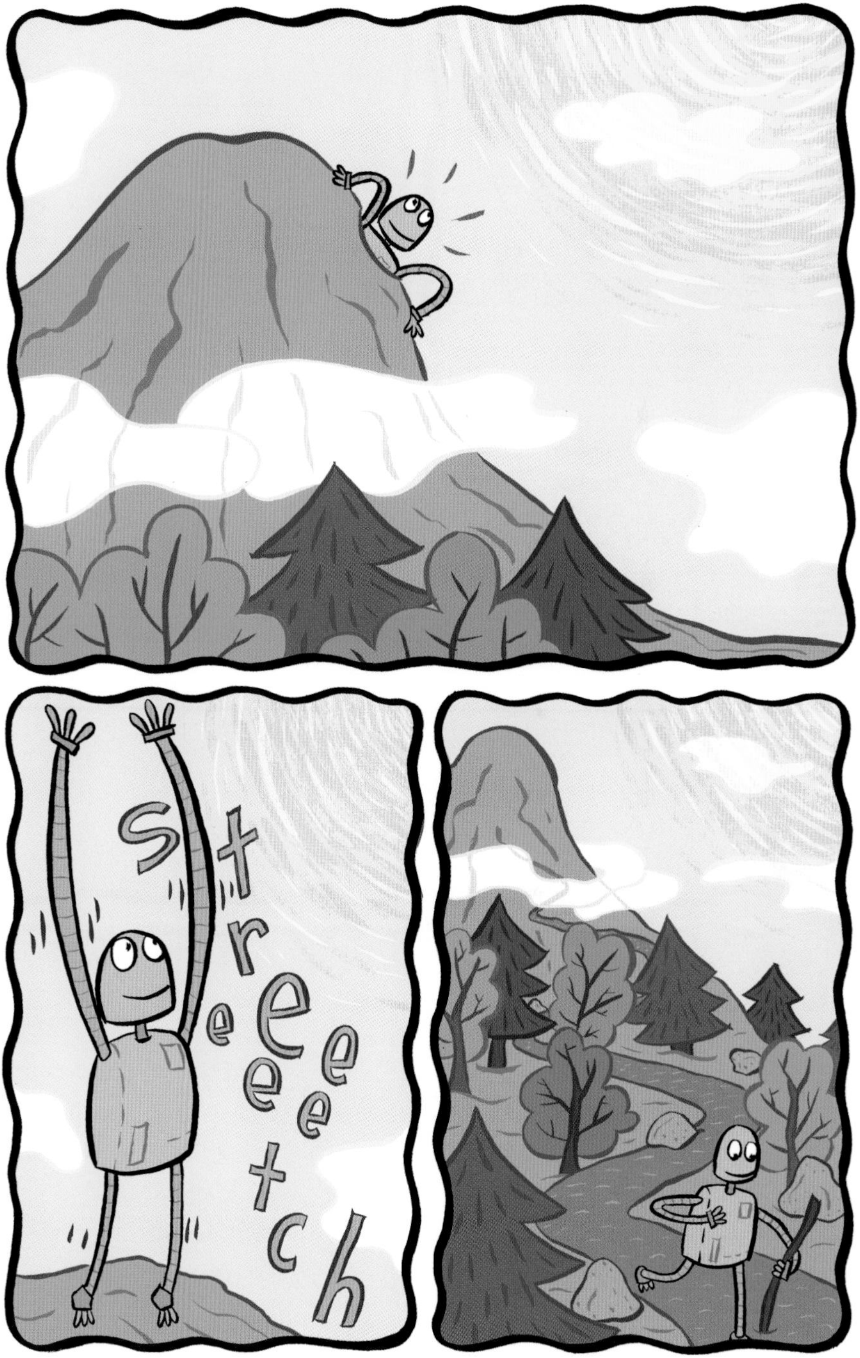

streeeeetch

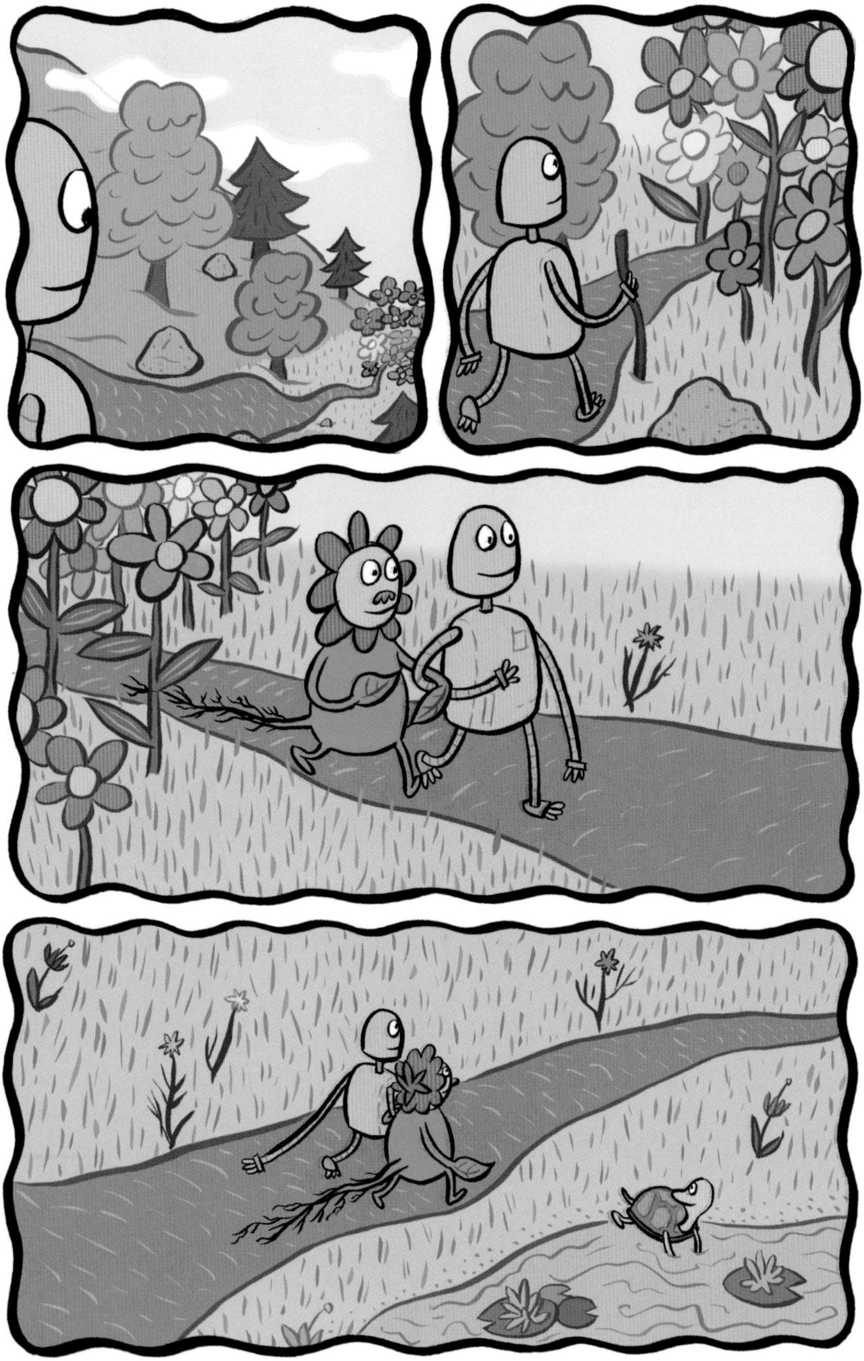

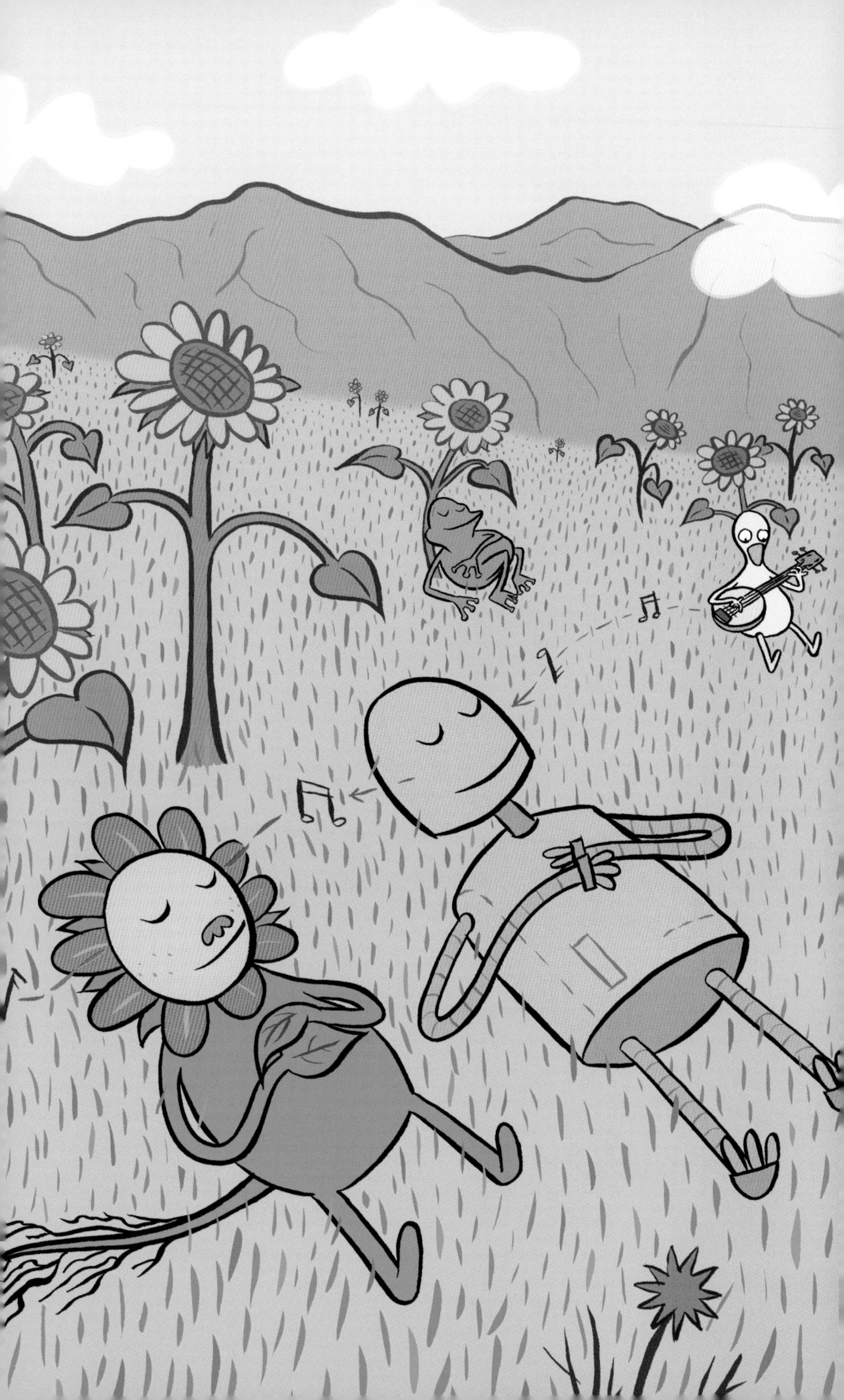

February

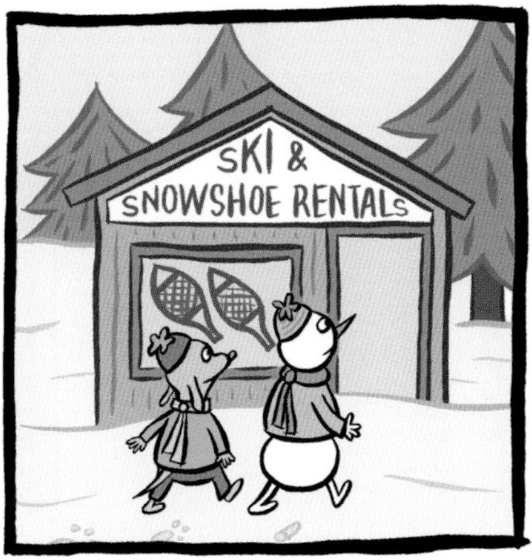
SKI &
SNOWSHOE RENTALS

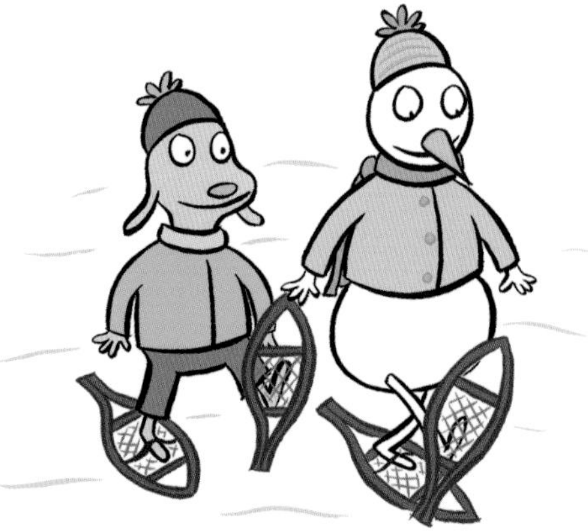

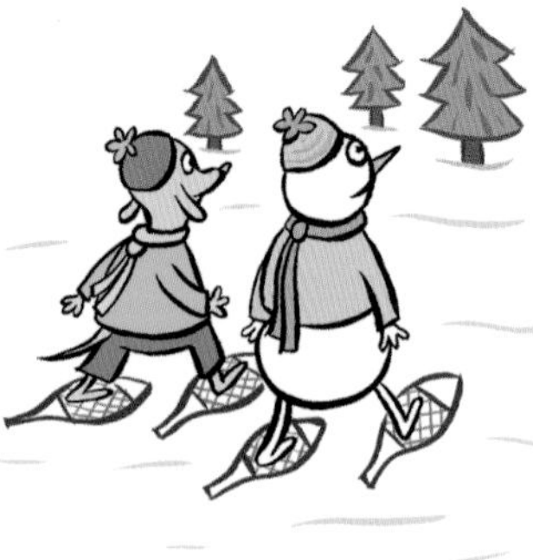

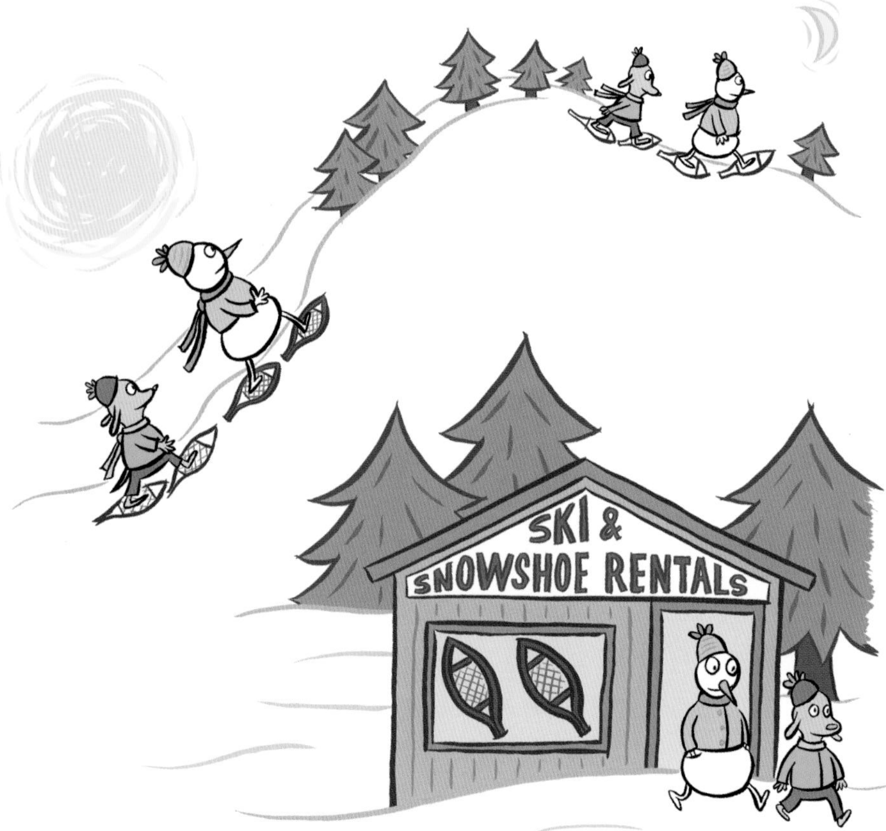
SKI &
SNOWSHOE RENTALS

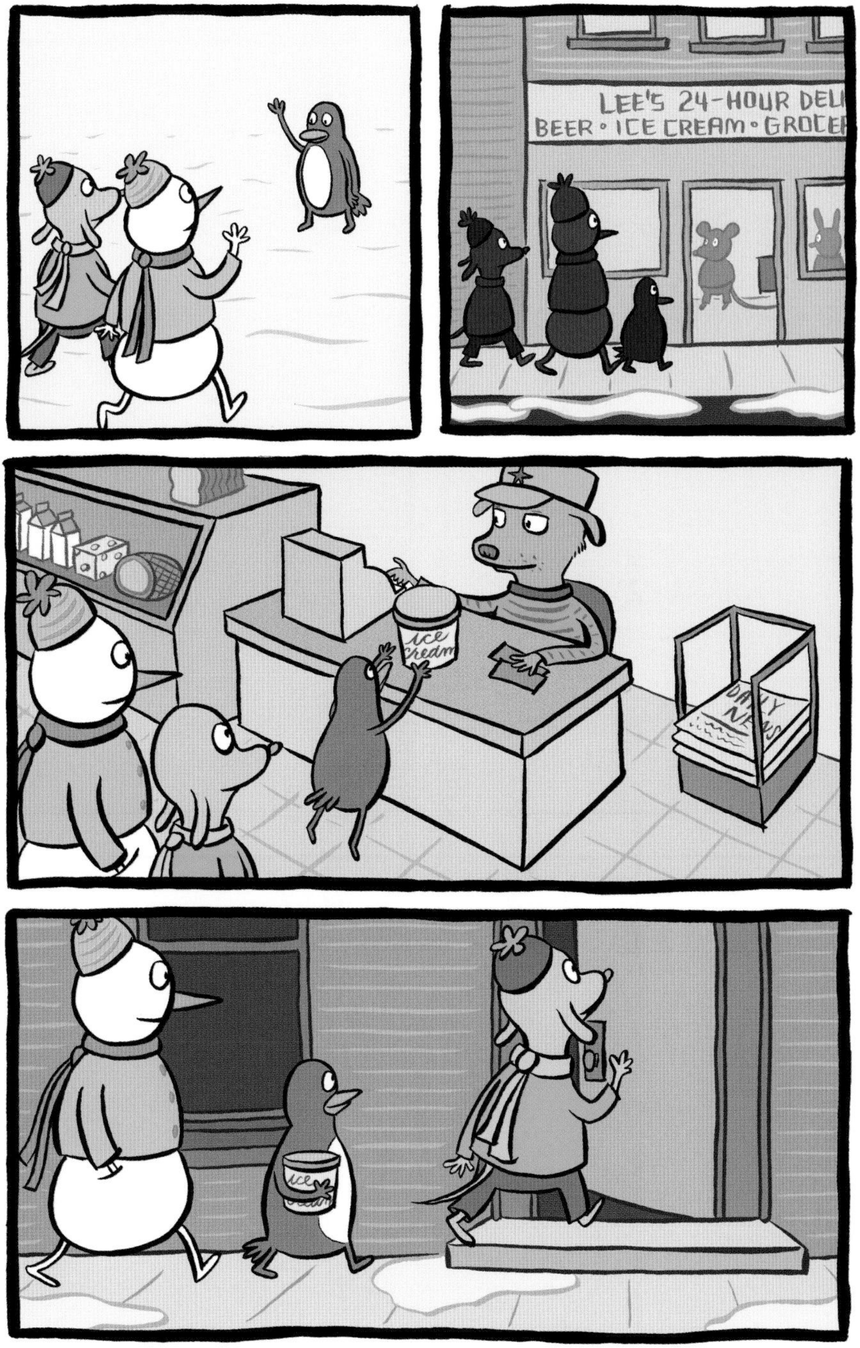
LEE'S 24-HOUR DELI
BEER • ICE CREAM • GROCE
ice cream
DAILY NEWS
ice cream

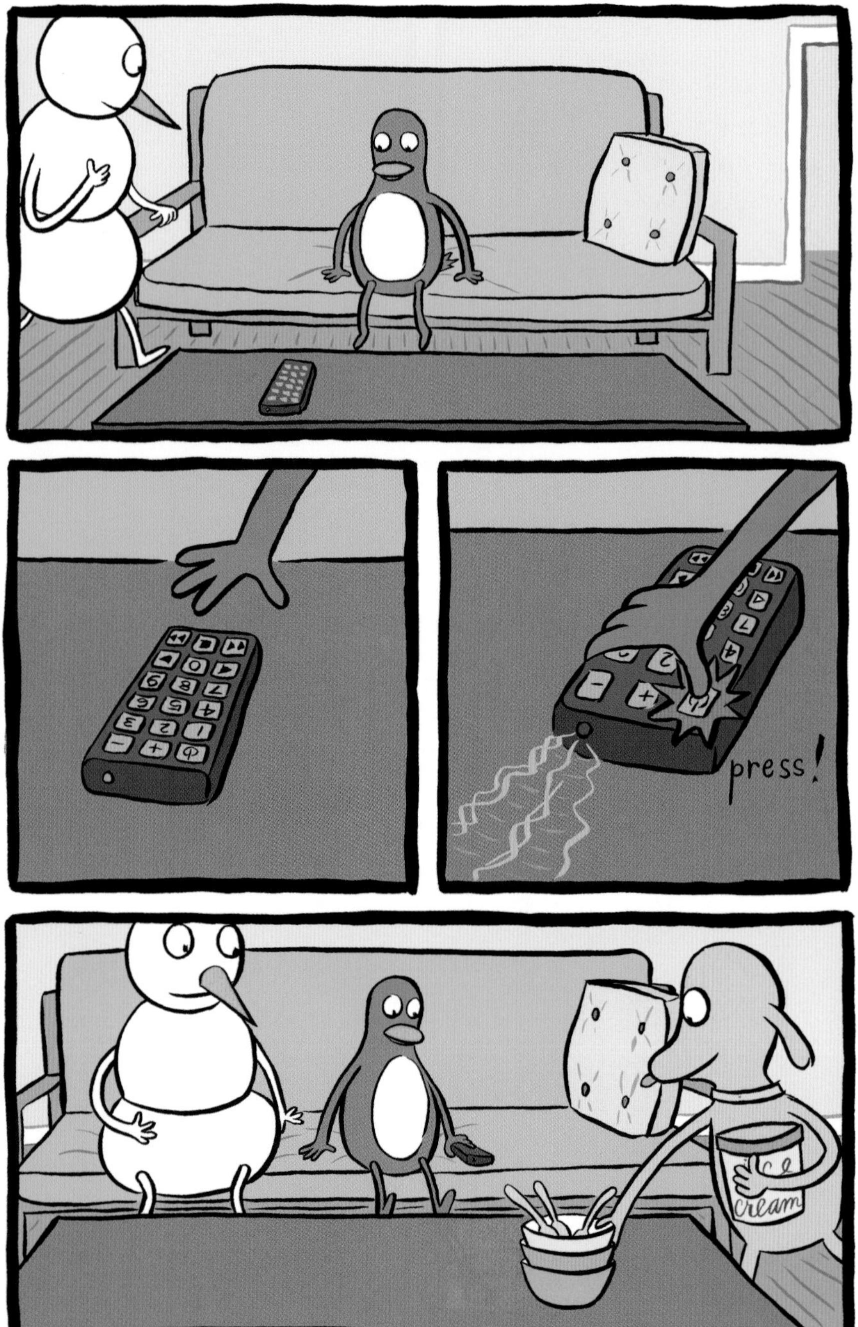
press!
cream

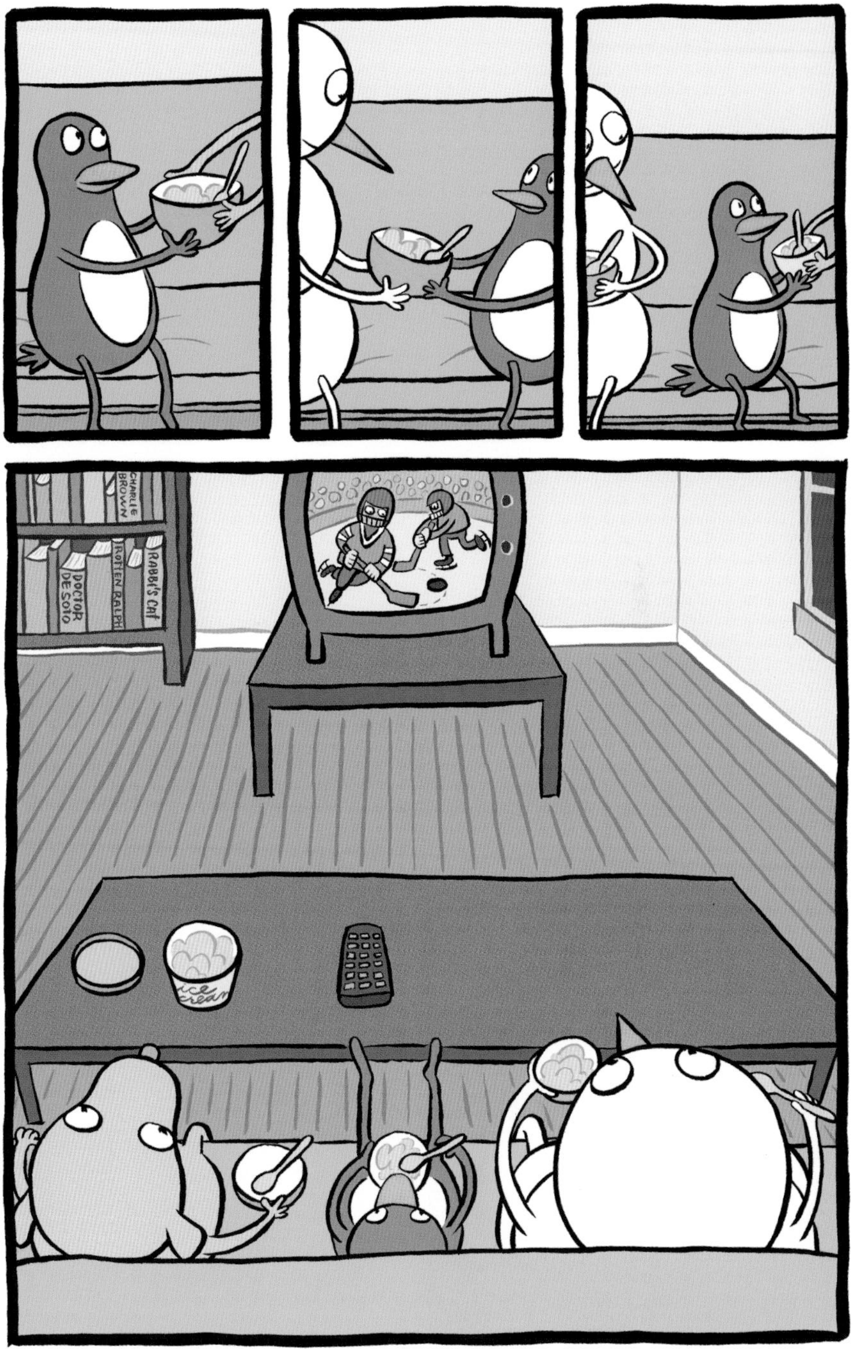
CHARLIE BROWN
DOCTOR DE SOTO
ROTTEN RALPH
RABBI'S CAT
ice cream

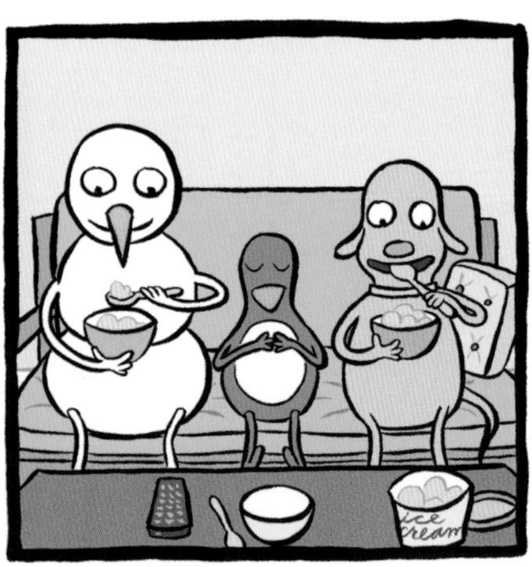
ice cream

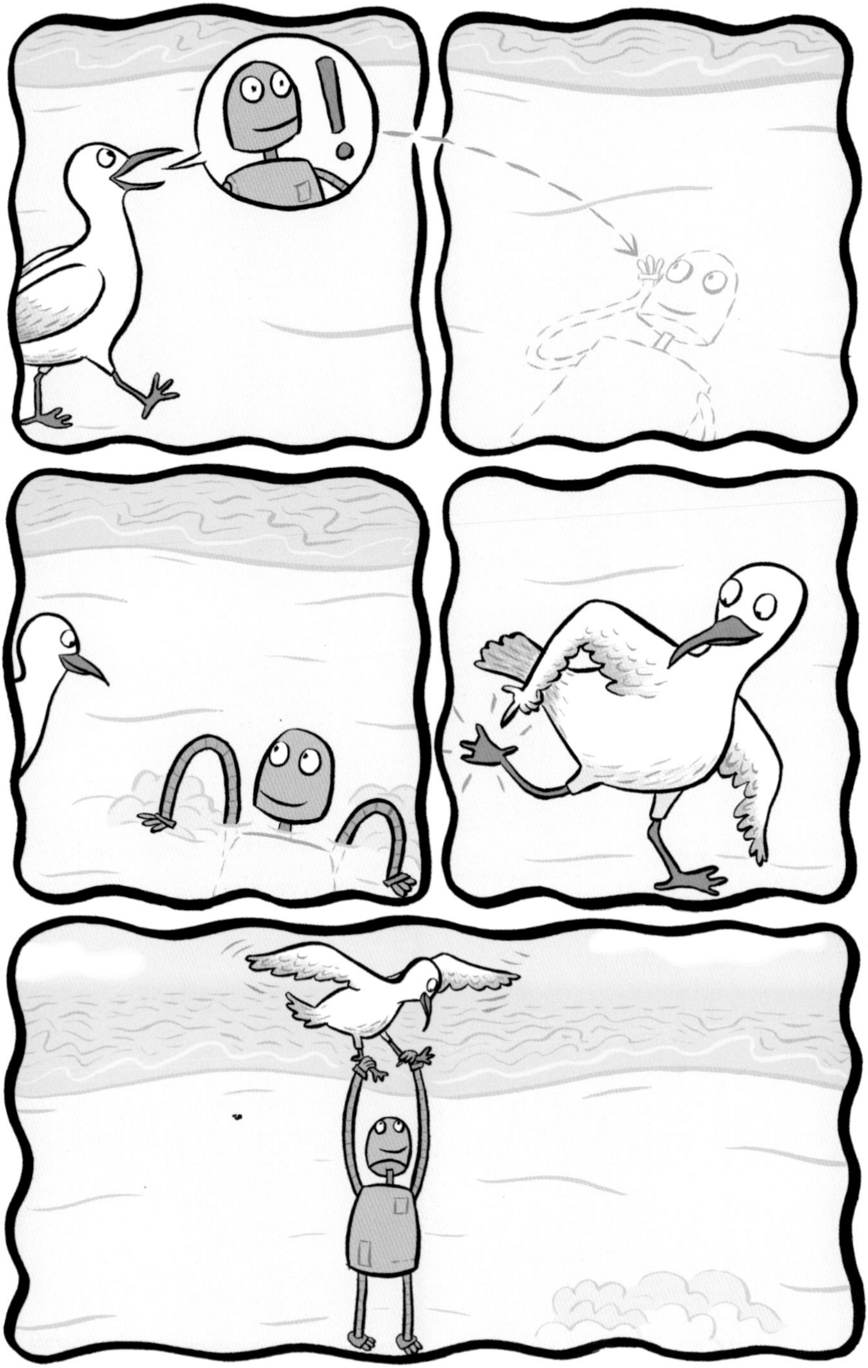
!

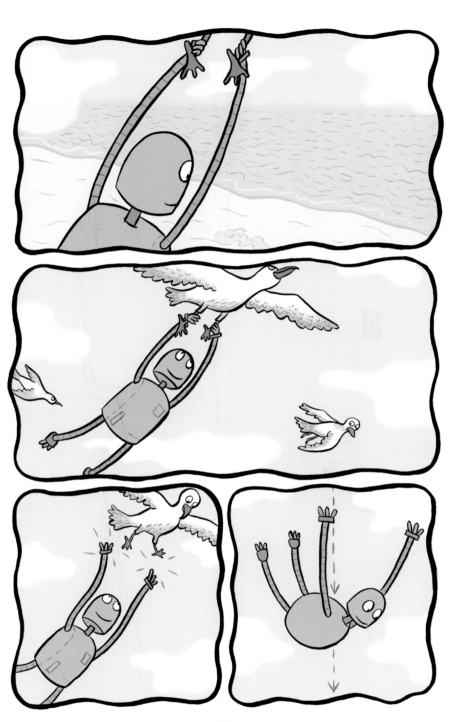

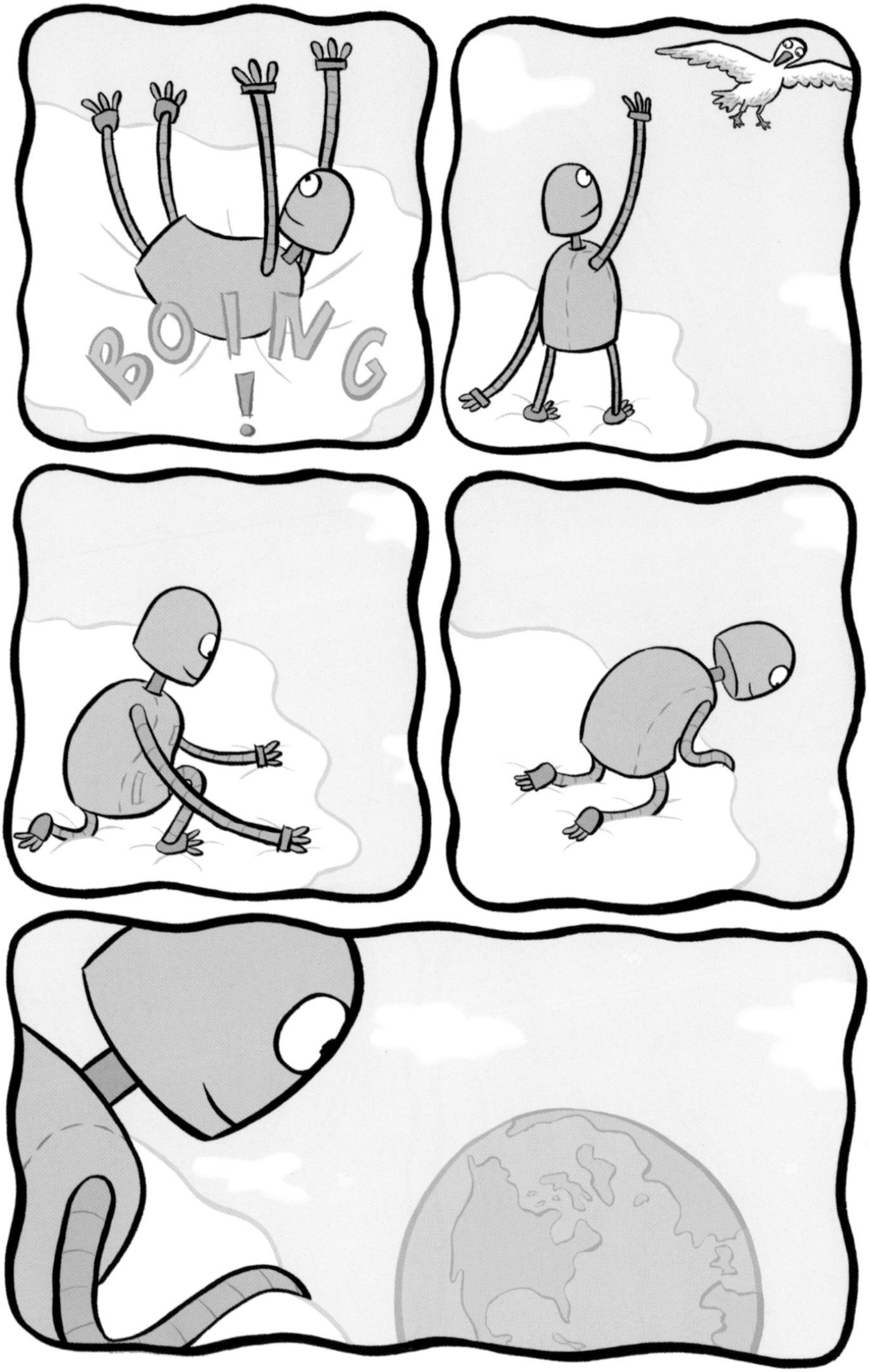
BOING!

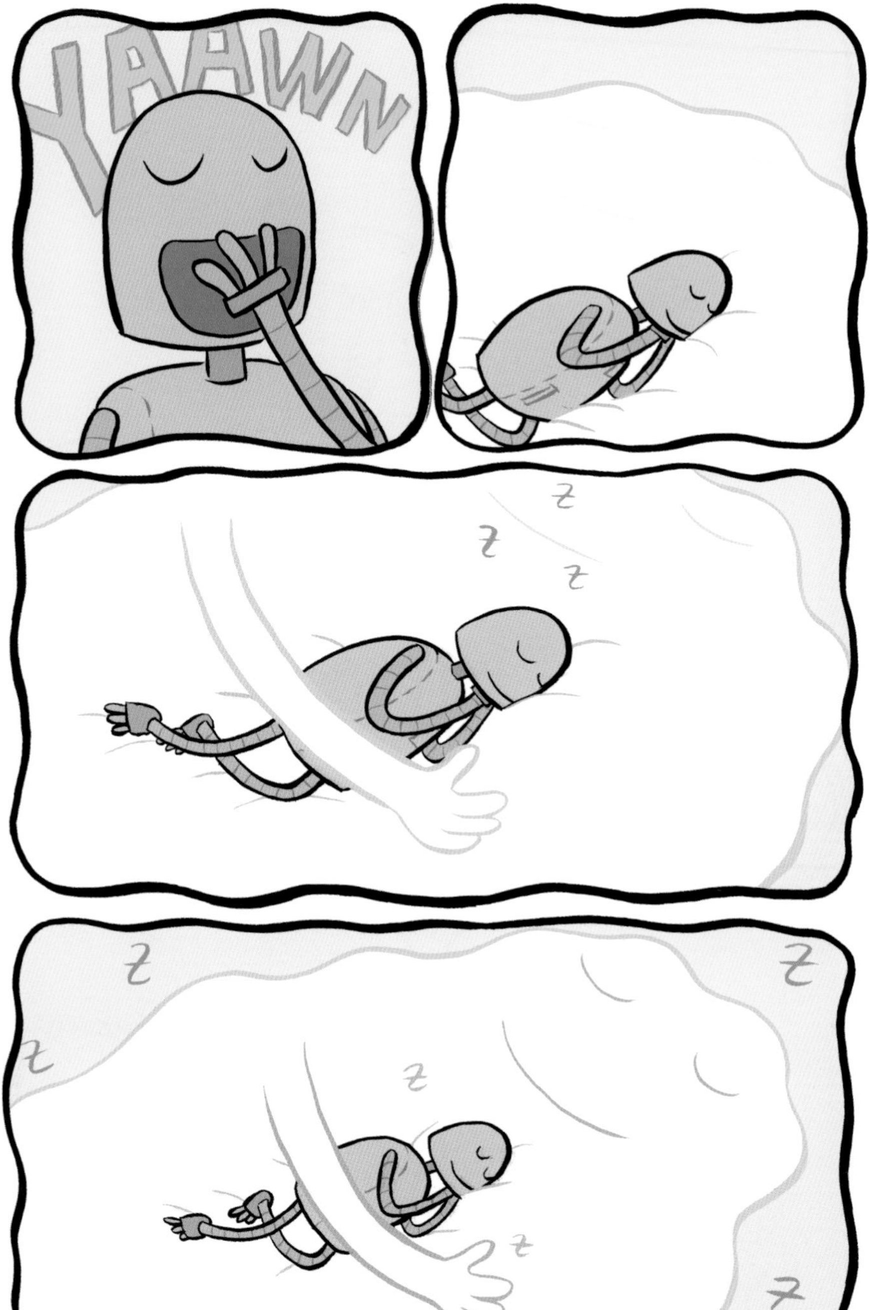
YAAWN
Z
Z
Z
Z
Z
Z
Z
Z
Z

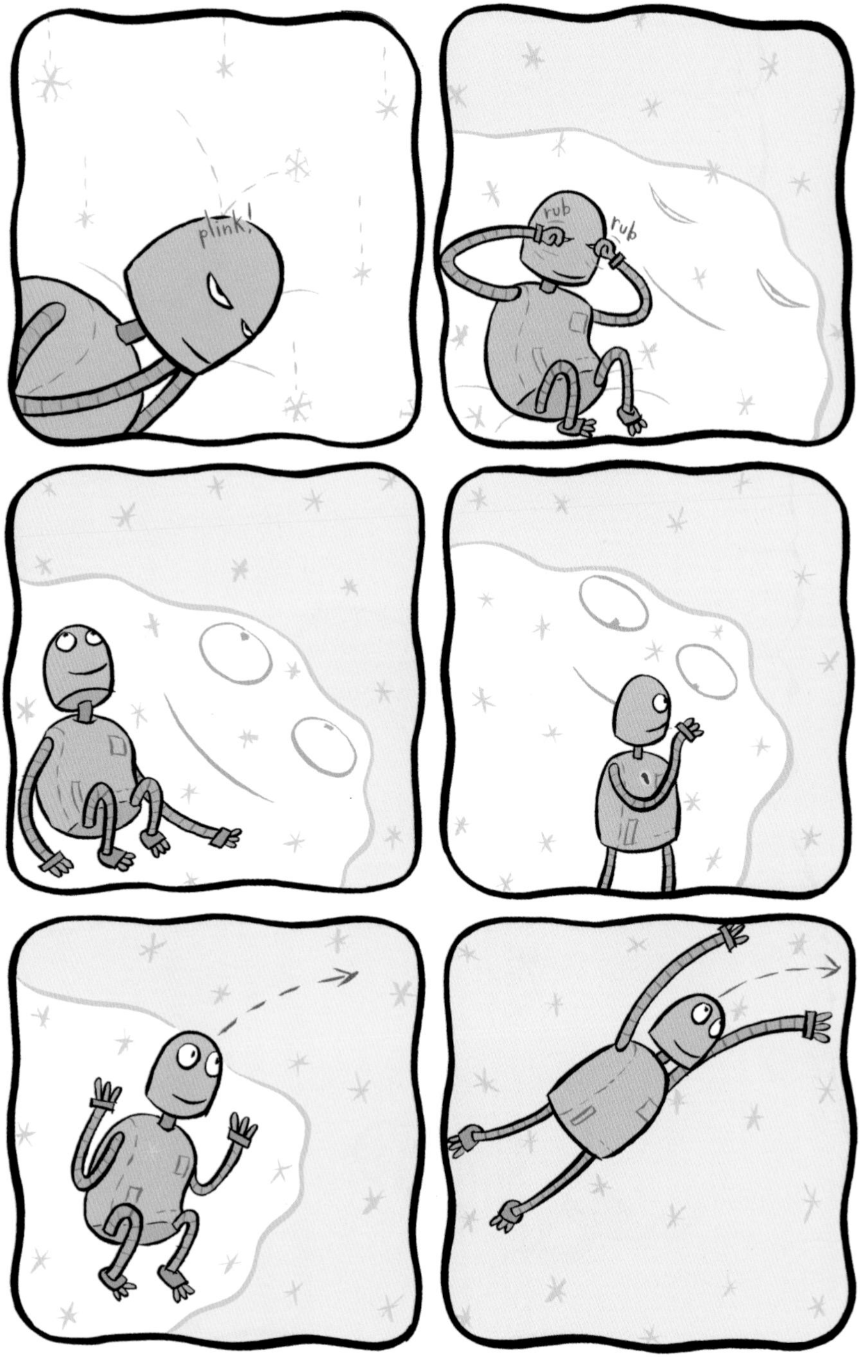
plink!
rub
rub

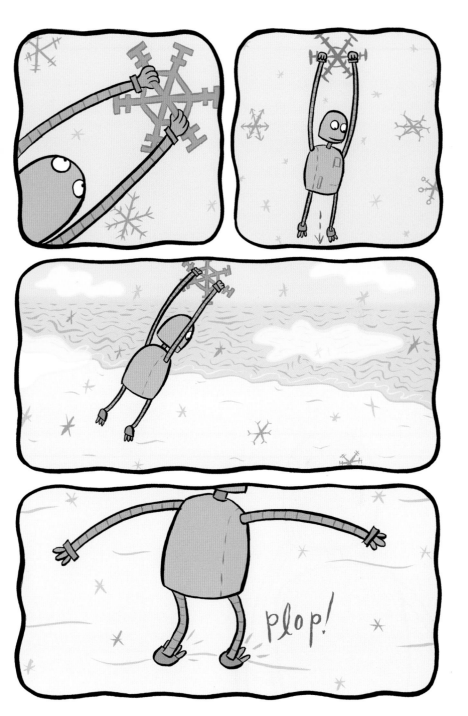

plop!

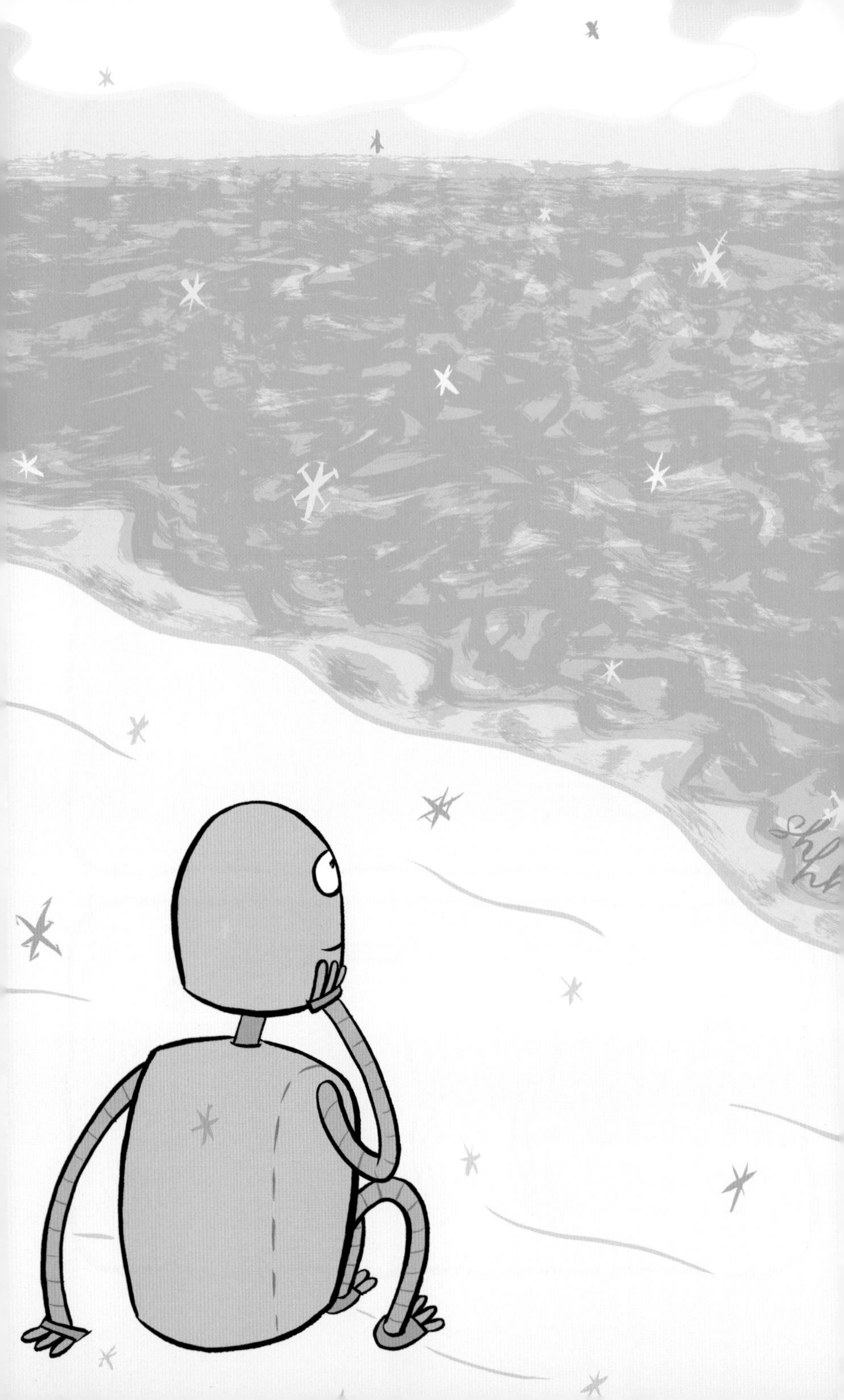

March

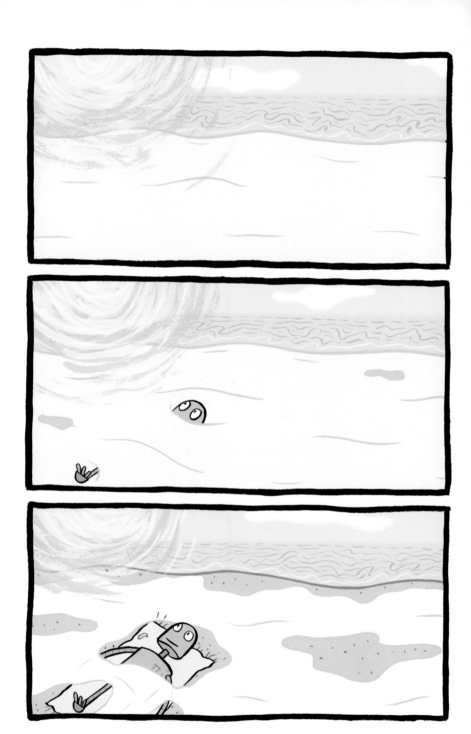

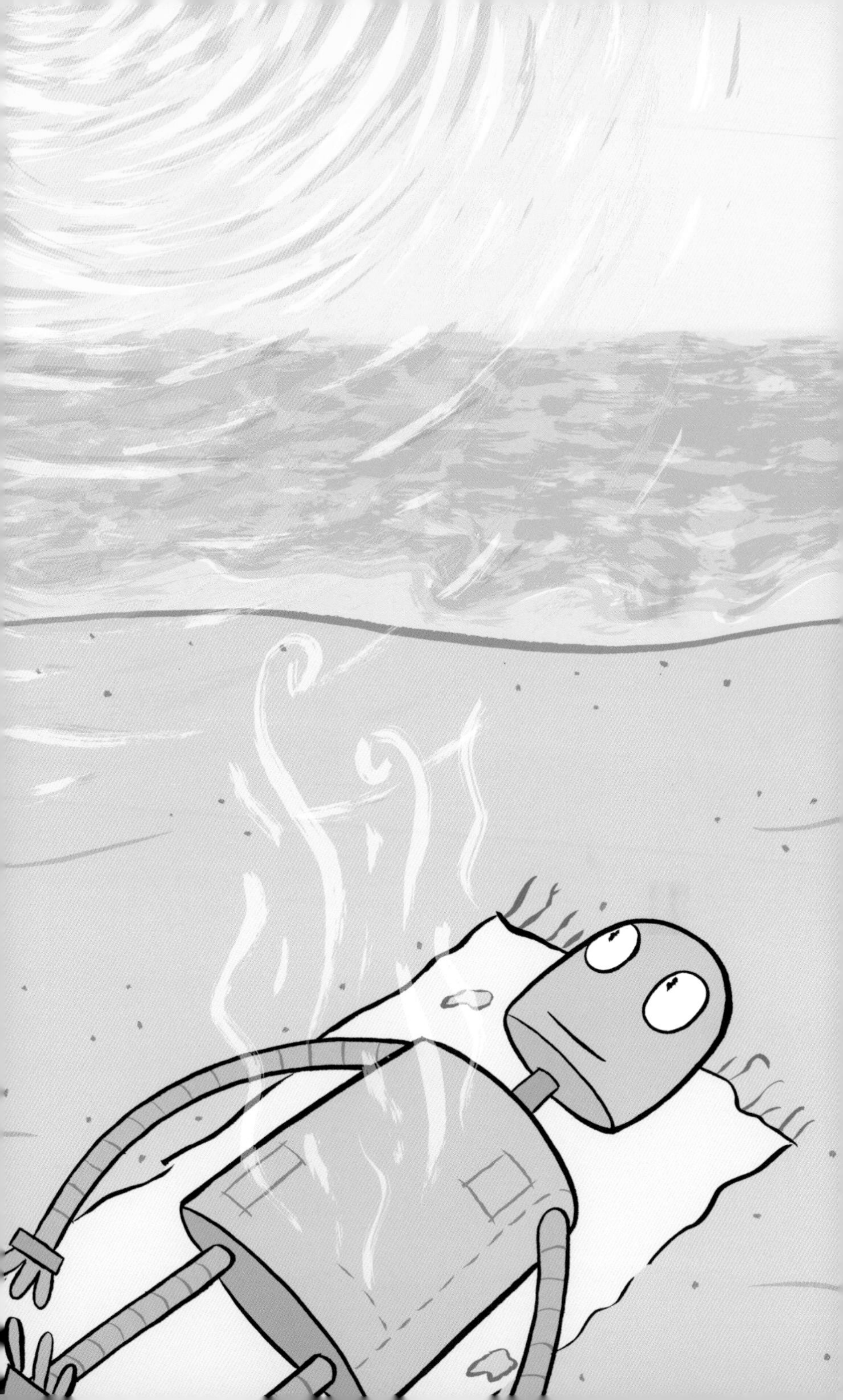

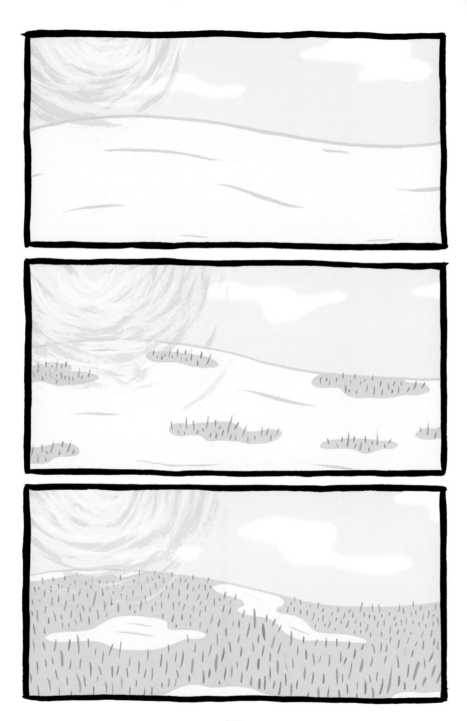

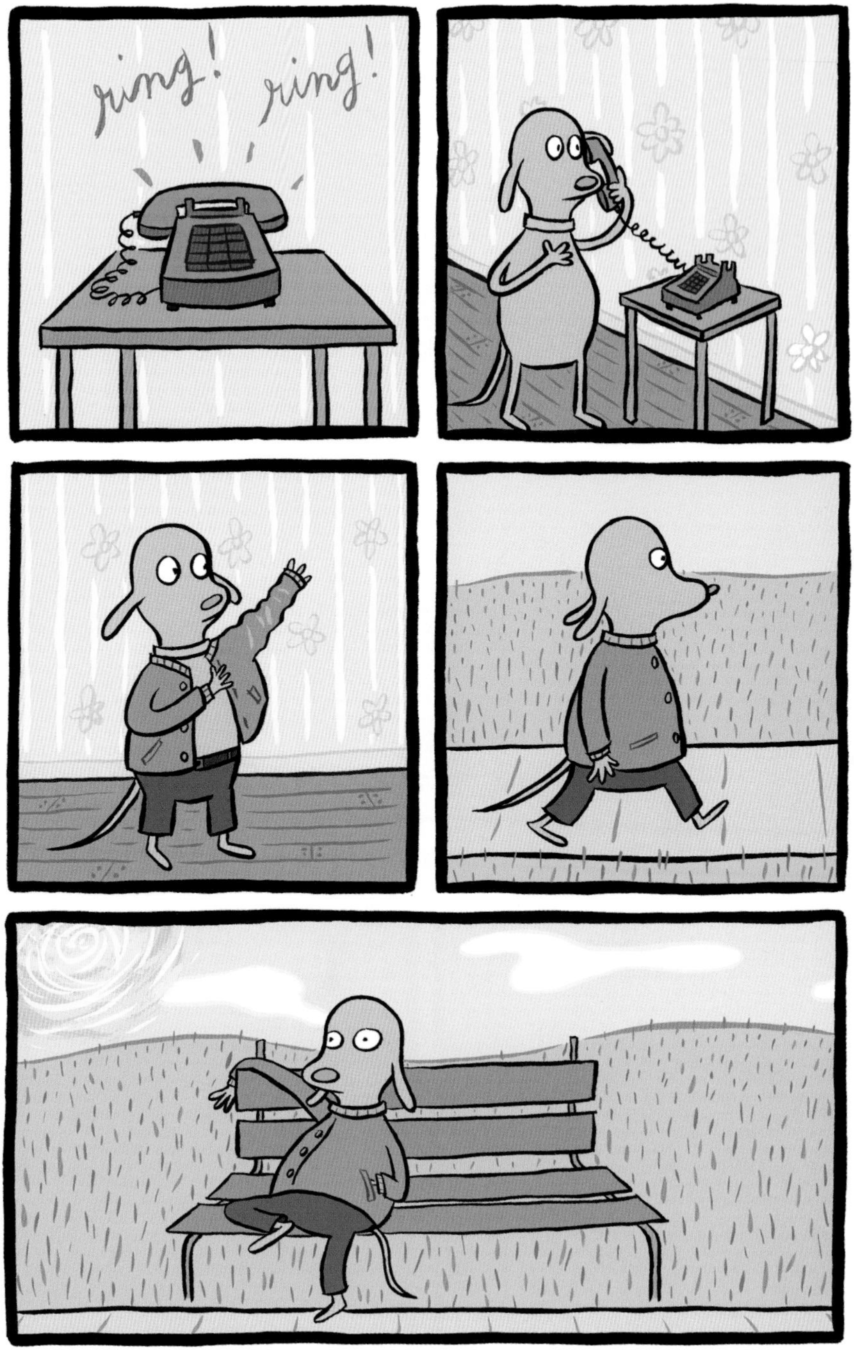
ring! ring!

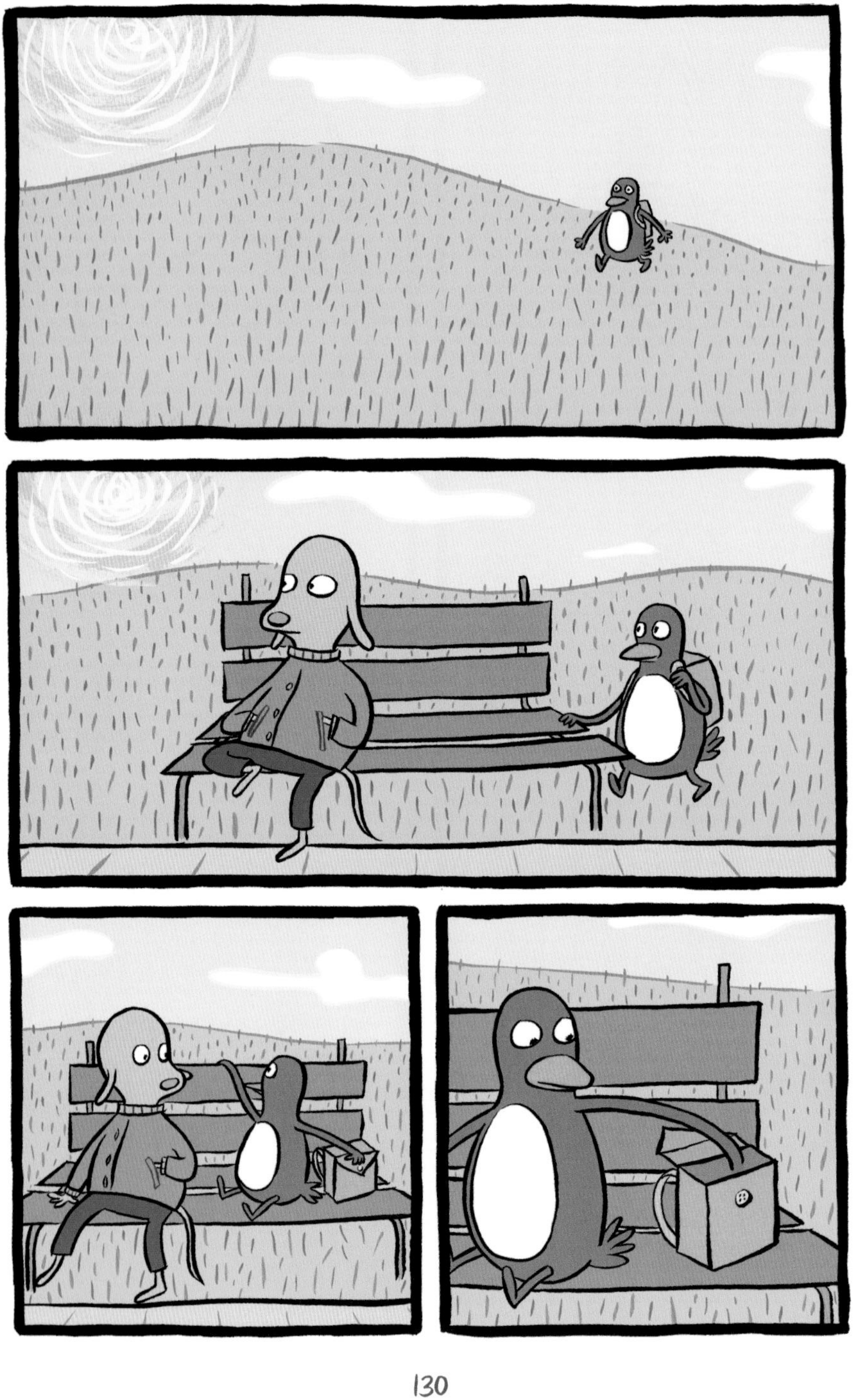

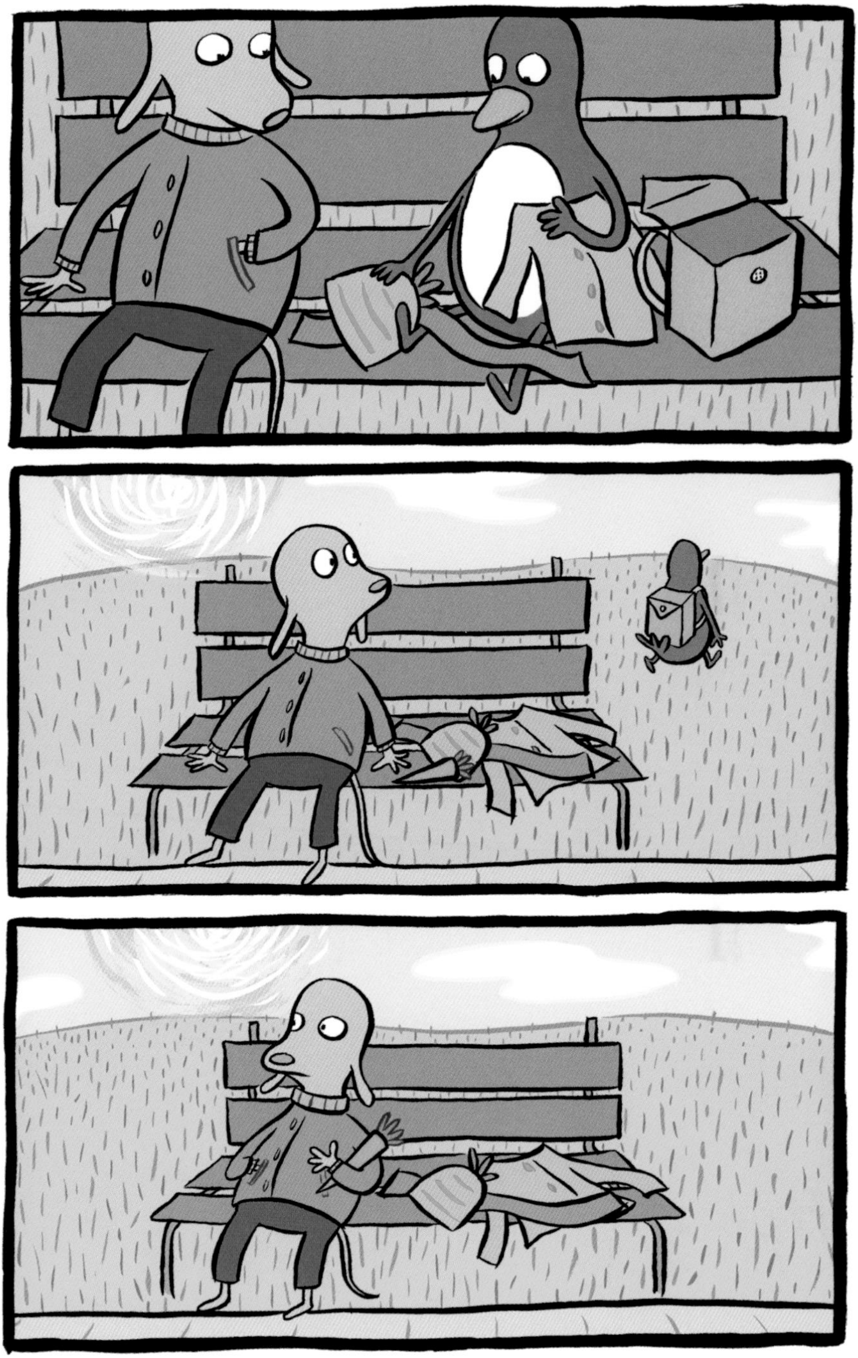

April

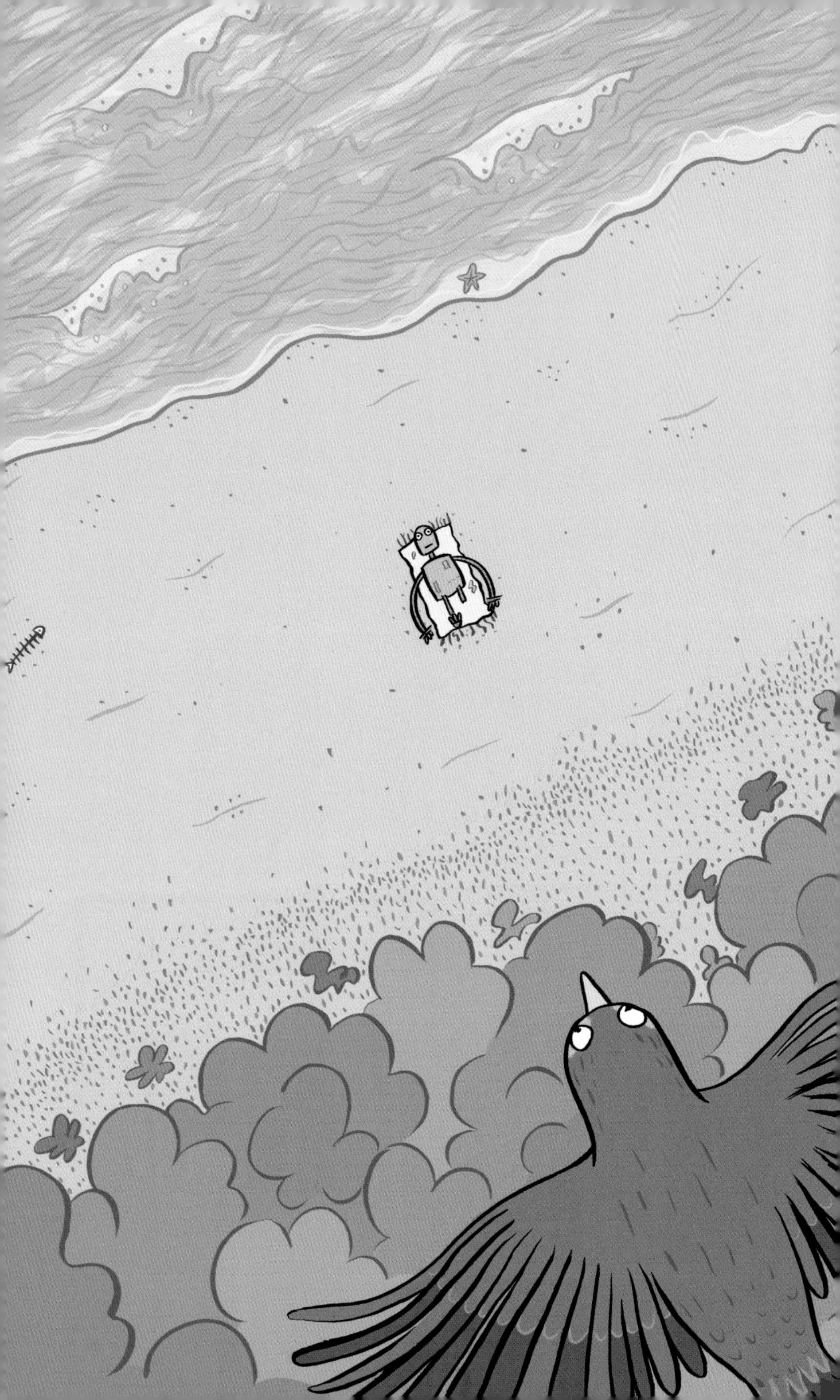

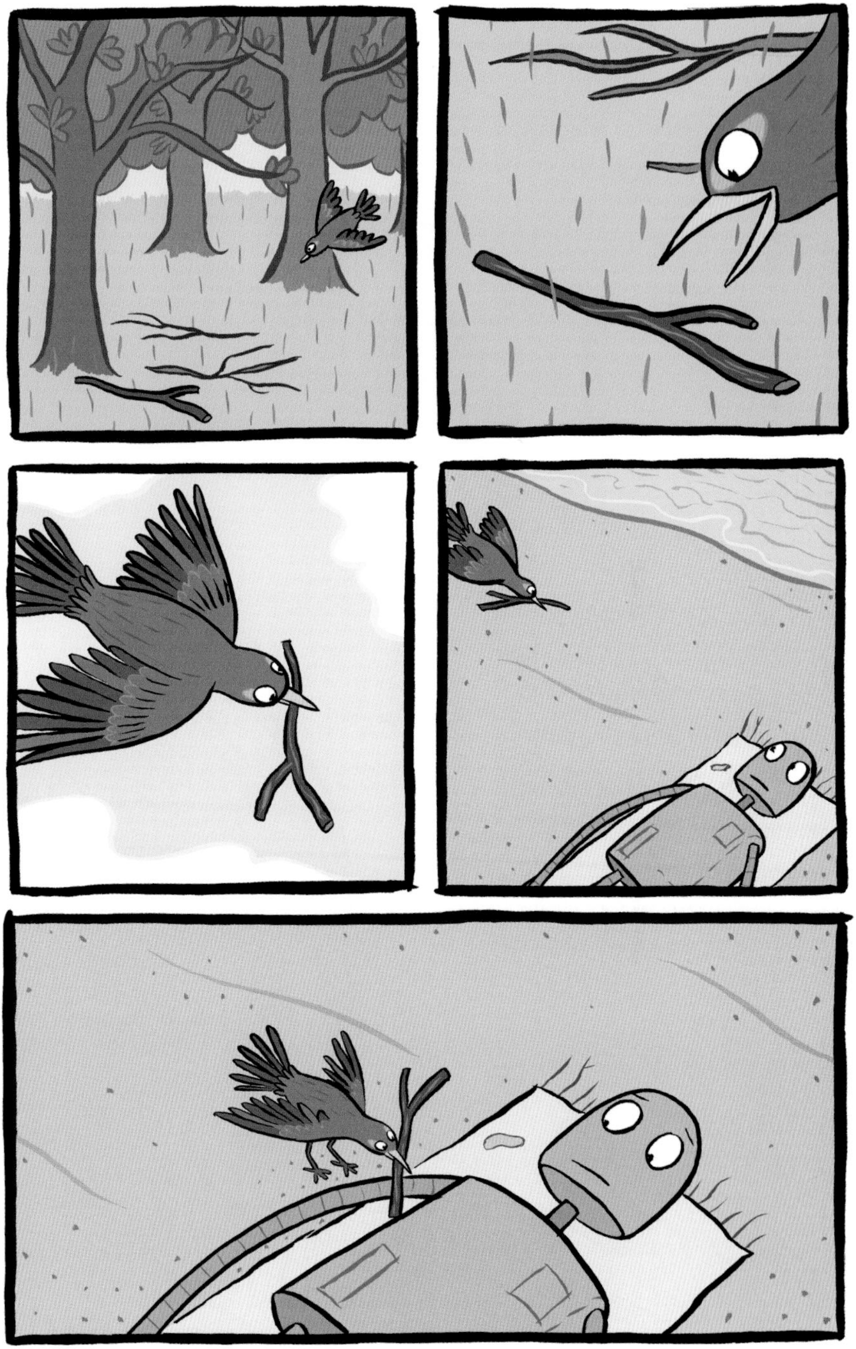

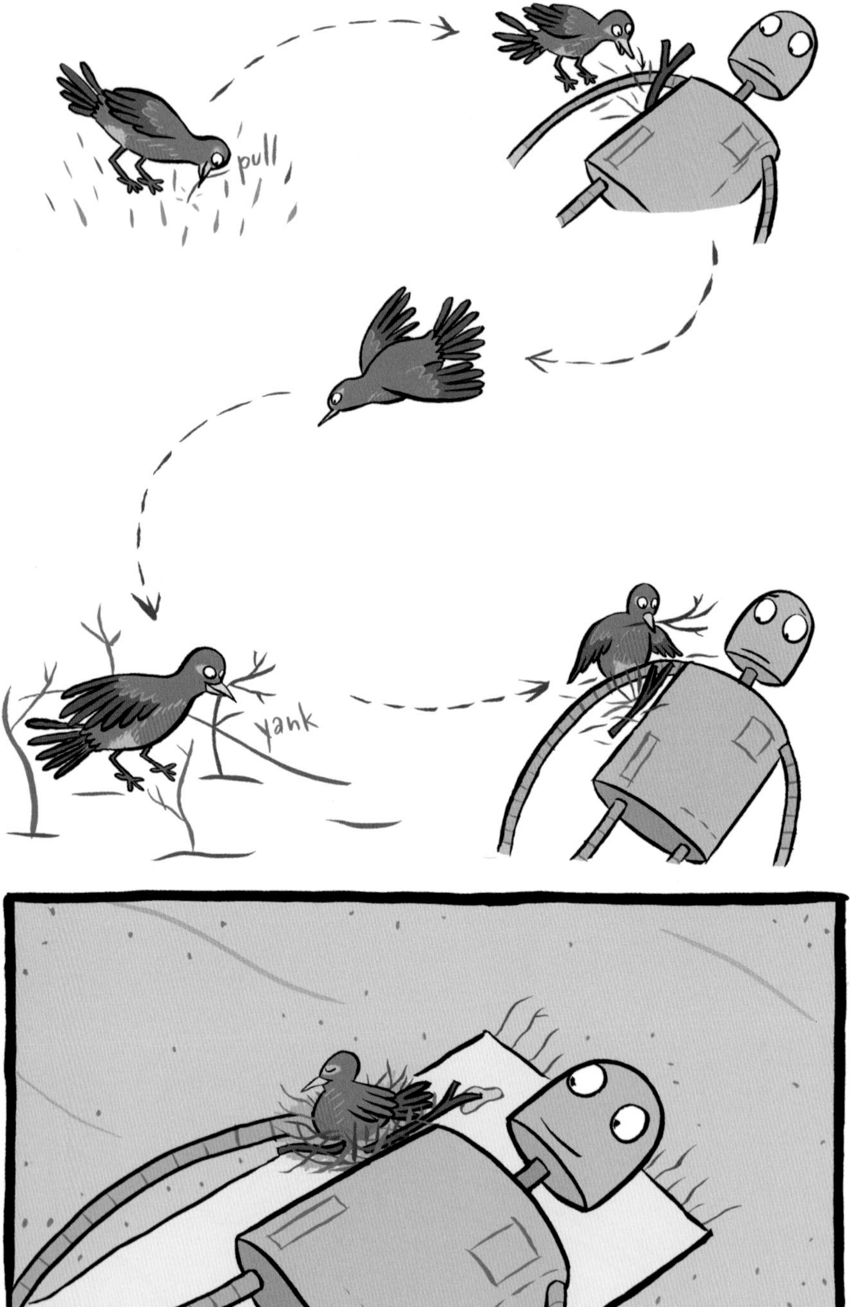
pull
yank

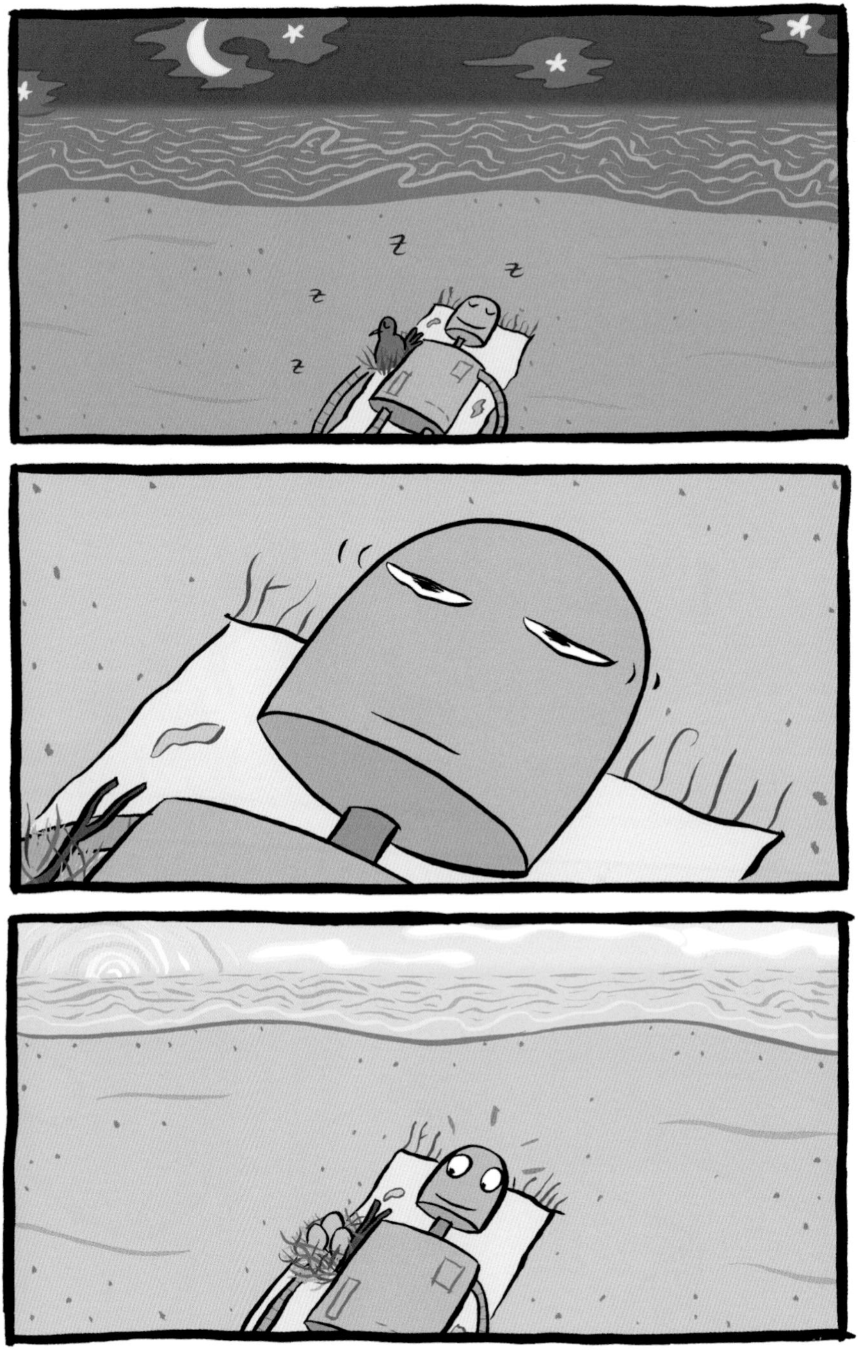
z
z
z
z

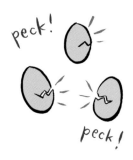

peck!

peck!

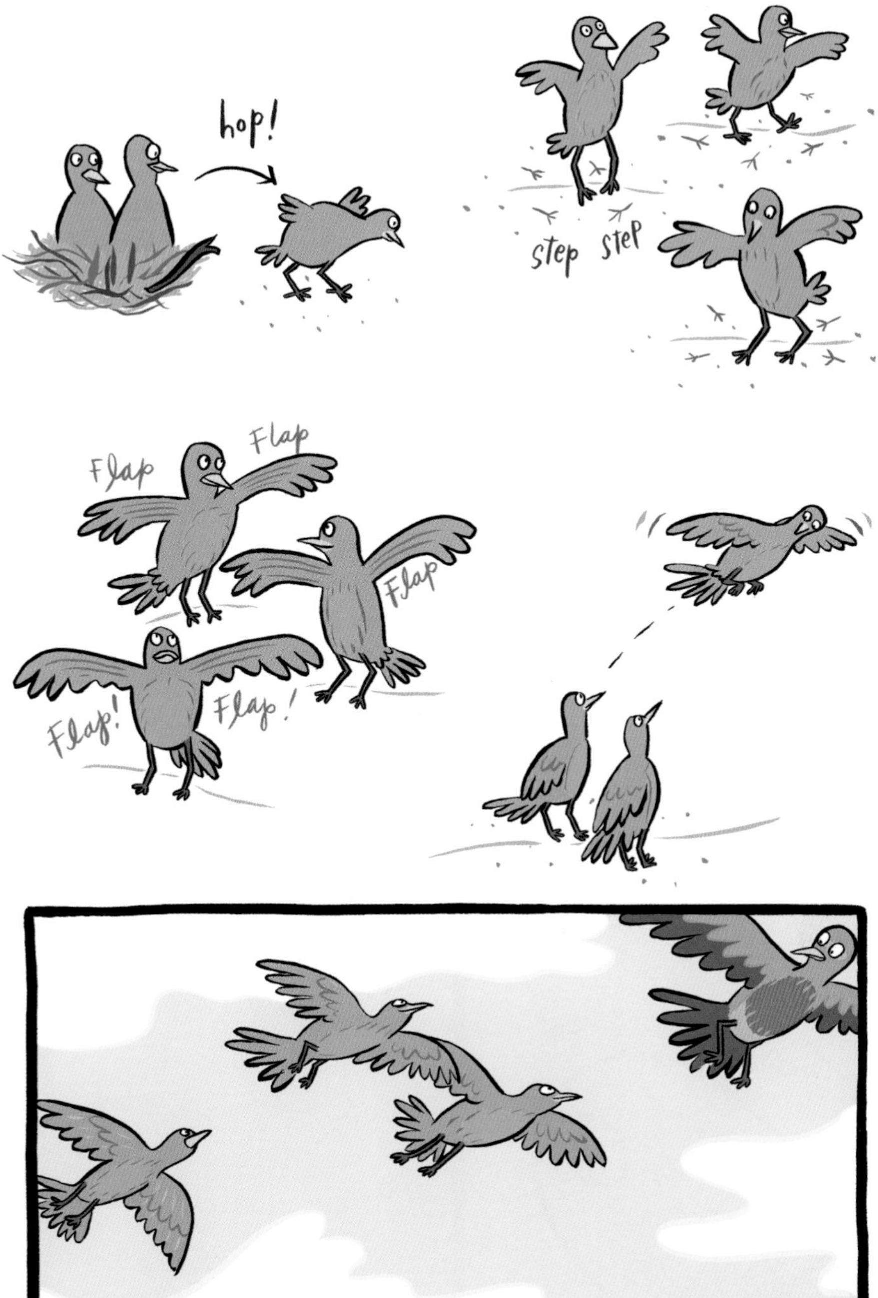
hop!
step
step
Flap
Flap
Flap
Flap!
Flap!

May

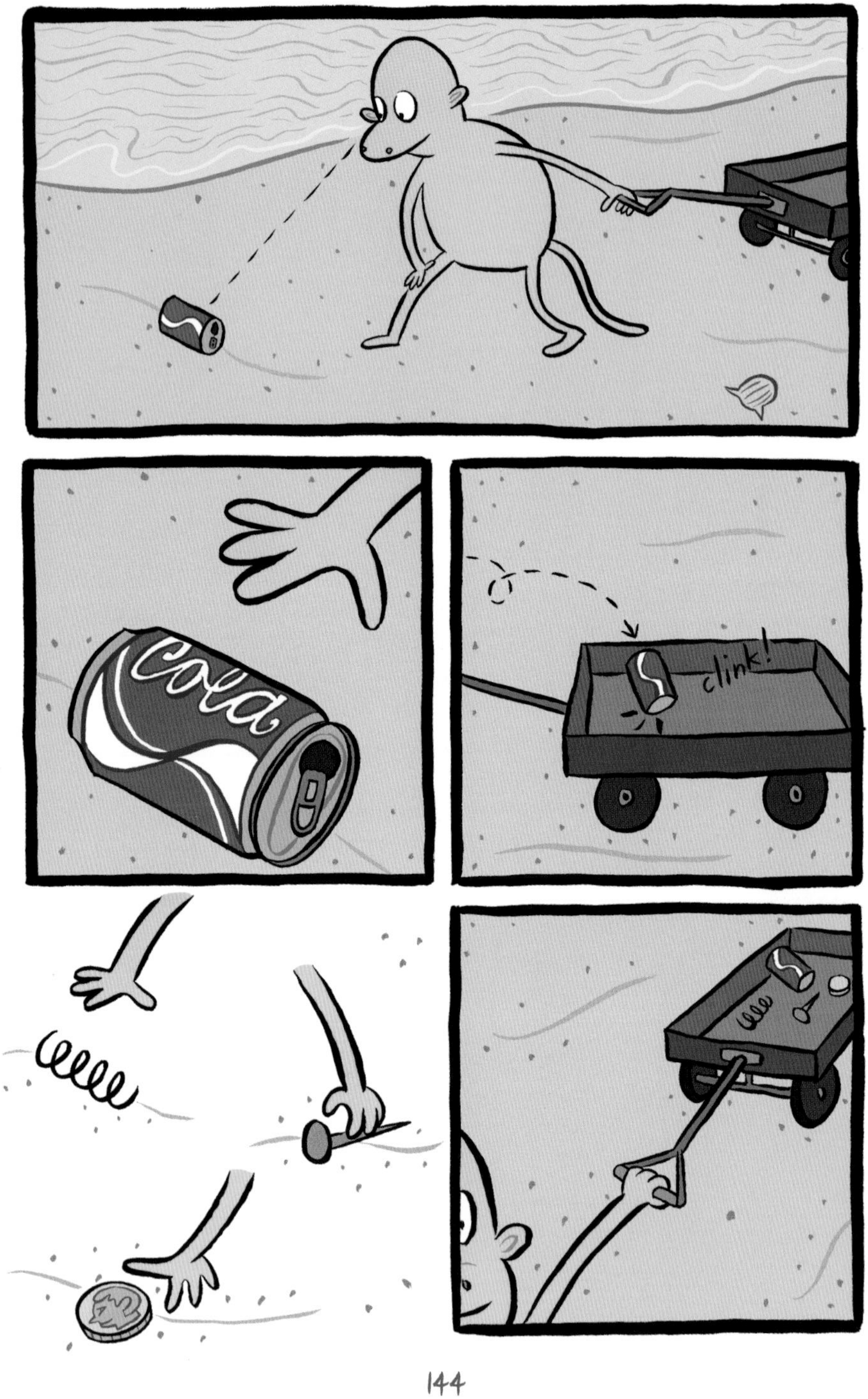
Cola
clink!

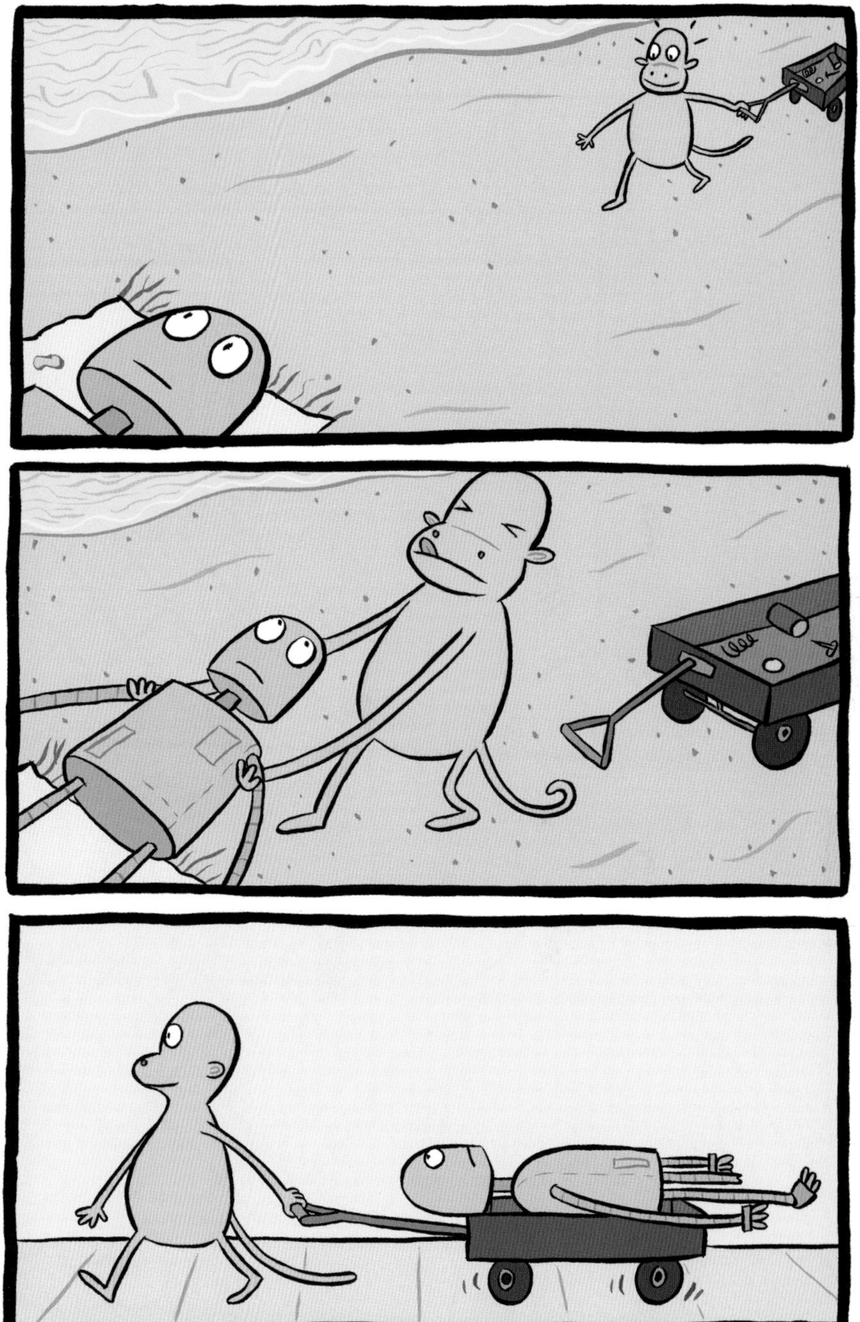

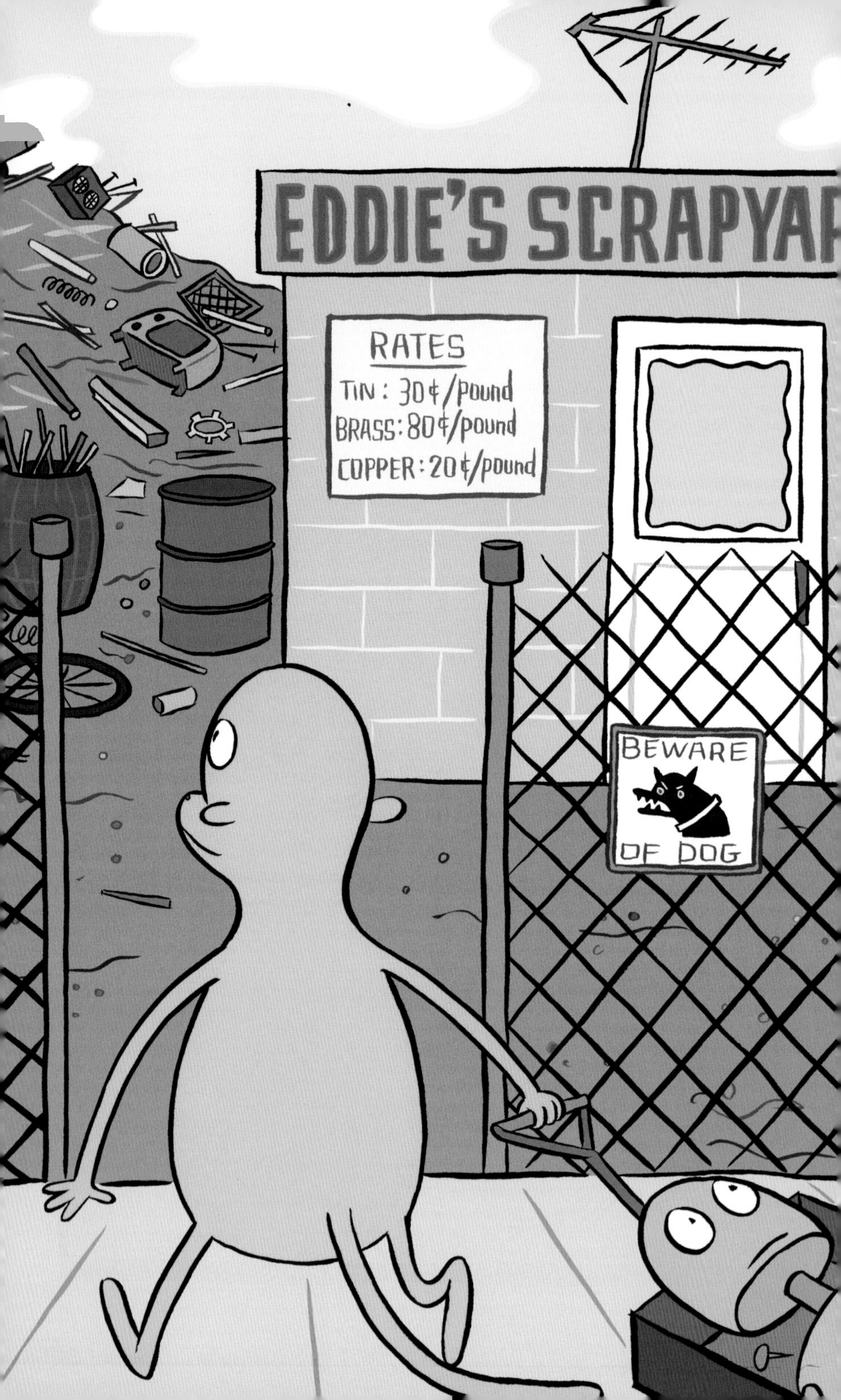

EDDIE'S SCRAPYAR
RATES
TIN: 30¢/pound
BRASS: 80¢/pound
COPPER: 20¢/pound
BEWARE
OF DOG

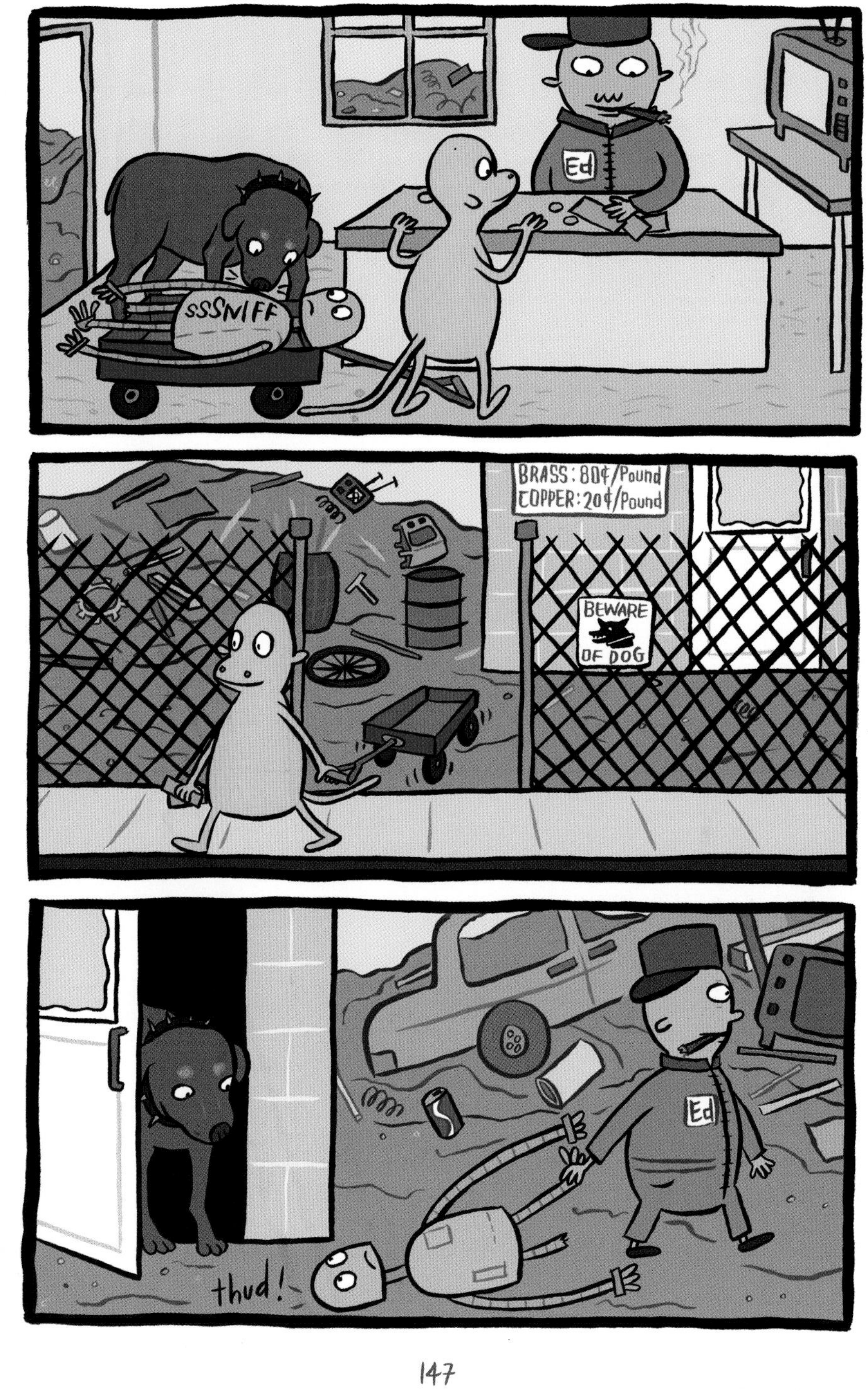
Ed
SSSNIFF
BRASS: 80¢/Pound
COPPER: 20¢/Pound
BEWARE
OF DOG
Ed
thud!

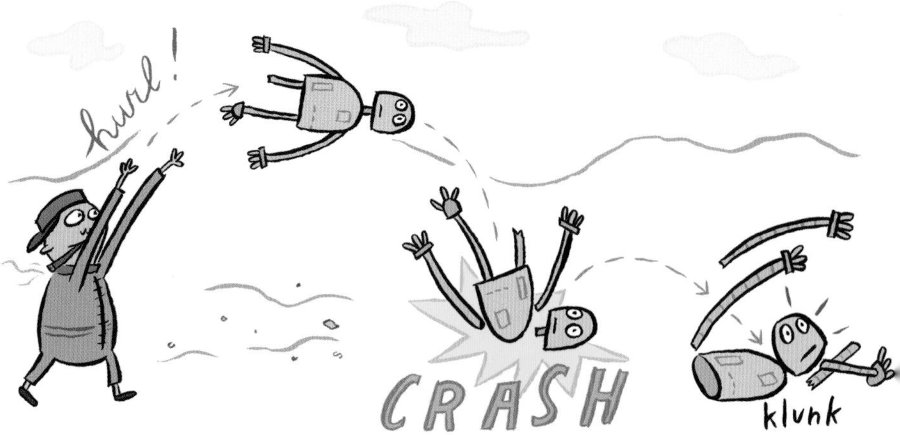
hurl!
CRASH
klunk

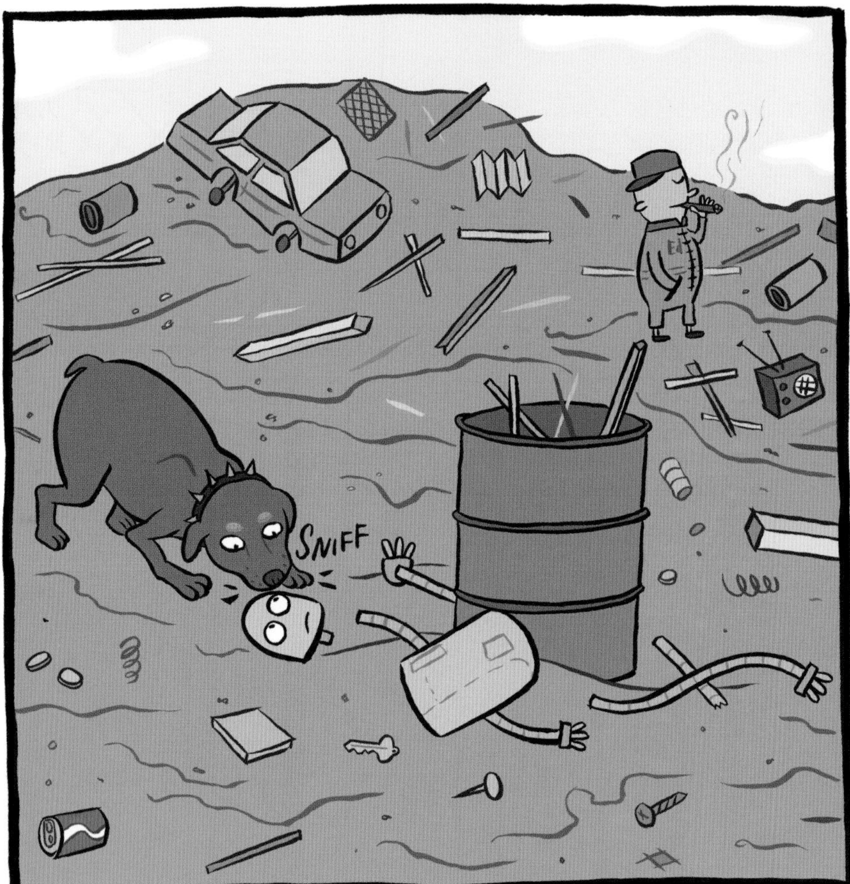
SNIFF

June

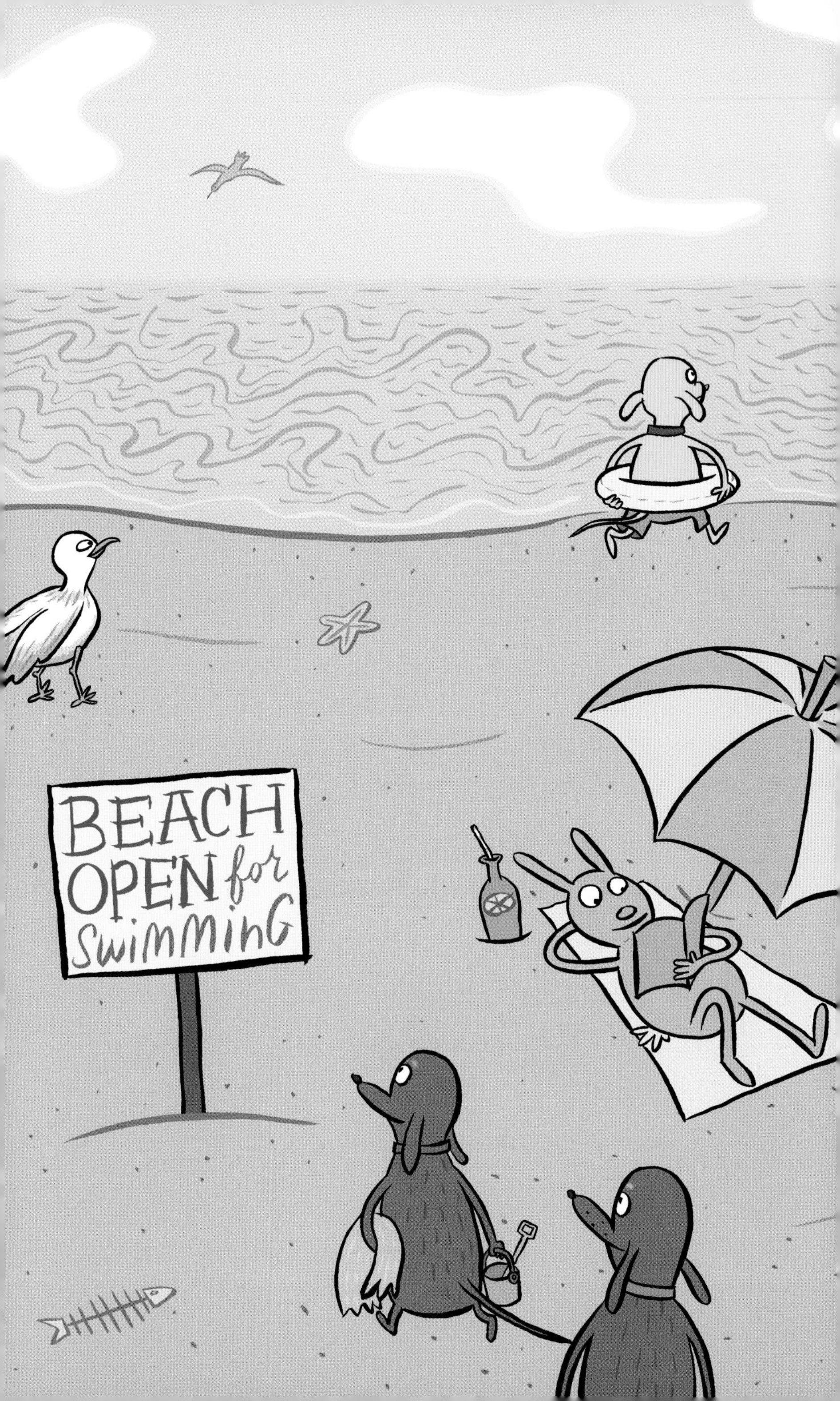
BEACH
OPEN for
SWIMMING

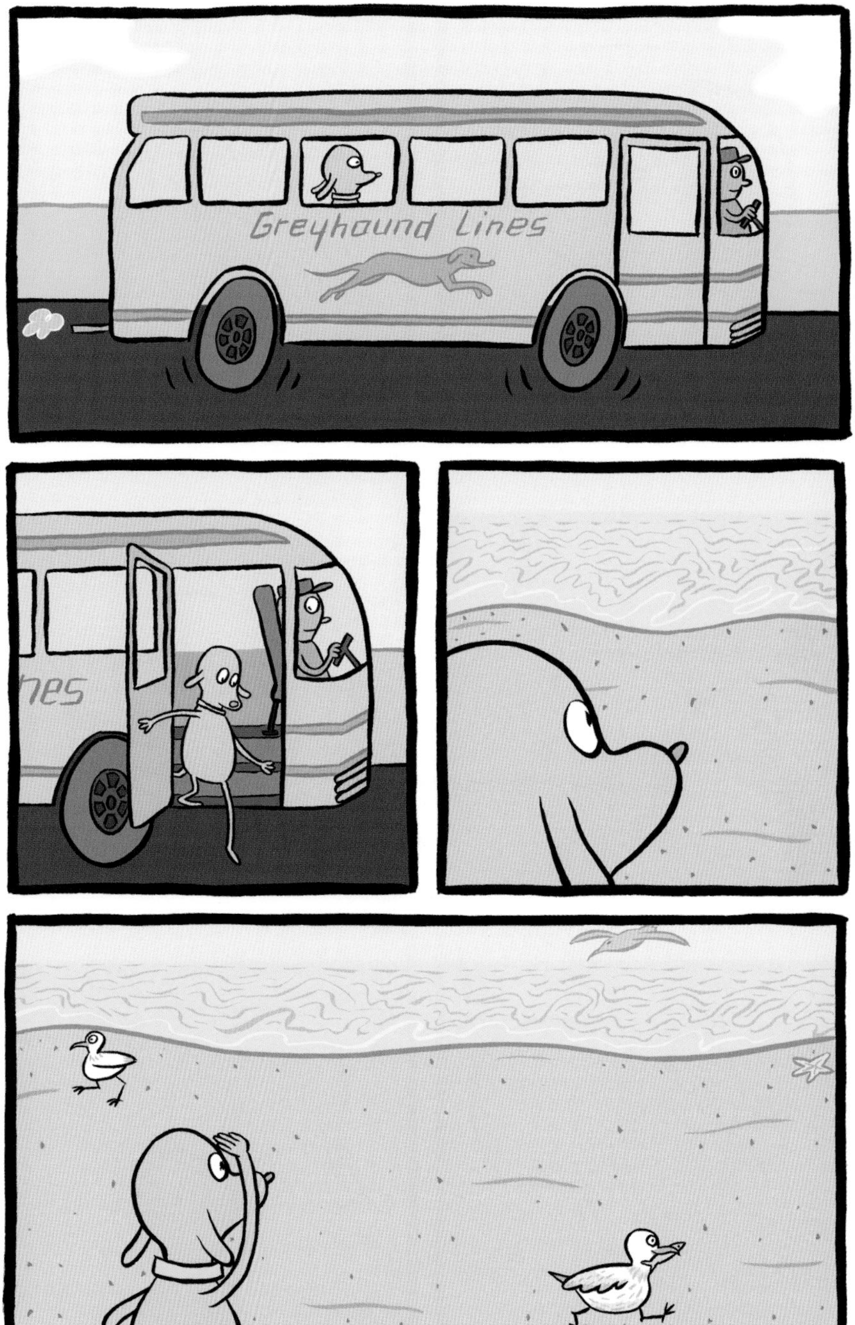
Greyhound Lines

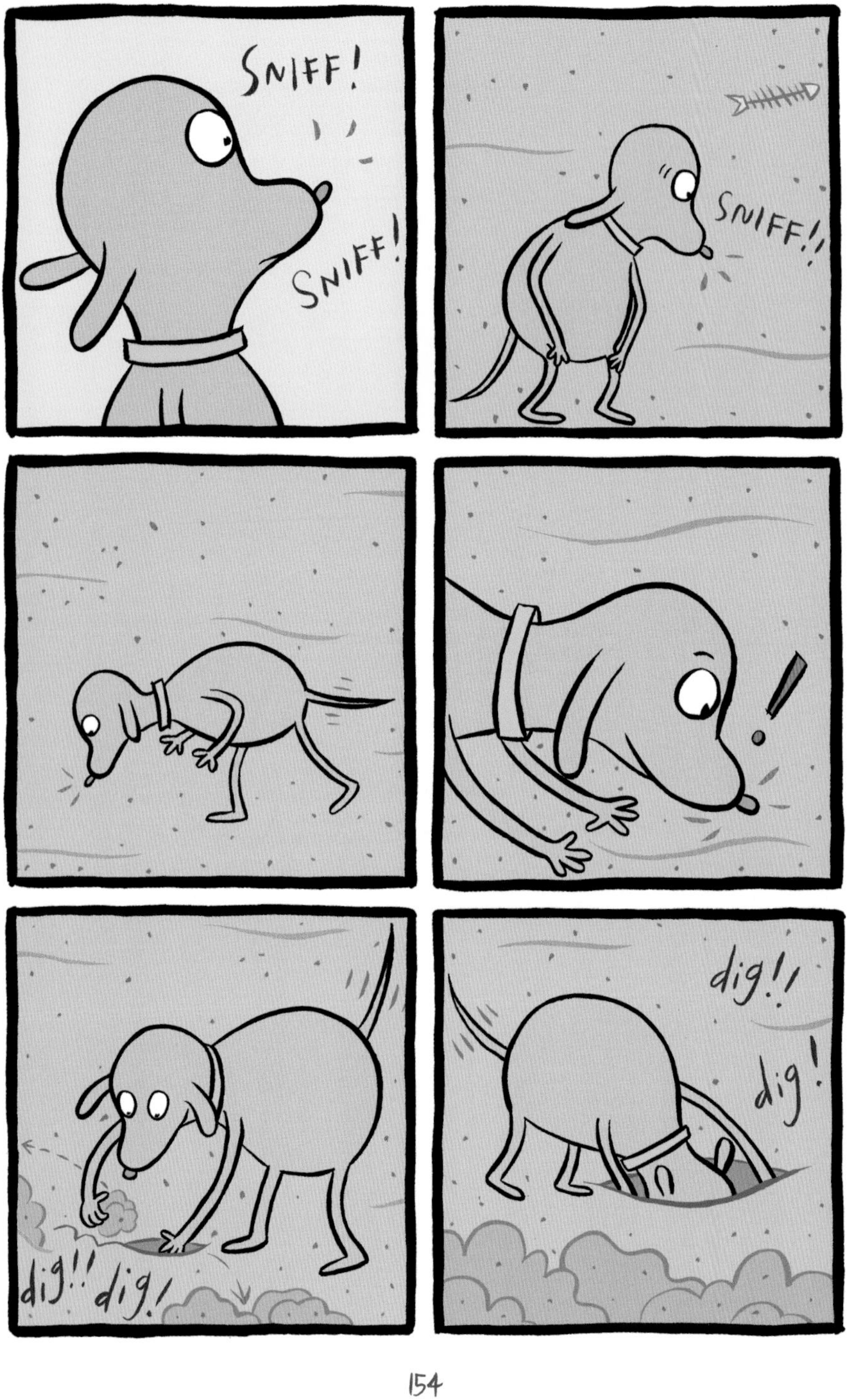
SNIFF!
SNIFF!
SNIFF!!
!
dig!! dig!
dig!!
dig!

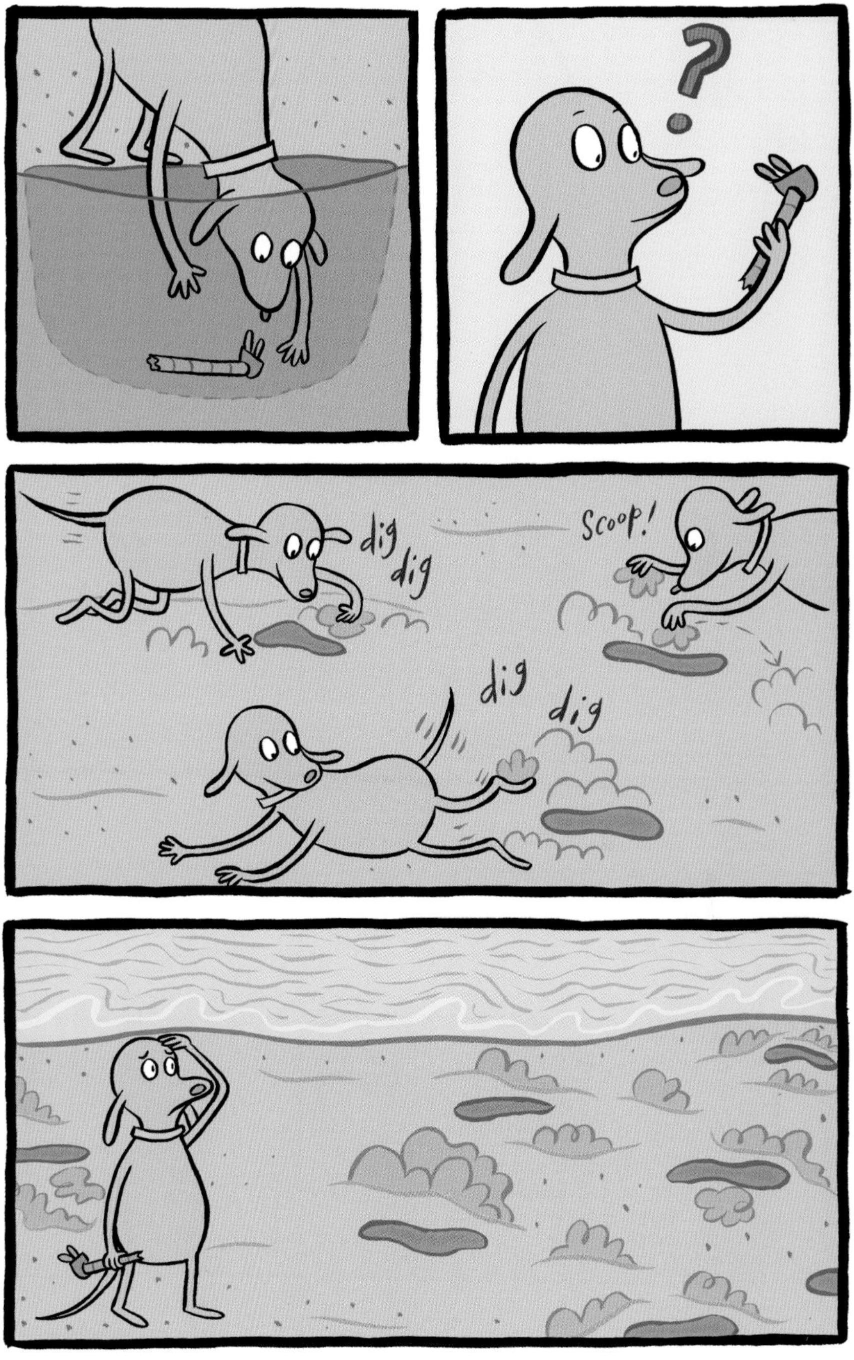
?
dig
dig
scoop!
dig
dig

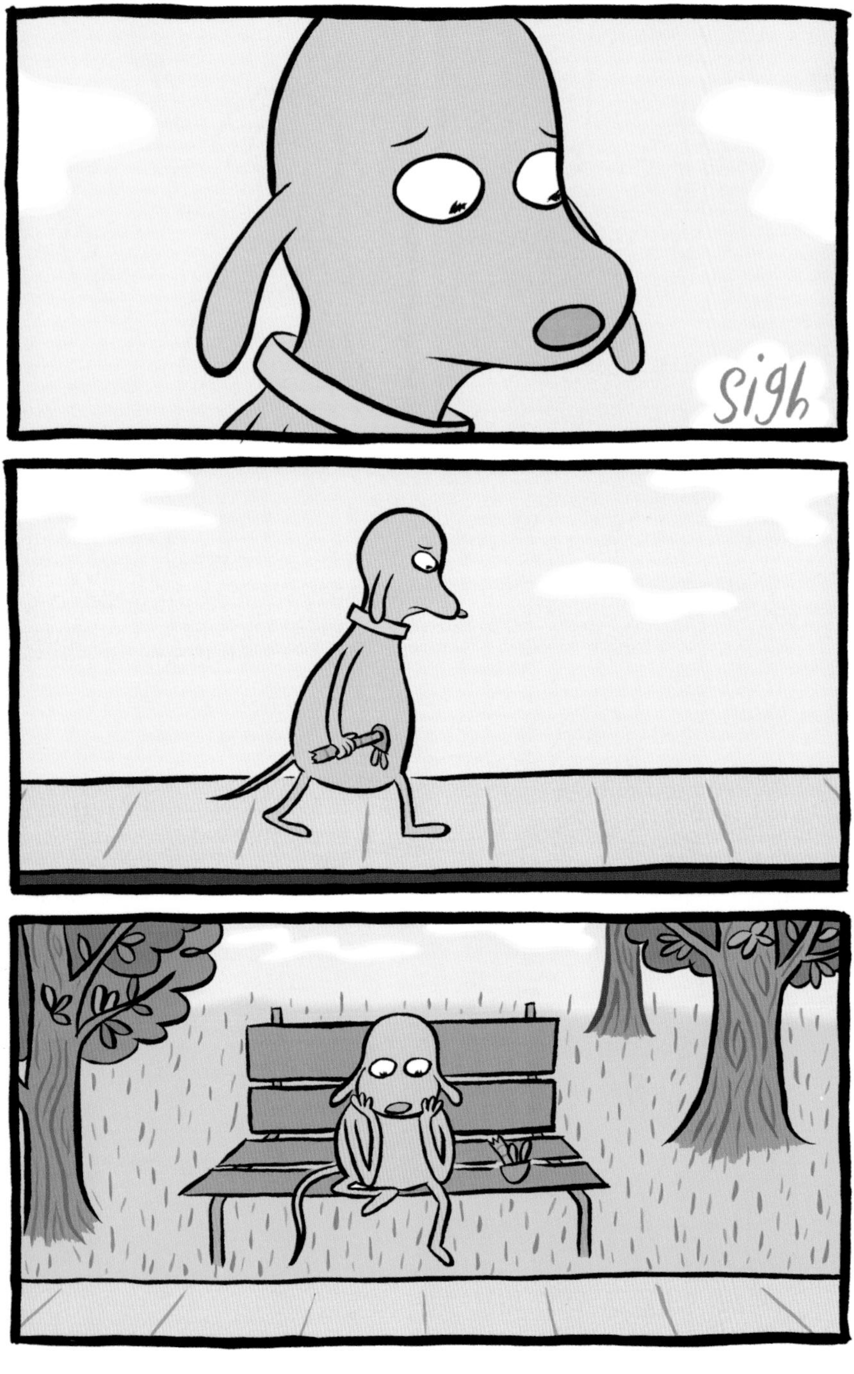
sigh

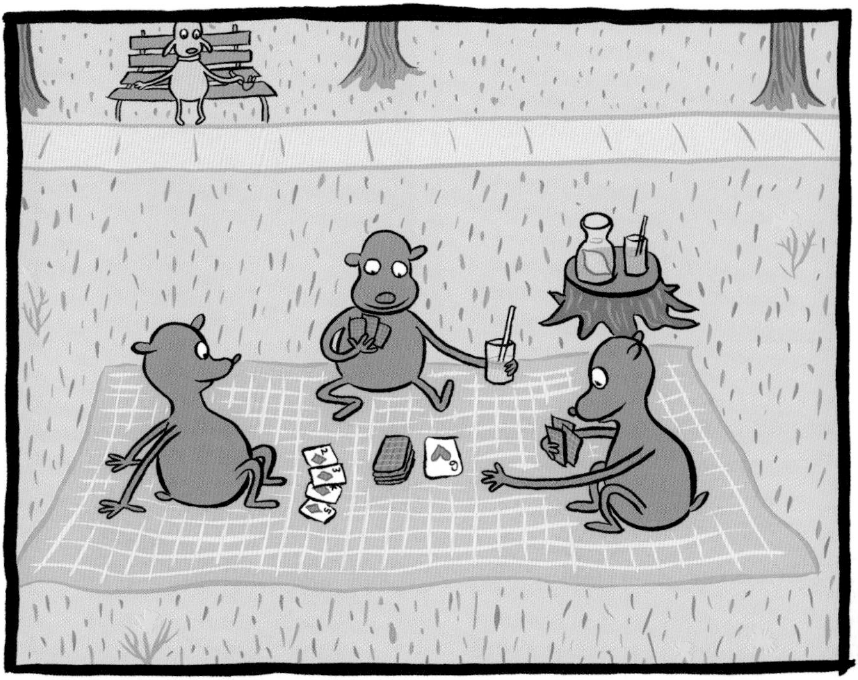

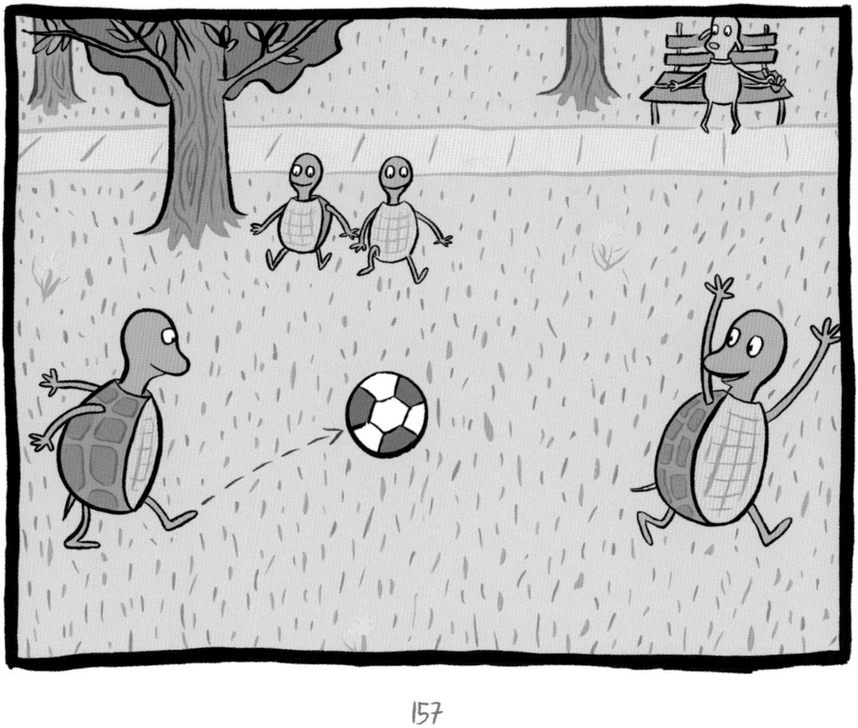

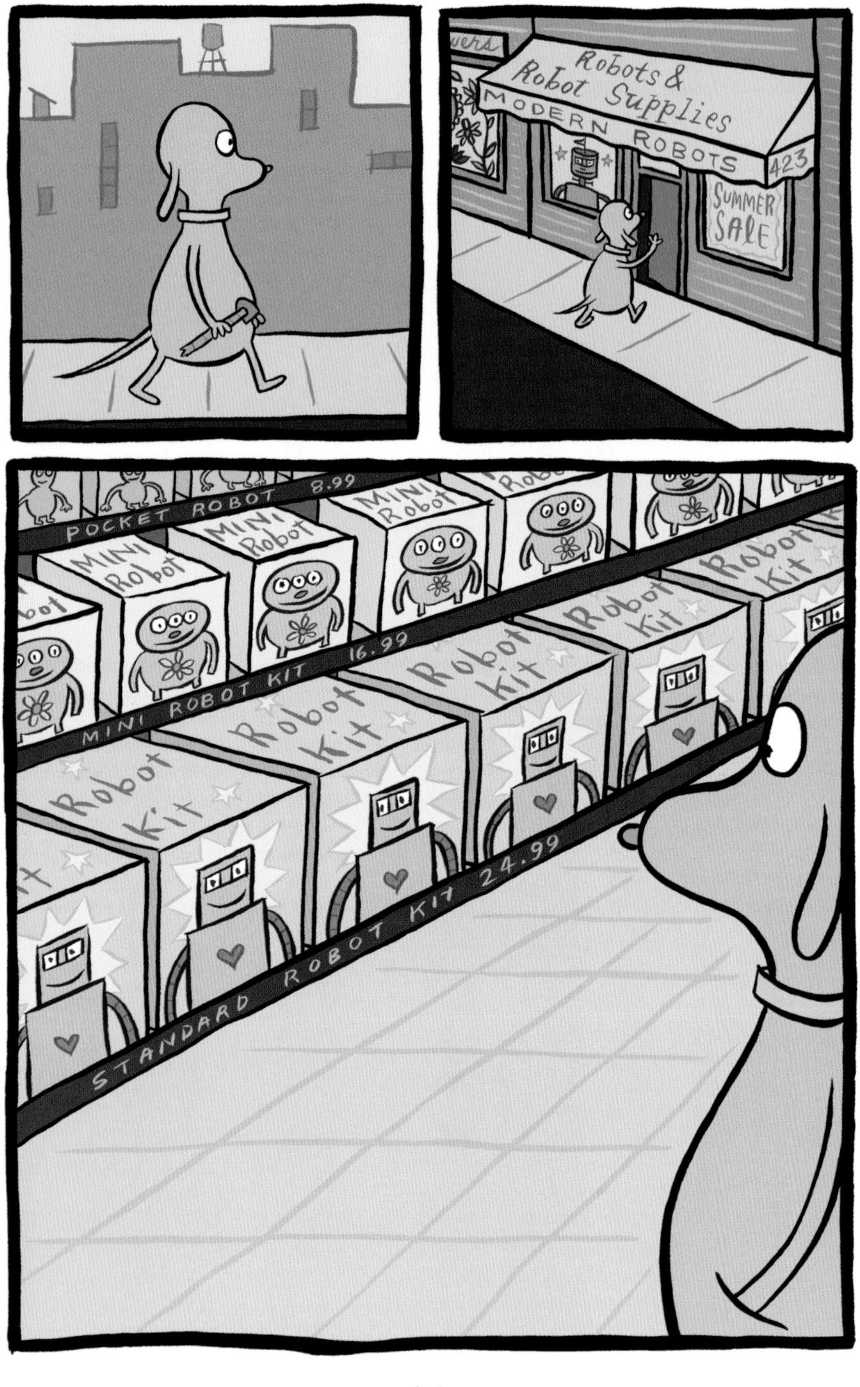

Robots & Robot Supplies
MODERN ROBOTS
423
SUMMER SALE
POCKET ROBOT 8.99
MINI Robot
MINI ROBOT KIT 16.99
Robot Kit
STANDARD ROBOT KIT 24.99

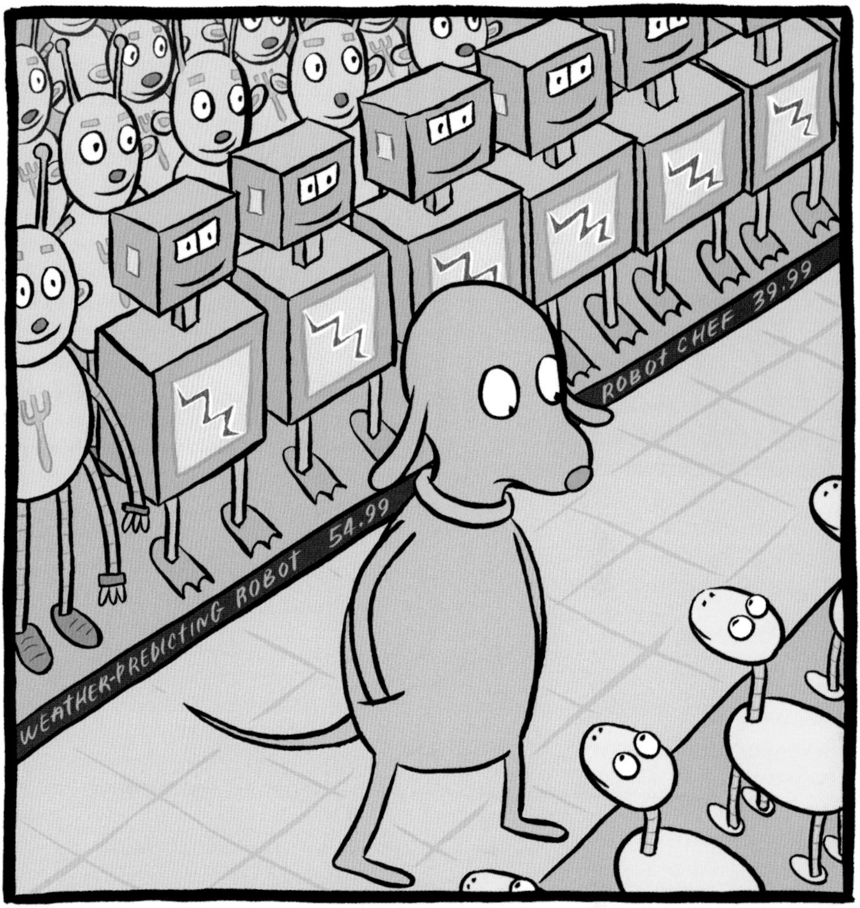
WEATHER-PREDICTING ROBOT 54.99
ROBOT CHEF 39.99

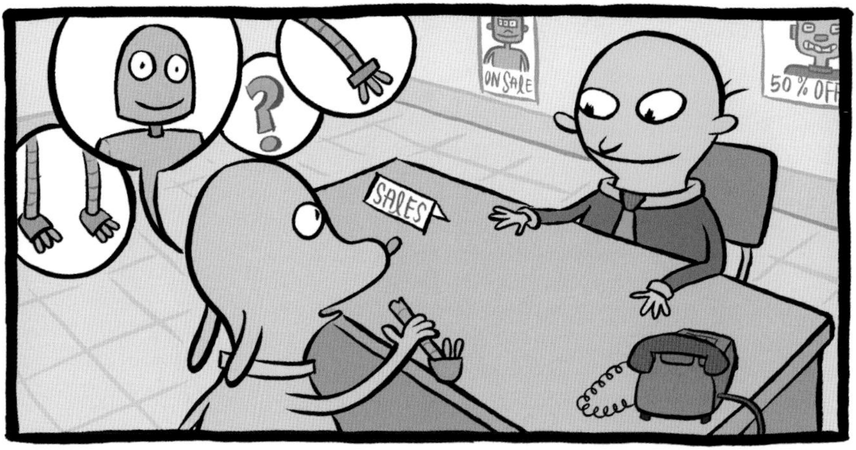
ON SALE
50% OFF
SALES

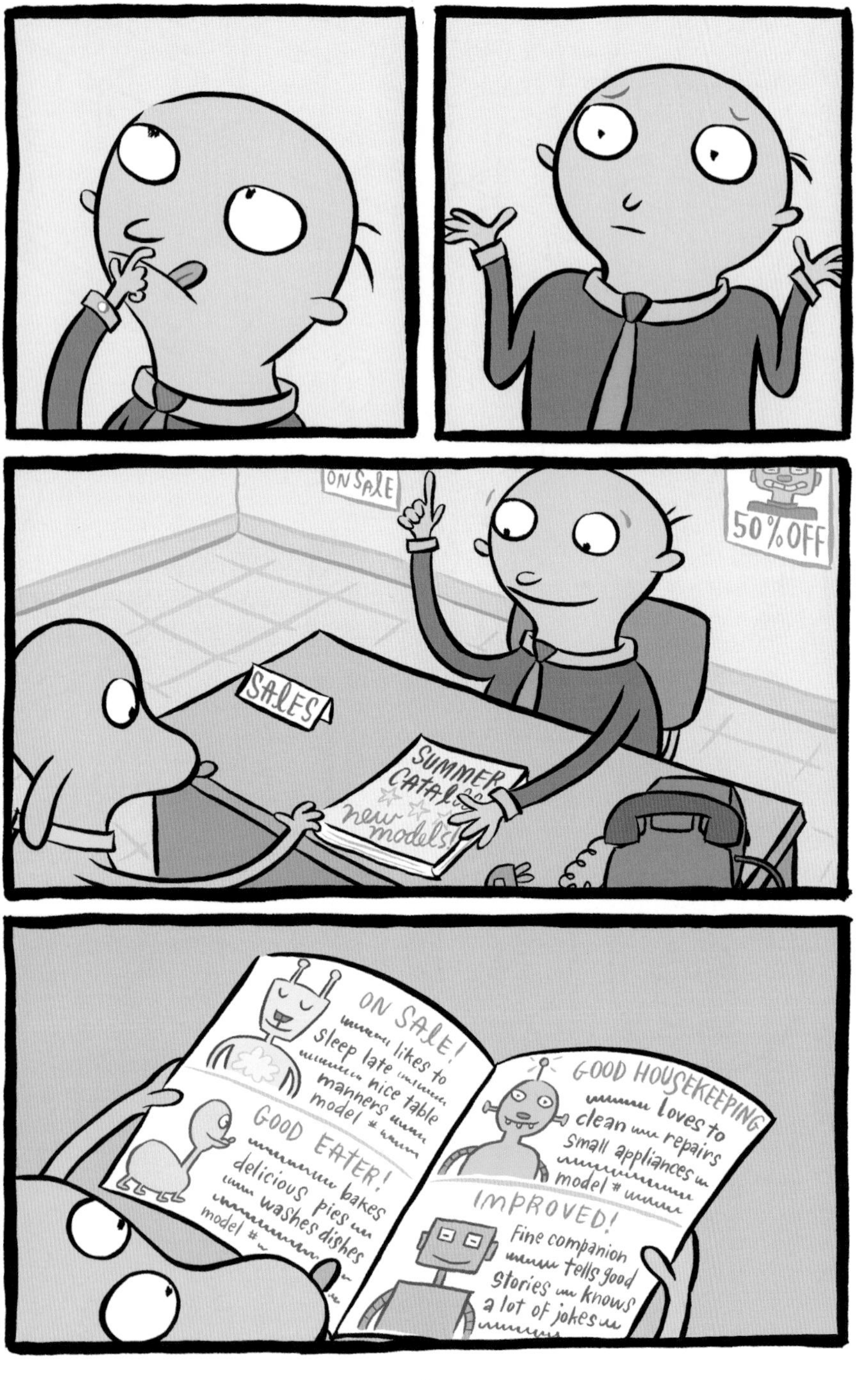

ON SALE
50% OFF
SALES
SUMMER CATALOG
new models!
ON SALE!
likes to
sleep late
nice table
manners
model #
GOOD EATER!
bakes
delicious pies
washes dishes
model #
GOOD HOUSEKEEPING
loves to
clean
repairs
small appliances
model #
IMPROVED!
Fine companion
tells good
stories
knows
a lot of jokes

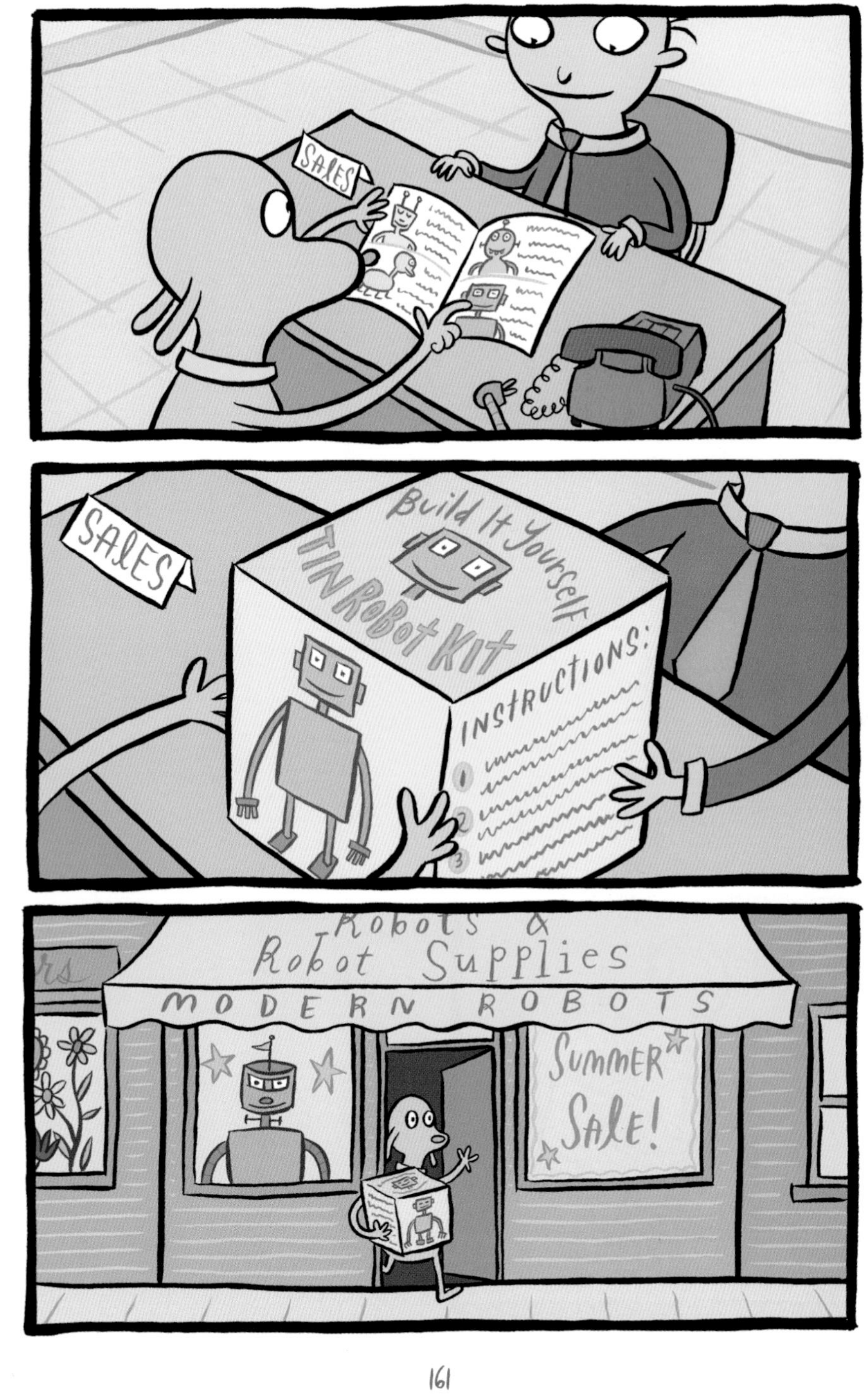
SALES
SALES
Build It Yourself
TIN RoBot KIT
INSTRUCTIONS:
1
2
3
Robots &
Robot Supplies
MODERN ROBOTS
SUMMER SALE!

July

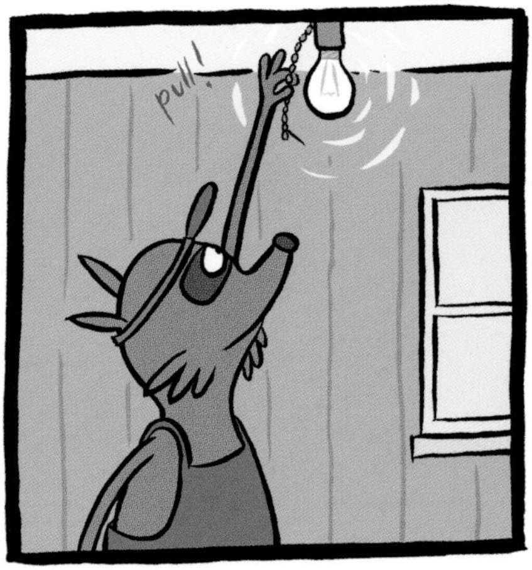
pull!

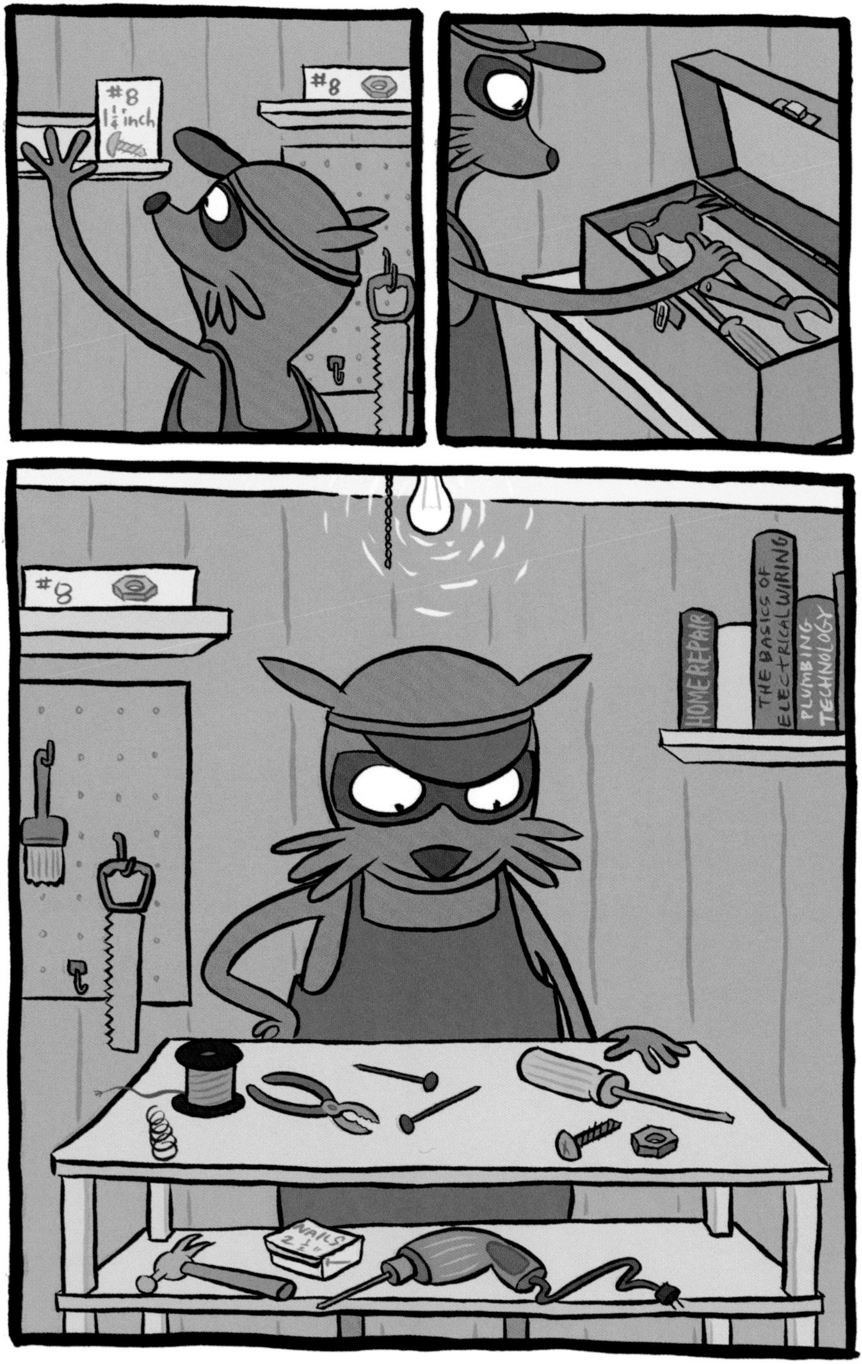

#8
1¼ inch
#8
#8
HOME REPAIR
THE BASICS OF ELECTRICAL WIRING
PLUMBING TECHNOLOGY
NAILS 2½"

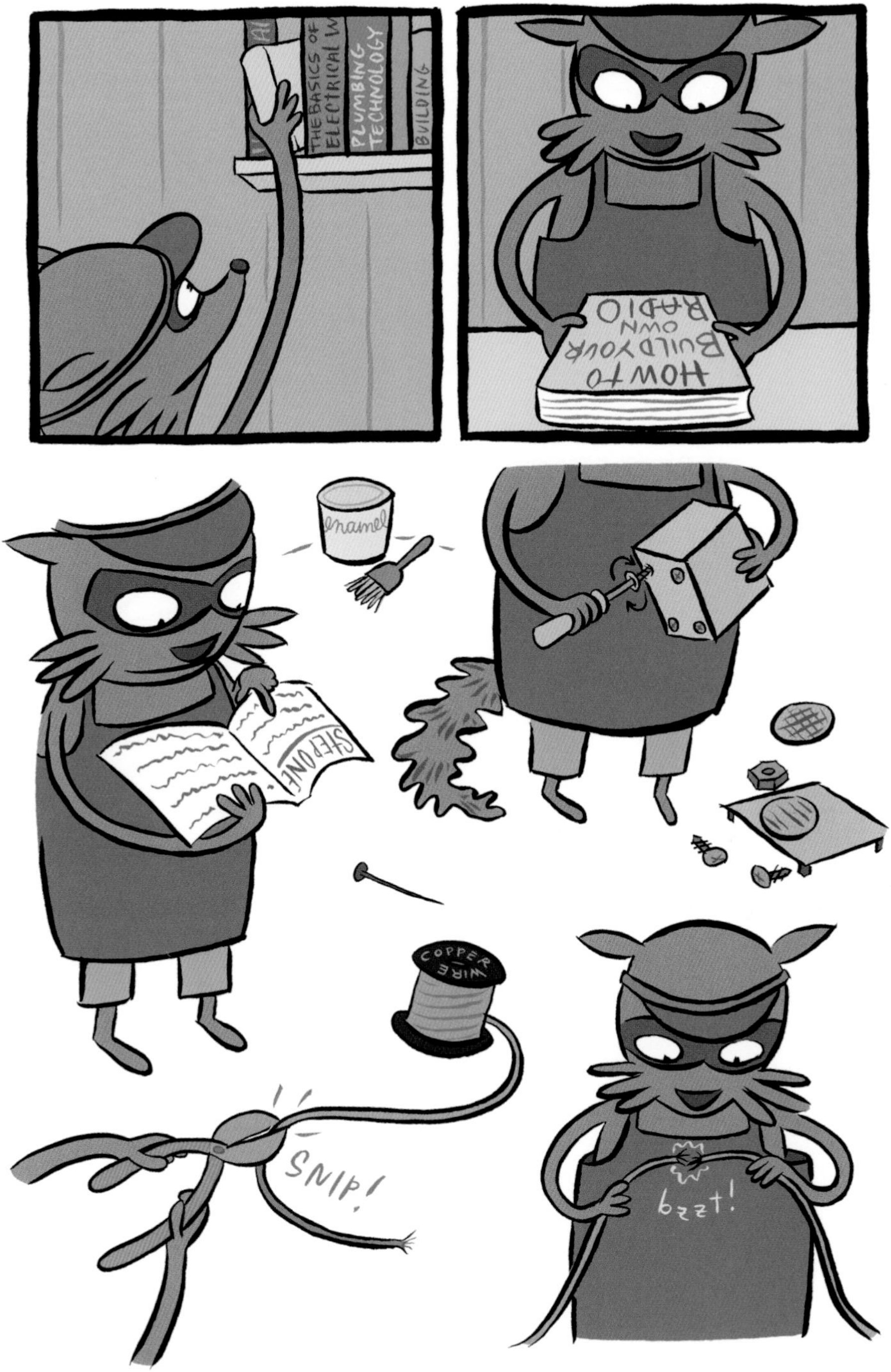
THE BASICS OF ELECTRICAL W
PLUMBING TECHNOLOGY
BUILDING
HOW TO BUILD YOUR OWN RADIO
Enamel
STEP ONE
COPPER WIRE
SNIP!
bzzt!

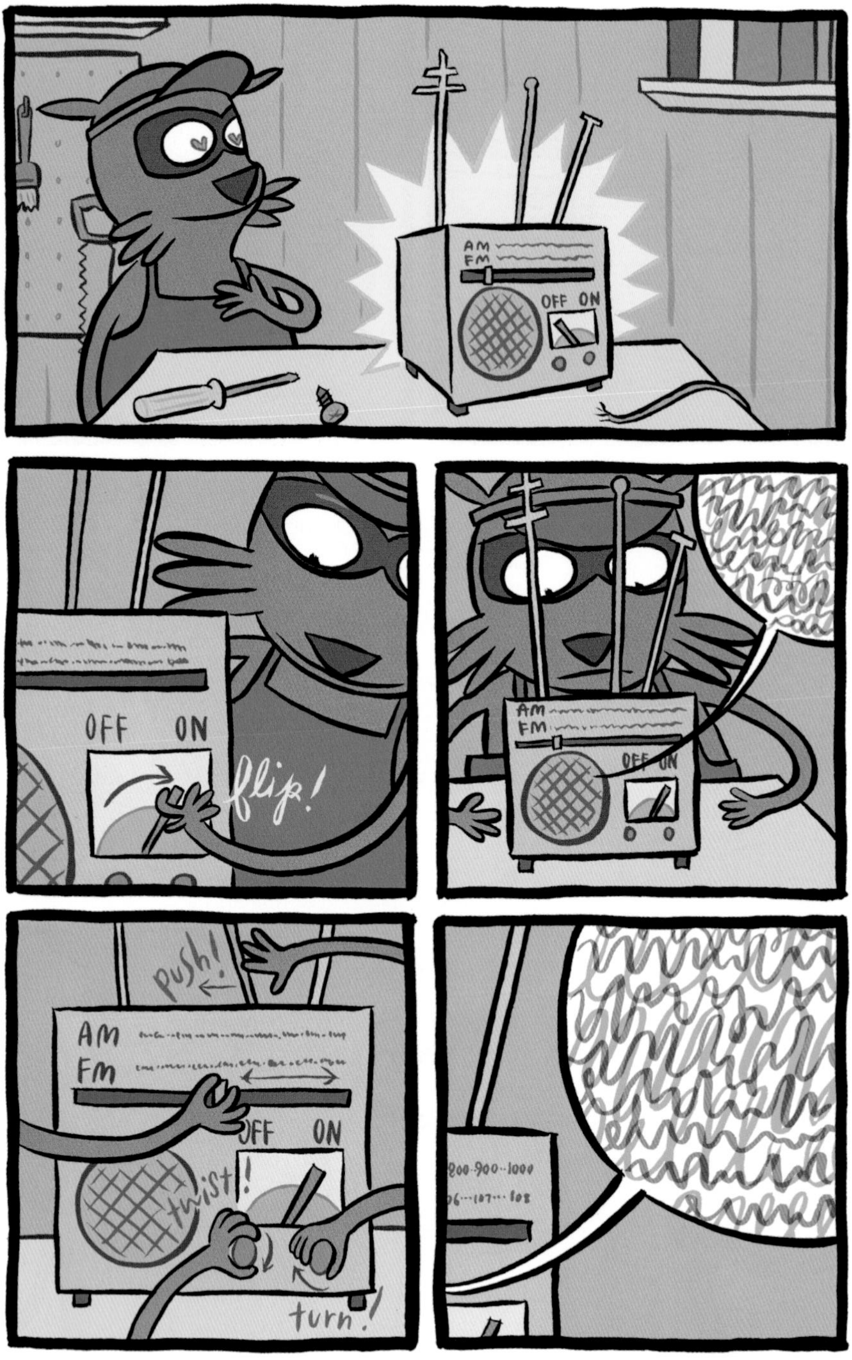

AM
FM
OFF ON
OFF ON
flip!
AM
FM
OFF ON
push!
AM
FM
OFF ON
twist!
turn!
800··900··1000
06···107··· 108

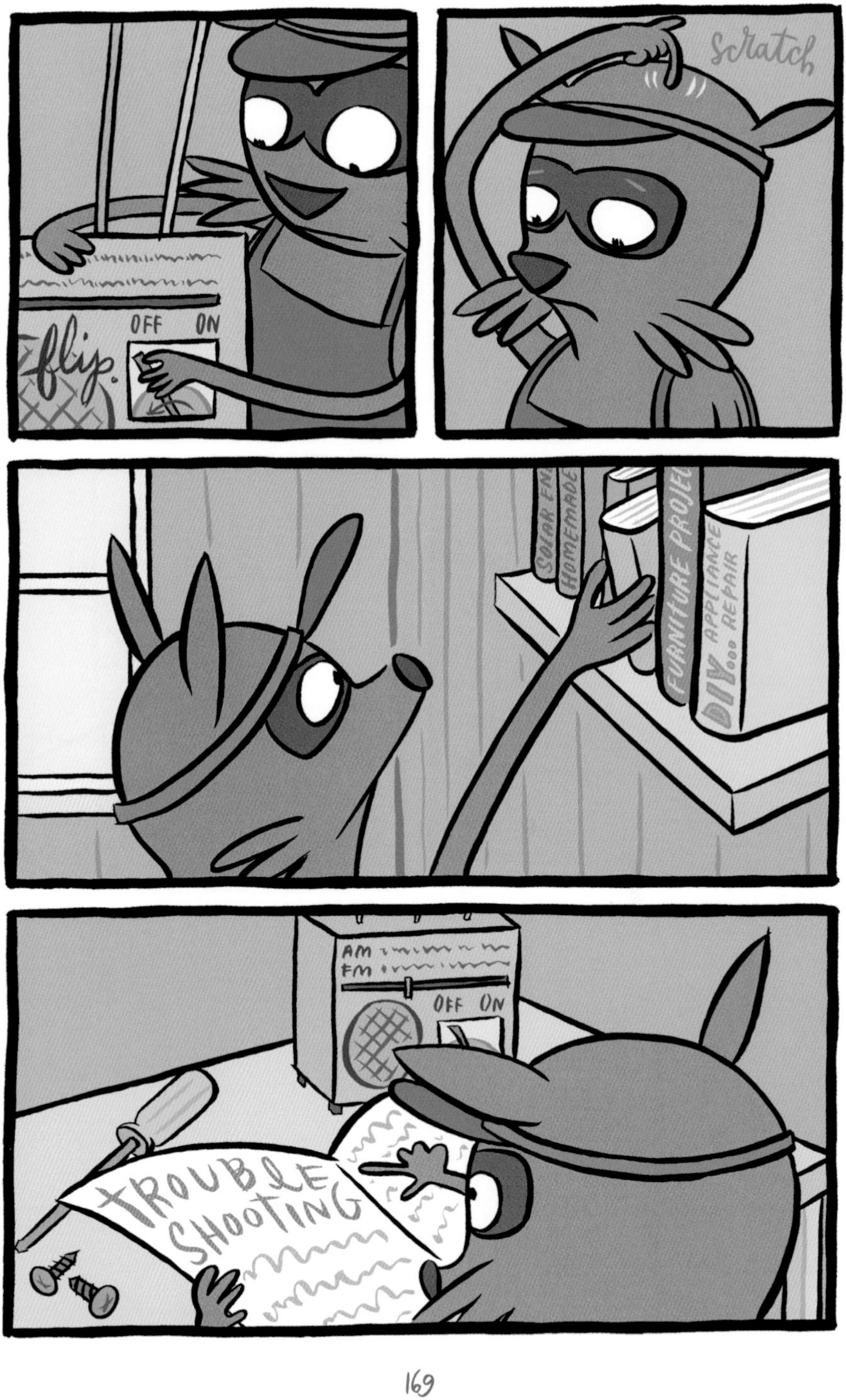

flip.
OFF ON
Scratch
SOLAR EN
HOMEMADE
FURNITURE PROJEC
DIY... APPLIANCE REPAIR
AM
FM
OFF ON
TROUBLE SHOOTING

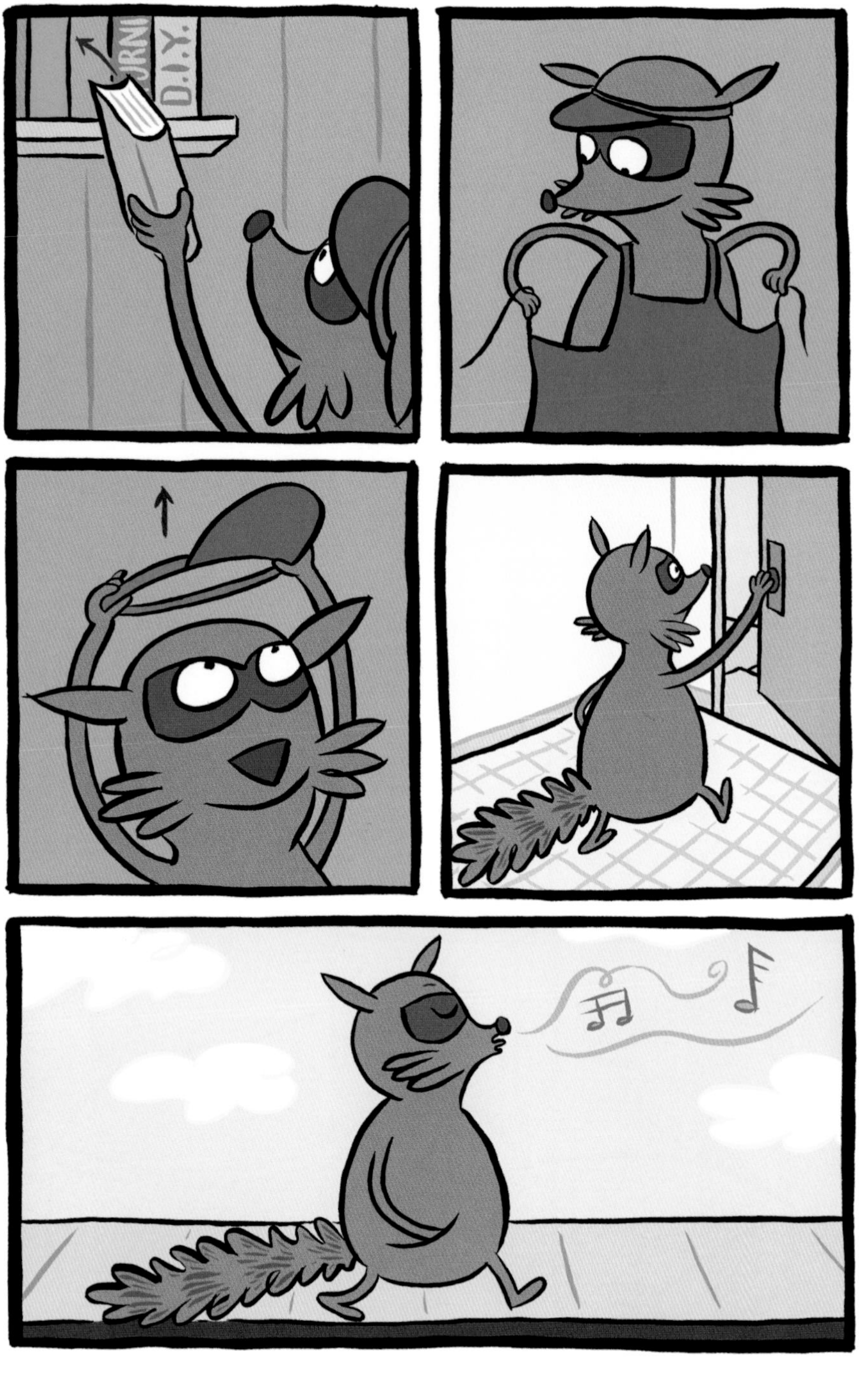
D.I.Y.

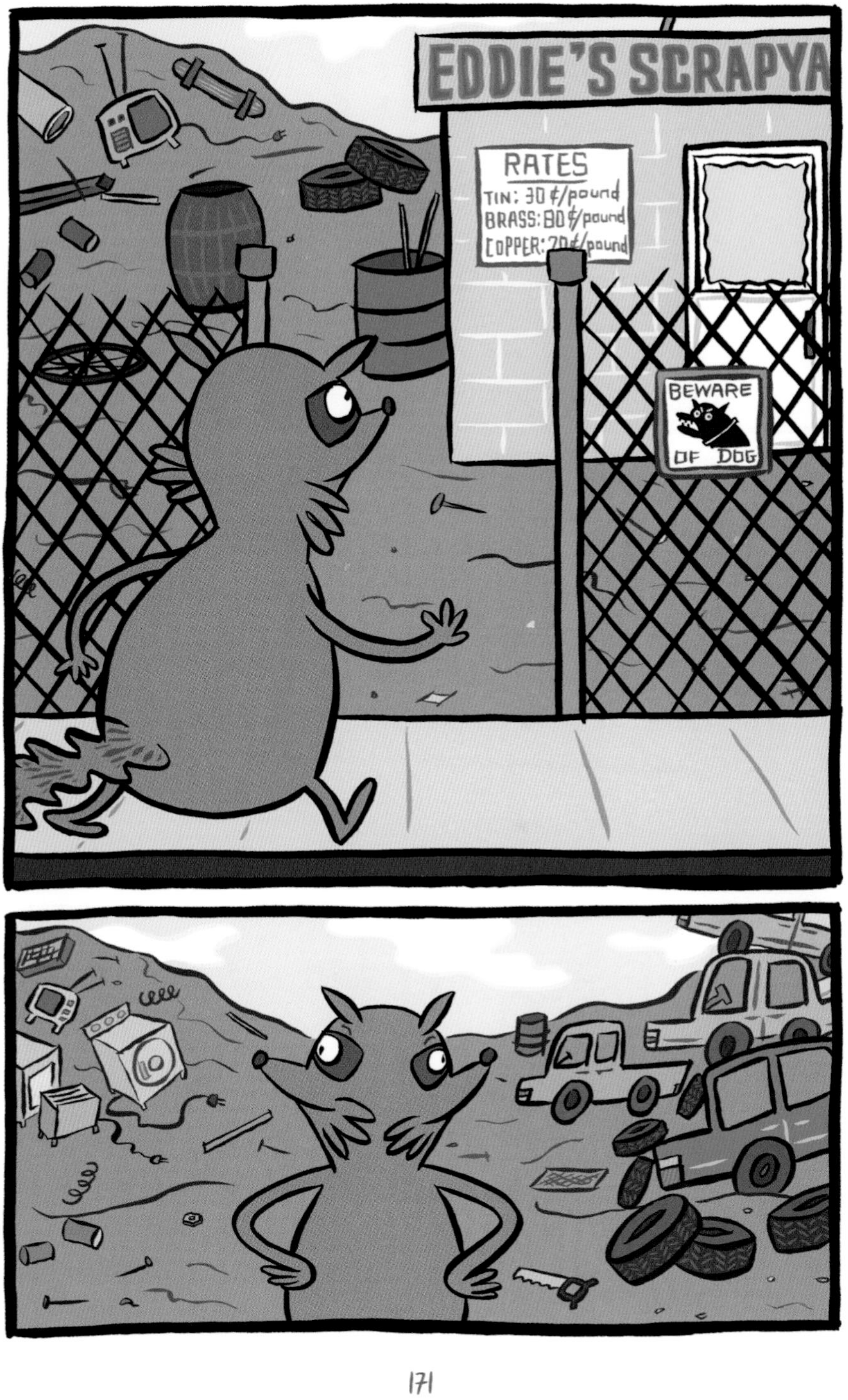
EDDIE'S SCRAPYA
RATES
TIN: 30¢/pound
BRASS: 80¢/pound
COPPER:
BEWARE OF DOG

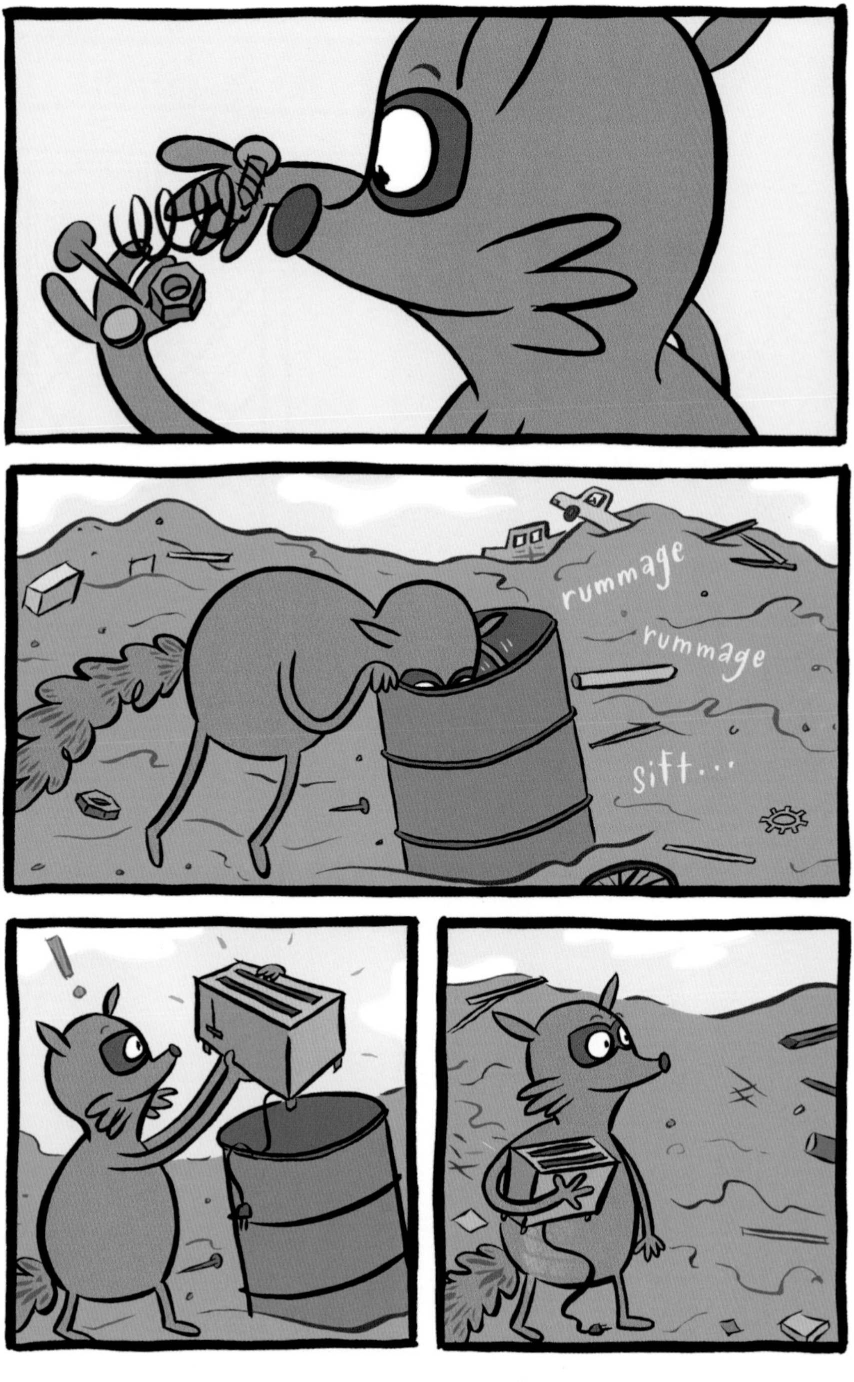
rummage
rummage
sift...

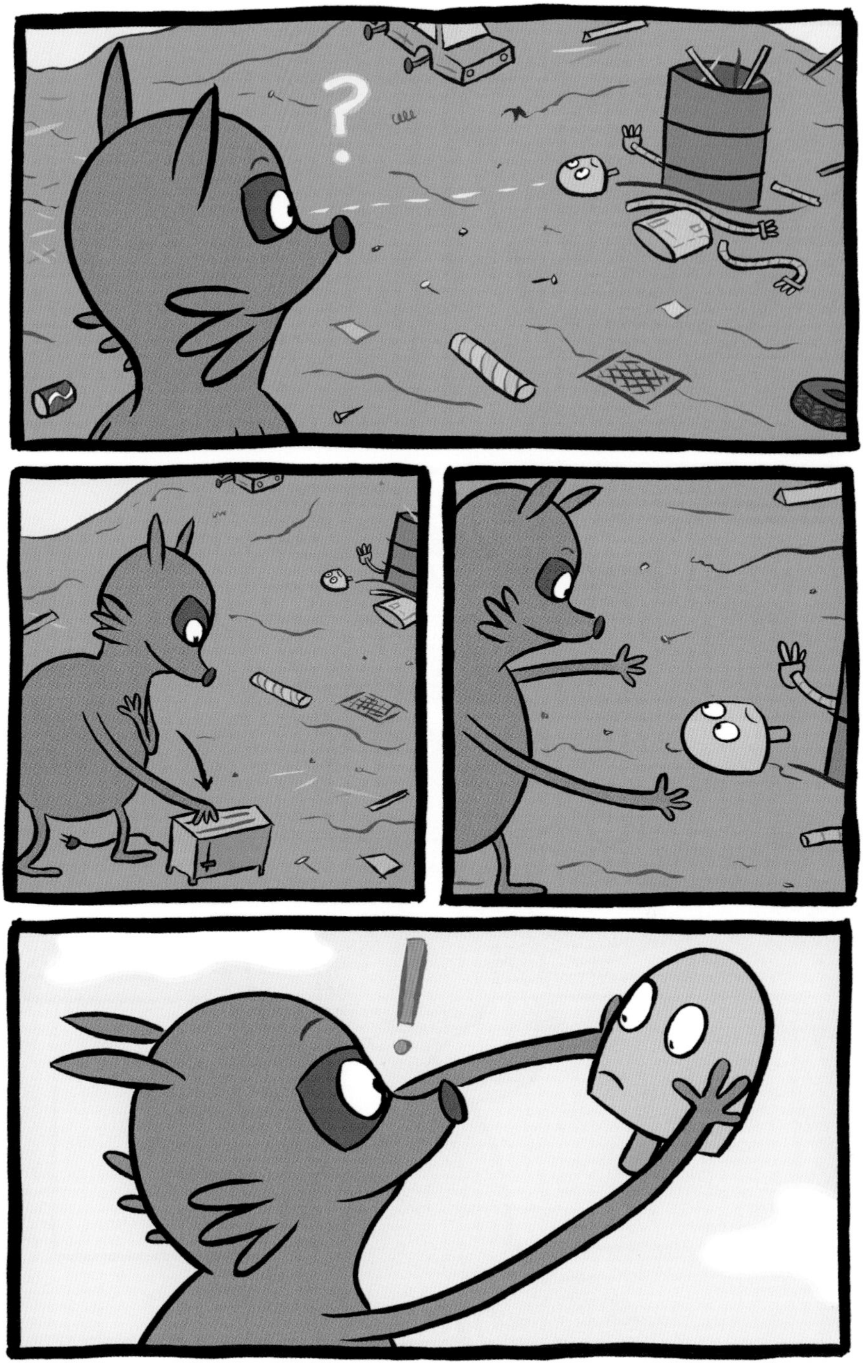
?
!

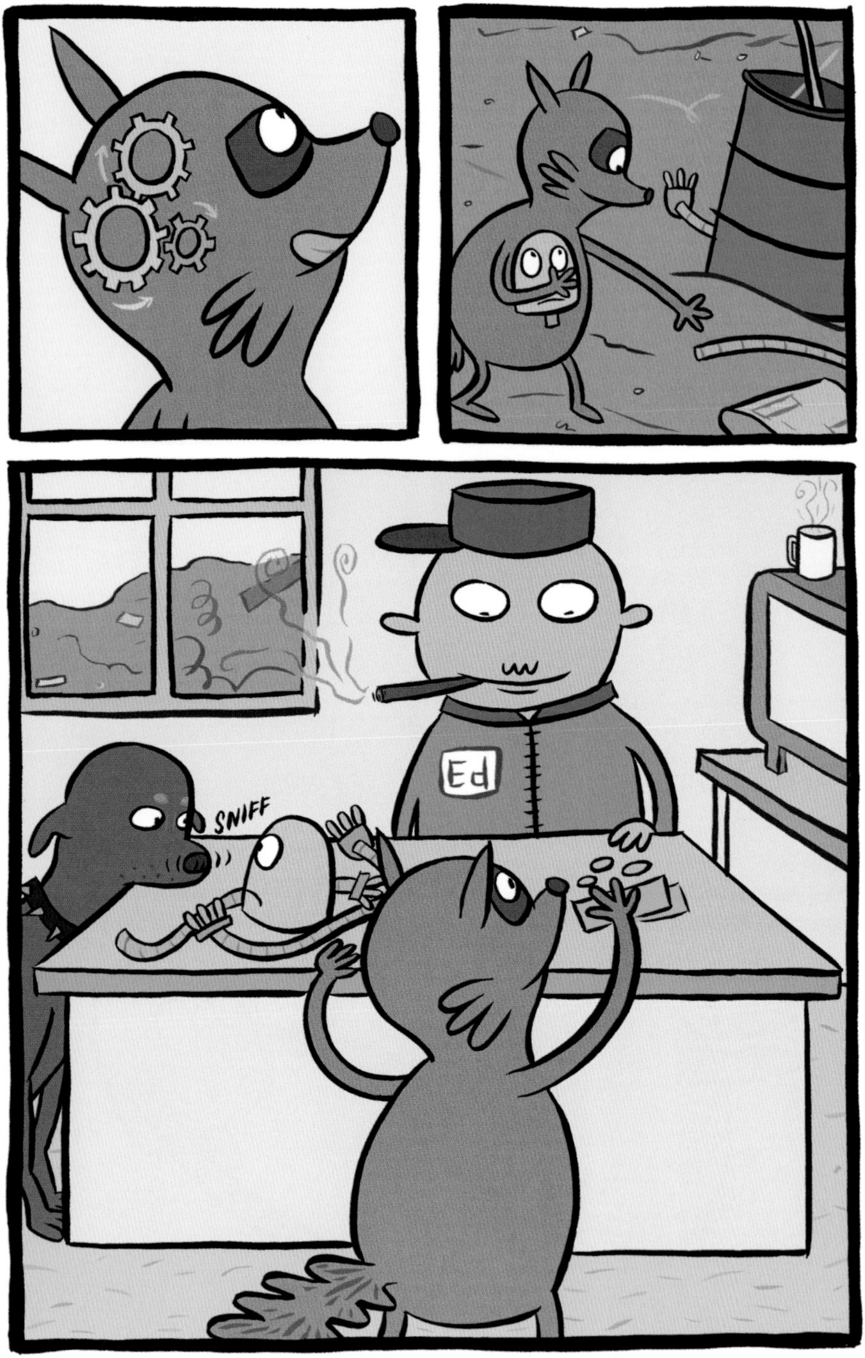
Ed
SNIFF

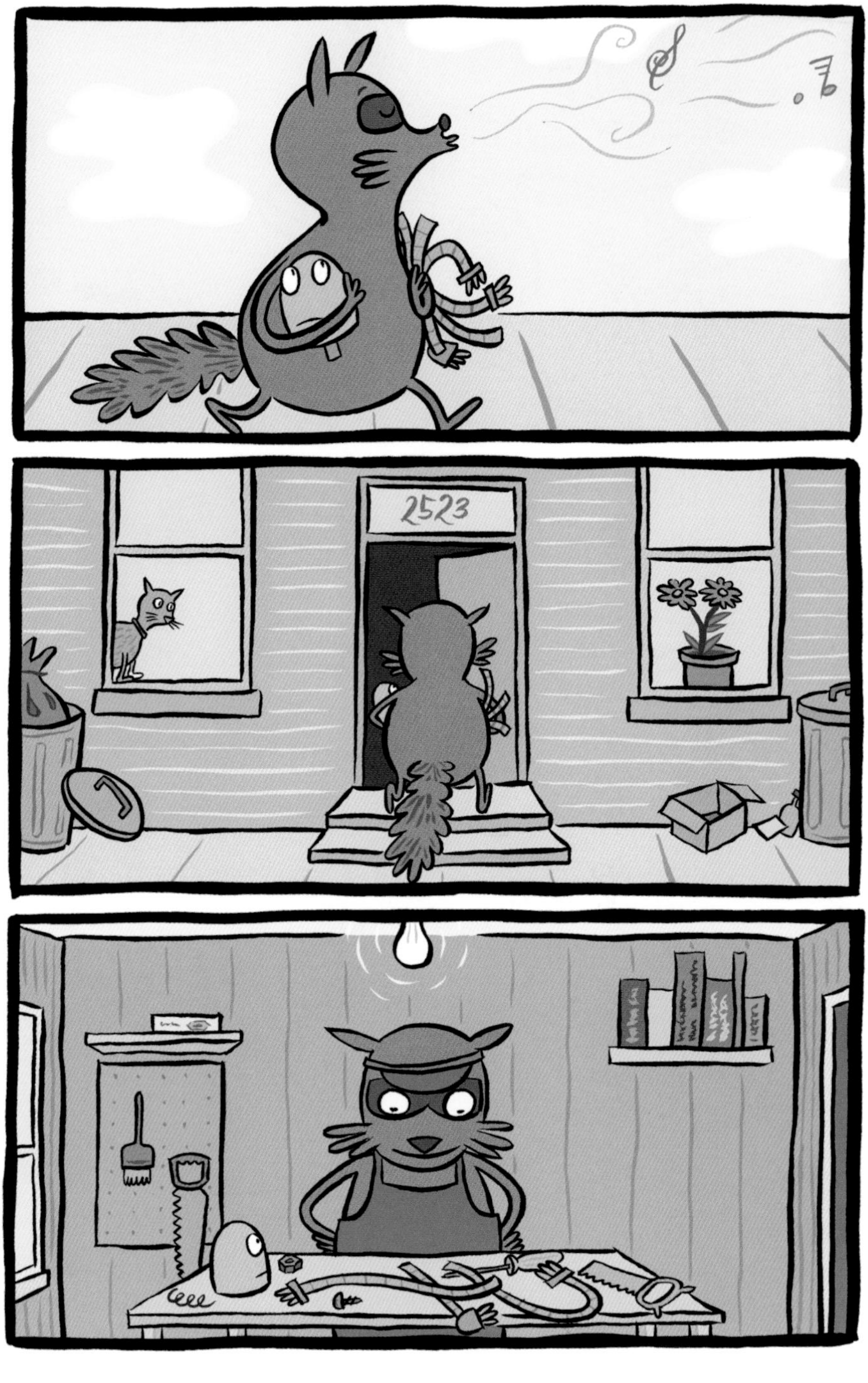
2523

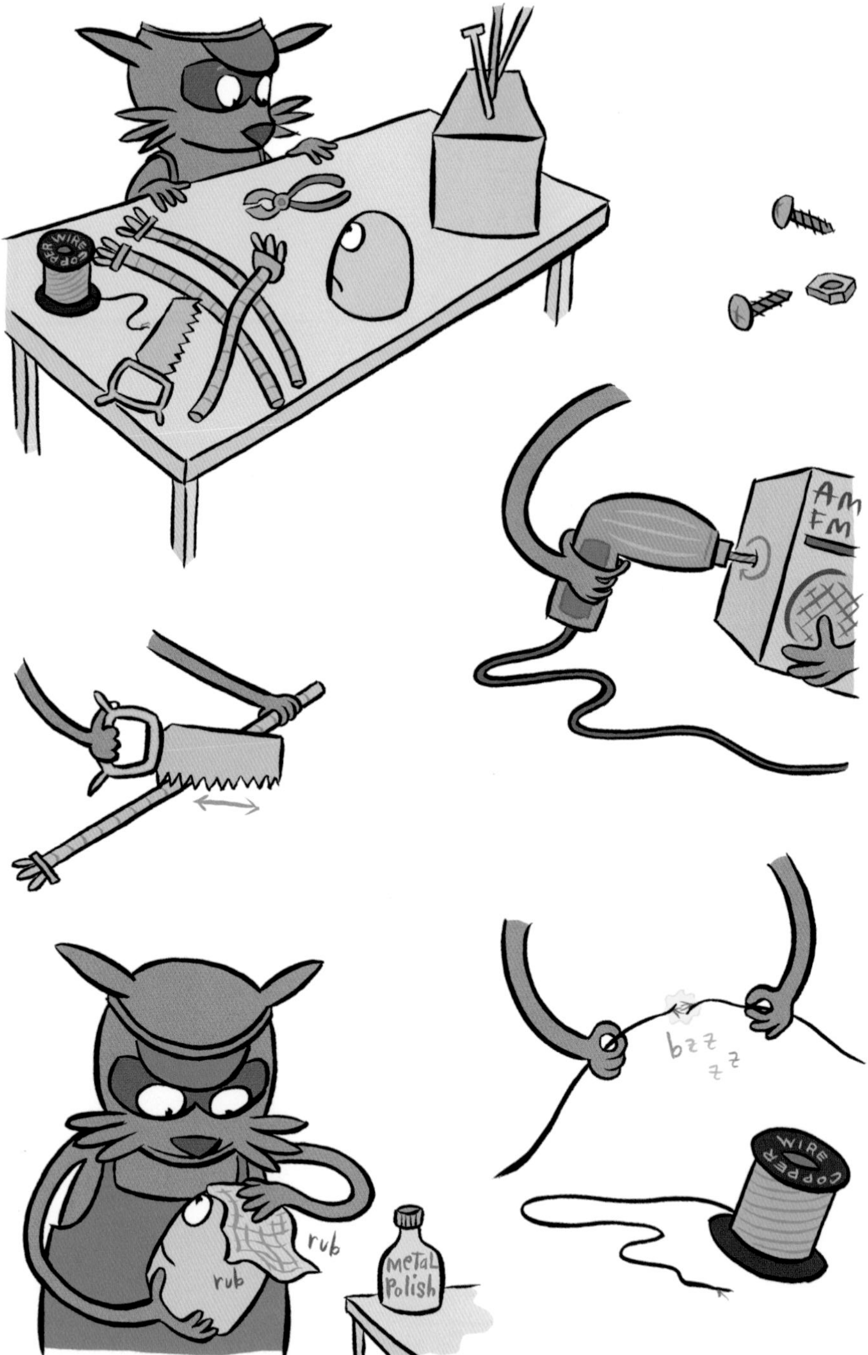
COPPER WIRE
AM
FM
bzz
z z
rub
rub
Metal Polish
COPPER WIRE

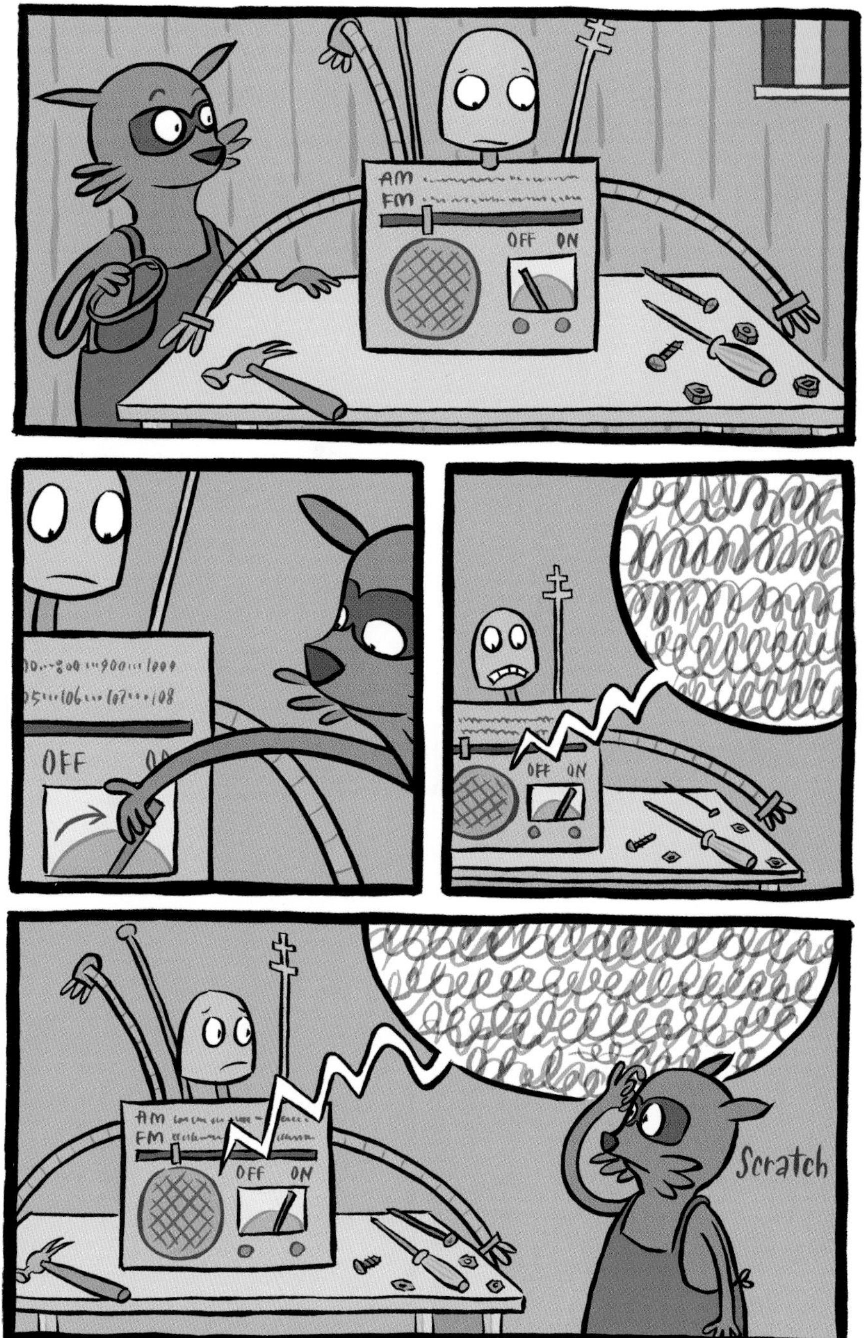
AM
FM
OFF ON
OFF
OFF ON
AM
FM
OFF ON
Scratch

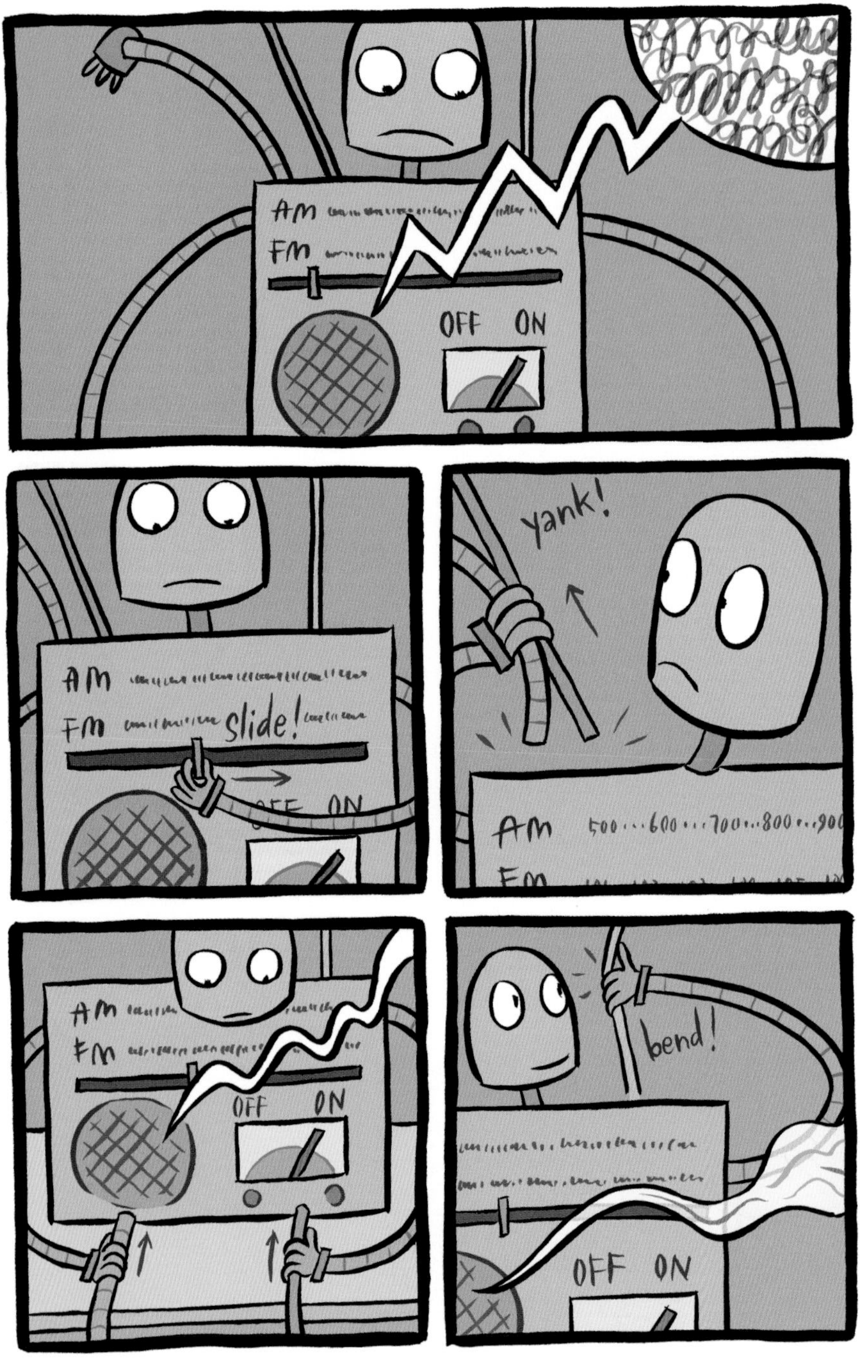
AM
FM
OFF ON
AM
FM slide!
yank!
AM 500...600...700...800...900
AM
FM
OFF ON
bend!
OFF ON

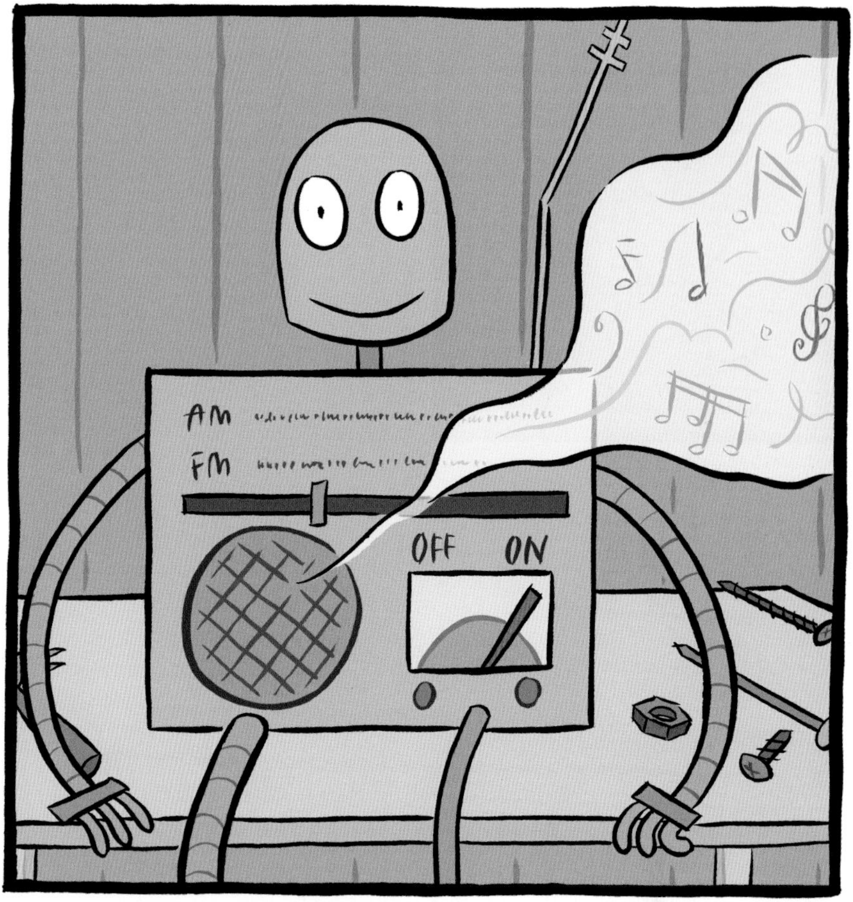
AM
FM
OFF ON

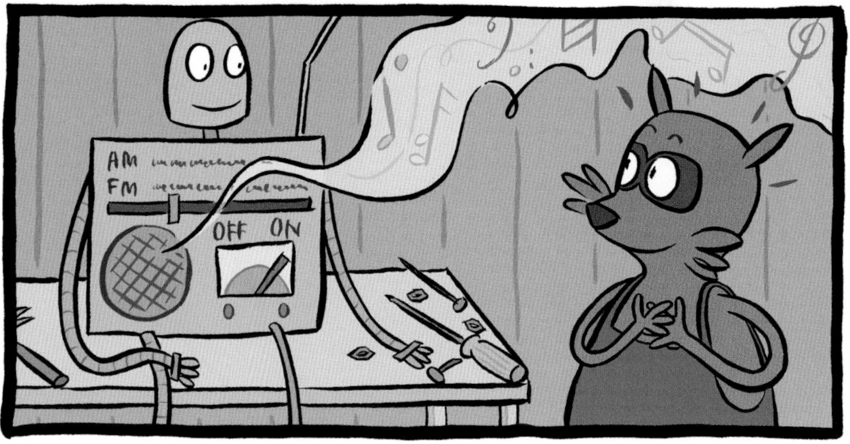
AM
FM
OFF ON

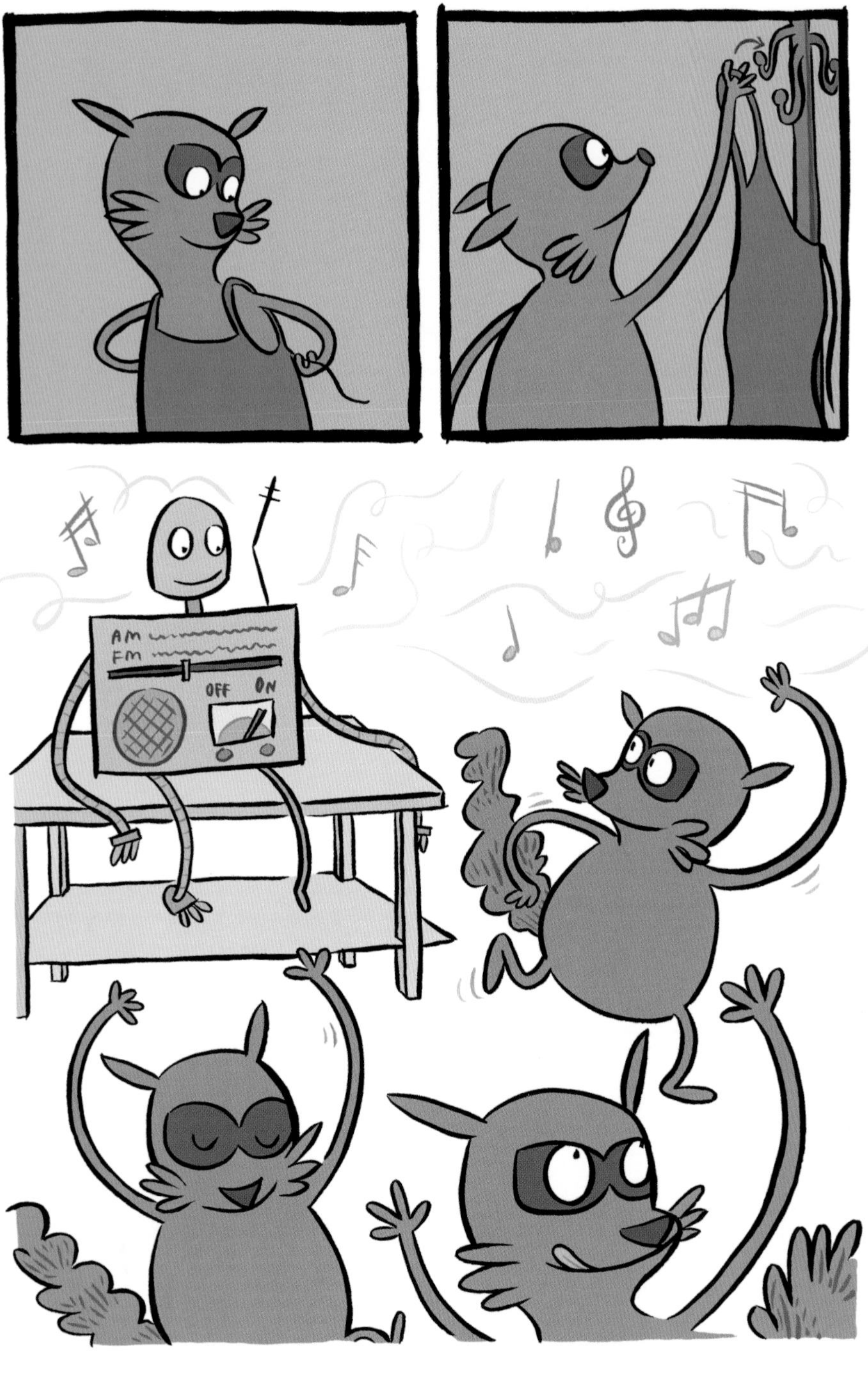
AM
FM
OFF
ON

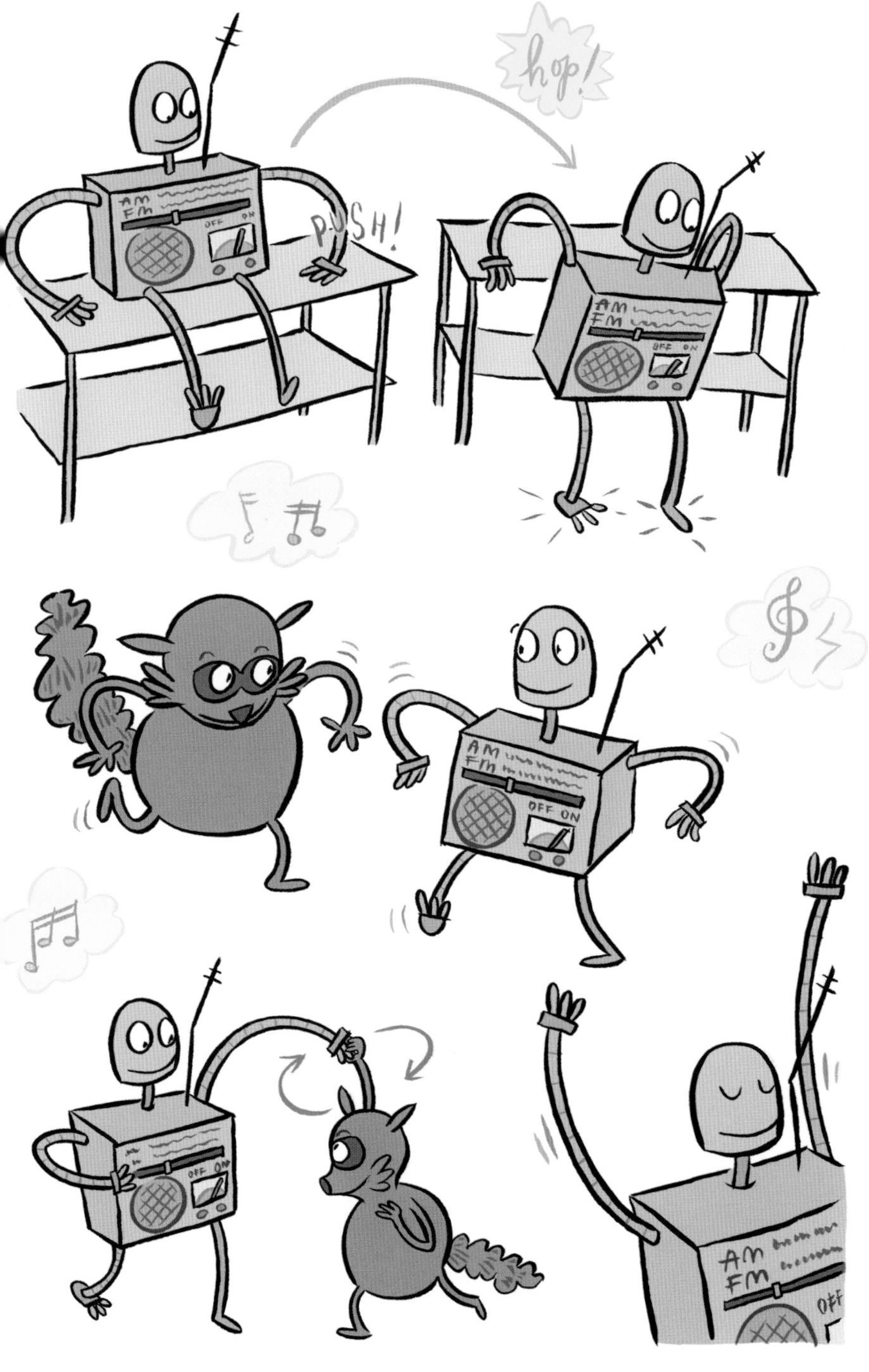
hop!
PUSH!

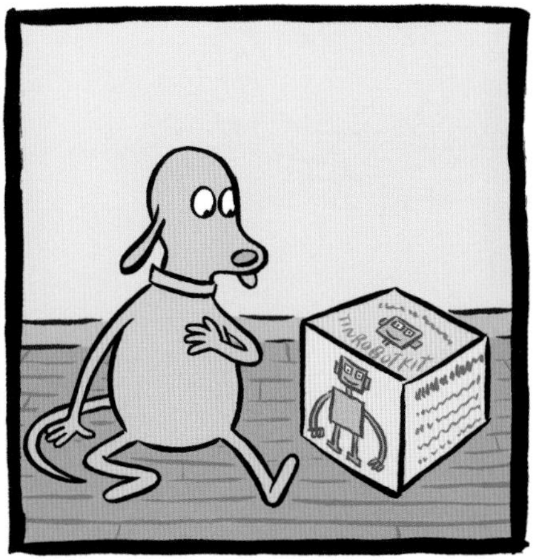
TINROBOTKIT

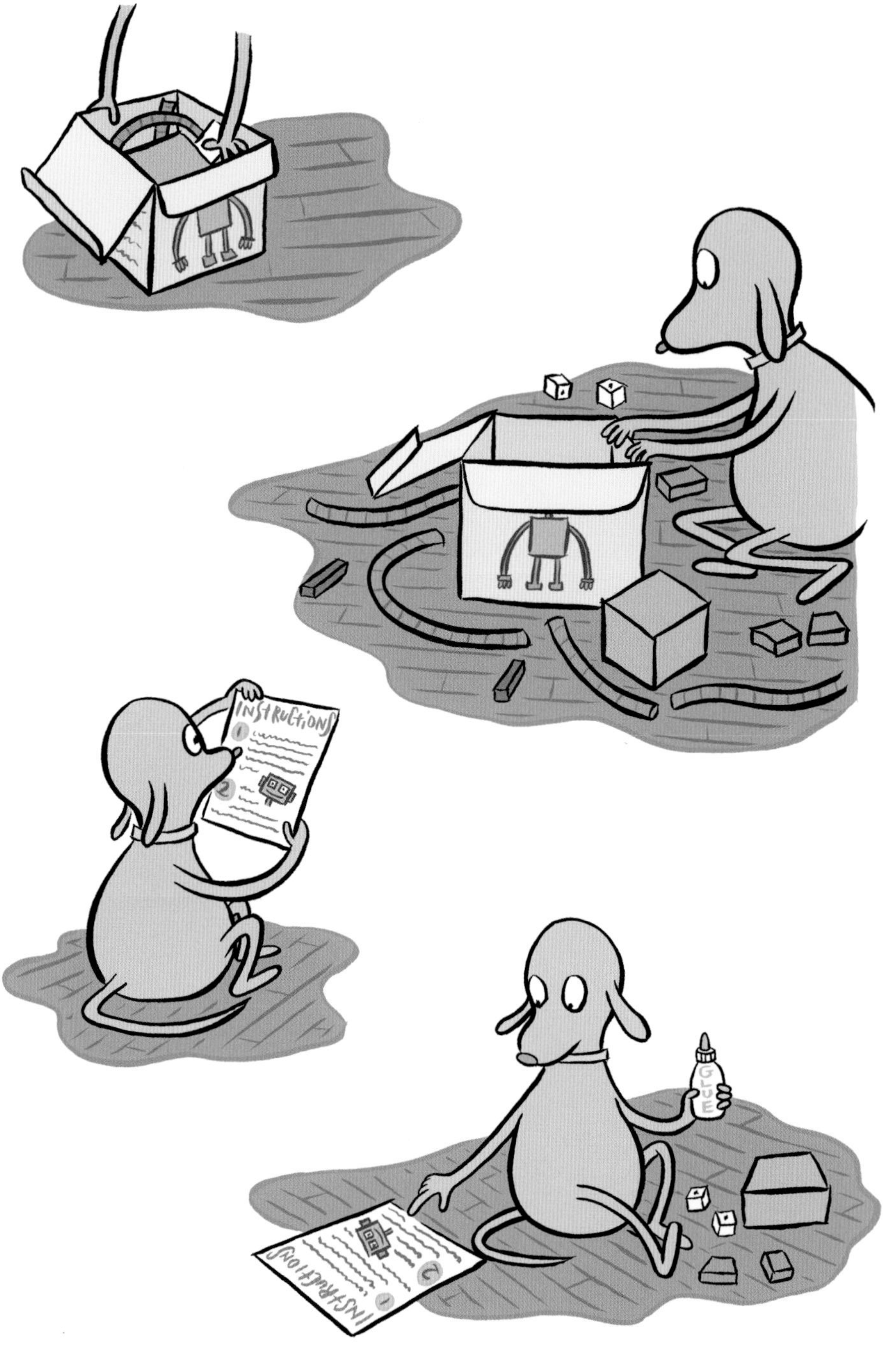
INSTRUCTIONS
GLUE

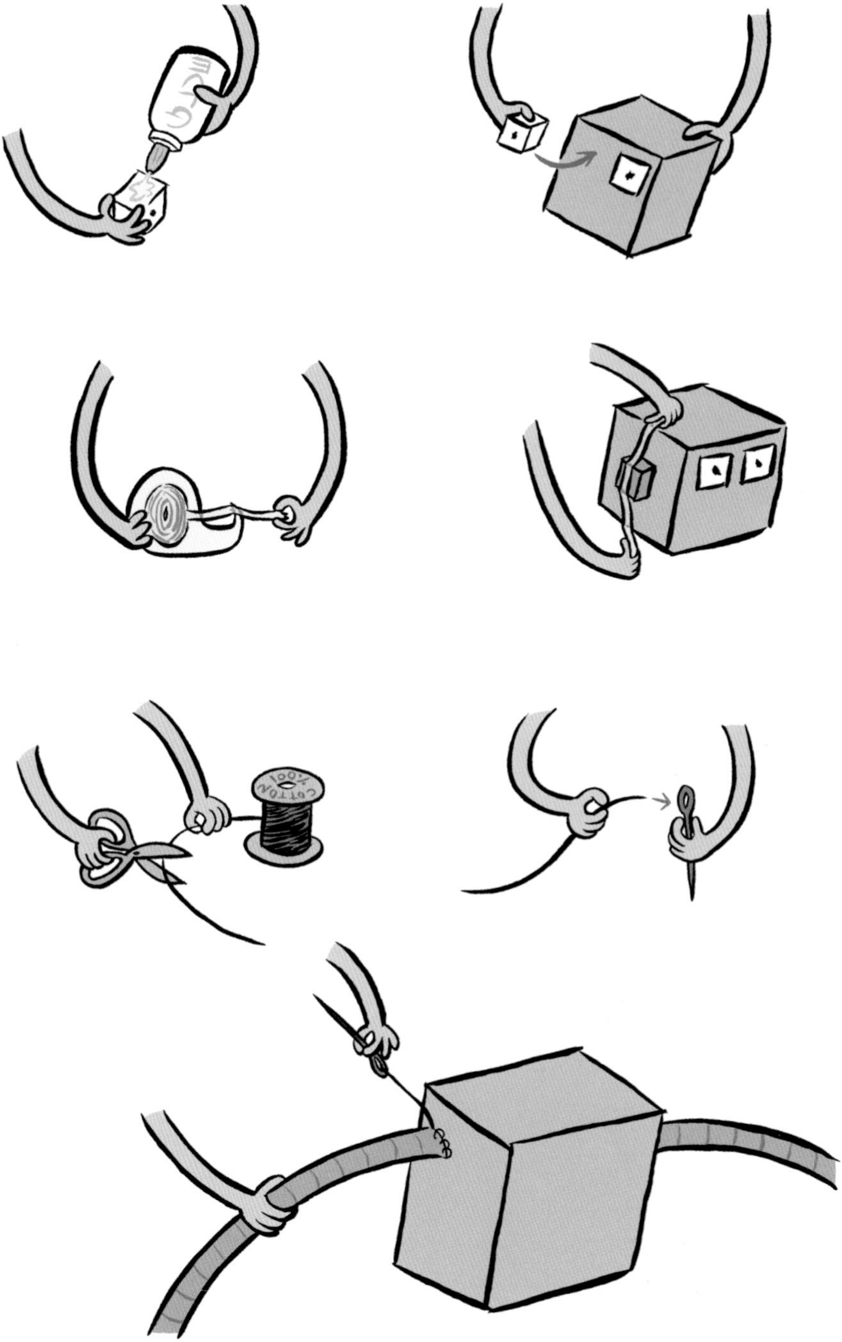
100%
COTTON

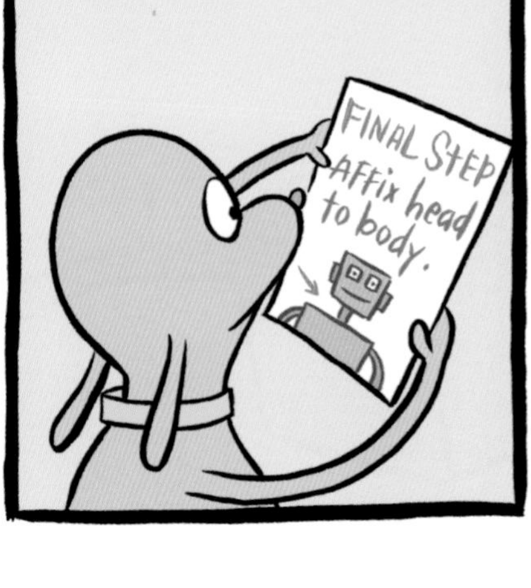
FINAL STEP
AFFix head to body.

August

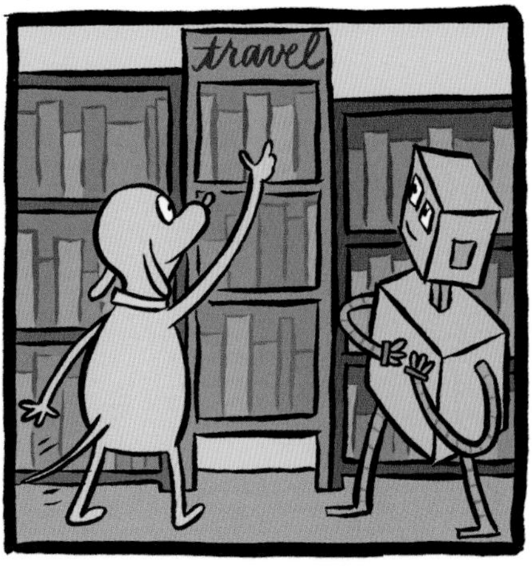
travel

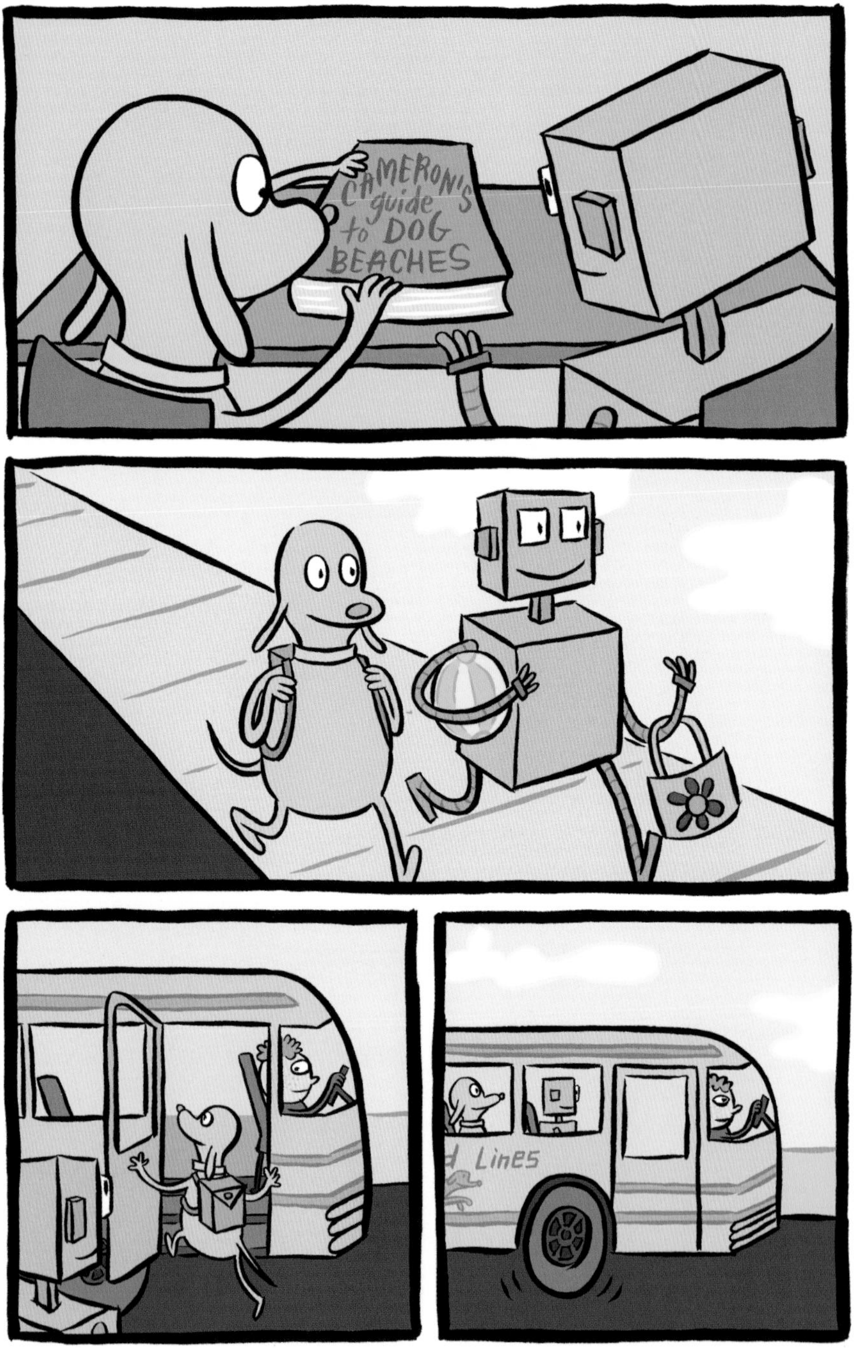
CAMERON'S guide to DOG BEACHES
d Lines

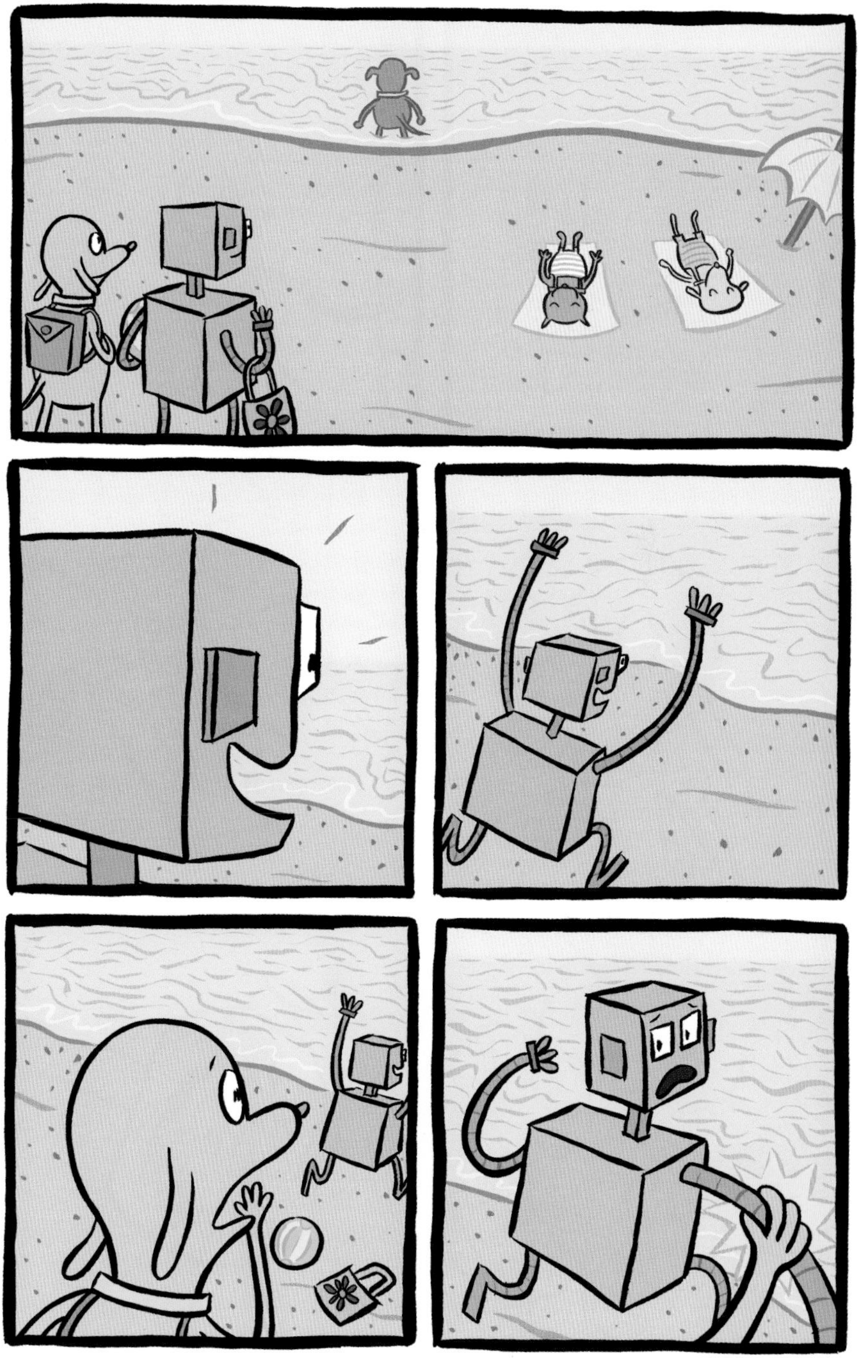

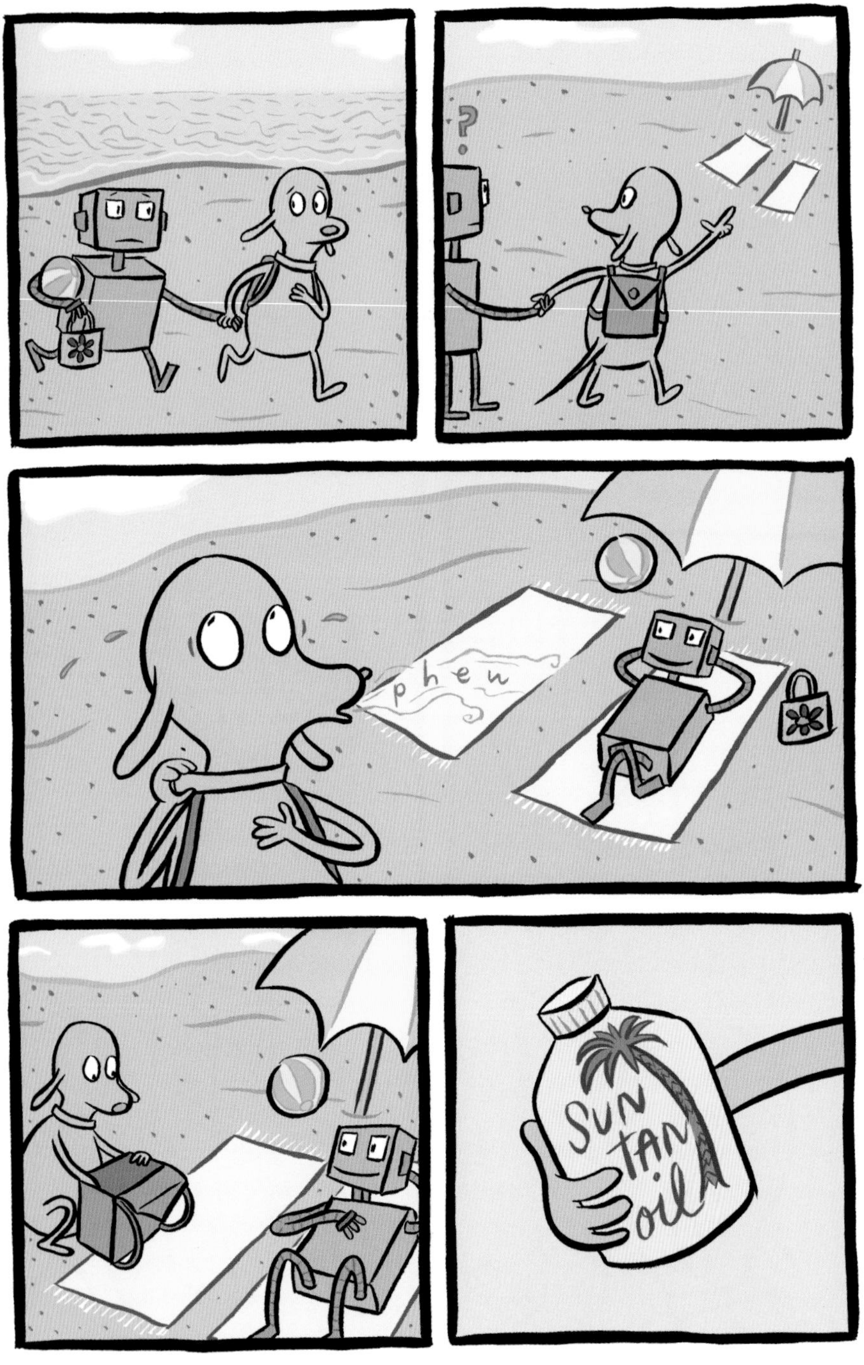
?
phew
SUN TAN oil

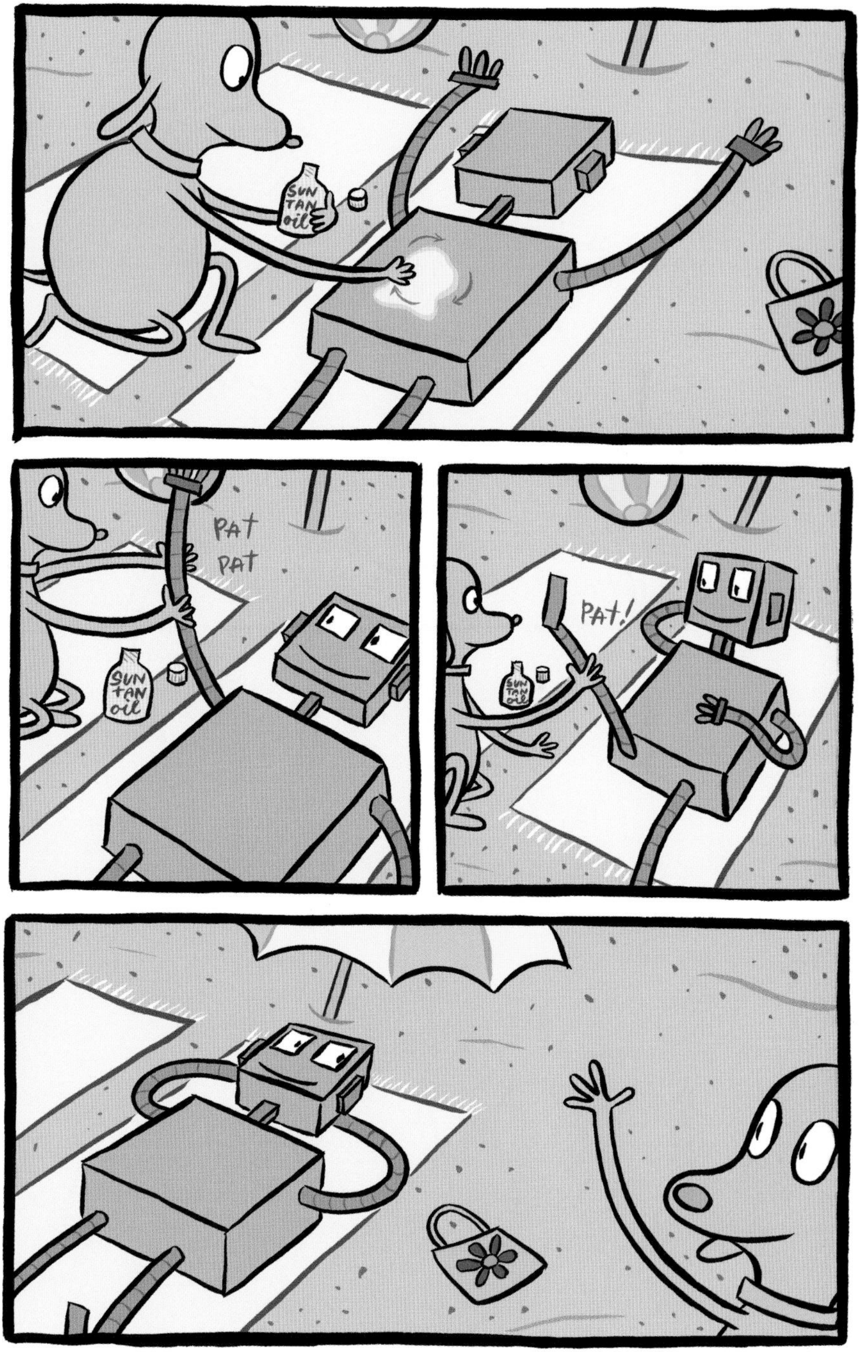
SUN TAN oil
PAT PAT
SUN TAN oil
PAT!

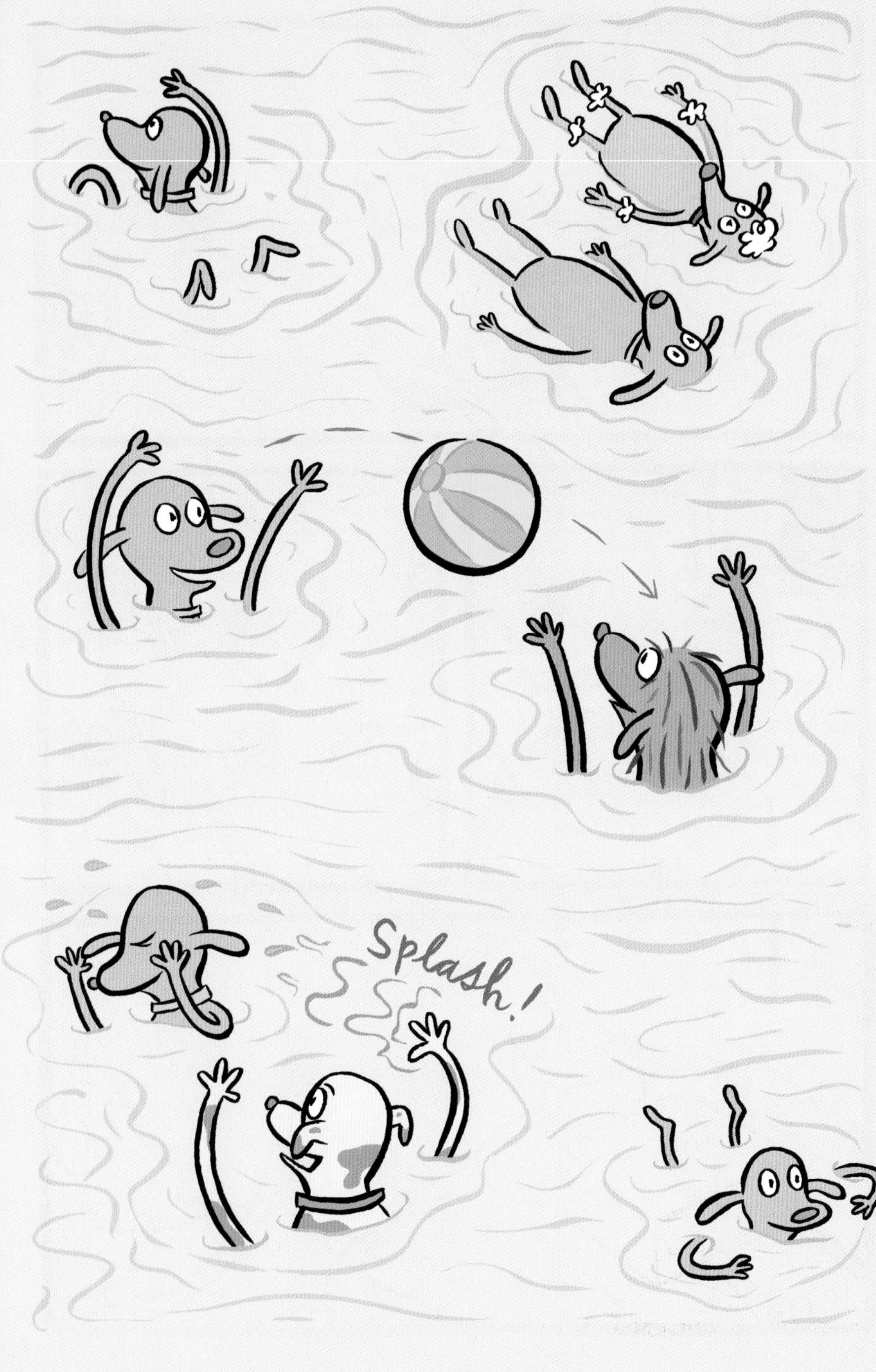
Splash!

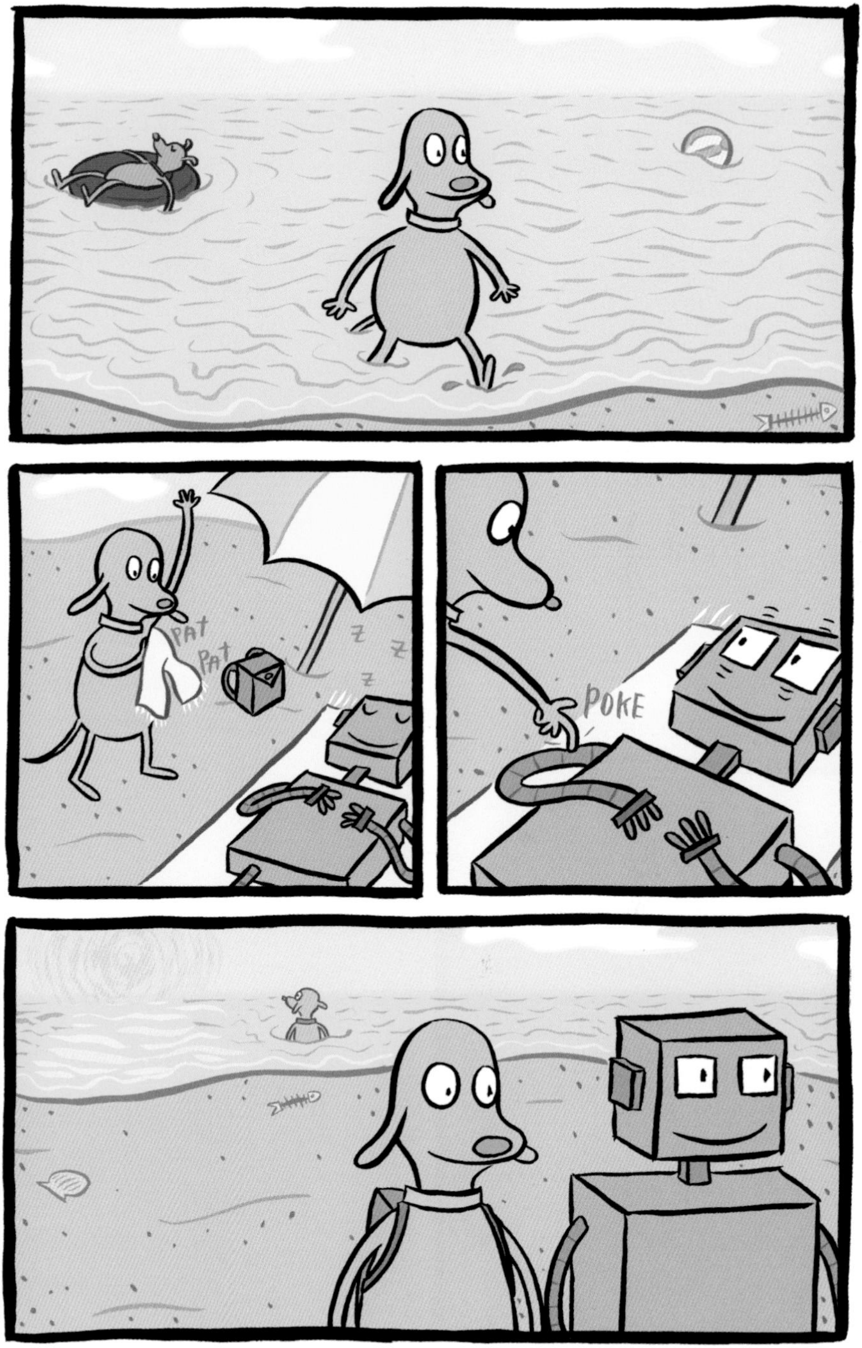
PAT
PAT
Z
Z
Z
POKE

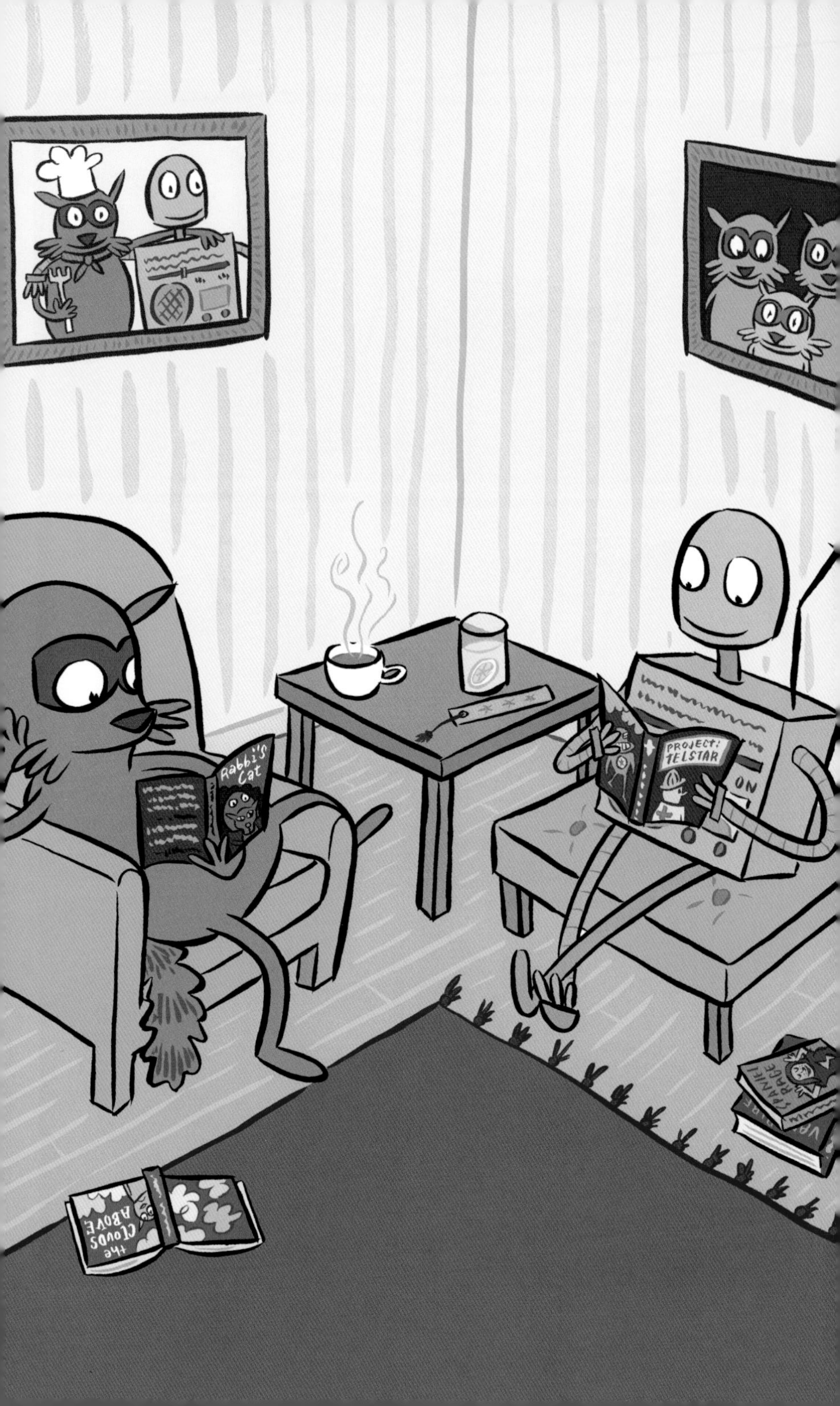
Rabbi's Cat
PROJECT: TELSTAR
ON
the CLOUDS ABOVE

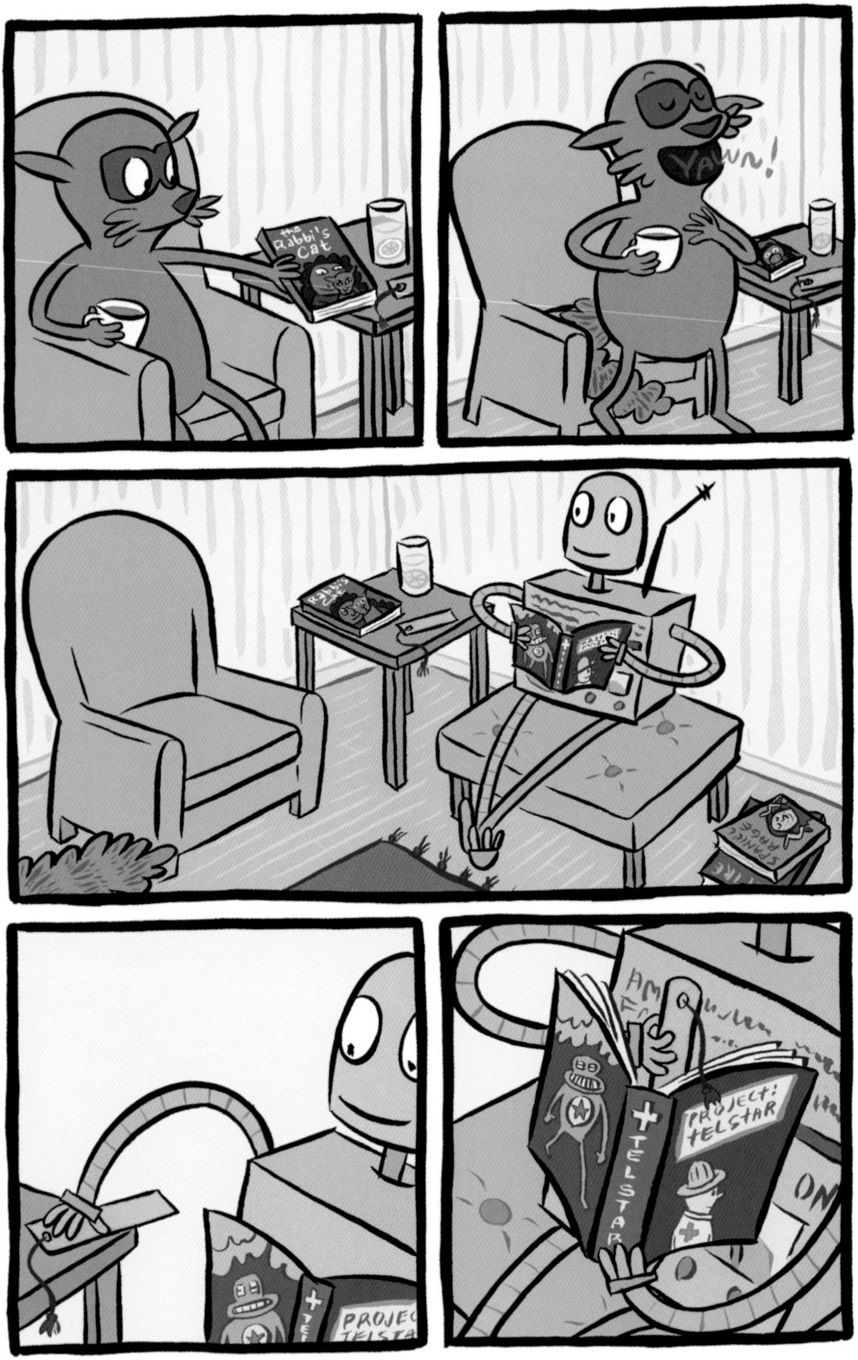
the Rabbi's Cat
YAWN!
SPANIEL RAGE
TELSTAR
PROJECT: TELSTAR

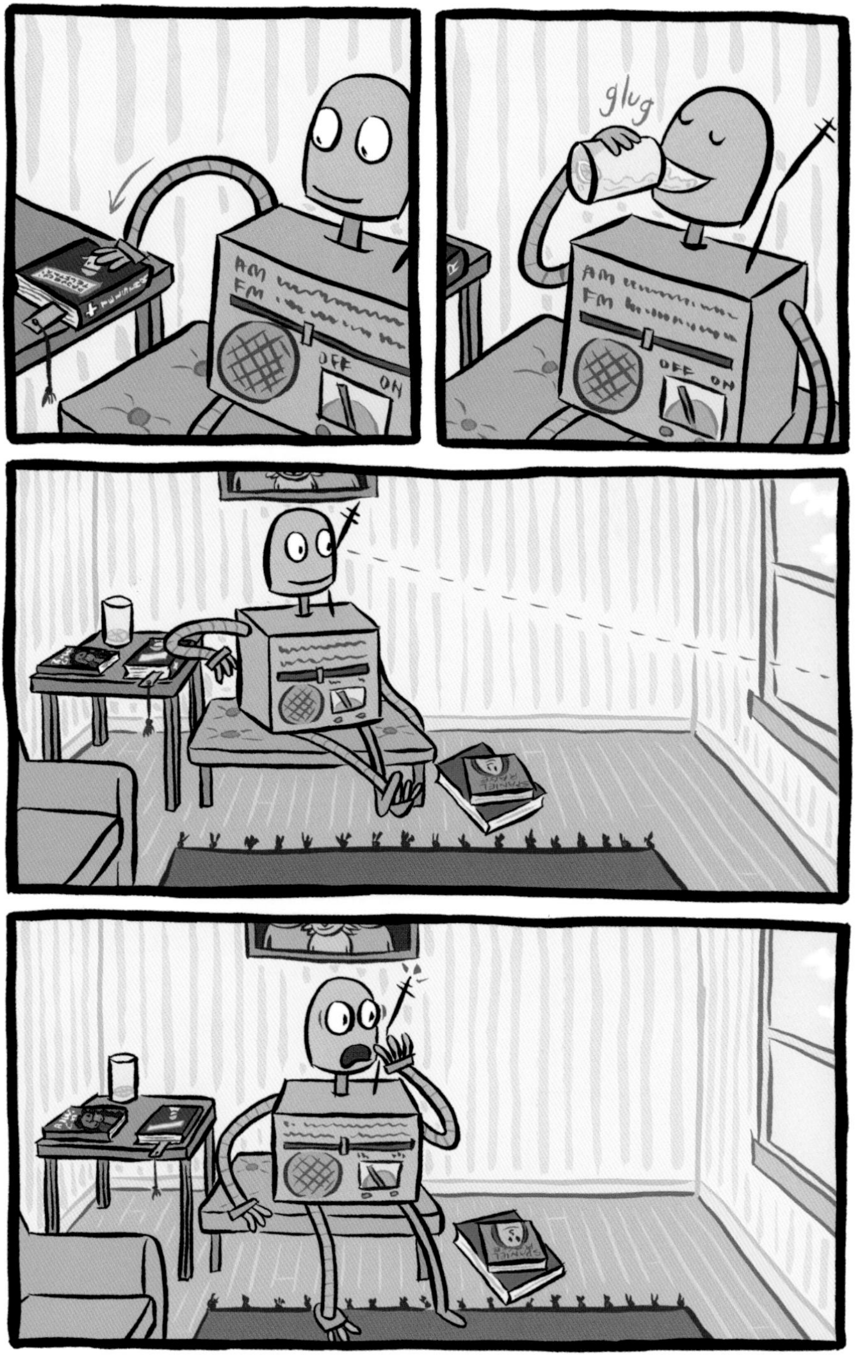
AM
FM
OFF
ON
glug
AM
FM
OFF
ON

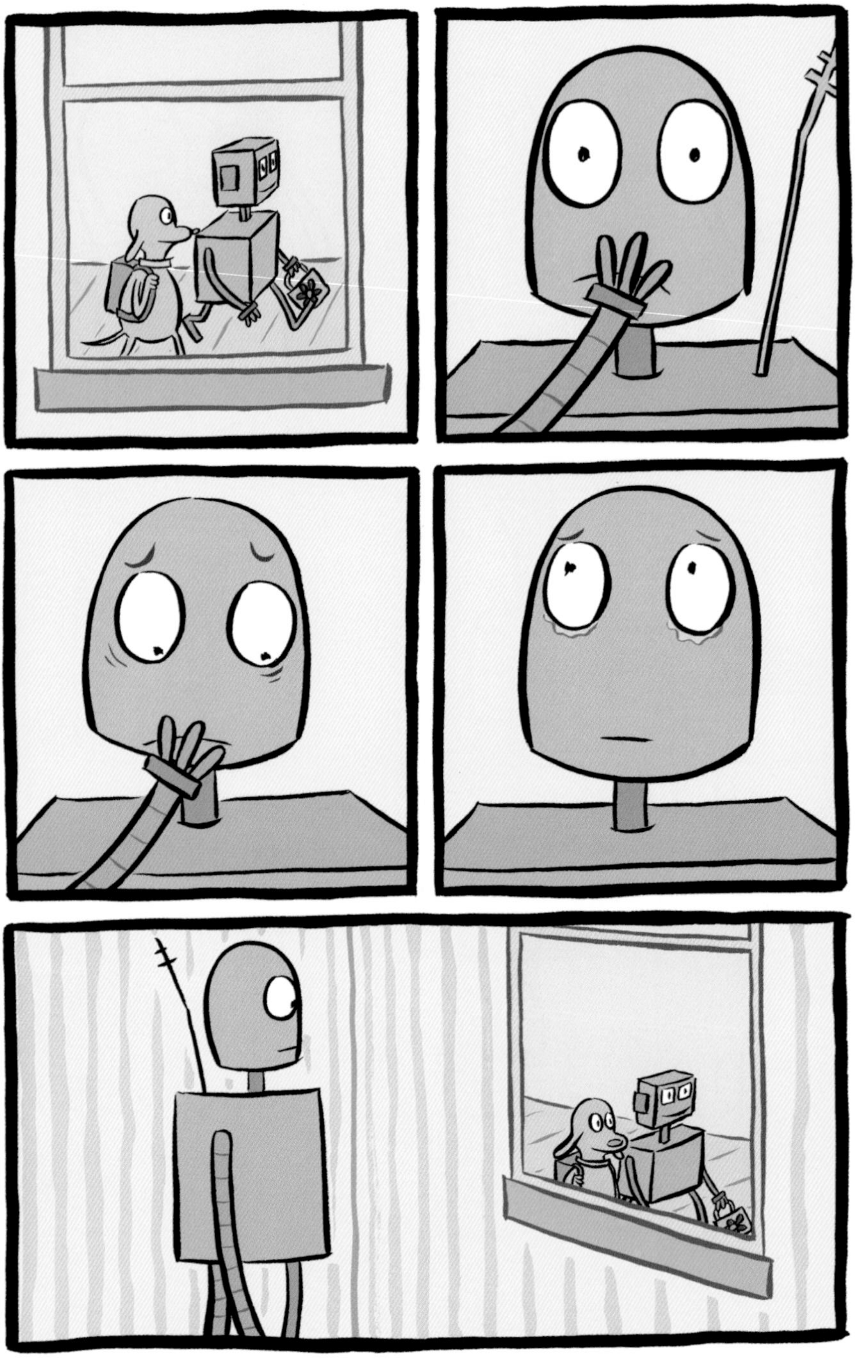

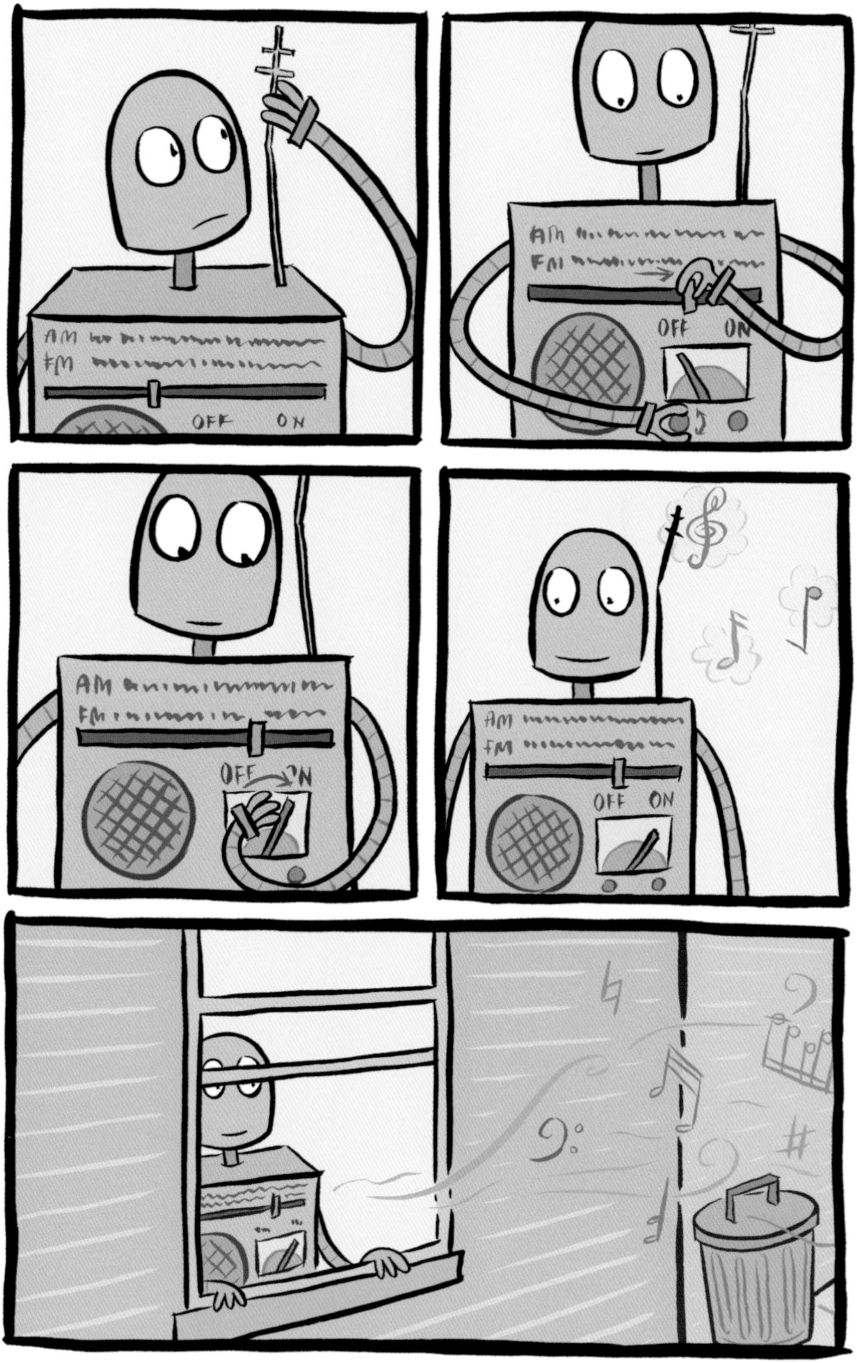
AM
FM
OFF
ON

Bonus
Materials

An Interview with
Sara Varon

When you were growing up, what first inspired you to draw?

Sesame Street and the Jay Ward cartoons (*Underdog*, *Tennessee Tuxedo*, *Tooter Turtle*) I watched as a kid were really formative to my sensibility. Also, the Richard Scarry books that I read.

Besides comics, what other kinds of art do you make?

A medium I always love working in is printmaking, especially silkscreen or letterpress. Printmaking is very physical—with silkscreen you're pulling your prints and with letterpress you're cranking the Vandercook printing press (that's the kind of press I usually use) and then you're taking your prints back and forth to the drying rack. I always have a hard time sitting still, so a medium where I'm moving around a lot is perfect for me. Another thing I really love about printmaking is that it is very much about color, and I love thinking about color.

How is making a graphic novel different from making a picture book?

At first I did short stories, so it was hard to do a long story for my first graphic novel. But now that I've done a few graphic novels, I find it's harder to work on a short story. Picture books are so distilled, nothing extra. They have to be perfectly concise. But what I like about the graphic novel is that you can make a whole world; you can put in all these extra details. There can be side stories and characters that are not that important but are really fun. You don't have that freedom in a picture book.

What are your hobbies?

I do a lot of running, and I find that this is a great time to think about stories and details. I usually run in Prospect Park, which is really convenient because I don't have to worry about crossing streets, getting lost, or getting run over by cars. (It's just a big loop with no car traffic.) So I can really lose myself in thought.

What technique do you use to draw your comics?

I draw on paper, with a brush and ink. Then scan it and color with Photoshop.

What inspired you to create a story about a dog and a robot?

It might sound a little silly, especially if you're not a fan of dogs, but I made the comic after putting my dog to sleep. Even though she was old and sick, I felt like I was abandoning her after she had been such a good and loyal pal, so, I guess I was kind of like the dog, and she was like the robot. Although I wasn't aware of it at the time of making the story, in retrospect I think I was pulling from that experience.

Why are there no words in *Robot Dreams*?

I am kind of quiet and not particularly articulate, so it's nice to have an alternative to telling stories with words. My stories are very simple, so they can be told easily with just pictures and pantomime. Usually I just make a list of characters or situations, and I figure out how to link them. Then I write them out as short sentences, break them up into separate pages, and draw thumbnails.

Is it harder to make comics with words in them?

No, one is not harder than the other. But I prefer the wordless stories because I am better at them. Words are not my strong suit.

Robot Dreams is about friendship, both the good and the bad. Is friendship important to you, and do you think you're a good friend?

I had a teacher who said that every artist has a theme they kind of stick with throughout their life, and I think friendship is mine. I'd like to think I am a pretty good friend. I was born in the year of the pig (according to the Chinese zodiac), and a characteristic of pigs is that they are supposed to be good friends to have. I'm a very loyal friend, kind of like a dog. I was an outsider growing up and didn't have many friends, so I know firsthand that a good friend is hard to find and something worth keeping, even through different stages and places in your life.

Why do your stories usually star animals, or baked goods, or robots?

I think it's kind of instinctive for me to use animal characters. The thing I like about them is that they are not boys or girls and have no ethnic or age identity, so I think that makes them more universal. Also, they can be symbols for certain character traits. For instance, everyone knows that a tin robot would rust if he goes swimming, so I don't have to explain it. Since my stories are really simple, using a specific animal can be a device for providing background info on a character.

What do you hope your readers will learn from *Robot Dreams*?

I hope that kids will relate to the ups and downs of friendship. Kids can be so mean to each other, and when you're small everything seems so significant, so I hope it will help them realize that people come and go, and everything moves forward.

Discussion Questions

1. Dog never meant to be cruel, but he wasn't a good friend to Robot. He abandoned Robot on the beach, and was never able to rescue him. Imagine you are Dog, and you are trying to rescue Robot. How would you do things differently?

2. Throughout this book, Dog is searching for the perfect friend. He makes new friends, but they aren't the right match: The duck family flew away in the fall, and dinner with the anteaters gave him a stomachache. What animal do you think would make the perfect friend for Dog?

3. In *Robot Dreams*, friendships change, and sometimes they end. Has this ever happened to you? How did it make you feel?

4. Robot spends months alone on the beach, dreaming of escape. Some of his dreams are realistic: If he had chosen to sunbathe instead of swim, he wouldn't have rusted. But some of his dreams are fantastical, like when he got a ride from a seagull. Create another dream for Robot. Write a little story about how he might escape the beach. Your story can be realistic or fantastical.

5. *Robot Dreams* takes place over the course of a year. How did the author depict the passage of time?

6. At the end of the book, Robot looks out the window and sees Dog again. Dog has a new robot friend. How do you think that made Robot feel?

7. *Robot Dreams* is a story told in pantomime, which means there are no words. Sara Varon relies on hers characters' facial expressions and body language to tell the story. Imagine that this story had words. Pick two characters and write a conversation for them.

8. Do you think this story has a happy ending, a sad ending, or something in between? How did the ending make you feel?

Process Images

Thumbnail

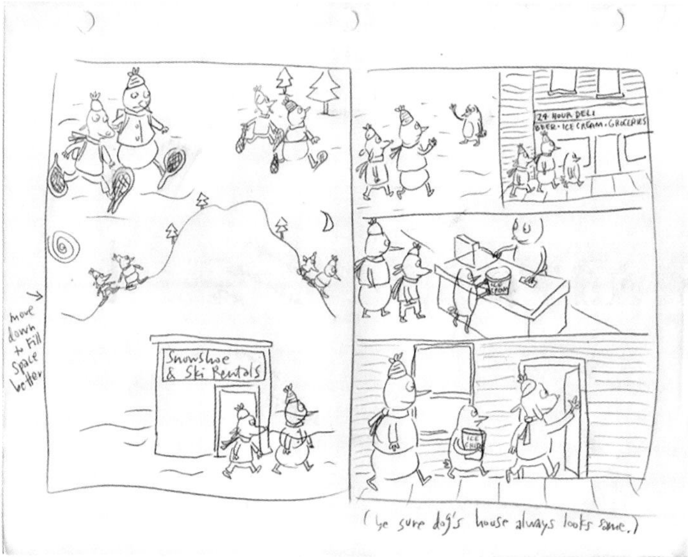

move down to fill space better
Snowshoe & Ski Rentals
24-HOUR DELI
BEER • ICE CREAM • GROCERIES
(be sure dog's house always looks same.)

Inked Page

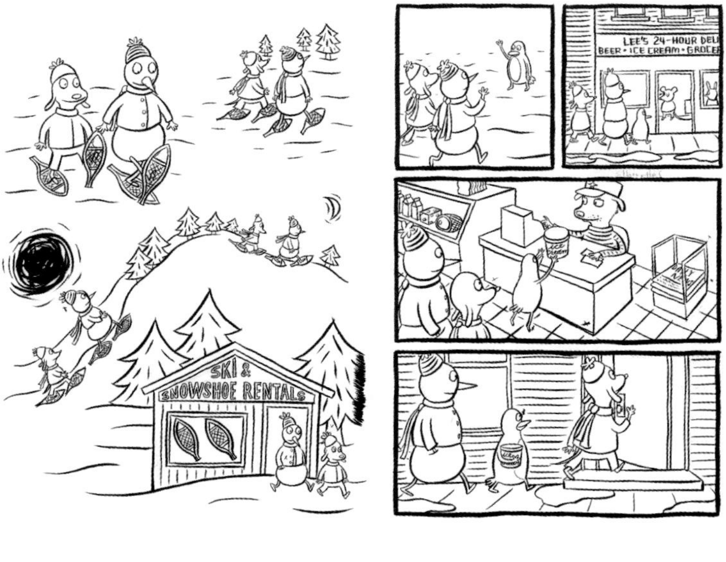

SKI & SNOWSHOE RENTALS
LEE'S 24-HOUR DELI
BEER • ICE CREAM • GROCER

Thumbnail

Inked Page

keep reading for
a behind-the-scenes look at
the original robot story,
which now appears in
Sweaterweather.

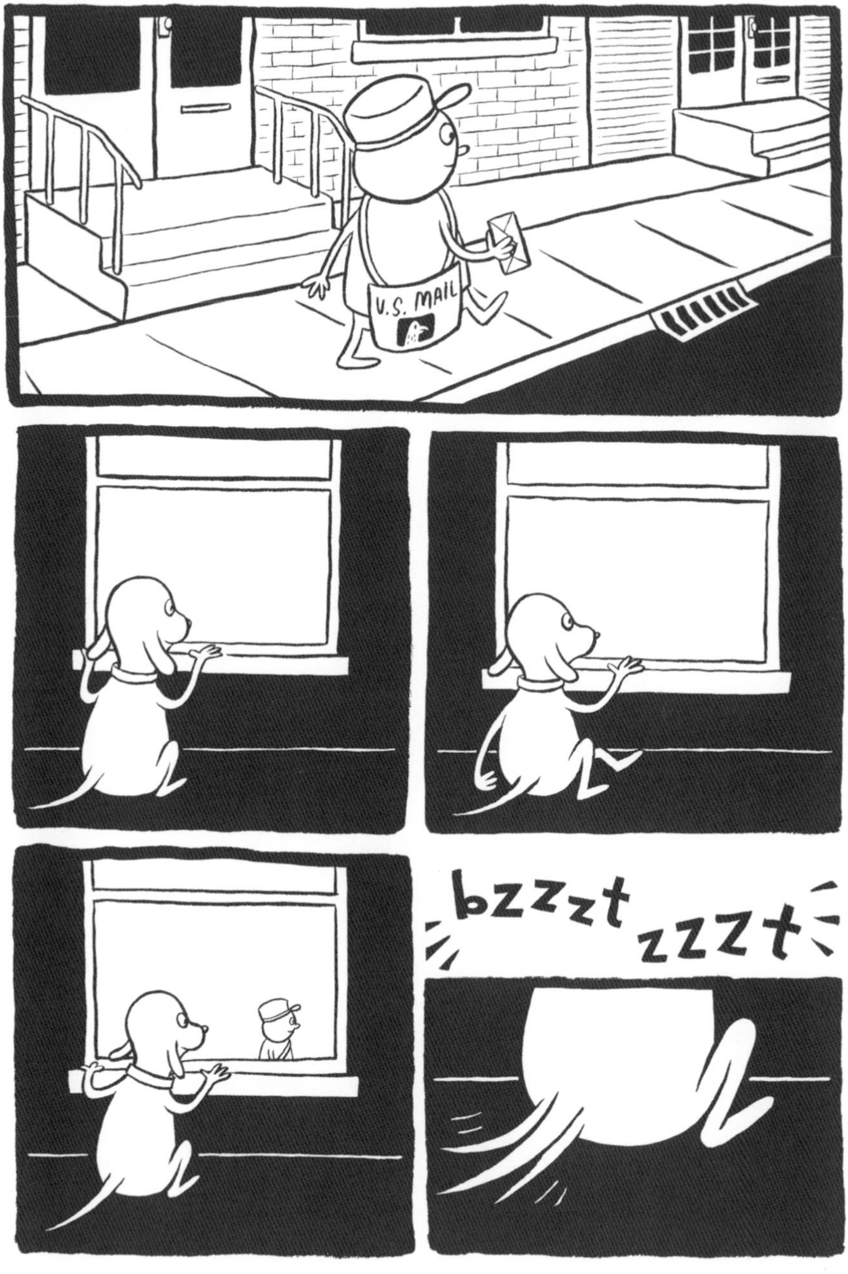
U.S. MAIL
bzzzt zzzt

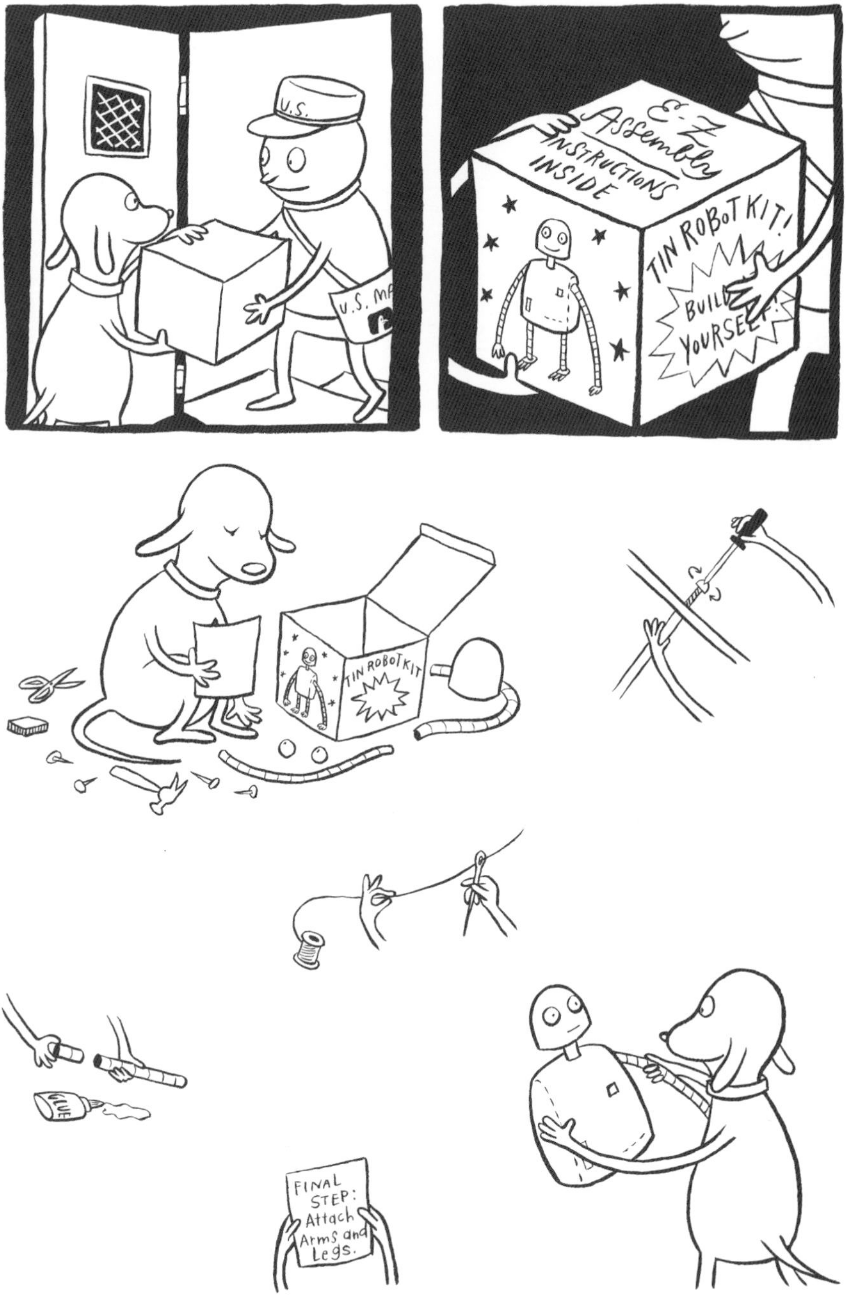
U.S.
E-Z Assembly
INSTRUCTIONS INSIDE
TIN ROBOT KIT!
TIN ROBOT KIT
GLUE
FINAL STEP: Attach Arms and Legs.

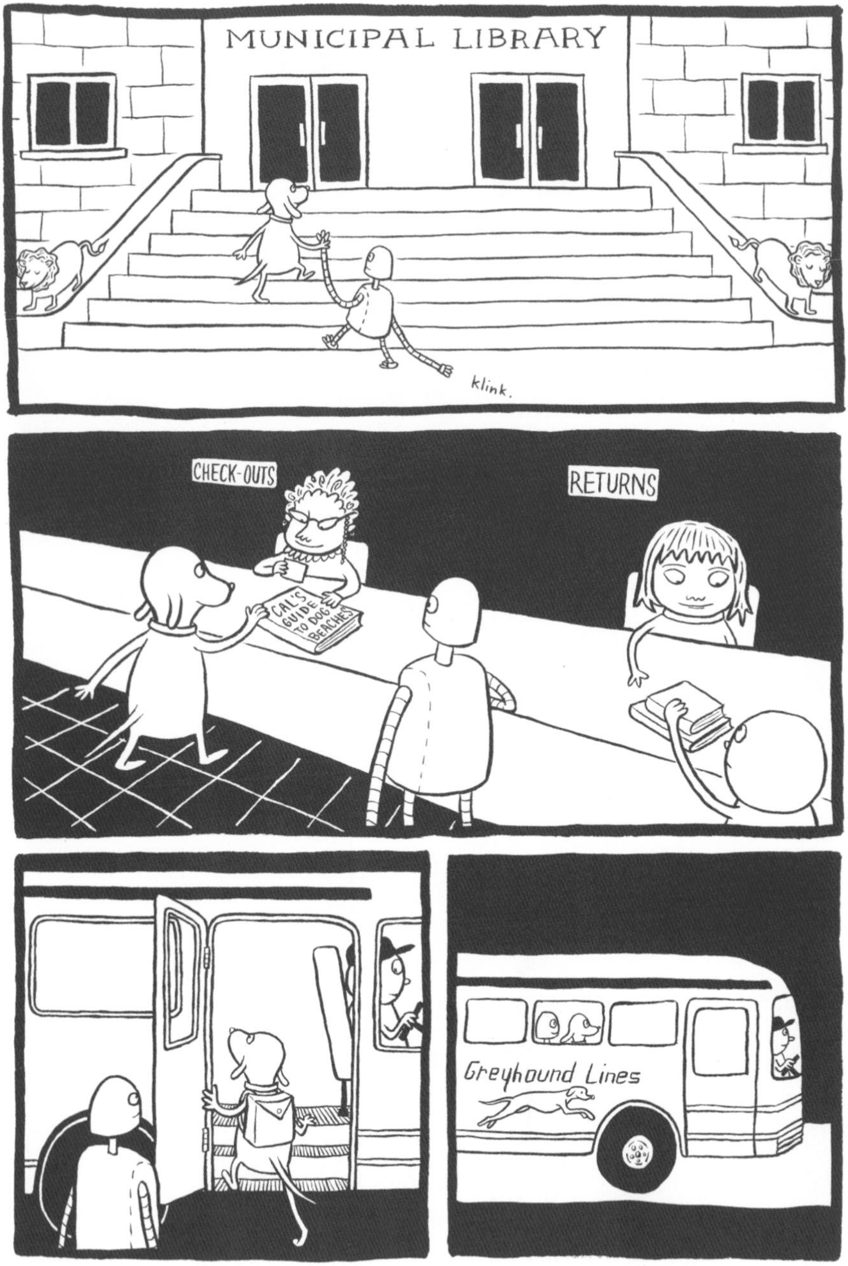
MUNICIPAL LIBRARY
klink.
CHECK-OUTS
RETURNS
CAL'S GUIDE TO DOG BEACHES
Greyhound Lines

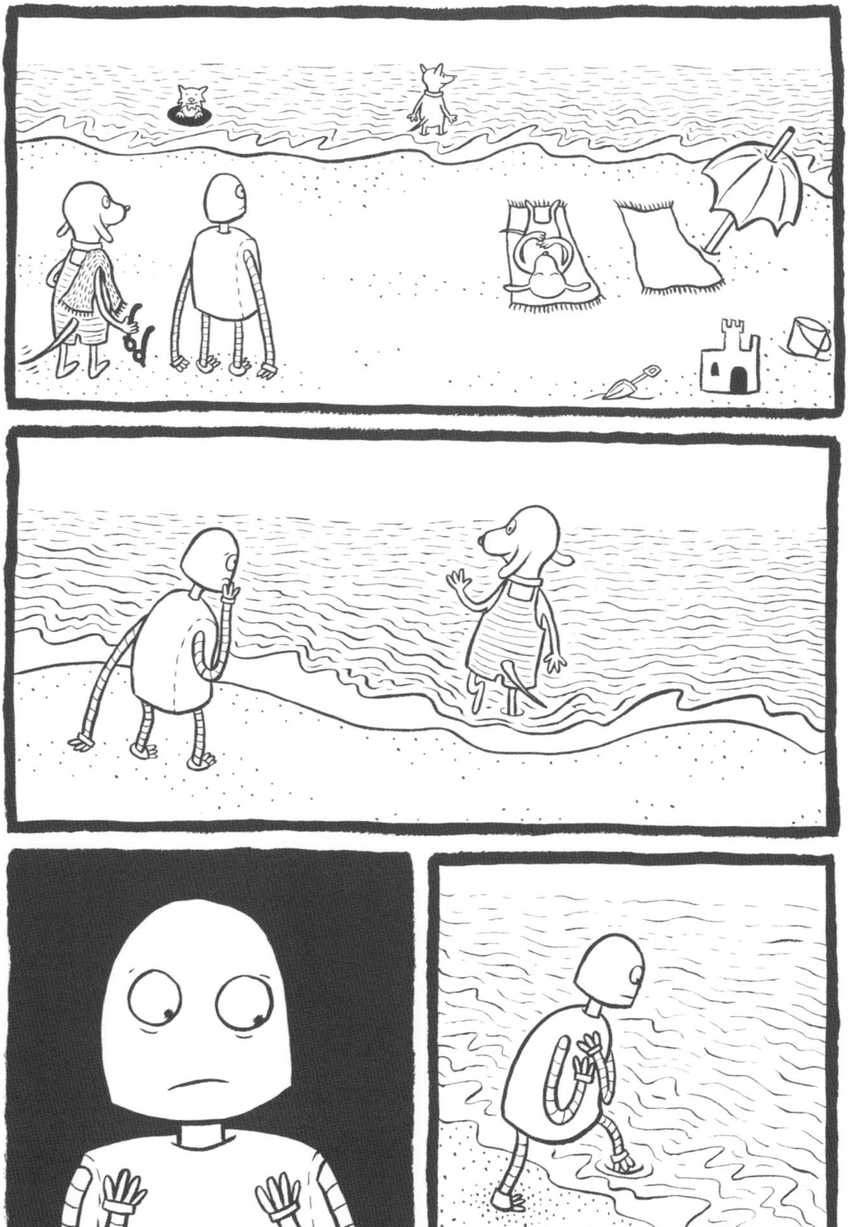

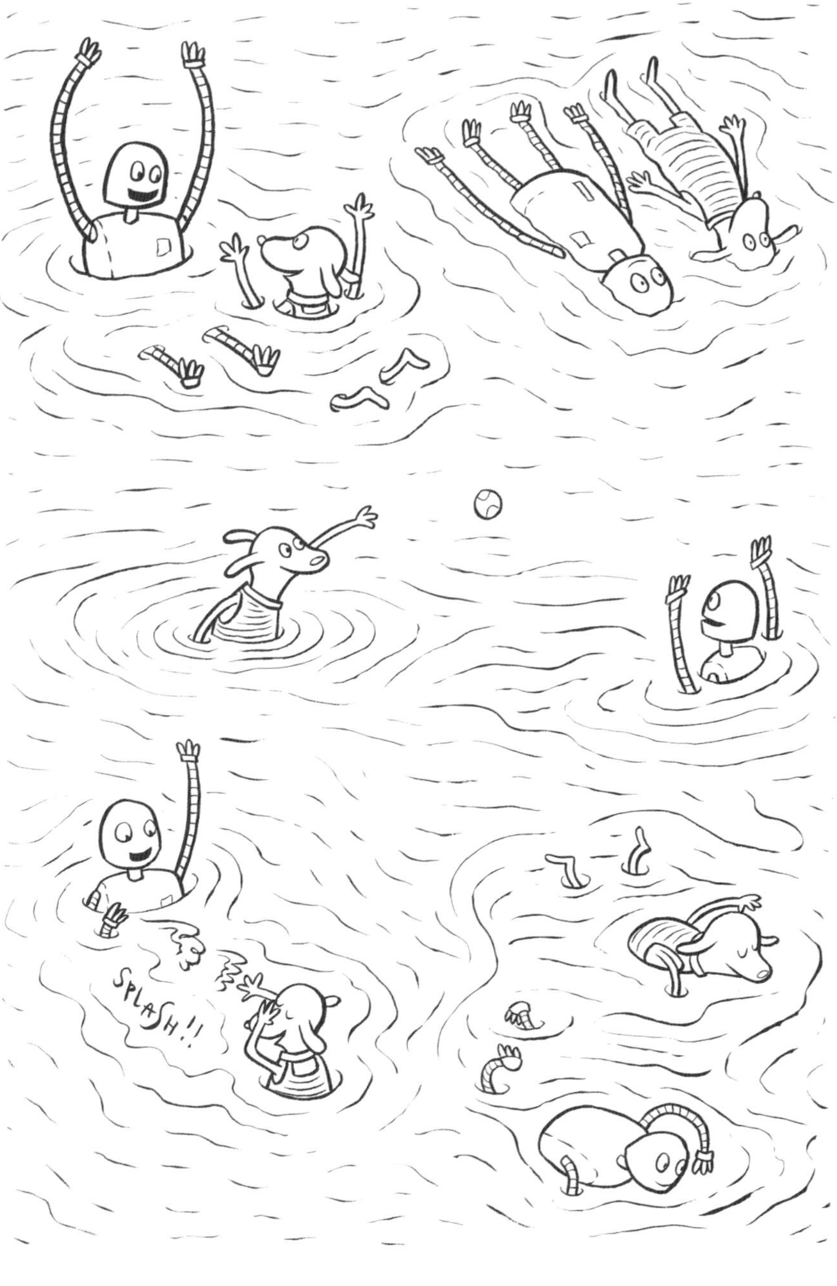
SPLASH!!

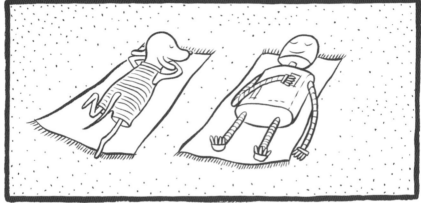

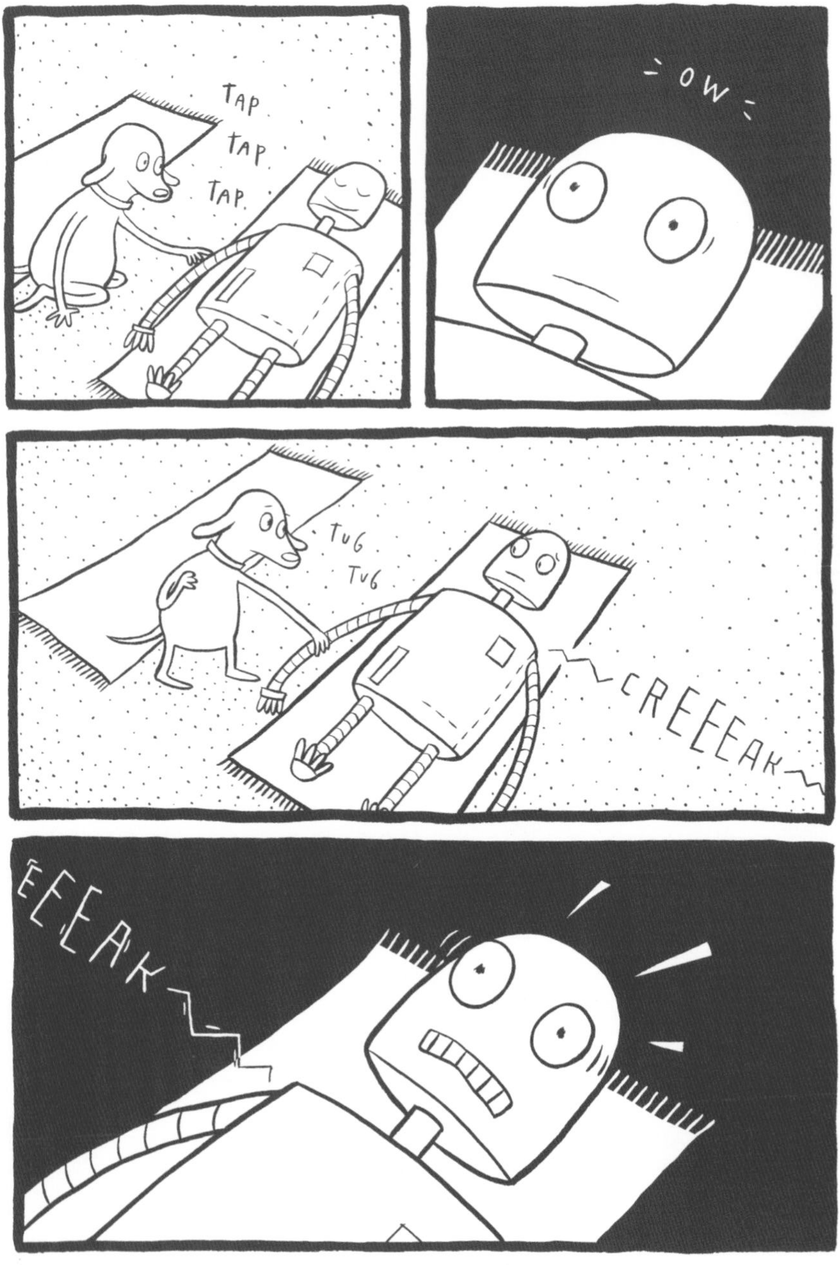
TAP
TAP
TAP
OW
TUG
TUG
CREEEAK
EEEAK

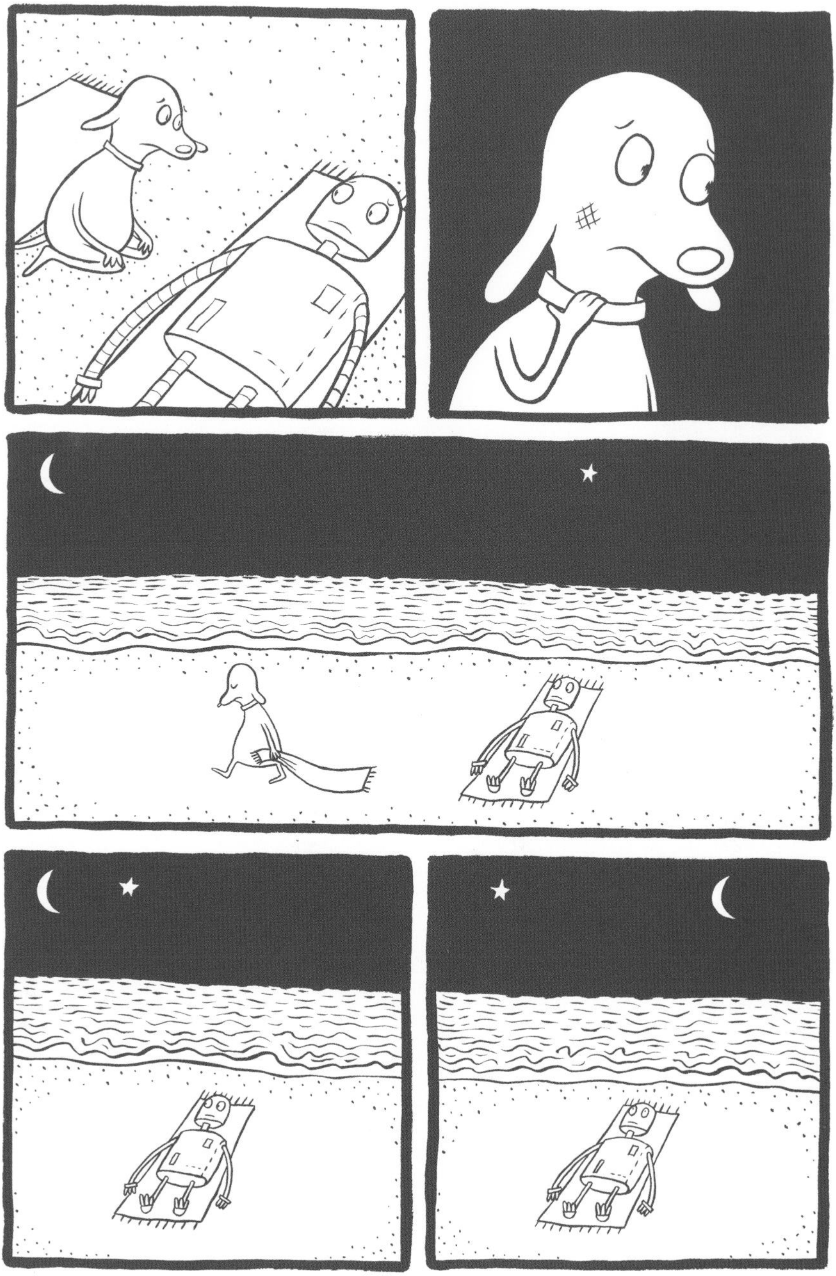

Also by Sara Varon

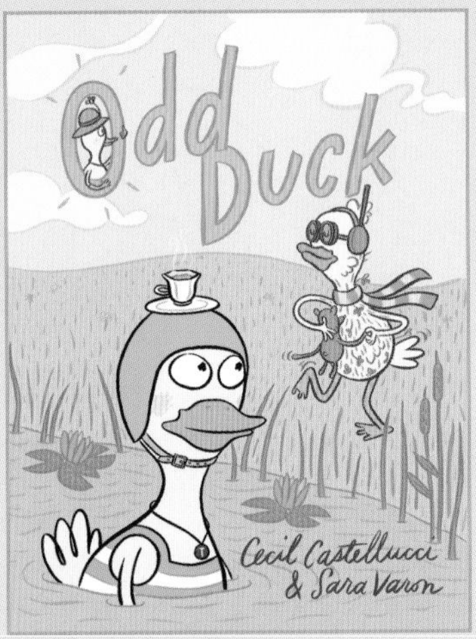
Odd Duck
Cecil Castellucci
& Sara Varon

Odd Duck

Written by Cecil Castellucci,
illustrated by Sara Varon
ISBN 9781596435575

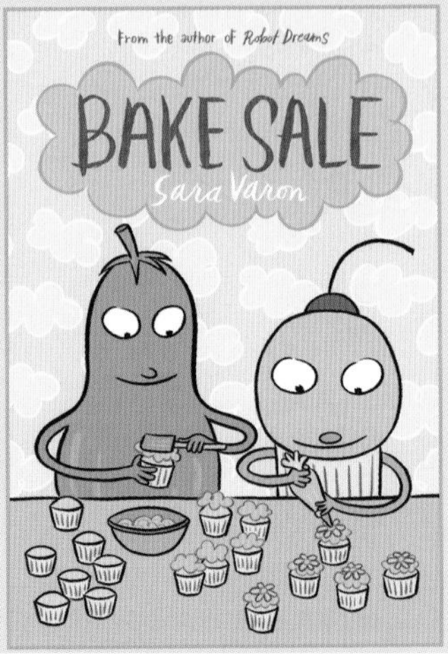
From the author of Robot Dreams
BAKE SALE
Sara Varon

Bake Sale

ISBN 9781596434196

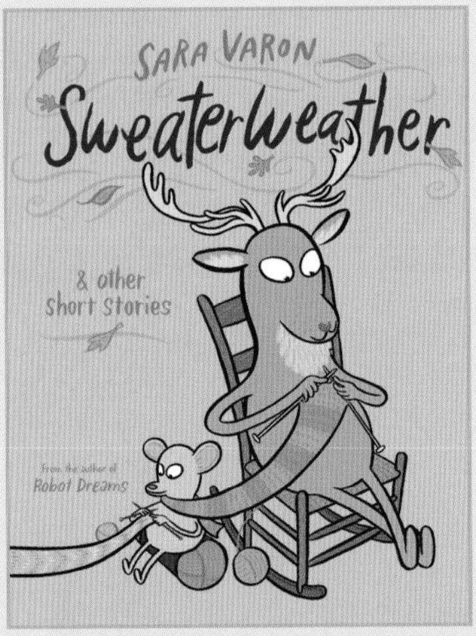
SARA VARON
Sweaterweather
& other
Short Stories
From the author of
Robot Dreams

Sweaterweather

ISBN 9781626721180